The
Wedding
Season

ALSO BY KATY BIRCHALL

The Secret Bridesmaid

Jane Austen's Emma (Awesomely Austen-Illustrated and Retold)

Morgan Charmley: Teen Witch

Hotel Royale: Dramas of a Teenage Heiress

Hotel Royale: Secrets of a Teenage Heiress

Superstar Geek

Team Awkward

Don't Tell the Bridesmaid

How to Be a Princess

The Wedding Season

KATY BIRCHALL

ST. MARTIN'S GRIFFIN
NEW YORK

First published in the United States by St. Martin's Griffin, an imprint of St. Martin's Publishing Group

www.stmartins.com

Designed by Devan Norman

Library of Congress Cataloging-in-Publication Data

Names: Birchall, Katy, author.
Title: The wedding season / Katy Birchall.
Description: First Edition. | New York : St. Martin's Griffin, 2022. |
  Identifiers: LCCN 2021061807 | ISBN 9781250845962 (trade
  paperback) | ISBN 9781250845979 (ebook)
Classification: LCC PR6102.I724 W43 2022 | DDC 823/.92—dc23
LC record available at https://lccn.loc.gov/2021061807

Our books may be purchased in bulk for promotional, educational, or business use. Please contact your local bookseller or the Macmillan Corporate and Premium Sales Department at 1-800-221-7945, extension 5442, or by email at MacmillanSpecialMarkets@macmillan.com.

First U.S. Edition: 2022

10 9 8 7 6 5 4 3 2 1

This book is dedicated to all those who work in weddings, an industry hit so hard by the 2020 pandemic.

Thank you for all you do to give others their perfect day.

The Wedding Season

PROLOGUE

Has anyone seen the peacocks?"

I look up from examining a selection of napkins. "Excuse me?"

"Have you seen the peacocks?" my brother repeats.

"What peacocks?"

"The peacocks I hired. I've lost them."

"Adrian, what are you talking about?"

"I hired some peacocks to roam about the lawn. It was meant to be a surprise for the wedding tomorrow. It's your wedding gift from me." He grins proudly. "Guessing you didn't put that on your gift list. Talk about an original idea."

I narrow my eyes at him. "You hired peacocks to roam the lawn at my wedding—"

"Cool, right?"

"—as a surprise present."

"You are welcome."

"And they've gone . . . missing."

"I wouldn't say missing exactly, more like they've roamed a bit further than expected."

I purse my lips. My best friend, Ruby, standing next to me, clears her throat and tries to look busy with the napkins.

"So," Adrian prompts, "have you seen them?"

"No, we haven't seen any peacocks here in the marquee," I hiss through gritted teeth. "Adrian, are you *kidding me*?"

He looks confused. "About the peacocks? No. They're genuinely around here somewhere. Also, get this. Did you know that they're actually called peafowl? The guy I hired them from told me this. Peacocks are the male ones, and the females are called peahens. *Peahens!* Who knew?!" His face suddenly lights up. "Hey, do you think they might be in the house? People have been leaving that door open all day."

Ruby glances at my expression and quickly jumps in. "Good idea, best to check inside the house. And . . . uh . . . maybe while you're in there, you might want to check that all the bedroom doors are closed, so that if the peacocks do somehow get in, they don't go near Freya's dress or anything like that."

I think my eyes must be bulging unnaturally out of my head as I try not to explode at my idiot younger brother, because Ruby takes another look at me and suddenly adds, "Go *now*, Adrian," in a very urgent tone.

Adrian swans out of the marquee toward the house, swiping one of the favor bags from the wicker basket by the exit on his way out. Ruby immediately turns to face me, putting her hands on my shoulders and looking me in the eye.

"Breathe with me," she instructs, inhaling and exhaling deeply.

"The day before my wedding, he sets *peacocks* loose in the house?"

"Technically he set them loose in the garden," Ruby corrects, trying her best to make it seem less of a big deal. "They won't get in anybody's way. And I'm sure he'll find them before tomorrow. You have to give it to him, it is an original gift."

I shake my head in disbelief.

"I think we should put the peacocks out of your mind and

focus on what's really important," Ruby declares. "Like which napkin you're going to use. White *or* almost-white *or* cream."

I sigh and turn my attention back to the napkins. "It has to be . . . the almost-white napkin."

"If you'd chosen the white, we wouldn't have been able to stay friends." She grins at me and gestures around the marquee. "Look at this, Freya. Everything is perfect. Surely we can go relax with a glass of champagne now?"

I turn to admire the setup as dozens of people busily put the finishing touches to it all. It's mad to think how my dad's garden has been transformed in just a few hours ready for tomorrow. I've always thought that the lawn here was the perfect open space for a marquee, and since we're in the middle of the tranquil Berkshire countryside, it's an idyllic setting for a country garden wedding. When Matthew proposed, we didn't even bother considering any other venues. And looking round at everything now, I'm confident we made the right decision. It's really starting to come together. All the effort and time I've put into this wedding, all those tiny, teeny, ridiculous details—who knew how many different types of paper stock an invitation could be printed on?—have all been worth it.

The marquee is beautiful, the fairy-light canopy overhead is magical, and even though the flowers won't be arriving until first thing tomorrow, I already know they're going to be spectacular because the florist, Lucy, is a genius and I completely trust her. She insisted on being here today with her colleagues to map everything out and make sure her vision was going to come to life as she'd planned it. (A woman after my own heart.)

The table settings look great and, now that the napkins have been chosen, are almost completed. The stage is ready for the band, the photo booth set up exactly where it should be in the corner, the favors sorted in the basket by the exit—one down, thanks to Adrian, but that's okay because I intentionally ordered spares, just in case—and the table plan, beautifully illustrated by this local artist I tracked down on Instagram, is propped up neatly on the easel. There's also a large rustic crate just inside the door with a pile of cream knitted throws in case it's a little chilly tomorrow, while in the house are forty giant umbrellas I ordered for the guests on the off chance that it rains when we're doing the photographs outside (though when I last checked the weather forecast, ten minutes ago, it was still saying it will be mild and sunny). But you can't be too careful—and I've really tried to think of everything.

"Don't worry, everyone, I am here and ready to help," announces Leo, Ruby's boyfriend, as he enters the marquee, rubbing his hands together.

"You're a few hours late," Ruby complains, watching him saunter toward us. "Everything is done!"

He gives her a mischievous grin. "Then I'm right on time, if you ask me. Sorry, the train was delayed this morning and it was a little tricky getting a taxi from the station. You were right, Rubes, I should have got yesterday off work too and driven down with you Wednesday night. But, I'm here now!"

"When will you learn I'm always right?" Ruby sighs as he throws his arm round her waist and gives her a kiss on the cheek. "Make yourself useful and get us hard workers a drink, will you? Really the least you could do."

"Not for me quite yet," I remark, focusing my attention back to the table settings and nervously checking them over once again. "There's still a few things I need to cross off the list."

"She's joking, right?" Leo asks Ruby, before turning back to me. "Freya, it's the day before your wedding. Aren't you supposed to be relaxing?"

"I don't think there are many brides who spend the day before their wedding relaxing, Leo," I point out, getting my phone from my pocket to run through my checklist. "I'm almost certain that, traditionally, the day before is reserved for freaking out."

He snorts. "I don't think you've ever freaked out in your life, Freya. What could you be worried about right now?"

"Well, my brother has lost the peacocks—"

"The what?"

"—and I need Matthew to run through some things with the catering manager, because we have to confirm timings."

"Speaking of the groom, where is he?" Leo asks.

"He's with his parents. They went for lunch together."

Leo raises his eyebrows. "Where? Please don't tell me they went to the Crown. I cannot see Matthew's parents enjoying the cuisine on offer there."

Leo has a point. He and Ruby have come to stay at my dad's a few times and they're well aware that the Crown is the nearest pub in the area—it's the nearest anything in the area—but that the food there is both limited and questionable. We're almost certain that the landlord buys a selection of ready-made meals from the supermarket, whacks them in a microwave, and serves them up for a tenner. Matthew's mum, Gail, is very prim and proper. There's no chance she'd touch anything put in front of her in the Crown. I doubt she'd risk perching on one of the chairs, let alone eat the food.

Although Matthew loves it here at Dad's, he's really a city boy at heart, whether he admits it or not. He likes to go on about how one day he'd love to escape to the countryside, but first he'd have to give up the luxury of the huge variety of restaurants and bars on our doorstep in London, and—considering that eating and socializing are basically his favorite things to do—I can't exactly see that happening for a long time.

"I think they went for lunch in town, don't worry," I assure Leo. "They'll be back soon."

"You know what I've been thinking? How nice it is that you and Matthew are opening the Wedding Season and we're closing it," Leo announces.

I frown at him. "The Wedding Season?"

"Yeah. We have nine weddings this year." Leo exhales, shaking his head. "It's mad."

"Welcome to your midthirties, Leo," Ruby remarks with a grin.

"Midthirties?! I'm thirty-two! That's pretty much late twenties!" he protests.

"Sure, keep telling yourself that," she says, patting his arm.

"I think we have eight weddings this year, including ours," I say, leading them over to the bar to check that the staff will have everything they need tomorrow.

"Exactly, a whole season of weddings." Leo nods. "Hence my point. Here we are, kicking off the Wedding Season with yours in March, and we're bringing the season to a close in September. It's going to be a big year."

"Look at us, all grown up," Ruby comments, studying tomorrow's cocktail menu written on the chalkboard. "I'm going to be a mess tomorrow. Waterproof mascara at the ready."

"You think you'll shed a tear saying your vows, Freya?" Leo asks curiously.

Ruby snorts. "Have you met her? Heart of stone, that one."

"So sweet of you to notice," I say dryly. "I hope that's a line from your maid of honor speech."

"Nah, going for something a little less emotional and gushing." She grins, turning back to Leo. "If anyone's going to cry tomorrow, it will be the groom."

Leo's face brightens as he spots someone at the entrance to the marquee. "Speak of the devil!"

Matthew shuffles in, dodging out of the way of the catering staff as they carry things in, and almost knocking into the florist, who is going through the fixings and weight loadings of the hanging flowers with the owner of the marquee company.

"S-sorry," he says, looking flustered as he stumbles away from them and clumsily knocks into a couple of milk churns. They clang as one wobbles into another.

"There you are," I say, laughing as he quickly steadies the churns. "Those are for the flower arrangements that will be just outside the entrance to the marquee. We're going to have two there and then some at the top of the path by the gate. What do you think?"

"Uh, fine," he says, distracted.

"Before I forget, I know your dad was worried about the boutonniere, but tell him not to worry, I've triple-checked with the florist and she's confirmed that he definitely has one waiting for him."

"Can we . . . talk?" Matthew says, his brow furrowed.

"Hey, you're sweating. Are you okay?" I ask, suddenly alarmed. "Oh no. You're not coming down with something, are you?"

"You want me to get some paracetamol?" Ruby offers, overhearing as she approaches.

"Hey, Matthew!" Leo grins, giving him an enthusiastic slap on the back. "How are you feeling, mate? The place looks great, you two have smashed it."

"Yeah, because Matthew had so much to do with it," I comment playfully.

It's been a running joke between us that Matthew's involvement with the wedding started and ended with him proposing. Every time I've tried to get his opinion on anything, he's brushed it off, insisting he's happy with whatever I want.

"Freya, I really need to speak with you," he says to me in a serious tone.

"What is it?" I ask, as Leo and Ruby share a concerned look.

"Are you still worried about insulting your uncle by sitting him on table nine? Because I really don't think he'll—"

"It's not that."

"Well, what then?"

His eyes dart frantically around the marquee, and he anxiously runs a hand through his hair, making it stick up all over the place. As he does so, we're asked to move aside so staff can carry in the crates of glasses to go behind the bar.

"Look, can we go somewhere private?" Matthew snaps, shooting glares at the staff as they pass. "It's so busy in here."

I frown at him. "Um, sure. Leo and Ruby, are you okay to hang here for a bit and then we'll do that drink?"

"Of course. We'll make sure everything's under control here, you don't worry about a thing," Ruby assures me. "See you in a bit."

I follow Matthew as he storms out of the marquee and marches toward the house. The back door to the garden is propped open and we head in. In the kitchen we pass Dad and Adrian, who are having a hushed conversation. Adrian straightens and plasters a smile on his face as he sees me.

"You've found those pesky peacocks, yes?" I prompt, raising my eyebrows, as Matthew continues out of the kitchen and through to the hall.

"Absolutely, sis!" Adrian calls out after me. "Everything is under control."

"I don't believe you!" I singsong back over my shoulder.

"Love you, too!" he replies.

I shake my head, unable to stop a small smile as we stop by the stairs. My brother may be an idiot, but he's a lovable one.

"I know the whole peacock thing is a bit crazy," I say, as Matthew leans on the banister. "But I'm sure that Adrian will . . . Oh hey, Aunty Em!"

"There's the beautiful bride-to-be!" my aunt trills from the top of the staircase. "And the handsome groom! You all set for tomorrow?"

"Everything's looking great! You need anything?"

"Just running through my reading," she tells us, as Matthew stares down at the floor, his foot tapping in irritation. "Your uncle is having a cup of tea with the vicar in the sitting room. What a lovely woman! She's been telling us all about her sermon tomorrow. It's going to be so moving."

"Ah, she's great, isn't she?" I smile up the stairs.

"Is there nowhere private in this place?" Matthew mutters under his breath.

Looking as though he might lose it at any second, he grabs my wrist and pulls me a few steps down the hall and yanks open the cupboard under the stairs, then ushers me in. He follows, shutting the door behind him. Startled, I feel for the switch on the wall and turn on the light. It's so cramped in here, with all the household bits like the hoover and brooms that Dad shoves in here out of the way, we're pressed right up against one another.

"Matthew, what are you doing?" I whisper, pushing away the mop handle that falls on my shoulder. "Why are we in a cupboard?"

"I couldn't hear myself think out there," he growls.

"Yeah, well, if you wanted some space we could have driven somewhere," I point out, wrinkling my nose at all the spiderwebs in the corners. "There are much nicer places to get away from everyone."

"This couldn't wait."

He bites his lip. He's really making me feel on edge. The way his mannerisms are so jerky, the beads of sweat forming on his forehead, his eyes darting around.

"Matthew, what is it?" I ask in concern, reaching for his hands. "Is it the peacocks?"

He pulls his hands out of my grasp. "Peacocks? What? No! This isn't about peacocks. Why would this be about peacocks?"

"You know what, you look a bit frazzled, so there's no need for you to know. Let's just say there's a peacock situation, but it's being handled."

He stares at me in bewilderment and then suddenly it's like he just gives up. His hands fall to his sides, his shoulders droop, his head bows. He exhales, shutting his eyes tight together.

"I can't do this," he whispers.

"Can't do what? Matthew, are you okay? What's wrong?"

"I'm so sorry," he whimpers, suddenly looking completely helpless. "I've known it for a while. I should have told you. I've spoken to my parents about it just now and they . . . well . . . I have to tell you."

I reach for him but he recoils as much as he can in such a small space, his foot knocking into the hoover. It switches on and he desperately searches for the power button. I calmly reach over and turn it off for him.

"Matthew, what's going on? You're worrying me. Whatever it is, you can tell me." I smile at him with encouragement. "We can sort it together."

"I can't do this," he croaks. "I can't do any of this. Not anymore. I can't go through with the wedding."

I stare at him, unable to speak.

"I'm so sorry, Freya," he says slowly but surely, lifting his eyes to meet mine. "It's over."

CHAPTER ONE

When you get dumped the day before your wedding in a broom cupboard, suddenly everything seems a bit shit.

I never imagined my world would come completely crashing down like this, but if I had, I never would have considered it might happen in a broom cupboard. I had a mop handle literally resting on my shoulder. My right foot was balanced on the dustpan and brush on the floor. There were about a hundred gross spiderwebs hanging around my head. And barely two inches away from me was my fiancé—the man I'd spent the last twelve years with; the love of my life, whom I was due to marry the very next day—who had decided that this was the best place to tell me that, actually, he'd changed his mind.

A *broom cupboard.*

My brain couldn't process the information at first. I made him repeat himself. You know, just to torture myself as much as possible. Apparently, I wasn't content with how he'd spelled it out the first time, when he said very plainly he couldn't go through with the wedding. No, I made him say it again and again, each time expecting his words to make sense.

But there was no sense to be made. All Matthew did was stand in that broom cupboard and repeat that he'd had doubts for a while, but that he didn't want to believe them. He'd hoped they would just go away, and when they didn't he had no idea what to do. As the wedding crept toward us, he'd tried to work out a way to tell me that he wanted out. Only he could never quite muster the courage.

Suddenly, it was the day before and he couldn't bear to cause me pain, but he knew he had to do it, otherwise it would be even crueler to go through with the marriage. So, he took his parents to lunch and he was honest with them. And they told him that he absolutely had to tell me. That day. Right there.

"They told you to tell me this in the broom cupboard?" I managed to whisper. Gail and Andrew loved me, how could they have encouraged their son to call off our wedding in a broom cupboard?

"What?! No, no, course not," he confirmed, his brow furrowing. "They didn't mention the broom cupboard specifically. This was the only private place on offer."

But as Matthew continued to say how sorry he was and how even though he loved me, he just wasn't in love with me anymore, I went strangely numb. And because I wasn't saying anything—on account of the bizarre, dazed state I seemed to have entered—Matthew just continued to make his case, and each reason he listed as to why he was breaking up with me was subconsciously logged away in my brain to scrutinize at a later time.

He believed he could be happier. We'd met when we were so young, we'd never had a chance to see what else was out there. What if, he kept saying. What if this wasn't as happy as we could be? What if there was something more?

"I can't do this, Freya. I can't do this. It doesn't feel right anymore. I'm so sorry."

Finally, tired of repeating himself, Matthew moved on to logistics. He courageously stated that he would help in any way possible to make the whole process easier on me.

I stared at him, still numb. "The process?"

"Of canceling the wedding."

Oh. Right. That process. God. I was losing Matthew, and the

wedding I'd just spent eleven months planning was now off. We were going to have to let everyone know that I had been dumped in a broom cupboard, less than twenty-four hours before I was supposed to walk down the aisle.

We'd have to ring round the guest list, make sure nobody made the unnecessary journey, and tell everyone already here to head home. The marquee would have to be taken down, the catering team canceled—not to mention the florist, the band, the bar staff, the vicar, the church string quartet, the wedding-car company, the minicabs, the photo-booth guy.

"And what about the peacocks?" I whispered.

"I'm sorry?" he said, kicking the hoover to one side.

"The peacocks. They're missing."

"Freya, what are you—"

"The peacocks that were meant to roam around the lawns tomorrow," I said, firmer now, irritated that he wasn't getting it. "If the wedding is off, we have to find them so they can go home."

Matthew stared at me like I had lost my mind. Which, I think it's safe to say, I had.

"Peacocks? That's what you're worried about, the peacocks?" His jaw clenched. "I've just told you the wedding's off and you're . . ."

He trailed off then, before sighing and shaking his head. "Look, Freya, this is kind of what I'm talking about. We don't . . . mesh well anymore. You're so pragmatic all the time. So together. Which is great. For you. But I'm, you know—" He searched for the words. "—I'm all over the place. Temperamental. Emotional. We can't be good for each other. We just can't. We don't make sense."

He paused, biting his lip. I went ahead and stared at him some more.

"Freya, you have every reason to hate me," he continued dismally. "I wish beyond measure I wasn't doing this to you. I'm a stupid bastard who should have said something sooner. I'm so sorry. But I also know I'm doing the right thing. I think . . . I think one day you may thank me."

There was a long silence after that. He tried to wait it out, but he gave up and asked if I was okay. Then, when I still wasn't responding, he begged me to say something, to tell him what he should do.

I asked him to leave me alone in the broom cupboard.

He was a bit confused I think, but he nodded, told me he was so sorry once more, and then opened the door.

"I'll . . . I'll go speak to your dad," he said softly. "Get the ball rolling."

Of canceling the wedding. He'd get the ball rolling of canceling our wedding.

I asked him to close the door. When he did, I reached up and turned off the light and then slid down to sit on the floor, next to the dustpan and brush. The mop fell forward, bouncing off the back of my head and resting on the floor. I sat there for a while, wondering if there was really a need for me to leave this cupboard ever again.

Perhaps I could stay here forever. It wasn't so bad. Sure, it smelled kind of musty and was already inhabited by a number of spiders, but once you got over all that, it really could be considered quite a cozy and convenient living space.

After a while, the door gently opened and Dad sat down next to me. He put his arm around my shoulders. I rested my head against him and closed my eyes.

"Dad," I whispered into the darkness, "I don't want to see anyone."

"I assumed as much," he replied. "Adrian's sorting it."

"How did this happen?"

"I don't know," he said, holding me close. "I just don't know."

We stayed there for a long time until Adrian rapped his

knuckles on the door and reported that everyone was gone. It was just us three. Together, he and Dad lifted me to my feet and practically carried me up to my bedroom and sat me on the bed.

They reluctantly left the room after I insisted, slowly shutting the door behind them. And finally safe in the knowledge that I was alone, I began to cry, my body heaving with alarmingly uncontrollable sobs as it began to sink in what was happening.

My whole world had just fallen spectacularly apart.

Dad keeps bringing me walnuts.

It's been a week since the broom-cupboard breakup, and every single day my dad has dutifully brought walnuts up to my room. Apparently, he googled ways to help someone get through a breakup. An article he read stated that there are certain foods that can help improve the mood and one of them is walnuts.

So, now I am surrounded by little bowls of walnuts. They are literally everywhere I look. I don't understand where he's getting all these walnuts from.

"Thanks, Dad," I say, when he appears in my doorway carrying yet another bowl. "But I'm not hungry. And I've already got the ones you brought in this morning."

"I'll just pop these here in case you need another snack," he insists, coming over to place them on my desk next to my keyboard. "So! How's work going?"

"It's fine."

He nods. "Are you sure you should be working, Freya? It's great that you can work from home, but your boss did say you could take some time off and I think it might be a good idea to—"

"No, Dad, I need to work," I tell him firmly, my eyes fixed on my screen as I scroll through my emails. "It's keeping me busy and distracted. It's getting me out of bed in the morning."

"Yes, but . . ." He trails off, searching for the right thing to say.

I sigh and swivel in my chair to face him. "Dad, honestly, I'm fine. I don't need any time off."

"If you're sure," he says sadly.

I offer him a small smile. "Look, Dad, you don't need to worry about me. I'll be fine. I'll head back to London in a week or so. I just wanted to give Matthew time to . . . clear out all his stuff from the flat. You know, so I don't have to see it when I get home and be reminded of . . ."

Him. Our life together. Our future.

I trail off and swallow the lump in my throat, hurriedly turning back to my laptop. God, I hate this feeling. I hate how much it aches all the time.

I can't get rid of this stupid, fucking ache.

It might seem strange, but at thirty-two, this is my first ever heartbreak. I started dating Matthew when I was twenty years old and before then I didn't have any serious boyfriends. He was my first love. Whenever I told anyone that, they always said how lucky I was. But now, the fact that I've never loved anyone else feels like a curse. Because I have no idea how to cope with a breakup. I didn't realize it felt like this.

How can someone be the most important person in the world to you and then, just like that, they're gone from your life? Vanished? Except you know they're actually still out there, somewhere. They've just chosen not to be with you. And you're supposed to keep going on with your life. You know everything about that person, but all of a sudden, you're not allowed to know them at all. It's like grieving the death of someone, but they're still alive and kicking.

I can't get my head round it. It can't really be happening. It just can't.

He'll realize what he's done. He has to. This is a gigantic, cruel, mortifying mistake, and he'll realize that soon. We'll be fine once he's got his head sorted. Until then, I've landed on the temporary solution of hiding away from the world and everyone in it. I can't let them see me like this.

Before my heart got shattered in a broom cupboard, I'd have described myself as an energetic, busy person. I'm good in the mornings, able to push myself out of bed when the alarm first goes off, unlike Matthew, who presses Snooze several times. Usually I'm out on a run before he gets up. I'm not exactly good at running—or any kind of exercise, to be honest—but I like the quiet, solitary time to get my thoughts in order, and I always feel much more ready for the day after my five-kilometer loop.

Once home, I'd get in the shower, get dressed, do my makeup, and then make the coffees while Matthew took his turn in the bathroom. He'd take any old mug, but I always have my coffee in the flask that Ruby bought for me as a joke, which has HOT STUFF written across it. I inexplicably love that flask, and if I don't have my morning coffee in it, I worry I'm going to have a bad day. (I know this seems like a stupid superstition of mine *and yet* the morning Matthew broke up with me? I had my coffee in one of Dad's mugs with a flamingo on it. That's proof right there.)

By the time I'd leave for work, Matthew would just be out of the shower and getting dressed. He's a graphic designer, and his office is in South London and a quick commute from ours, so he has the luxury of leaving just half an hour before he needs to be there.

"Love you," I'd tell him every morning, handing him his coffee and kissing him on the cheek.

"You too," he'd reply sleepily.

A matter of habit for some couples, maybe. But it had never felt that way for me.

Anyway, I haven't been able to force myself out for a morning run since the wedding-that-wasn't. I can't even muster the energy to bathe properly. I just stand there in the shower, letting the water splash on the top of my head. I mean, it's tragic. If I had more energy, I'd feel ashamed of myself, but there's just no room for that right now.

As I have temporarily lost any kind of enthusiasm for personal hygiene, my skin is retaliating by completely breaking out, just to kick me when I'm down. It's cruel really. All those years of being so regimented with my skin-care routine—double cleansing, a vitamin C serum, careful moisturizing—it's all gone out the window. The idea of washing my face twice is *too much*.

It's all gone to shit. All of it. My love, my life, my combination skin.

On what would have been our wedding day, I literally only left my childhood bedroom to go to the bathroom and, even then, I pretty much crawled on all fours to get there. At one point, Dad was standing on the landing and he actually had to step aside to let me crawl past him along the carpet to the loo. He stood watching me go, not saying a word.

I imagine, one day, we'll laugh about that.

When they took the marquee down the next day, I closed all the curtains in the house so I wouldn't accidentally see it being dismantled. I curled up in my bed with my headphones on, blasting music into my ears to block out the banging and clanging of all traces of the wedding being removed.

On Monday, I mustered the energy to go downstairs for lunch. Adrian and Dad tried their best not to make a big deal of it, but it was obvious that they were freaking out. As I sat at the table, glumly pushing food around my plate, they sat tensely, glancing at each other wide-eyed and attempting unnaturally cheery conversation.

"Aren't those birds singing today?" noted Adrian, a guy who has never noticed birds tweeting in his life. "Ah, nature."

"Yes, nature." Dad nodded, trying his best. "It brings so much."

"Yes."

"Hmm."

They both turned to look at me. I didn't say anything, my eyes fixed on my plate, too tired to participate. There was an awkward silence until Adrian couldn't take it anymore.

"I think I can hear a bumblebee!"

"Extraordinary!"

The conversation continued in this vein until I thanked them for lunch, put my plate in the dishwasher, and headed back upstairs to the safety of my depressing little den. I have managed to conjure better conversational skills since then, but it's all so tiring. I still feel exhausted. *All. The. Time.*

I decided I didn't want to take any time off work. I had booked two weeks off for the honeymoon, but I called my boss, Phil, on Tuesday morning and asked if I could carry on as if nothing had happened. By then, I'd spent three days in my room wallowing, and I needed something to take my mind off the horror that was my life.

"If you're sure you're okay to work?" Phil asked, sounding *very* uncomfortable.

Phil is an awkward person at the best of times, so the idea of talking to me at such a somber time must have been excruciating for him. At sixty-one, he's a bit older than the rest of the team, and being naturally shy and quiet, he doesn't enjoy the socializing side to work, so it's not like we know each other very well. He's very much the sort of person who likes to march into his office in the morning, do his job, and leave.

"Of course I'm okay!" I insisted, sitting slouched on my bed in just my underwear, slipper socks, and Matthew's old Foo Fighters T-shirt, while sticking a twisted bit of tissue up my nostril. When I was crying earlier, I blew my nose so hard it bled. "Why wouldn't I be okay?"

"Oh. Well. I . . . ahem . . . I was very sorry to hear about . . . what happened. Very sorry."

I felt the stab of humiliation, the idea of everyone in the office talking about it. Feeling sorry for me. The idiot who had no idea her relationship was over until the day before her wedding.

I still can't believe that idiot is me.

"Thanks, Phil, but I'm fine."

"If you think work could be a good distraction . . ."

"I do."

"But you must look after yourself, Freya," he said in a firm tone, which was really quite sweet of him. "You take things at your own pace."

"I promise I will."

Which was a lie, of course. You can't really do my job at your own pace. I'm a brand manager for Suttworth, the biggest drinks company in the country, and it's not like people stop selling and drinking alcohol across the UK just because I'm having a life crisis. But I do have a brilliant team who are helping me out, and since I can stay home for now, I don't have to be presentable, which definitely works in my favor. I had also made sure that things were all sorted and under control before I left the office last week, to much prenuptial fanfare. They decorated my desk in white balloons and silver confetti and cracked open the champagne.

I was the excited bride-to-be off for a few days of wedding prep before jetting off on a honeymoon to Barbados.

Ugh.

Anyway, these walnuts everywhere around my room really don't help much. Earlier, I tried to eat one by lobbing it at my open mouth half-heartedly and I missed. It hit the corner of my lip and then dropped to the floor. I stared at it and then wailed, "Whyyyyyy?"

It was a low point.

"Well," Dad says suddenly, clapping his hands together as he glances around my bedroom, "if you feel like a break from work, then let me know."

"I will," I say, clicking on a spreadsheet for no reason at all, just to have something I can pretend to examine. "Thanks, Dad."

"I did actually come up here for a reason."

"You've already delivered me the walnuts."

"Another reason," he says, forcing me to swivel round to face him again. "As Adrian has to fly back to New York tomorrow morning, I wondered if you might want to invite Leo and Ruby over. You know, for some company."

"I really don't want to see anyone."

"I think it would be a good idea."

"I have you for company," I point out.

He smiles modestly. "I'm hardly good fun. You need people to help lift those spirits."

"My spirits are perfectly lifted."

He sighs and gives me a pointed look. "Freya, I know you put on a front—" He holds up his hands as I open my mouth to protest. "Please. I know what you're like. You take after your old man, pretending everything's fine when it isn't. Not talking about stuff." His eyes fall to the floor and his voice softens. "It's all very well, but trust me, it's important to . . . to let things out once in a while. I understand you don't want to dwell on it, but don't sweep over it. Not something like this. You're allowed to lean on people. What else are we good for if not to be there in times of trouble?"

I take a deep breath. "All right, Dad. I'll ask Ruby and Leo to come for the weekend. Things must be bad if you're talking about being there in times of trouble."

"Thought I'd take a stab at being sincere."

"You pulled it off nicely."

"Don't expect it to happen again."

"I'm pleased to hear it."

"So, you'll invite Ruby and Leo?" he prompts.

"I'll message them now."

"Good stuff. I'll let you get back to work." He heads to the door and then hovers there, glancing back at me. "Oh, your mum called again. She said you haven't been answering her calls to your mobile."

"She's not really the person I want to speak to at the moment."

"I understand, but she's your mum. She's worried. She wants to be there for you."

"That's new for her," I say breezily.

"I know she can be a bit . . . well—" He searches for the word and gives up. "—you know. But she really regrets how things are with you and Adrian, and she's trying her best to make it better. Just because you're all grown up now, doesn't mean she doesn't worry. You should have heard her when I phoned her to let her know that . . . you know . . . things weren't going ahead—" He frowns at having to even allude to it. "She was in bits for you. She really wanted to extend her stay for a couple of weeks, so she could be in the area, near to you. It took a lot of persuading to get her to head home. I think she just wants to make sure you're okay. Even just a message would suffice."

I take a deep breath. "Fine. I'll send her a text."

"Good." He smiles warmly at me. "You just have to keep putting one foot in front of the other."

I blink at him. "What?"

"In life," he says, as though that clears everything up. "One foot in front of the other. You'll get there. I know you will."

***

Reasons NOT to call Matthew:
* He destroyed the life we'd built together in one fell swoop
* He dumped me in a broom cupboard
* He canceled our wedding
* He completely humiliated me, and I don't know how

I'll *ever* face friends and family again without feeling embarrassed about the whole thing
* He cost me a lot of money by canceling the wedding *one day before*, rather than three months before, when we would have lost deposits but not entire costs
* He's a fucking selfish little wankface and I hate him

Reasons to call Matthew:
* I love him and miss him and I don't understand how this happened

Conclusion:
* Chucked my phone out the bedroom window
* Decided to listen to "Total Eclipse of the Heart"
* Realized all my music is on my phone
* Remembered that I just threw my phone out the window
* Wailed "*Why is the world so shit?*" at the top of my lungs
* Remembered I have a laptop
* Used my laptop to play "Total Eclipse of the Heart"
* Sobbed into my pillow
* Problem solved (for now)

CHAPTER TWO

"How can we ruin Matthew's life?"

Leo and I share a look as Ruby paces around my room, swigging from a bottle of beer. There is a *lot* of alcohol stacked up in Dad's garage. A whole wedding's worth, in fact. It took Ruby about ten minutes after she arrived to head straight there and return with a box of selected beers and wine to fill the fridge. Thanks to my job, we also had a huge supply of spirits ready to go behind the bar, so I won't have to buy any alcoholic beverage for a couple of years at least.

That is potentially the one good thing that has come out of this whole mess.

The unlimited supply of wine.

"I'm being serious," Ruby says, her forehead furrowed in concentration. "We need to get revenge. I'm not talking about murdering him or anything. Just something we can do that completely destroys his life forever."

"Well, I'm glad you cleared up the murder question," Leo mutters.

"Death would be too easy a way out," Ruby seethes. "There are worse things we can do."

Leo looks mildly panicked.

Dad was right to insist I invite friends down for the weekend. I am grateful to have them here, especially after the goodbye with Adrian in the early hours of this morning. I felt so adrift watching him get in the car to go to the airport. We've always been close and he's been such a rock the last few days.

Ruby and Leo have really made me smile today, like properly smile, and laugh, too, and that makes me feel a tiny bit hopeful for life in general.

Not much. But still.

Ruby, Leo, and I were all in the same halls in first year of university and bonded straightaway, becoming close friends right from fresher's week. We ended up living together for the rest of our three years there, and moved to London together, too. We've seen each other through it all: boyfriends and girlfriends, break-ups, exams, new jobs, family dramas.

A few years ago, when Leo and Ruby kissed on a drunken night out, I was (a) shocked that they were attracted to one another, even after copious amounts of vodka, (b) horrified that they could risk our beautifully balanced friendship group, and (c) confused, because when I really thought about it, they actually seemed like a great couple. How had I not considered it before?

Luckily, they weren't confused at all. They both admitted they'd had feelings for each other for a while and they'd be stupid not to give it a go. I was worried that I would become a major third wheel, but actually our dynamic didn't change all that much. Maybe it was because they made sure not to make me feel like that—Ruby and her parents flew out to Mauritius every year to see her mum's family, and the first time Leo joined them, I was invited along, too. I did consider saying no at first and leaving them to it, because I didn't want to take the spotlight off Leo, but then I thought, *hello*, who turns down a trip to Mauritius?!

Ruby, Leo, and I have always very much had a "Three Musketeers" mentality when it came to our little clique. Matthew was welcomed as my other half, but he always had his own group of friends he'd spend most of his time with. Once we moved to London, he got closer to them and we'd hang out together as couples, but he'd also respect that Leo, Ruby, and I had a dynamic he wasn't part of. Matthew loved Leo and Ruby, and they loved him, but the three of us were the originals, and nothing was ever going to change that.

Anyway, Leo and Ruby have turned out to be the perfect match and here we all are today, still best friends, the two of them engaged to be married in September. It was fate that we were all getting married the same year.

Matthew really screwed us on that one.

"We could frame him," Ruby muses, as I snuggle down further into the duvet.

I have yet to get up, but they don't care. Leo is under the duvet with me and Ruby is drinking beer at 11:00 A.M.

There's no judgment in our friendship triangle.

"What do you mean?" Leo snorts. "Like, for a crime?"

"Exactly." Ruby nods slowly, her eyes freakishly widening with her evil-genius plotting. "It's simple. We frame him and he goes to prison for the rest of his life. Then who's laughing?"

"I don't think anyone's laughing, Ruby," Leo points out. "And if we're going to frame him, we'd need to find a crime to frame him for."

"Not a problem." Ruby shrugs. "We could rob something. A bank! Let's rob a bank! And leave his fingerprints everywhere!"

Leo blinks at her. "That's . . . stupid."

"You know, Leo," she begins, narrowing her eyes at him, "you could be a little more supportive, rather than just lying there like a slug, making cynical and rude comments."

"I'm also lying here like a slug," I point out.

"Yes, but you're allowed to be a slug," Ruby says, coming over and stroking my hair. "You can be a perfect little slug for however long you want."

"All right," Leo sighs next to me. "How about we egg his house?"

Ruby rolls her eyes. "What are we, eight years old?"

"You were egging people's houses at the age of eight?"

"Look, Leo, let's not lose focus," Ruby demands, brushing off his question and going back to her pacing. "We can't egg his house because in case you've forgotten, he doesn't have one. He's moved back in with his parents for the time being. And as much as I hate him right now with every fiber of my being, his parents seem nice. Sorry, Freya."

"Don't be," I say glumly. "They are nice. They're really nice."

Leo rests his head on mine, not saying anything.

Ruby sits down on the bed. "Have you heard from Matthew at all?"

"Not really," I admit. "He phoned last Saturday to make sure I was okay."

"He thought there was a chance you'd be okay on the day that would have been your wedding? How thoughtful." Ruby shakes her head. "I am so angry at that man."

"Dad wouldn't let him speak to me. He was manning my phone. When I got it back, I called Matthew maybe five billion times, but he didn't pick up." I hesitate, picking at my nails. "Then he messaged saying he thought it would be better if we cut off contact for a bit. Took some space. That hasn't stopped me from calling him about twice a day. I threw my phone out the window to stop myself from doing it, but about ten minutes later I ran down to the garden to find it. It had landed in a hedge and was fine. I called him straightaway and it rang out. I'm pathetic."

"No, you're not. Anyone would be the same after what's happened," Leo says, Ruby nodding in agreement.

I sigh heavily. "I just . . . I know it's not over yet. We always work things out eventually. Everything will be fine once he's had a bit of time."

Ruby blinks at me, her eyebrows knitted together. "Wait. You don't think it's over?"

I throw my hands up, exasperated. "We were together for twelve years. Twelve years. You don't throw that all away, right? He got cold feet about the wedding, which can happen. It's a big deal. There's a lot of pressure. I get it. But we are meant to be together. He'll realize that soon enough."

"Freya . . ." Ruby begins cautiously.

"He made a snap decision. He hasn't thought this through. He'll have some time away and then he'll realize. And yes, I'm devastated that he ruined our wedding and humiliated me in front of . . . well . . . everyone. But, at the end of the day, we love each other. He knows that."

Ruby and Leo share a look. I know what they're thinking, but I also know I'm right. I've had all week to think about this. Matthew clearly panicked and broke up with me on a whim. We were together for all of our twenties, it's normal that he'd worry that he'd somehow missed out. But I don't believe that he doesn't love me.

Why would he go to the trouble of giving me an engagement ring in the first place if he doesn't? It's not like I forced him to. That was all him.

"Freya," Ruby starts again, clearing her throat, "would you even want him to come back after what he's done to you?"

"I know it sounds mad," I say with a shrug. "But, yeah. I can't imagine my life without him. This week has been torture. I haven't gone a day without speaking to him for twelve years. And now, it's just cold turkey. It's horrible."

"Matthew broke up with you the day before your wedding," Ruby emphasizes, as though I don't know that. "He doesn't deserve to ever speak to you again. He is a selfish, spineless—"

"I think what Ruby is trying to say," Leo says, shooting her a look of warning, "is that you've been through a lot. A huge life change. And you should be focusing on looking after yourself right now, rather than waiting for him to come back. We all just want you to be okay."

I shift slightly to face him. "'We all'?"

"You have a good support network and everyone is here for you, whatever you need."

I slide my head further down into the pillow glumly. "Everyone is gossiping about me, aren't they? It's mortifying. I haven't been able to face replying to any messages. They're all so pitying."

"That's not at all how it is," Ruby says in her most serious tone. "Everyone thinks Matthew is the worst. No one is talking about you as if it's gossip. It's just . . . shit."

"But it will get better," Leo adds brightly. "You'll get through this and be stronger for it."

"Just like Britney and Kelly Clarkson and all the greats say," Ruby adds solemnly.

I manage a smile. "You're right. Anyway, enough chat about me. Let's talk about you guys. How has your week been? And how are wedding plans?"

Leo looks horrified. "Freya, we are *not* talking about our wedding plans."

"Come on, Leo, it's not like I can avoid weddings altogether. The season, remember? I have eight. Wait—" I hesitate. "Seven. It was eight including mine."

"You don't need to think about any of that stuff right now," Ruby tells me gently.

"Fine, but eventually I'll have to. Of course, the year that I get jilted at the altar is my busiest wedding year yet." I let out a deep sigh. "That *was* a good thing. It was supposed to be the best year of my life."

"We're here with you every step of the way," Leo reminds me.

"Exactly," Ruby says firmly. "We'll work out a plan to help you get through the season in one piece. You leave that to us. And technically you weren't jilted at the altar. So that's something."

"Yes, there is that, I guess. A broom cupboard is much more discreet. He didn't give me the chance to get in the dress."

Ruby winces, glancing up at where it's still hanging on my wardrobe in its bag.

I know it sounds materialistic, but part of me can't help thinking that one of the saddest things about the wedding going up in flames is that I didn't get to wear the dress. The dress it took me seven bridal shops to find. An ivory crepe gown with a crisscross bodice and off-shoulder sweetheart neckline and a very gentle, sloping A-line skirt. It really is beautiful.

"Do you want me to hide it away somewhere?" Ruby offers.

"No, it's fine. I'll keep it here, just in case."

"Well, let's not think about stuff like that," Ruby says abruptly. "Let's watch trashy movies and eat loads of delicious food, and drink in the mornings. One day at a time, yeah?"

"Exactly," I nod, gazing up at the dress bag. "One day at a time."

Ruby reaches over, squeezes my hand, and then sits up straight. "Now, Leo and I prepared a little something to help cheer you up and remind you that everything is going to be okay."

Leo groans, covering his face with his hands. "No, Rubes. You're not actually going to make me do this."

"Yes, Leo, I am," she says through gritted teeth, jumping to her feet. "Because Freya needs some laughter."

"Why do I have to do this?"

"Leo, come get into position right now."

As Leo reluctantly gets out of bed and goes to stand next to her, I look from one to the other in confusion. "What's going on?"

"You'll see," Ruby declares, connecting her phone to my speakers and putting her beer bottle down.

Leo puts his hands on his hips and shoots me an apologetic look. "This wasn't my idea."

"We've been working on this all week," Ruby informs me. "Are you ready?"

"I guess so."

She presses a button on her phone and then shoves it down on the desk. Britney Spears's "Stronger" starts blaring out of the speakers, and Ruby and Leo launch into a dance routine. I use the words "launch" and "dance routine" lightly. I burst out laughing as Ruby bops about with full enthusiasm, all the while encouraging Leo, who half-heartedly joins in with the arm movements and hip swings. I sit up to appreciate the full show, unable to stop giggling.

"You see?" Ruby cries happily. "I told you it would cheer her up! Now, Leo, ready for the *Dirty Dancing* lift?"

"Rubes, I really don't think—"

She runs full pelt toward him and he does his best to lift her before they collapse in a tangled heap on the floor. I shriek with laughter, clutching my stomach. In that moment, everything seems just that little bit better, and that means a lot.

Because a few days ago, in the worst moments, I wasn't sure I'd ever feel like laughing again.

CHAPTER THREE

A week later, I return to the London flat.

Standing in silence in the middle of the hall with my bags at my feet, I instantly regret insisting I do this alone.

All my things are just where I left them back when I was in control of my life, before my blissful ignorance was shattered. But all of Matthew's things are now gone, leaving bizarre empty spaces scattered around the flat. Like the photo frame of his parents, making the mantelpiece look uneven. The PlayStation that sat under the TV stand, gone. The bookcase has random gaps in it where his biographies used to fit. He only read biographies.

Part of me didn't think he'd actually go through the effort of moving out. Part of me thought he'd walk in here and be reminded of the life we've built together, which would make him realize that he was making a huge mistake.

"Oh my god," I whisper out loud as something dawns on me, "he took Percy!"

Okay, I was sad there for a second. But now I'm *furious*. I get my phone out of my pocket and call Ruby. She answers on the second ring.

"Hey! Are you at the flat? Are you all right?"

"He took Percy!"

"Huh?"

"Percy! He took him!"

She gasps. "No!"

"Yes!"

"That *fucker!*"

"I know! I can't believe it! He just took him! He's gone!"

"Surely you should get custody!"

"Obviously! What do I do?"

I hear Leo in the background ask Ruby what's going on.

"Matthew took Percy," she explains to him while I wait. "Freya's just got back to the London flat and Percy's gone." There's a pause. "Come on, Percy! You know Percy! The plant!"

"Not just any plant," I huff down the phone. "A large Swiss cheese plant that I bought and I cared for! That is *my* plant! And he's taken him!"

"You're on speaker," Ruby informs me.

"Hi, Freya," Leo's voice comes through tinnily.

"Leo, can you believe this?! How could he? He just took Percy!"

"Hang on," Leo says cautiously, "didn't you give him the plant as a gift?"

There's a pause until Ruby snaps, "Oh shut up, Leo. What has that got to do with it?"

"I'm just saying," Leo explains, sounding as though he's beginning to regret getting involved in this conversation, "maybe Matthew thought Percy belonged to him because it was a gift for his birthday."

"Yeah, well, I thought we were getting married because Matthew proposed to me," I say grumpily. *"Things change, Leo."*

"You know what? You're right," Leo croaks, no doubt receiving a thump on the arm from Ruby. "He should have left Percy. The plant clearly belongs to you."

He quickly adds, "Matthew's an arsehole," just in case we weren't sure.

"Thank you, Leo," Ruby says curtly. "You just remember whose side you're on."

"Guys, what am I going to do?" I ask, devastated as I stare at the horrible empty space where Percy sat. "I need to get him back! But I can't ring Matthew! I promised myself I wouldn't contact him for a while after what happened last weekend."

There's a silence at the other end of the phone. I know that Leo is likely giving Ruby a pointed look. He still blames her for what happened, but in her defense, it really was all me. I didn't plan on doing it. It just sort of . . . happened.

I don't even have the excuse of alcohol, because I was sober.

Last Saturday night, we'd had dinner and Leo and Dad were in the sitting room, having a beer and discussing golf or something boring. Ruby and I were upstairs talking and I don't know how, but we sort of riled each other up and decided it might be a good idea to get in the car and drive to Matthew's parents' house to demand an explanation.

I'm almost certain it was my idea in the first place and, while Ruby didn't exactly do much to discourage me—"*Let's do it*" were her exact words—it definitely came from me.

We snuck out to my car, because we knew that Leo and Dad would talk us out of it.

As Ruby had been drinking since the morning, I was the one driving while she was in charge of the music. The whole journey we listened to such hits as Kelly Clarkson's "Since U Been Gone" and Gloria Gaynor's "I Will Survive," blasting them out full volume, singing at the top of our lungs. So, by the time I pulled in to his parents' drive, I was *pumped*.

"I can do this," I announced, turning off the ignition.

"You can do this," Ruby echoed.

I got out of the car and knocked on their door. They must have seen it was me through the window, because there was a noticeable pause in answering and when the door finally opened, Matthew was the one to emerge.

"What are you doing here, Freya?" he asked, giving me a sympathetic look. "You shouldn't be here."

Right off the bat, I'm furious. Because firstly, how dare he tell me what I should or should not be doing? And secondly, I don't need his pitiful looks. *I'm fine.*

"I deserve an explanation!" I announced.

"What?"

"You need to tell me why this has happened!"

He sighed. "I'm going to call your dad and get him to come collect you."

"I can drive myself home, thank you very much!"

"Okay, well then, I think you should go."

That's when I almost lost it. There he is, the love of my life, standing in front of me. And it's really hitting me that we've broken up and we're not getting married, and all the emotion is threatening to bubble over.

I had scrunched up my face as hard as possible, desperate not to cry. Ruby was out of the car at this point because she could see I was suddenly struggling. She put her arm around me, shot him a dirty look, told him *exactly* what she thought of him—which made him wince, because he loves Ruby—and then she said we should head home.

And do you know what Matthew said?

He said, "You'll be okay, babe."

Ruby tensed. I froze. His words were hanging in the air and he knew he'd made a mistake on so many levels. The tone, the endearment—the whole sentence stabbed me like a knife through the heart.

You'll be okay, babe. Are you kidding me? *Are you kidding me?*

It's safe to say, I saw red.

I shook off Ruby's arm from my shoulders, I strode right up

to him, and, before he had a chance to apologize, I karate-kicked him right in the balls.

Yeah. It was bad. Also, I use the words "karate-kicked" loosely. I tried karate when I was a teenager and quite enjoyed it, but haven't done it in years. My balance isn't what it was, and I'm not really flexible or elegant enough to pull it off. Still the energy was all there.

He doubled over, gasping in pain. Ruby yelped in surprise and then burst into hysterical laughter, yelling, *"Yes! Go Freya!"*

I think Matthew's mum must have been watching from the window, because she came frantically running out to his aid. As she flanked him, checking to see if he was all right, I cleared my throat.

"Sorry you had to see that, Gail," I told her. "Hope you've got some ice."

And then I turned on my heel and strode back to the car while Ruby cheered me on, like I was in some kind of film.

Of course, I regretted it as soon as we were home and the adrenaline had worn off. I was convinced I'd destroyed any hope of him coming back to me. No matter how many times Ruby said he deserved it, I didn't believe her. If he had been in any doubt over losing me, a karate kick in the balls was hardly going to help my case.

I made a vow to leave Matthew alone now, no matter how unnatural and painful it was. He was right. We did need space. I just have to trust he'll come back to me and, in the meantime, as Dad said, I'll keep putting one foot in front of the other.

Dad thought the karate-kick-in-the-balls story was the best thing he'd ever heard. Leo agreed that Matthew absolutely deserved it, but I think he saw how upset I was over the whole thing. He told Ruby off for sneaking out without his advice.

Ruby's told me she doesn't regret it, but I can tell from the silence down the phone now at the mention of the incident that it's still a point of contention in their household.

"Maybe Matthew has earned the right to Percy after I did that," I admit reluctantly.

"What about what he did to you? He hasn't earned the right to anything," Ruby insists.

"Percy aside, how are you doing in the flat for the first time since . . . everything?" Leo asks. "Are you sure you don't want us to come over?"

"I'm sure. Thanks, though."

"I really wish we could be with you," Ruby says seriously. "Just for the first night. Please, let us. It really wouldn't be a problem."

I smile into the phone. Ruby and I have had this discussion a hundred times over the past couple of days. She has, very sweetly, worked out a rota between her and Leo and my other two closest friends from university, Cali and Simone, to stay with me all week so that I won't be alone in the flat once. I had to really fight my corner to tell her that I wanted to be alone for the first night.

The truth is, I don't want anyone to witness any kind of meltdown. I can't let them see me fall apart and I can't promise that won't happen tonight.

"You're the best, Rubes, but please don't worry," I assure her once again. "I've done enough wallowing at Dad's. Time to get back on track."

"Okay, but it has only been a couple of weeks," Ruby says gently.

"I know." I glance at a picture of me and Matthew up on the wall. "I'm fine. Promise. I'll call you if I'm not. I'm going to order some delicious takeaway, have a bath, you know. Look after myself."

"Good. Call us straightaway if you need anything," Leo says.

"I will."

"And keep us updated on other things he took," Ruby adds. "We can make a list and steal it back if necessary."

"Will do. I'll speak to you later."

"Bye, Freya," Ruby says. "And don't go kicking anyone else in the balls unless I'm there to witness it!"

I laugh and hang up. The room is eerily quiet again. I take a deep breath and then pick up my bags to take them through to the bedroom to see what else has gone.

Might as well get this over with.

⌇

I can't believe it. He's taken the piece of art we got from Spitalfields market the day he proposed! We bought it from the stall of this super talented young artist and then a few hours later, Matthew got down on one knee, so I had the painting framed and put it up on the wall opposite our bed!

Did he think he was being nice by taking it?

He must have done. He must have thought it would be too weird to leave up there. Which he may have been right about. I suppose it would just be a painful reminder of that day.

But, still. I'm annoyed.

⌇

Shame. He's completely emptied his wardrobe. I was considering whether it might be fun to burn an item of his clothing like they do in films.

Though I do feel like I've had a bit of revenge by karate-kicking him in the balls.

Still, a bonfire of that disgusting brown jacket he loves would have been entertaining.

⌇

I see that he's made off with his bedside lamp. I suppose that's fine. It was on his side of the bed, so I guess that technically belongs to him. But now the room looks uneven and it's not like he was particularly attached to that reading lamp, it was just a plain one from IKEA that I bought. Not that I care. It's his right.

I'm sure he needs it for all those biographies he's clearly planning to read for a second time.

Personally, I think it's a little bit petty, but that's neither here nor there.

⌒

Typical. He's taken the chessboard.

You know, I was getting quite good at chess and I seem to remember it being a present from his dad to *both* of us. But whatever. I can't help but notice he's also gone off with Monopoly. Jenga has been left in the cupboard.

How thoughtful of him.

⌒

He took the nonstick frying pan.

He knew that was the only pan I cared about! He could have nabbed any of the other pots and pans and I wouldn't have minded, but that smart nonstick one was brand-new!! Okay, so he was the chef in the relationship, while I can't really cook, but that's *not the point*. I liked that pan. It was nice and easy to wash after he cooked with it.

I caught him trying to sneak it in the dishwasher one time. Seriously. Didn't he read the instructions on the bottom of the pan *explicitly* telling him not to put it in the dishwasher?!

He doesn't deserve that pan. He doesn't treat it right.

⌒

All the Tupperware is gone. All of it.

What the fuck.

⌒

He has also taken the electric whisk and the cheese grater.

The cheese grater. *Seriously?!*

Who is this monster?

I see he's helped himself to our alcohol collection. I think you'll find, Matthew, that we got those expensive spirits you have claimed as yours because of *my job*.

Luckily, I can stock back up with the twenty or so bottles of spirits I organized for the cocktails we didn't drink at the wedding we didn't have.

Speaking of which, now might be the time to have a splash of whiskey.

Bathroom is, thankfully, unscathed. He only took his cheap shower gel, razor, and toothbrush. He left that expensive moisturizer I gave him for Christmas last year in the cabinet. I just checked and he never opened it anyway.

Whatever. His skin doesn't deserve to be moist. I hope it's dry as a fucking bone.

Where's my Aesop hand cream? It's gone. He wouldn't dare. *He wouldn't dare.*

I am going to *lose my shi—*

Oh wait. It's here. Phew! Crisis averted.

And last, but not least, I've only just noticed he's seen fit to take the weighted owl doorstop his uncle got him that we used for the bedroom door. Wow.

Well, good riddance. It didn't even look like an owl. It looked like a knitted brown blob with googly eyes.

And I tripped over it like a hundred times a day.

So long, stupid googly-eyed blob. I shall not miss thee.

I've wandered into the bedroom again with my glass of Staeburn scotch—one of the brands I work on, a deliciously smooth and fairly gentle single malt with a hint of vanilla—and opened the drawer of his bedside table, to check if he missed anything. I wasn't expecting to find anything, considering he bothered to take the lamp on top of the table. It's unlikely he'd leave the contents of the drawer.

It's completely empty, except for the engagement ring box.

I stare at it. I didn't realize he'd kept it. I remember telling him to keep the box just in case I ever needed to take the ring off for washing up or something and wanted to place it somewhere safe. But considering I never bother to take my ring off, I'd forgotten about it.

As if when he came to clear out his stuff from the flat, he emptied this drawer and made the decision to leave this one thing.

I can't work out if it's deliberately cruel.

Slowly sitting down on the bed, I hold up my left hand. I haven't taken the ring off yet. Dad told me that Matthew was sorting returning our wedding rings, and as I hadn't had the chance to wear mine yet anyway, it didn't feel overly crushing. There were other things to worry about.

But the engagement ring is different. I've worn it every day for a year. I've got used to it. Like it belongs there. My hand would feel naked and weird without it.

Taking it off would make everything feel . . . real.

I close my eyes for a moment, and allow myself to think about the day that now feels like a lifetime ago, when Matthew and I went to a shop in Hatton Garden to pick out the ring. He (correctly) thought I'd want to choose the ring myself, so he proposed with a tasteful Astley Clarke milky moonstone placeholder ring with a thin gold band, which I wore for a couple of weeks until we were able to book an appointment with a jeweler. I honestly didn't know what I wanted until I saw this one. A solitaire diamond on a white gold ring. Classic, timeless, elegant. That's how it was described by the well-groomed man taking my finger measurement.

"This is beautiful," I said, admiring it as I slid it on and held my hand up to the light. "What do you think, Matthew?"

"If you like it, I like it," he confirmed.

We left the shop hand in hand. I beamed up at him, bursting with excitement. He laughed at my expression and kissed the top of my head.

I clench my jaw at the stabbing pain in my chest. Then, steeling myself, I open my eyes determinedly, down the rest of my whiskey, and twist the ring up off my finger. Opening the box, I carefully push it into its slot between the black velvet cushions.

I know I will wear this ring again.

I gaze one last time at the perfect diamond, brutally sparkling in the light.

I snap the box shut.

CHAPTER FOUR

I've taken up a new hobby.

Everything I've read about surviving breakups says this is what you should do. Apparently, this is the perfect time for me to create positive experiences for myself and try new things.

I've come to realize that, apart from my morning jogs, which I'm *very* gradually beginning to work back into my routine, I currently have no hobbies, so literally anything will be new and exciting to me.

I've been lucky to have company during this time of major life adjustment, thanks to Ruby, Leo, Simone, and Cali. I've barely had a night on my own ever since I returned to London a few weeks ago, and I know they've been working their arses off to keep me busy. We've had cozy movie nights, boozy dinners, and weekends jam-packed with activities. Simone even took advantage of my vulnerable state and dragged me along to an interactive theater performance with her, which is, quite honestly, my worst nightmare, but I didn't have the energy to protest.

It was a terrible experience, but I suppose it was better than spending the evening crying into a gin while watching psychological thrillers, a scenario I've found myself in more than once recently when I've been left to my own devices.

Simone found my awkwardness during the interactive show highly entertaining. Hailing from Leeds, she's a force of nature, strong-willed, loud, and fearless. Cali is more of a calming soul, very sweet and gentle-natured. Matthew once said Cali reminded him of a Disney princess and, you know what, I can see it. She's easygoing, optimistic, and the person you want to have a cuddle with when you're feeling blue. When it was her turn to organize an evening for me, we drank herbal tea, ate chocolate digestives, and watched old seasons of *Keeping Up with the Kardashians*.

Awkwardly, Cali's fiancé, Dominic, is close friends with Matthew. Cali felt the need to promise me over and over that she is *furious* at Matthew, she's completely on my side, and she doesn't want anything to do with him. It is, of course, going to be a very difficult situation for them as a couple, but there's nothing I can do about it.

When I first saw her, I wanted to ask Cali a hundred questions about Matthew—Is he upset? Does he miss me? Does he talk about me? Does he regret this?—but I can't. It wouldn't be fair to her.

And to be honest, I'm not sure I want to hear the answers.

At first, I considered whether something like yoga would be a good hobby for the present moment, but my one attempt didn't go so well. I had hoped that it would give my brain a nice hour off from its constant whirring, but all it did was heighten it. Yoga is so quiet and peaceful. It literally gives you the perfect opportunity to *think*. Every time the instructor went, "Clear your mind," in that whispery, gentle, mildly unnerving tone of hers, my mind went, *I wonder what Matthew is up to right now.*

"You learn to clear your mind," Ruby informed me over the phone, when I rang her afterward. "That comes with time and meditation practice."

"Does it work with every mind? Or is it just some minds?"

"You're worried that your mind can never be cleared?"

"Ruby, it was torture. I had to mentally start listing what I needed to get from Sainsbury's just to keep Matthew from creeping on in there. When the instructor came round with that weird bell thing at the end and told us to lie back and close our eyes, I was repeating to myself over and over, 'Don't forget the salsa, don't forget the salsa, salsa, salsa, salsa.' And I've just been into the local shop on my road, and you know what?"

"You've forgotten the salsa?"

"That's right. Because once I was out of the class, my mind was too busy freaking out about never being clear."

"What are you having tonight that needs salsa?"

"Doritos."

There was a pause at the other end of the phone. "Not for dinner, though, right?"

"Of course not," I assured her. "That's my side dish."

"What's your main?"

I hesitated. "Cheese."

"You know, instead of taking up yoga as your new hobby, how about you consider cooking?"

It was a strong suggestion. Sure, I could do a couple of staple meals, which mainly consisted of shoving something prepared into the oven, but I wasn't exactly adventurous. Since Matthew took the nonstick frying pan with him, I've been less inclined to hang around my kitchen (except for the fridge end), but Ruby was right. Cooking was not only a good idea for a new hobby, but it would also be advantageous to my health.

So, after I failed at yoga, I took a stab at cooking. That did not go well.

It turns out that timing is very important in cooking. You'd think I'd actually be very good at that side of things. I'm organized, sensible, and punctual, and my timekeeping skills are second to none. Too good, Matthew might say. Isn't that what he was hammering home in the broom cupboard? I'm too together for him. Too in control.

Apologies, Matthew, for not being a hot mess. Enjoy your new life of double-booking yourself for events, missing people's birthdays, and not knowing the upcoming bank holidays. Good luck trying to reserve an outdoor pub table on a Friday evening in the summertime, mate.

Anyway, timing. Key to cooking, I've discovered, especially a curry. But how can you possibly stay on top of getting whatever out of the oven, when you're busy chopping something else and also supposed to be smothering another thing in some sauce so it marinates?

I got so confused with all my different timers, I couldn't remember which alarm was for what thing. Safe to say that my first attempt was not a success. But these things are sent to try us, right? I wasn't going to give up on cooking as easy as I'd given up on yoga. At least the stress of it all had stopped me from thinking about Matthew. I was too busy trying not to set myself on fire. So, I would try again.

I thought maybe I'd aimed too high, so I went on to BBC Good Food and picked a one-pot recipe that was labeled as "Easy."

Those bastards. It was *not* easy.

Firstly, what the fuck is a cacciatore? I didn't even know what it was I was cooking, but the pictures looked nice, and the site sold it as a recipe that you just throw into a pot and Bob's your uncle, so I thought this was the one for me. I had to pop the onion in with the chicken that had been cooking away, and fry the onion until it was tender.

How do you know when the onion is tender?!

Was I supposed to stab it with a fork? How do you stab one of those fuckers?! They're all chopped up thinly like instructed. I wasn't going to pinch it with my fingers, because I'd rather not have burn marks, so I had to just guess. Do you know how stressful guesswork is for a control freak? *It is high-stress.*

So, then I poured in the wine, ready to let it "evaporate slightly." *What is "slightly"?!* How do I know when it has evaporated slightly?! Am I supposed to be able to *see* the wine liquid changing to a gas?! My vision is not that spectacular! It is human vision!

Seriously, who is writing this recipe, *a hawk*?!

Honestly, by this point, I was glugging the wine from the bottle, while also tipping it into the pot. The moral of this story is that people need to be *more specific* with their cooking instructions. I ended up eating my burned, dry chicken cacciatore from the pot, with onions that were so crispy they snapped between my teeth, while messaging Ruby to update her on my hobby status. Cooking was not The One.

You know, before I was dumped in a broom cupboard the day before my wedding, I was a great believer in everything happening for a reason. Now I strongly believe that many bad things happen simply because people like Matthew act like arseholes and ruin things for everyone else.

Argh. I miss him.

However, in this case, thanks to my cooking attempts not working out, I ended up stumbling upon the perfect new hobby for me.

Gardening.

It's going to become my thing. It has it all: calming vibes, feeling at one with nature, and satisfying results. We have a sort of small patio bit outside the flat, which is currently overrun with weeds and horribly neglected.

Matthew and I had planned on buying our own place together after the wedding. We wanted to get on the property ladder and we'd saved up, but we agreed that we'd focus on the wedding first and then we would start looking for somewhere to buy. It was exciting because, once we were engaged, chats about The Future seemed that much more real and within reach than before. Matthew must have felt that, too—only for him, that was a negative rather than a positive.

I love this flat, but because we rent it, it's never felt completely ours to do what we want with, and I suppose that attitude extended out to the patio.

But I have a feeling I might be a bit of a natural when it comes to this sort of thing. I'm going to work hard to transform this outside space.

"You can't buy a gardening fork and claim you're a gardener," Adrian says during a video call.

I prop my tablet up on the kitchen chair I've dragged outside so he can witness my first foray into this world of pleasant greenery and nature.

"I didn't just buy a gardening fork," I reply smugly, wiggling my hands into brand-new polka-dot gardening gloves. "I also bought these. And a cute little spade thing."

"A trowel."

"You're just jealous because you don't have a garden in New York."

"That is partly true," he admits with a grin. "But I'm not sure I'd call that there a garden. It's more like some slabs of concrete paving with borders."

"When I'm done with it, it will be a haven. I shall sit out here, listen to the visiting birds sing, and watch the world go by."

"It's surrounded by a wall. You'll be watching bricks."

"You know what I mean," I huff, opening a garden-waste bag. "How is it across the pond anyway? All good with you?"

"Work is busy, doing some long hours," he says, running a hand through his hair. "I'm missing home a bit."

"You always miss it for a week or so, and then you'll forget about dear old Blighty in the haze of New York's glamorous lights."

"I do love this city."

"Me too."

"You need to come visit me again soon, please. Hey, in your next parcel, can you send over some crumpets? And also chocolate buttons."

"How old are you, five?" I snigger, kneeling on the ground and pulling out my first weed, getting all its roots up, which is *extremely* satisfying.

I chuck it in the waste bag triumphantly. I am so into this gardening thing.

"When I called you two days ago, you were eating a Dip Dab," Adrian points out.

"That's true." I nod, clutching another weed in my grasp. "I'd forgotten how good Dip Dabs are."

"They are sensational."

"I'll make a note of crumpets and chocolate buttons," I assure him.

"Speaking of home stuff, I spoke to Mum the other day."

I pause midway through tugging up a weed and turn to face the screen. "Really? Like, did she leave a voicemail, or did you actually talk to her?"

"We actually spoke," he says.

I pull up the weed and chuck it in the bag, using the fork to start digging up the next one, which seems a bit trickier than the others. "What did she say?"

"She was calling about you. She wanted to know if you were okay. Apparently, you haven't spoken to her since . . . since it all happened."

"Or didn't happen, you mean." I stab at the soil. "I don't have much to say to her. But I have sent her a message or two, promising her that I'm fine."

"Yeah, but she knows you're not."

"I am fine."

"Come on, Freya." Adrian sighs. "You're doing amazingly and I'm really proud of you, but you've been through a lot. And I know Mum hasn't exactly been there for us in the past but—"

"You're on her side now?" I shake my head, finally pulling up this stubborn bloody weed, shaking the soil off the roots. "What did she say to you to manage that?"

"There are no sides, Freya, and you know that I'm not Mum's biggest fan. But she sounded genuinely worried, and we've both known for a while that she wants to make amends."

"Her idea of making amends is for us to travel to the Lake District to write poetry with her and Evan. If she wanted to make things better all these years later, she'd have made the effort to come to London once in a while."

"I don't think if we went there, we'd be expected to partake in their village poetry club," Adrian says, chuckling. "We may have to listen to a few verses, but I don't think it's mandatory. She says you're avoiding her calls."

"She's correct."

"Hear me out." He takes a deep breath and becomes serious for a bit, which is greatly unnatural for him. "The fact that it's been a few weeks and she's still hounding you, not to mention me and Dad, just to make sure you're okay—that has to mean something, right?"

"She's hounding Dad?"

I feel a lurch of guilt. We don't really talk about it, but I don't think Dad ever really got over Mum. He's never tried dating anyone else and it's been a long time since she left him for Evan. He says it's got nothing to do with her, he's just not interested in the dating game, but we all know how heartbroken he was when she walked out.

Dad wants us to be amicable with Mum. For a while, he's been saying how important it is that we make amends; he wants his children to have a relationship with their mother. But, even though he claims that he and Mum are on good terms now, he can't be loving the fact that she's calling asking about me.

"Dad doesn't mind," Adrian says, reading my mind. "He doesn't want her to bother you if that's not what you want. But after a couple of missed phone calls from her, I decided to pick up and have a chat. She sounds genuinely worried. I think it might be worth calling her. She's still our mum, you know? She's really upset that someone did this to you."

I let out a heavy sigh, wiping my forehead with the back of my glove. "Fine."

"You'll call her?"

"I'll pick up if she calls me."

"Good enough." He grins. "I have to head off to breakfast, but let me know how the gardening goes, yeah?"

"Thanks for calling. And, yes, will do."

"I'm very happy that you've found a hobby you're passionate about. Can I give you a tip?"

"I don't need any tips."

"When you touch your face with your garden glove on, you're going to get mud on your skin." He waves cheerfully at the camera. "Byeeeee!"

As he hangs up, I peer at the reflection of my face in the blank tablet screen and can see a smear of mud across my forehead from where I wiped it earlier. I roll my eyes in irritation, but I leave it, because it's not like anyone is going to see it. I stay focused on my weeding and turning the soil, and gradually the border of the patio starts looking much better.

It's very peaceful here in this little outside space. Matthew and I wasted it. Yeah, it's small, but with a little work and some bright, colorful flowers and plants, it will be quaint and cheery. We could have sat out here on some nice garden furniture if we'd bothered to buy any and enjoyed our little corner of sunshine. I think I could fit in a couple of chairs and one of those small, round garden tables.

I wonder why Matthew and I never sat out here. I've been doing a lot of this: wondering if we'd done things differently, whether the relationship might have worked out. I know that I'm supposed to focus on what's ahead, not dwell on the past. But in any other area of my life, if something goes wrong, I analyze it, so I know how to do better next time. How to not make the same mistake twice.

So, I guess the answer to why we didn't make the most of this patio is that we got complacent. After twelve years, it's easy to do. If we went to sit in the sunshine, it would be in a pub garden with our friends. We wouldn't bother to sit out here alone together, enjoying the tranquil warm evenings.

I wonder if that was my fault or his? If we'd done things like sit in a lovely little garden we'd worked on together, would that have made his future with me seem better?

If I hadn't karate-kicked him in the balls, I'd call him and ask.

It would be easier if I could just blame his change of heart on the neglected garden. But when I think about it, we did have date nights. We made an effort to book meals out every now and then. We had laughs. We were happy.

Why has he broken us?

I stab at the soil with the fork a little too enthusiastically, flinging the dirt as the prongs twist and lift up. I wince, brushing the mud off me.

That's when I notice it. The longest worm I have *ever seen*.

"*Ahhhhhhhhhhhhhhhh!*" I scream, jumping to my feet and stumbling backward, dropping the fork and letting it clatter on the ground.

Squealing and jumping up and down on the spot, I yank off the gloves and use my hands to frantically brush off my clothes and hair, suddenly feeling like there's worms all over me, even though I'm pretty sure there was just the one. My phone starts vibrating in my pocket and I quickly answer, still shuddering as I watch the worm move across the patio.

"Hey," Ruby says, "do you want to come over tonight for dinner and a delicious red wine that I've picked up?"

"A *worm just attacked me.*"

"What?"

"A *worm flung itself at me.*"

She gasps. "Are you serious? I didn't know worms could do that! They can launch themselves at you?! Gross!"

"Okay, technically I flung it at myself while gardening, but oh my god, it is the biggest worm I've ever seen in my life!"

"Did you just say you were gardening?"

"Yes! It's my new hobby."

"Your new hobby is gardening?" she asks in disbelief.

"*Can we focus on the worm please.*"

"Is it still on you now?"

"No, it's on the ground. *Bleugh.* Why do they move in that way? Like the head is going and then the tail has to catch up. Why can't they crawl like a normal bug?"

"You mean, like a centipede or something?"

"Oh my god, can you get centipedes in England? Do I have to keep an eye out for worms *and* centipedes when I'm gardening? What the fuck."

"You weren't prepared for this?"

"I didn't even think about it." I hesitated. "I was thinking about Matthew when the worm attacked me. I was wondering why we never sat out here."

"Maybe the universe was sending you a sign," she reasons. "When you think about Matthew, worms will fly at your head."

I sigh heavily. "Did you say something about red wine?"

"It cost twelve pounds, so you know it's classy stuff. Come round for sixish?"

"I'll be there."

"Excellent. You know, I can't believe you're gardening. For

what it's worth, I think it's a really good idea. I'm very excited about this new hobby of yours and lend it my full support."

"You do?"

"It's wholesome and good for the soul. My granny was a real gardening nut, she always said it was soothing. A bee stung her once, but she just planted more foxgloves. Apparently bees love them. I'm going to buy you a big sun hat with the string that ties round your chin. She had one of those and looked adorable in it."

"I'm thirty-two, Ruby. I don't think I need a sun hat with string that ties round my chin."

"How about next weekend, we come round to yours to sit in the garden and admire your work? Unless it's raining, in which case we can admire it through the window."

"I have Isabelle's hen do next weekend."

There's a pause before she carefully asks, "You're still going to that? Are you sure that's a good idea?"

"Yeah, course," I say, trying to sound more confident than I feel. "I want to be there for Isabelle. It's been a few weeks now, Rubes, I can't hide away from everyone but you lot forever. And it's a good way of easing me into the Wedding Season. It's coming at me, whether I'm ready for it or not."

"I guess so," she says, reluctantly. "Well, we can come over another time to admire your gardening prowess. You keep going with it."

I hesitate. "Even though there's a chance that worms will attack me?"

"Oh please, you spent twelve years putting up with Matthew." She snorts. "What's a couple of worms?"

CHAPTER FIVE

I'm so sorry, Freya. Breakups are just the worst," Isabelle tells me, adjusting her veil. "Honestly, I don't know how you're doing this. If I'd been through what you've been through, I'd be . . . like . . . dead on the floor."

I nod, taking a sip from my cup. "Mmm."

"You are so strong." She places a hand on my shoulder, her heavily mascaraed eyes gazing at me. "I want you to know we're all here for you." She hiccups loudly and then giggles. "Whoops! What's that you're drinking?"

"Prosecco."

"Can I borrow it? Only way to get rid of hiccups is to drink from a glass upside down."

"Don't you need water for that?"

"Yeah, but it's my hen do!" she cries. "So, prosecco it is!"

I smile and hold it just out of her reach. "Finish your pee first. Then you can attempt to drink this upside down."

"Smart thinking," she slurs, reaching for the loo roll.

Using the wall to balance, she stands up and smooths down the skirt of her dress before wobbling in her heels across to the sink to wash her hands. I stand up from the ledge of the bath I was perched on while waiting for her.

"I am so in awe of you, Freya. You should know that. We all are."

"Thanks, Isabelle," I laugh. "Come on, though, let's get back to your hen. I think they're keen to play another game. How are those hiccups? We can get some water first."

"No, I want to say this," she tells me firmly, turning off the tap and spinning round to jab her finger at me. "You are so amazing. You didn't have to come to this and yet here you are."

I had braced myself for a lot of this chat throughout the weekend. Isabelle kept messaging me saying there was absolutely no pressure for me to come on her hen, that it was surely the last thing I wanted, and she couldn't bear the idea of me forcing myself to go. Her maid of honor sent me a very sweet WhatsApp, too.

But even though anything to do with weddings is hard to swallow, I didn't want to miss this. They may be a bit silly, but you remember your mates' hen dos for the rest of your life. Isabelle is a really close friend of mine from school, and I want to celebrate her hen. However difficult it is.

So I told the MOH that she was very kind, but she didn't need to worry, I would be coming, and I sent the message in as bright and cheery a tone as possible. I added in a lot of emojis, so she knew everything was just fine.

The problem is, whenever Isabelle has a few drinks, she loves to have deep conversations. So, I've spent the majority of today warding her off the topic of Matthew-and-Me. I knew when she grabbed my hand and insisted I come with her to pee, she'd want to make a drunken speech in the loo, so I casually tried to shake her free, but her little hands are very strong and I couldn't pry those stubborn fingers loose.

"I couldn't do it," she continues, shaking her head dramatically. "But after everything that's happened to you, you're here for me. You're right there"—she points at me with her finger, her eyes glazing over as she hiccups—"and that means more to me than anything. I hope you know that."

"I do. Come on, let's leave the bathroom."

"I love you, Freya," she says, throwing her arms around me and hugging me so tight, she almost cracks one of my ribs.

"Love you, too," I wheeze.

She pulls away, cupping my face in her hands and giving my cheeks an affectionate pat, before letting me open the door for her. She barrels out and stumbles back into the living room of the Bath Airbnb, where she's greeted with cheers and whoops.

"There you are!" Kelly, the maid of honor, yells, grabbing Isabelle and plonking her down on a chair. "Right, time for another game. Top up your glasses, girls, and get ready to . . . pin the *junk* on the *hunk!*"

As the room descends into excitable chaos, I sneak out to the kitchen and through the back door into the garden, filling up my cup from the fridge on the way. Niamh, the other school friend here at the hen and therefore the only other person I know, is out there in the late-afternoon sunshine already, smoking.

She raises her eyebrows behind her sunglasses as I appear on the patio. "I didn't know you smoked."

"I don't," I reply as I make my way over to the garden furniture to join her. "I wanted some fresh air."

She smiles to herself. "Code for 'I needed to get the hell out of there.'"

"Nah," I laugh, sitting down. "It's a lot of fun, but I got cornered by Isabelle in the loo. She wanted to tell me how strong I am."

"Ah." Niamh takes a drag of her cigarette. "Classic Izzy. Loves a drunken heart-to-heart." She hesitates. "I forgot, we're not supposed to call her Izzy now, are we? She prefers Isabelle. Difficult to get out of the school habits."

"Yeah well, I can understand that. Remember when everyone at school went through a phase of calling me 'Feathers'?"

"Oh yeah," she laughs. "Because of the hat thing."

I nod, grimacing at the memory. One of many horrifying

moments I can blame my mother for. She showed up for the school Speech Day one year with the most gigantic hat on with plumes of feathers sticking out the top. The people sitting behind her were furious. She, of course, didn't notice their anger, or didn't care. All the kids laughed about it and I was mortified.

To be fair, at least she showed up for that Speech Day. I think it may have been the only school event of mine she attended. Naturally, she had to make a statement.

I still haven't spoken to her since Adrian's phone call. She called me while I was working earlier in the week, and I haven't quite mustered the courage to call her back. I promise myself I'll do it when I get home from the hen do, if only for Adrian's sake. And Dad's.

"How is your mum?" Niamh asks, exhaling. "You ever see her?"

"Not really."

Niamh nods. There's a few moments of comfortable silence before she says quietly, "So how are you, really? I didn't want to bring it up this weekend, but since we're here alone without the gaggle"—she jerks her head toward the house, where we can hear shrieks of hysterics as a blindfolded Isabelle tries to pin a penis on a ripped cutout fella—"I don't know, it would be odd not to say anything. But tell me if you don't want to talk about it."

"That's sweet of you. Yeah, I'm all right. I'm fine."

"Are you, like, actually fine? Or fine-but-not-really-fine?"

I smile at her. "Maybe in the middle of the two."

"Being here must be difficult." She waves her hand about. "Memories of your hen and stuff."

"A little."

Niamh takes another drag. "Want to change the conversation?"

This is what I like about Niamh. There's no bullshit with her. She's always been straight to the point. When we were at school and someone pissed her off, she'd tell them so. But she has this talent of not making it too harsh, although sometimes what she says can be hard to hear. It always needs to be said, though. She's blunt, but it's never gratuitous.

Having said that, she did once tell me that my eyebrows were a "unique" shape.

Make of that what you will.

"Yeah, best not to dwell." I give her a weak smile. "How is Freddie?"

"He's good. He's getting into golf, which is unexpected."

"I'm into gardening now."

"That is also unexpected."

I laugh, resting my head back on the chair. "Not long now until your wedding. How are you feeling about it?"

"Yeah, it's fine. Our wedding planner at the hotel in Dublin is amazing. She's basically doing everything."

"Oh good."

We fall into silence. She doesn't want to talk about her wedding, and I'm not sure I want to hear all that much about it. Which I hate, by the way. I hate that Matthew's actions have made me dread these huge, exciting events in my friends' lives.

"Did I ever tell you about the time I proposed?" Niamh asks suddenly.

"What?" I stare at her. "I thought Freddie proposed to you."

"He did," she confirms. "But I wasn't talking about Freddie. I was talking about my ex, Jules."

"You proposed to her?"

"Yep. On a picnic blanket in Richmond Park, surrounded by deer." She smiles to herself. "It was extremely romantic, if I do say so myself."

"What happened? You've never told me this before!"

She shrugs, stubbing out her cigarette. "I've never told anyone before, except my parents. I bought her a ring and proposed the weekend before her birthday. She said yes, everything was perfect, and then the next day she changed her mind. We broke up that evening."

My jaw drops to the floor. I feel such an overwhelming mixture of emotions: horrified that I didn't know any of this about such a close friend, and sad that she went through it.

"But . . ." I search for the right words to say. "Niamh, I'm so sorry."

"It was a long time ago."

"Why did she say yes and then change her mind?"

"Apparently, she said yes because she was caught up in the moment and she knew it was what she should say. Then she lay awake all night knowing in her gut that she wasn't being truthful to either of us. I was heartbroken, obviously. At that point, it was the happiest night of my life, and she'd been in turmoil. Everything I thought was forever was gone in a flash."

I glance down at the ground. We both know how it feels, then. Niamh reaches for her cigarettes and lights another, before continuing.

"Look, it's a long time ago and obviously now I'm crazy happy with Freddie, but I thought you should know. I'm sure people keep saying this sort of shit to you and it means nothing, but I know firsthand that it really does get easier. It doesn't feel like it at the time, but things do get . . . brighter again."

"I'm clinging to that hope. I appreciate you telling me all this."

"Don't you go spreading it round."

"My lips are sealed." I pause. "Thanks, Niamh."

"Always here for you, Feathers."

I nod and we go quiet again, looking out across the manicured lawn. Whoever owns this house has done a very good job with the garden. The beds running along the edges are bursting with colorful flowers, and there's a tasteful fountain in the middle of the patio, the trickling water lending the garden a calming, tranquil ambience.

"I kicked Matthew in the balls," I blurt out.

Niamh splutters, the smoke billowing around her face. "You *what*?"

"I kicked him in the balls," I repeat.

"What the!" She sits up, pushing her sunglasses back to sit on top of her hair. "You're joking."

"Nope. Ruby was with me. I lost my cool."

"Bloody hell, Freya, that is *brilliant*. Tell me he doubled over in pain?"

"He did. He couldn't speak. His mum had to help him back into the house."

She bursts out laughing. "The *one* time you lose your cool and I'm not there to see it! If I wasn't so happy that it happened, I'd be fuming! Well played!"

"It wasn't my proudest moment."

"Trust me, Freya, if anyone deserves it, it's him." She sits back in her chair, looking baffled. "That is amazing. Hands down, that's going to be the best thing to happen all year. Nothing will beat that."

"Um, how about your wedding this summer?" I laugh. "That's got to win, surely."

"My wedding is not going to beat you kicking Matthew in the balls," she states in her most serious voice. "Did Ruby film it?"

"Thankfully, no. It really wasn't planned."

"You're my new hero, Freya Scott. I want you to know that." She laughs, and points her cigarette at me. "You know what you should do?"

"What?"

"Buy yourself a big, statement ring."

"What do you mean?"

"For that left hand," she explains. "When you feel the time

is right, you should go buy yourself a big, gorgeous ring to sit on the middle finger of your left hand. Then, every time you look at that hand, you won't feel sad. You'll feel proud."

"Proud of what exactly? Kicking someone in the balls?"

She chuckles. "Proud that you got through this."

I glance down at my finger, the indent from the ring still lingering. The back door suddenly swings open and Kelly bursts out into the garden.

"This is where you're hiding!" she cries happily, clapping her hands together, her maid of honor tiara wonkily sitting on her head. "Isabelle's been looking for you both. She wants you to have a go at pinning the junk to the hunk. Totally understand if you want a time-out though, we can always move on to 'Mr. & Mrs.'"

"We were just having a smoke," Niamh explains, stubbing out her cigarette. "But I am *so* ready to pin the junk to the hunk. What do you reckon, Freya?"

"Born ready," I declare, jumping to my feet.

"Apparently, when it comes to junk," Niamh says to Kelly with a grin as we head back into the house, "Freya knows exactly where to aim."

CHAPTER SIX

I t comes out of nowhere.

One minute I'm having a nice time, fully under the impression that I'll emerge from the hen do unscathed, and the next minute I'm engulfed by an overwhelming sense of loss. It's *not* a good time to fall apart. I'm surrounded by a wonderful bunch of people having brilliant fun. I don't want to ruin it. And, perhaps more than that, I don't want anyone to see me crumple into a mess.

I've never been one for public displays of affection or emotion. I know I can sometimes come across as cold. I once had a performance review in an old job where an anonymous colleague had described me as "standoffish" and "hard to read."

(Fuck you, Jeffrey. I know it was you who said that. Just because I didn't fawn all over your homemade almond brownies that one time like everyone else. They were dry, Jeffrey. Dry.)

I'm aware it's something I should work on. There's no denying that Matthew was the chattier one of the two of us when it came to socializing and meeting new people, and I've always envied Ruby for being so open and warm and bubbly. People are instantly drawn to her. She's never reluctant to show how she's feeling. When she and Leo started dating, I was involuntarily engrossed in their relationship, because she told me absolutely everything: how she got major butterflies in her stomach when he smiled, how vulnerable she felt after telling him she really liked him, how irrationally angry he made her.

I never really wanted to show anyone the intricacies of my relationship with Matthew, not even Ruby or Leo. We never argued in front of anyone, but we never kissed in front of them, either. And that was all me. It's not that I desperately wanted to be private, I just didn't think our relationship needed to be on display. We were happy and fine. We had arguments, like every couple, but they weren't important enough to talk about or dwell on. They were over stupid stuff (like how he couldn't just close cupboard doors, he apparently had to slam them).

I'm good at holding it together. And for some reason, I'm determined not to let anyone think otherwise. So when I'm suddenly struck by this all-consuming emotion in the middle of Isabelle's hen do, I have to get out of the room. Clutching my stomach—because it genuinely feels like a physical pain that is going to cause my legs to buckle from beneath me—I stumble out of the door and close it firmly behind me, before scrambling up the stairs to the bedroom I'm sharing with Niamh as fast as I can.

I shut the door and inhale deeply, tears rolling uncontrollably down my cheeks. With my back to the door, I slide down until I'm sitting on the carpet and hug my knees to my chest, pressing my forehead against them as I quietly cry alone.

There had been a few moments throughout the day that had caused a pang to the heart, but I genuinely believed I had shaken them off. The first wobble happened when, after discovering that I was truly terrible at pinning the junk on the hunk (I pinned it to his left nipple), Kelly jumped up and announced it was time for "Hen Confessions."

"Each of you has to write down a funny or outrageous story that's happened to you," she informed us, handing out pieces of paper and pens. "It can be anything. Drunken night out, embarrassing moments, relationship disasters. And then Isabelle has to read them out and guess the hen who wrote it!"

I took a swig of my prosecco and stared at the blank piece of paper in my lap. A lot of the other hens were giggling as they scribbled away; some were even gasping and pointing at each other, saying "I know what you should write!" and then whispering in the other's ear, prompting hysterical laughter from both parties.

I guess I had quite a good one. Being dumped the day before your wedding in a broom cupboard was certainly outrageous and also ticked the box for a relationship disaster. But I'm not sure it really matched the tone of the afternoon. I decided it would be best for me to stick to the drunken-night-out idea and started thinking back on any funny stories I could use in this game.

And that's when I got the first major wave of emotional nausea. Because as I racked my brain, I realized that, aside from my childhood, almost every single memory involved Matthew.

I met him when I was in first year and he was in second. Leo, Ruby, and I had already formed our little friendship gang and Ruby announced that she was going to join the drama club. She forced me to come with her to the audition, because she was so nervous. We were sitting outside the studio where the auditions were being held and she was reading through the script. There were a few people lined up down the corridor and it was eerily quiet as the acting hopefuls all read through the few lines they'd been given.

"Everyone here looks very professional," Ruby whispered. "Maybe we should go home."

"You look as professional as everyone else."

"Yeah, but they all look edgy. They look like drama students. I'm not cool enough."

"You're very cool," I assured her. "Stop being ridiculous."

"What if they ask me about my music taste?"

"Who would ask that?"

"The third-year students holding the auditions," she whispered, agitated. "They might ask some questions after to see if I'm cool enough to hang out with them."

"If they do that, they're wankers."

The guy sitting next to me snorted into his audition sheet. He caught my eye and smiled. I remember thinking straightaway that he had really nice, long lashes framing his light green eyes. He was a lot more gangly then—it was a good few years before he started bulking up at the gym, something he does almost every evening now—and his mouse-brown hair was styled with too much wax. He had a spattering of freckles across his nose and an endearingly wonky smile.

He got Invisalign braces the year before he proposed. I never told him this because of the money he spent on them, but I preferred his smile before his teeth were straightened and whitened.

"Name an edgy band," Ruby demanded as the person in front of her was called into the audition room. "Quick."

I sighed. "I don't know any edgy bands. I'm not sure I know what you mean by 'edgy.'"

"Someone cool and non-mainstream. Someone no one else has heard of."

"If you need someone that no one has heard of, why don't you just make up a name?"

Ruby gasped. "Freya, that is a *genius* idea."

(It turned out to be a terrible idea. Although her music taste wasn't asked about during the audition, the topic did come up when she got a small part in the play and they were all out for a cast bonding night. Apparently, one of the guys she was speaking to went home and set about googling, but couldn't find a trace of this amazing singer-songwriter she banged on about all night, Elvis McGee.)

While Ruby was in the audition, the guy next to me asked me what role I was going for. I promptly informed him that I was merely there as moral support. He asked why I wasn't interested in the stage. I told him I was not an in-the-spotlight kind of person.

He tilted his head at me when I said that and went, "Are you sure about that?," with that unique smile that made my heart somersault. It was cheesy and ridiculous and wonderful.

That was how it all started; a couple of terms into my university education and I'd already met The One. I know some people think relationships can affect how much fun you have at uni, but it wasn't the case for me. Matthew made my experience. All of my best memories involve him in some way. But we also weren't stuck together like glue—I was very strict about not spending all our time together. I never wanted to become one of those couples who never saw their friends. I was intent on doing things "sensibly," i.e., not moving in together too soon, making sure we kept up our own individual passions and interests, putting in time with friends without each other. I listened to all the warnings in movies and books about whirlwind romances, what happens when couples move too fast and isolate themselves from their friendship group—if everything falls apart, what happens then? Who do you turn to? People talk about "following your heart" as you fall madly in love, but I wasn't the sort of person to throw caution to the wind.

And it worked.

Loads of couples we knew broke up after university, but not me and Matthew. We happily kept going, all the way through our twenties. We saw each other through everything; we were together for every milestone. I organized a huge party for his twenty-fifth birthday; he took me for a fancy dinner at the Ivy when I got the job at Suttworth; we've been on long weekends around the UK, trips abroad, family holidays. Everything was great; our relationship was calm, solid, and drama-free. I never questioned it. We were all set.

"Like a tortoise," I told him after a couple of very strong cocktails celebrating our engagement.

"Sorry?"

"You and me," I slurred, leaning into him. "We're strong and steady, like a tortoise."

"Is that right?" He took a sip of his beer. "How sexy."

It was drunken silliness, but it was also true. We'd made it so far, it seemed impossible that we would fall at any hurdle.

Life is full of surprises.

"Freya, have you got your story?" Kelly asked with a bright smile, jolting me from my depressing stroll down memory lane.

I noticed that all the other hens were looking at me expectantly. I was the only one still holding a piece of paper, so they must have already handed theirs over. I tried to answer but my throat had tightened.

Because Matthew was my story. And now he's gone.

"What about Isabelle?" Niamh announced, causing the heads to swivel toward her. "She surely has to write a story, too. Please tell me that you have all heard about the guy she met in Ibiza? The nickname 'Gladiator Gordan' ring any bells?"

Isabelle shrieked with embarrassment and covered her face with her hands, while the other girls immediately started hounding her to tell them the story. I gave Niamh a grateful smile and pulled myself together to concentrate on Isabelle's hilarious antics with Gladiator Gordan, who was so muscly he could throw her about the dance floor, and the bedroom, like she was a feather. When it came to reading through the confessions, I was ready to enjoy myself again and had managed to quickly jot down a few lines about the time I went to the theater, fell down the steps while looking for my seat, causing a ripple of gasps through the audience, and then, when I scrambled to my feet and people could see I wasn't actually hurt, received a round of applause.

Just the memory of it makes me break out in a sweat, and it was thirteen years ago.

The next wave of just-bearable agony enveloped me during the classic hen game "Mr. & Mrs." Kelly had filmed clips of Isabelle's fiancé, Ryan, answering certain questions, and before playing each one, Kelly would read out the question and Isabelle had to guess what Ryan had answered.

The way Ryan spoke about Isabelle, laughing bashfully as he answered prying questions about her likes and dislikes, their sex life, what he loves most about her, and what their future will look like—it reminded me of when Ruby played the clips of Matthew answering these exact same questions on my hen do.

He'd said all the right things, acted precisely how he was expected to. All my friends went "aw" and placed their hands on their hearts, when at the end he said that he hoped I was having the best time on my hen do and he couldn't wait for our big day.

I hadn't thought about those clips of Matthew playing this game until that very moment. My chest tightened at the horrifying realization that he'd known even then he wasn't going to marry me. But he still sat in a room with Ruby and looked straight at the camera and said he couldn't wait to marry me with that charming smile of his, knowing that I would watch it, surrounded by my closest friends. He fooled all of them, too.

Bloody hell, that hurt.

When "Mr. & Mrs." came to an end, I found myself almost gasping for air, but I was relieved it was finally over and we could move on. I sat in the corner next to Niamh, who could see I needed a moment, so she didn't bother me, chatting away to others nearby, while I pressed down on the inner corners of my eyes with my thumb and forefinger, barring any tears that were threatening to form. I could *not* make this about me. It would be the worst thing I could do to Isabelle, and, I told myself firmly, it would have been better for me not to have come at all if I was going to make her think I was having a miserable time.

I had committed to this hen do. I shook my head as if that might shake Matthew right out of there, took a deep, calming breath in, and asked Niamh to top up my prosecco. She promptly did so, we clinked cups, and then I threw myself into the fun and cheery conversation she was having with Isabelle's cousins.

But there was one more stab to the heart to come. We had all gone upstairs to our allocated bedrooms to get ready for the night out. Niamh and I had done our makeup side by side and we'd been joking about how we used to attempt makeup back at school. We were not very good at it then. The photos capturing that bright blue eyeshadow smeared right up to our eyebrows do not lie.

I came downstairs in a good mood, excited for a girls' night out in Bath. We still had half an hour before we needed to be anywhere, so the people who were ready were milling about in the sitting room, chatting.

"Before we go, can everyone please write in Isabelle's hen book!" Kelly called out over the room, gesturing to where it was on the table. "I'm just going to go get dressed."

People had crowded the book at first, eager to look through the funny photos of Isabelle through the years that Kelly had sourced for this collection. I waited until the coast was clear and then took it to a chair in the corner of the room, so I could flick through it quietly as the crowd in the sitting room got drunker and rowdier.

Isabelle was a super cute baby. There were some hilarious pictures of me and Niamh with her at school, including the blue-eyeshadow moments. Smiling down at the images, I turned the pages until I got to the back, where Kelly had left a bunch of blank pages for us to write in. At the top of each one it said, "My message to Isabelle," and then, leaving a gap for a few lines, it stated, "My advice for the bride," followed by another gap.

I clicked the pen and wrote a short and, quite frankly, hilarious message about how she might not remember, but she'd lost a bet to me that she made in year seven, when she declared she'd marry one of the cast members of *The OC*, so I expected her to cough up that Freddo chocolate bar I'm owed. Then, without being overly gushy, I finished by saying how proud I am of her. She knows what she means to me, I didn't feel the need to write it.

My pen hovered over the next gap. "My advice for the bride."

A lump formed in my throat. How could I possibly give her any advice? What did I know? Here's some advice, Isabelle: Make sure the guy you're marrying wants to marry you. Just because he's given you a ring and you've planned a wedding *does not guarantee* that the marriage will go ahead.

I was blind.

That was the moment it overwhelmed me; after a day of building up, it all came bubbling over.

Now here I am on the floor of the bedroom, my head buried into my knees, my face wet with tears. I've finally given in to the sadness.

After a while there's a knock on the door.

"Freya, you in there?" Niamh asks. "Are you okay?"

"Yes, of course! Just . . . uh . . . sorting some things. Is it time to go?"

"You've got about ten minutes."

"Okay, thanks. I'll be ready."

"See you downstairs!"

I thank her and listen to her footsteps grow quieter as she walks back down the stairs. I sit in my crumpled heap for a couple of minutes, feeling sorry for myself, and then reach for my phone and call Ruby.

"Hey, you okay?" she asks straightaway when she picks up.

"Fine. I just . . . you know . . . I'm fine."

"Oh, Freya," she says, understanding immediately. "Want us to come pick you up?"

"I'm in Bath."

"So? There are roads that connect London to Bath, you know."

I chuckle, wiping my cheek with my palm. "You're the best. Thanks, but it's okay. I'm driving back in the morning. It's really good fun, too. It's just . . . you know. It's a lot."

"I can imagine."

"I don't want to feel like this."

"I know," she says in such a gentle tone, it makes my eyes well up again. "You have to allow yourself to mourn it. But it will start getting easier. You have to believe that. Look how far you've come already!"

"Niamh said something along those lines to me earlier."

"She's a wise one. Is Isabelle having a good time?"

"Yeah, really good." I take a deep breath. "Right. I should go sort out my makeup before we go. I have to work out a way of not thinking about Matthew tonight."

"He's a fuckface. He doesn't deserve your thoughts."

"Ruby, if I can barely make it through one hen do without feeling like this," I begin, closing my eyes in despair and leaning my head back against the door, "then how the hell am I going to survive the Wedding Season?"

CHAPTER SEVEN

On the way to Ruby and Leo's the following week, I have a very awkward encounter. Thankfully, it's not Matthew. But it is his best man, Akin.

He's with his girlfriend, Sarah, and I don't see them straightaway because I'm walking along with my head down, busy messaging in the group chat to ask if Ruby and Leo want me to pick up anything last minute for dinner. I glance up midtyping to check I'm not about to walk into a lamppost and instead discover I'm about to walk into something—someone—a lot worse.

"Freya! God, hi!" Akin blurts out, as we both stop short of smashing into each other.

I inhale sharply at the sight of them and stop still, fingers poised over my phone. I haven't seen them since the breakup. I got a really sweet message from Sarah after the event, but nothing from Akin. I found that hurtful, because even though Akin is Matthew's school friend and best man, I've known him for a long time and thought we were close. I appreciate he's in an awkward position, but come on. He might have checked in, shown some compassion to me and still retained his loyalty to his best friend.

"Hey," I say, lowering my phone and thanking my lucky stars that I made the effort to put makeup on for a meeting with clients at work this morning.

If I'd bumped into them any other day this week, it would have been another story. Since the breakup, my standards of what is socially acceptable to wear in public have really taken a downturn. In fact, on Sunday, when I got back from the hen do and was hungover and braless, I wandered down to Sainsbury's wearing pajama shorts and a poncho.

"Hi, Freya." Sarah smiles at me warmly. "How have you been?"

"Good, thanks. Yeah, great. Really good. What about you?"

"Good, thank you," she replies, as Akin shifts his weight from one leg to the other, clearly squirming at being in this unfortunate position.

"Great."

"Are you headed out tonight?" she asks. "You look amazing!"

"Thanks! Yeah. Yeah, I am."

I decide not to add where I'm going. No harm in providing a bit of mystery. I could be going on a date for all they know! How do you like that, Matthew, huh? I could be on my way to meet an intelligent and funny hunk who owns a castle! Yeah!

I'm not sure where that castle idea has come from, but it would be nice.

"How are you, Akin?" I ask pointedly, as he attempts to avoid eye contact.

"Yeah, I'm good, been super busy." He clears his throat, then turns to Sarah. "We should get going, though, because we're late . . . for the . . . for that thing."

"Sure." I nod as Sarah narrows her eyes at him. "Have fun at your thing. Nice to see you, Sarah."

She gives me an apologetic smile and I dart round them, marching away down the road, adrenaline pumping through my veins at how awkward that situation was. I turn the corner and stop, leaning against a random wall and taking some deep breaths.

A really horrible side to breakups is losing friendships, too. I didn't just get cut off from Matthew, I got cut off from his parents and those whom I met through him. There are some people I know I'll stay in touch with—the true friends—but I appreciate there are others I'll have to let go. Although, after total silence from Akin, I'm not sure I mind losing him.

There's loyalty and then there's spinelessness.

My phone starts vibrating, still clutched in my hand from when I was messaging Ruby and Leo. I check the screen to see who it is and groan. Mum. I consider letting it ring out, but I still haven't spoken to her and I might as well get it over with now when I have the excuse to hurry off as I reach Ruby's flat.

Plus, I've just had one awkward conversation, might as well have two. Out of the pan and into the fire, as they say.

"Hi, Mum."

"*Freya!*" she cries in surprise, causing me to hold the phone away from my ear to protect my poor eardrums. "Hello, darling! It's me! Mum! Oh darling, how are you?"

"Fine, thank you. How are you?"

"I've been so worried about you! You poor, poor thing! Are you coping okay? Do you need me to come stay with you? Do you want to come here to the lakes for a bit? Get away from it all! I can't believe what you've been through, you poor thing!"

Ah, Mum.

One of the things that bug me about her the most is how whenever we talk, which is rarely, she pretends as though we're close friends who chat all the time. Even when I make snide comments—which I admit that I do, because it's hard not to be angry at someone when they take no responsibility for their mistakes—she pretends that she doesn't hear them or just glides over them and moves on to another point in the conversation.

It feels like a performance. She's always cheerful, eccentric, fun Meredith. Nothing ever seems real with her. Maybe it's because she wants to gloss over all the horrible, messy bits of the past and start afresh now that Adrian and I are grown-ups. But that's not how life works.

We can't pretend that she didn't walk out on us. It's not like she'd been all that present before, but when she left Dad and went to live with Evan, it was like she'd forgotten she had a family at all. She met Evan when she was working as an events coordinator for an environmental trust and he was leading one of the tree-planting projects her company was helping to fund.

I know.

Not exactly the sexy scenario that one might imagine would ignite a passionate love affair, but there you go.

I was fifteen and Adrian was eleven, and all of a sudden our mum was just—gone. She didn't visit, she didn't beg us to come see her at weekends, and neither she nor Dad really gave us much of an explanation as to what went wrong. We were upset and confused, but it was as though she didn't care. The only silver lining to those years is that they brought Adrian and me closer together, forcing us to rely on each other in ways we might never have done otherwise.

The truth is, Mum had never been naturally maternal. She loved going out, being the life and soul of the party. She had loud, flamboyant friends, and a busy social calendar. I'm not sure she ever really wanted children. She married Dad when she was pregnant with me. He was the one who brought us up, even when they were together. He got us ready for school, cooked all the meals, took us out for trips on weekends, came to every school event. He was a single parent long before she left.

Mum and Dad are so different, it's a miracle they lasted as long as they did—though it's not as if they ever argued. In my head, they got on well. Mum made Dad laugh all the time. But after the divorce, when I thought properly about it, I realized he was always making excuses for her. When she promised to be somewhere, it was very likely she wouldn't show. When she moved to the Lake District with Evan, she didn't even bother to promise anymore.

"Yeah, it's been tough, but I'm okay," I tell her, looking down at the pavement. "Thank you for all the calls and messages. Anyway, I'm just off to meet—"

"I want you to know how sorry I am that this has happened," she says, and I'm affected by the tone of desperation in her voice. I understand what Adrian was getting at now. It does sound like she means it, but she's an awfully convincing performer. "I can't even imagine what you've been through. How have you been coping?"

"Fine," I assure her. "Keeping busy."

"That's important. You have good friends around you to support and look after you?"

"Yep, I do."

"Thank goodness. I mean it, Freya, if you want to get away from London and have a break here, you're welcome any time. We'd love to have you. The walks around here by the lakes are good for the soul. They bring so much peace."

I purse my lips. "Thanks for the offer, but I can find peace here."

"Have you been eating okay? Sleeping all right? I can recommend some meditation if that might help?"

"Actually, I've tried that and I don't seem to be able to switch my brain off. But, as I say, I'm fine."

"I've sent you a little care package. Have you got it?"

I raise my eyebrows in surprise at this information. "You sent me something?"

"Yes, it should have got to you by now. Lots of nice things to pamper yourself with and enjoy. You haven't got it? I hope it hasn't got lost in the post."

"When did you send it?"

"A couple of weeks ago."

"What? It definitely should have arrived by now. You sent it to the right address?"

"Yes! Your Peckham one!"

I hesitate, my heart sinking. I don't know what I expected.

"That's my old address, Mum. We moved to Forest Hill two years ago."

"Oh, you're joking! What a shame! Someone else is enjoying your lovely care package!"

Of course, that's what's upsetting to her. Not that she didn't remember I moved house. Not that she didn't bother noting down my new address. It's that someone else might be using the bubble bath she picked out. I shake my head.

"Thanks anyway, Mum," I say, because I can't be bothered to have any kind of negative conversation right now after my run-in with Akin. "I have to go, I'm heading to Ruby and Leo's for dinner and I'm late."

"Oh! Of course, you go have a lovely evening. But maybe one day soon we can have a proper chat? Maybe a video call? It would be lovely to catch up, darling. It's . . . it's been a long time. And as I said, maybe you could think about coming here. Or I could come to you."

"Honestly, I'm fine."

"Times like this, a person needs their mother."

It's a comment that's meant to be sweet and lovely, but it stings so badly, I have to close my eyes and bite my lip so I don't say something I'll regret. I don't need her ever. She forced me to be that way.

"I have to go," I manage to croak. "Bye, Mum."

"Bye, darling," she trills as I hang up the phone.

The still painful memory of the exact moment I realized I could never, ever rely on my mum—that I would never let myself rely on her again—flashes across my mind as I shove the phone back in my pocket.

I was seventeen and on a school trip in the Peak District, where my year group was spending a few days to celebrate the end-of-term exams being over. It was all organized fun—some sightseeing, outdoor activities, toasting marshmallows at night around campfires, that kind of thing.

Dad was still a bit of a mess at that point. It had only been two years since Mum left and he hadn't quite got his head round anything yet, plus he was working all the time, and looking after two moody teenagers. It can't have been easy. But he was determined to be a "good dad," which meant encouraging me to keep up with Mum, regardless of his personal struggles with her.

The summer camp where my school class was staying in the Peak District was about two and a half hours' drive from Mum's—a lot closer than the five hours between her and Dad's. He thought it was the perfect opportunity for us to meet. He was so adamant that in the end I gave in—I called Mum and we organized a plan. Instead of me getting the coach back home to Berkshire with everyone else, Mum would pick me up, and I'd go stay the night with her and Evan. The following afternoon she'd drive me to Manchester, and I'd get the direct train from there to Reading, where Dad would pick me up.

The final morning, I stood waiting with my bag outside the camp. The teacher in charge waited with me, and the coach with all the other students loaded onto it waited, too. The teachers—responsible adults that they were—weren't going to leave me in the middle of the Peak District without ensuring that I'd been picked up by my mother.

After a half hour passed, I called her house, but there was no answer. By the time an hour had gone by, it was obvious that I'd been stood up.

The most humiliating part of the whole debacle wasn't that Mum didn't show—it was that everyone else in my class knew exactly what was happening. I'll never forget that feeling of shame as kids started grumpily calling out from the coach that they were bored and it was time to go, and couldn't they just leave me and I could call when my mum finally arrived?

And when Mum finally called in a fluster to explain—something had come up, she'd lost track of time, then she couldn't find her phone and, would you believe it, there was nightmare traffic, but not to worry because she was on her way and couldn't wait to see me—I was already on the bus on my way home. I snapped at her down the phone, hung up, texted Dad to explain what had happened, and then sat on my own looking out the window, trying to ignore the mixture of sympathetic looks and snide comments coming from my classmates.

When the coach got back to the school, Dad was waiting for me with Adrian.

"I'm so sorry, Freya. This is all my fault," he said desperately, after hugging me hard. "Are you okay?"

I could see how terrible he felt, and I couldn't bear the idea of telling him just how awful it had been.

"I'm fine! It's really not a big deal, Dad," I insisted with a cheerful expression. "And it's not your fault! The bus was waiting and everything, so it's not like I was stranded. It's good to be back. Come on then, Adrian"—I ruffled my brother's hair—"you can spend the way home telling me how much you missed me."

With the subject successfully brushed over, we headed to get fish-and-chips, and Dad's mood lifted as I filled them in on the fun parts of the trip. Mum sent me a breezy message saying she was sorry that our plan hadn't worked out but she couldn't wait to spend time with me soon, whenever that might be.

But she didn't call at all that week, not once, to check that I was okay. That's what really stung me: not her absurd lateness, but the fact that she seemed absolutely clueless about how it would make me feel.

And it still stings now when I think about it. All these years later.

The anger fuels my walk to Ruby and Leo's flat and I'm there in no time.

"Why do you have crazy eyes?" Ruby asks on opening the door.

"I just bumped into Akin."

"Shit."

"And then I got a phone call from my mum."

"Fuck."

"She said, 'At times like this, a person needs their mother.'"

"I was going to pour you a glass of wine, but tell me if you want the bottle," she says wisely, standing aside so I can barrel through the door.

"Hey, Freya," Leo calls from the kitchen, waving at me in his oven gloves as I hang up my coat. "Did I just hear you say you bumped into Akin? What was that like?"

"He looked like he wanted to melt into the pavement," I reply, coming over to give him a hug.

"Did you ever hear from him?" Ruby asks, pouring me a hefty glass of red.

"Not one word." I slump down on their sofa, gratefully accepting the glass of wine from Ruby, taking a sip before continuing. "Thanks so much for having me over! How are you two? How's your week going?"

"We have no news," Ruby says, coming to sit next to me, offering me a bowl of crisps to snack on. "Except for the fact that Leo went swimming once this week and now he thinks he's Michael Phelps."

"I've bought some new goggles," Leo informs me proudly.

"Cool." I nod. "I didn't consider swimming when coming up with a new hobby."

"Swimming is too much hassle," Ruby opines, leaning back on the sofa. "There's so much pressure to keep the pace when you're in your designated lane. Last time I went, I kept getting overtaken and that was in the slowest lane possible."

Leo chuckles. "Ruby brought the average age of the slow lane down a couple of decades."

Ruby glares at him. "New goggles do not mean you're a pro. So you pipe down and focus on the lasagna, please." She sighs and then moves the focus back to me. "Are you okay after your phone call with your mum? Sounds intense."

"It's like she's on another planet. She has no awareness of anything. In her little bubble with Evan, she feels as though she can get away with saying whatever she wants. Just because my wedding was canceled does not mean she gets to shower me in motherly love."

"Did you say that to her?"

"No, course not." I shrug. "I told her I was fine and that I had to go. She's a nightmare."

"Maybe you should tell her how you actually feel."

"Yeah, because that would change everything." I roll my eyes. "Trust me, there's no point. Anyway, let's not waste any more time talking about my mother. Or Akin. Please tell me something lovely about your lives. Besides the swimming, of course."

"Can we just cheers to you bumping into Akin and handling it like a boss?" Ruby proposes.

"I'll cheers to that," Leo adds, rushing over with his freshly poured wine.

"How do you know I handled it like a boss?" I laugh.

"Because it's you," Ruby says, and without any further explanation, she holds up her glass for the two of us to clink. "Cheers!"

"Cheers!" Leo and I chorus.

It's the start of what steadily becomes a rowdy evening. I shouldn't really be drinking on a weeknight, especially after the hen last weekend, but I throw caution to the wind. It's not like I have anyone to get home to.

"Maybe I'll get a cat," I ponder aloud after we've finished eating, plodding back from the kitchen table to the cozy armchair by their window.

"Are you a cat person?" Leo asks, plopping down next to Ruby on the sofa. He sits a bit too enthusiastically and almost spills his red wine as it sloshes around his glass.

"I could be. And it would be nice to come home to a friendly, fluffy animal that is happy to see me."

"I think it's a great idea," Ruby says sincerely, getting bolder and more reckless with every sip of wine. "Why not? Really, why not? You can do what you want now. You get to focus on you. You want a cat? I say, get a cat."

"I can't believe you bumped into Akin today," Leo says, shaking his head. "What are the chances?"

"Actually quite high. He lives a few roads away from yours. I should have prepared myself better."

"Did you tell him you were on your way to see us?" he asks.

I shake my head. "I said I was going out, but I didn't say where or with whom. You know, I thought a bit of mystery surrounding my life couldn't hurt."

"Yes, well played," Ruby says, pointing her wine at me. "Now, he probably thinks you're out on a date."

"If it was super awkward seeing Akin, how bad is it going to be when I have to see Matthew?" I get a shiver down my spine at the thought.

"You never have to see Matthew again!" Ruby declares defiantly.

"Actually I do." I sigh heavily. "He's going to be at Cali and Dominic's wedding. I can't ban him from going to a wedding of a mutual friend. At some point we're going to be in the same room."

"You have to hold your ground and simply focus on how much better off you are without that scheming little weasel." Ruby narrows her eyes.

"How am I supposed to do that? How am I going to concentrate on anything else but him?" I groan, draining the last of my wine. "How do I keep him out of my head at all these weddings?"

Leo reaches for the bottle to top us up. Ruby looks thoughtful and then her face lights up.

"I've got it!" she announces, pushing herself up off the sofa and putting her glass down on the side table. "Hang on a second."

She hurries out of the room, returning a moment later carrying marker pens and an A3 pad of paper.

"Hey!" Leo frowns at her. "What are you doing with my special art pad?"

Leo has always been fairly artistic and, about a year ago, he proclaimed that he'd like to get back into it. He bought all the materials and I genuinely believe he had good intentions, but twelve months later, he's yet to attend any of the life-drawing classes that he banged on about joining or produce a new piece of art.

"I need to borrow it," Ruby replies simply, taking the lid off the purple pen and flipping the pad to the first page.

"What do you need it for? That's proper art card, Ruby," Leo huffs, as I smirk into my glass. "You can't just doodle on it for no reason."

"Who said anything about doodling? And there is a reason for using it, a very good one in fact," she replies haughtily. "We are going to sit here and come up with the plan."

"Plan for what?"

"Freya needs to survive the Wedding Season," she announces, her eyes flashing dangerously at me. "And, together, we're going to work out how."

CHAPTER EIGHT

I burst out laughing, but Ruby looks deadly serious. She starts writing at the top of the paper and then holds it out so we can see what she's written: "How to survive the Wedding Season."

"You're kidding, right?" I ask nervously.

She stares back. "Do I look like I'm kidding? I've written the title at the top of the page, Freya"—she taps it with her finger—"and I've underlined it. You don't underline titles at the top of the page unless you're serious about them. Didn't you learn anything at school?"

"I think a wedding survival guide is a good idea," Leo pitches in. "To be honest, I think I could use one, too."

"This isn't about you, Leo," Ruby teases. "This is going to be a personal guide just for Freya. Something for you to focus on during each wedding and keep you distracted."

"Distracted from the miserable mess of my life."

"No, you do not have a miserable mess of a life," Ruby corrects sternly. "Firstly, you're on a different path to what you expected, that's all. And secondly, you're a gardener now. And gardeners have got their shit together. That's a well-known fact."

"How do we go about working out this plan, then?" Leo asks curiously.

"Well, we start with getting Freya's permission to create the Wedding Season survival guide," Ruby declares, pointing the pen at me. "Without your full support, there's no point in doing this. You have to be all in."

I sigh and then take a swig of wine. "I'm in. Why the hell not?"

"That's my girl." She grins, before pulling her legs up so she's sitting cross-legged on the sofa, resting the pad of paper on her knees. "Okay, now that permission is granted, we need to know what the first wedding is. We need details."

"Okay, the first wedding of the season." I get my phone out and open my calendar. "It's Obi and Eva's on twenty-first May."

"Of course!" Ruby starts writing. "A perfect start! It's in London, so not far from home, and Leo and I will be there, too."

Leo nods at me knowingly. "We can give you moral support."

"What can your first task be?" Ruby asks, glancing up from her work.

"Task?" I blink at her. "What are you talking about?"

"The task that you'll be undertaking in order to survive the wedding."

"How is giving me a task for the wedding going to help me survive it?"

"Because that's the best way to distract you. You need something to focus on, a challenging activity that you have to complete. What did you expect this survival guide to entail?"

"I don't know." I shrug. "I thought it was going to be top tips or something. Pleasant musings, positive sayings to think on, practical things to do to pick me up when I'm down. That sort of thing."

Ruby rolls her eyes. "You've essentially described the book we have in our toilet. Ah! I've decided on your first task," she says, cutting me off before I can protest any further. "For the first wedding of the season, you shall: be the last person on the dance floor."

Before she starts writing it, Leo says, "Ooh, make it 'the last person standing.' I think that sounds better."

"You are so right," she agrees, looking at him in wonder.

"Nice, Leo! You got that, Freya? Your first task is to be the last person standing."

"You have to be joking." I look at them as though they've both lost their marbles. "I'm the last person to be the . . . well, the last person standing! You know it, too. I don't do dance floors."

"Oh, excuse you, Miss Priss," Ruby says, putting on a silly high-pitched voice. "If you don't do dance floors, I'm afraid you're going to have to learn then, aren't you?"

"Don't write that one down," I instruct as Ruby completely ignores me and begins scribbling it in her loopy handwriting. "Ruby! There's no chance I can be the last one standing. Maybe make it 'the last one sitting.' That I might be able to pull off."

"Ooooh. Yes. That sounds super fun," she says sarcastically, before raising her eyebrows at me. "The whole point of this is that you're doing something different! Something challenging! You need to feel like you've really accomplished something! For Obi and Eva's wedding, you *have* to be the last one standing, no excuses. No leaving early, no sitting on your own in the corner with a bag of jelly beans and cola cubes—"

"Okay, that was one time, at Lana's wedding, and that pick 'n' mix stall was insane."

"—and no avoiding the dance floor because you're embarrassed. This will ensure that you have the best time possible. It will help you to throw off those inhibitions and lose yourself in the moment. You won't have time to let your mind drift, because you'll be too busy throwing shapes to the sweet-nectar vocals of Jason Derulo!"

"I think Ruby is right," Leo adds. "Besides, being the last one standing is a new thing for you. Maybe, thanks to this task, dance floors will become your thing," he says optimistically.

"Yes!" Ruby holds her hand up and high-fives Leo. "Okay, so you will be the last one standing at the first wedding. Now, we're getting somewhere. Let's talk about wedding number two."

"That would be Isabelle's, the one who I just went on the hen do for in Bath," I inform them. "Her and Ryan are getting married in Devon, on eighteenth June."

"Okay, so obviously a little trickier, because it's one of your school friends." Ruby prods Leo's arm with the end of the pen. "This has to be a good one because we won't be there to support her. So put your game hat on."

"Got it, got it," he replies, his forehead furrowed in deep concentration. "How about . . . you have to kiss a guy?"

"No!" I recoil in horror. "That is *way* too soon!"

"Yeah, Leo!" Ruby whacks his arm with the pen now. "That is way too soon! What is wrong with you?"

He holds up his hands. "Okay, okay, just a suggestion! I mean, it's not totally out there." He hesitates, glancing nervously from Ruby to me. "Is it?"

I can't even imagine kissing anyone who isn't Matthew. It seems totally alien to me and, weirdly, even after everything that's happened, I would feel like I was cheating somehow. I don't want to kiss anyone else.

I don't want him kissing anyone else.

"Let's move on," Ruby suggests, noting my pained expression.

"Let's," Leo says, with a vigorous nod. "Okay, so the second task . . ."

"How about getting a guy's number?" Ruby says.

"I don't think she's there yet," Leo snaps, shaking his head at her.

"By then you may be, I reckon, Freya. And if you're not, then it doesn't matter. You don't have to do anything with the number. It's just a fun game that could encourage a bit of flirtation. When was the last time you had a bit of a flirt with someone?"

I consider Ruby's question. "Is it flirting if you're in the queue for self-checkout and you're not really concentrating and the guy behind you points out that there's an empty till at the end and you share a moment?"

"No."

"Well in that case, then the last time I flirted was probably with the hot guy in that French petrol station. Remember him?"

Ruby blinks at me. "That was two years ago and we didn't know what he was saying."

"Yeah, but you could tell it was flirtatious."

"Wow. It's even worse than I thought." Ruby tuts. "For the second wedding of the season you will be using your flirting skills to get someone's number. Don't worry, we will make working on those skills a priority between now and then."

"Wait. I think instead she should have to get someone's cuff links," Leo interjects smugly. "When you think about it, she could make up that she got someone's number or get the number without flirting skills. You know, for practical reasons."

"Hey!" I frown at the two of them. "I would not cheat. And Ruby, don't think I didn't notice your little comment about working on my flirting skills. I am extremely charming when I want to be."

"Oh yeah?"

"Yeah!"

She grins mischievously. "Then it won't be a problem getting a guy's cuff links from Isabelle and Ryan's wedding."

"Good one!" Leo lifts his hand and they high-five.

"All right, that's enough of the dorky high-fives," I huff, prompting them both to look quite rightly embarrassed. "Fine. That won't be a problem. Let's move on to wedding number three. Dominic and Cali's mid-July. Matthew will be there."

Leo grimaces. "Are you sure he'll still be going?"

"I know how excited he was for it, so I doubt he'll easily duck out of that one. He'll probably think enough time has passed too," I reason. "It's mid-July."

"You know what, Matthew being there is not a problem," Ruby announces. "This wedding is abroad *and* Leo and I will be there too. It's a double win. Where better to see Matthew for the first time than in the South of France where you'll be tanned and gorgeous and glowing and in little summer dresses that will make the boys go wild?"

Leo clears his throat. "Maybe that's enough wine for you, Rubes."

"I think what you have to do for wedding number three is—" She pauses for effect, beaming at me. "—secure a good-night kiss."

"*What?*" Leo throws his hands up in the air. "You just bit my head off for suggesting that!"

"Yeah, for wedding number two, Leo! We're now talking about wedding number three! It's completely different."

"Did you not witness Freya's reaction?" He tells her urgently, glancing at me, "I don't think it's appropriate to suggest—"

"Maybe it's a good idea," I say thoughtfully, swirling my wine around the glass like a Bond villain.

"*Are you serious?*" Leo runs his hands through his hair and then crosses his arms in a strop. "I don't get it. I really don't get it. You two are a mystery."

"Just keeping you on your toes, Leo," Ruby says, giving his arm a comforting pat. "A good-night kiss in July in France. What do you reckon, Freya?"

"I say, I'm in. And if Matthew finds out about it, that might not be such a bad thing."

"Exactly! Who cares?"

"He doesn't own my lips anymore."

"He definitely does not own your lips."

"Secure a good-night kiss. Write it down."

"I'm writing it down," Ruby confirms, as I take a triumphant sip of wine.

Leo sighs. "It's hard not to feel left out when your weird brains connect like this."

"We're on to wedding number four now," Ruby says. "Whose is that one?"

"My other school friend," I reply, consulting the calendar. "The wonderful Niamh and her fiancé, Freddie. They're getting married in Dublin end of July. You won't be at that one, so I'll be on my own."

"I think the next task needs to be a bit more out there, a bit more fun," Leo suggests. "It's Ireland, you can't be boring."

"Yes, we can't let the Irish down with this task." Ruby chuckles. "You know, I watched this thing recently and one of the Spice Girls admitted that when they were on tour, they would run naked down the hotel corridor."

"They did not!"

"True story," she insists. "It couldn't be more perfect."

"Wait." I put my wineglass down. "What exactly are you saying?"

"If you're going to take inspiration from anyone, it may as well be the Spice Girls," Leo says, sharing a knowing look with Ruby. "Your task for the fourth wedding of the season will be running down the hotel corridor naked."

"*What?!* No way. Absolutely not!"

"Oh come on, Freya, it's brilliant! You'd never dream of doing anything like that normally!" Ruby points out.

"*No one* would dream of doing anything like that normally!"

"But think about it, you're not going to have time to think about anything sad when you're busy working out the best moment to run down your hotel corridor naked."

"This is a *wedding*! You can't just run about naked!"

"We're not saying you do it at the wedding," Leo corrects. "We're saying you do it back at the hotel you're staying in."

"That's just splitting hairs!"

"Have you ever been skinny-dipping?" Ruby asks, leaning forward with intrigue. "I seem to remember that coming up before and you admitted you never had."

"Why would anyone want to go skinny-dipping? It's ridiculous."

"It's fun and freeing," Leo tells me. "We went skinny-dipping in Portugal last year, didn't we, Rubes?"

"Okay, gross." I wrinkle my nose. "Don't tell me stuff like that. I don't want to know. It's not a big deal that I haven't gone skinny-dipping and it's not crazy to be against running down a hotel corridor naked. What if someone sees?!"

"You have to make sure no one does." Ruby sighs impatiently. "It's either skinny-dipping in the Irish Sea, which will be *cold*. Or, having a little stroll down the hotel corridor naked, with no one there. What will it be?"

I stare at her, my jaw on the floor. She stares back with a deadpan expression. I'm about to do some more protesting when I have a flashback to the broom cupboard and Matthew's stinging comments. I'm so in control. So together. Not spontaneous and fun like the girl he should be with.

"Fine, I'll do it," I proclaim. "Put it down."

"Brilliant." Ruby scribbles it across the page, while Leo looks impressed by my decision. "Okay, the fifth wedding."

"That would be Carley and Rachel's wedding on the thirteenth August in Norwich."

"Rachel's your cousin, right?" Leo checks.

"Yeah, Aunty Em's daughter. You met her at our engagement party, remember? The only people I know there will be family. Obviously my dad and my brother. And unfortunately, my mum is invited, too."

"That's an easy task then," Leo says confidently. "You have to make a speech."

"What? Don't be stupid."

"You said yourself, you and Rachel are close," he points out.

"It wouldn't be mad for you to make a spontaneous speech at your cousin's wedding, would it?"

"Um, *yes*? There are certain people who make speeches at a wedding, Leo, and they are selected by the bride and groom. I can't just grab the microphone and say a few words."

"Why not? I think it's a lovely idea," Ruby says encouragingly.

"Have you forgotten how much I hate public speaking?" I appeal to her sensible side. "I'm awful at speeches! I can barely speak up in a team meeting without my mouth going really dry in the lead-up."

"Hence, why it's a great task for you! These are supposed to be challenges, Freya. If they were easy, there would be no point. You can't be thinking about Matthew when you have an entertaining and witty speech to prepare!"

I groan. "I can't make an entertaining and witty speech."

"That's what you think." Ruby begins writing. "Maybe by the end of the summer, you'll think differently."

"I really hate you both."

"Wedding number six," Leo says, ignoring me. "We're on the home stretch now."

Glaring at him, I pick up my phone and scroll through the calendar. "Next up is Andy and Roshni's wedding in St. Ives, end of August, the twenty-seventh."

"Will Matthew be at that one?"

"No, he was invited, but he doesn't know Roshni that well. I used to work with her. He's missing out because it's going to be a beautiful, big Indian-Anglo fusion wedding."

"I've got an idea," Ruby begins carefully. "Do you think Roshni would let you keep the plus-one?"

"I'm not sure, maybe. I don't actually know anyone else going, so it would be nice to bring someone. I haven't exactly raised it with her yet, because . . ." I hesitate. "Wait. Why would you ask that?"

"Task number six: you have to bring someone unexpected as your plus-one."

Leo gasps. "That is a *great* one!"

"That is not a great one. Who on earth would I ask?"

"It's unexpected!" Ruby exclaims. "You're going to have to think about it and find someone. Maybe you'll meet someone through completing these other tasks. Who knows?"

"So I can't ask one of you?"

"No, you cannot. I'm writing it down."

"Good one, babe," Leo whispers audibly to her.

"And last but not least, wedding number seven?" Ruby asks, looking up from the pad.

"That would be on the twenty-fourth of September. Yours," I reply.

"Oh, right! Course!" She turns to Leo. "What do you think?"

"I think we wait," he says, stroking his chin. "We wait until she has successfully completed all six tasks, and then we choose the perfect conclusion. We need time to come up with it."

"Yes, I agree," Ruby says. "It has to be the perfect ending. You happy with that, Freya?"

"Not much I can do about any of this."

"Then, we're done!" Her eyes twinkle with excitement. "Trust me, you won't give a hoot about stupid Matthew or what happened with your wedding. You'll be too busy completing these wonderful, exhilarating challenges."

She holds up the plan so we can admire it all together.

"What do you reckon, Freya?" Leo chuckles. "You feel ready to take on the Wedding Season?"

"I said I'm in, so I'm in," I reluctantly confirm, burying my head in my hands. "And something tells me I'm going to deeply regret this."

HOW TO SURVIVE
THE WEDDING SEASON

WEDDING ONE
Obi and Eva
Be the last one standing

WEDDING TWO
Ryan and Isabelle
Bring home a pair of cuff links

WEDDING THREE
Dominic and Cali
Secure a good-night kiss

WEDDING FOUR
Freddie and Niamh
Run down the hotel corridor naked

WEDDING FIVE
Rachel and Carley
Make a speech

WEDDING SIX
Andy and Roshni
Bring an unexpected plus-one

WEDDING SEVEN
Leo and Ruby
Watch this space . . .

CHAPTER NINE

O n the morning of Obi and Eva's wedding, I feel positive about the day ahead.

In some ways, it's a good thing that Matthew isn't here getting ready with me. I can take as long as I like in the bathroom, for example. There are no impatient knocks on the door while I'm showering; no yells for me to "hurry up" because he needs to grab his beard trimmer. I don't get told off for the fake tan all over the bedsheets from last night's careful application, and no one gruffly mumbles that I'm "hogging the full-length mirror" when I have to check which shoes go with which dress.

As I finish curling my hair in my cozy dressing gown, I consider these advantages. I hate getting ready in a rush. I like to give myself lots of time just in case I change my mind on what I'm wearing, or if I make mistakes with my makeup and need to reapply. I hate rushing out the door frazzled in a whirlwind of last-minute stress. Matthew always teased me about taking so long. But it's not like he would just throw something on at the last minute and casually stroll out the door. He liked to take his time with his appearance, too, which is why me hogging the bathroom would stress him out.

I'm learning that it's important to acknowledge positives after a breakup along with all the painful stuff, so as much as I miss Matthew, there's no denying I've had a bloody good time peacefully applying my makeup while listening to an uplifting nineties-pop-star playlist.

Look at me, single and taking as long as I want. I saunter into the bathroom and spritz some perfume on my wrists. Lovely. I check my reflection in the mirror with no one nudging me out of the way so he can check his nostril hair is under control. Fabulous. This is so great.

I go to check the time on my phone charging by the bed.

Oh. *Bollocks.*

How is that the time?! I swear it's only been about five minutes!! Leo and Ruby will be here any minute to pick me up in their Uber! *And I'm in my dressing gown!*

A car horn beeps outside.

Double bollocks.

I run around the room, tripping over the wire of my hair tongs not once, but *three times*, until I unplug it in fury. I ignore my phone ringing and then the doorbell ringing as I throw my dressing gown off and grab the blue dress I'd splashed out on for the occasion. Yanking it off the hanger, I slip it on and then remember it has the main zip over the bum and then all these delicate hook and eye fastenings up the back to the neck.

Facing away from the mirror, I look over my shoulder and, clumsily reaching for and clasping the tiny little hook at the bottom, I attempt to attach it. I miss. I miss again.

It's so tiny, I can't see it in the mirror, so I forget about trying to look at my reflection, and instead rely on touch. I feel where the hook is. I feel where the opposite eye is. Aaaaand *hook*! Bugger it. Missed. Okay, there's the little hook. There's the little hole. If I just touch them together and then carefully move the hook up, it should just simply slide in. Easy. Aaaaaand . . .

Oh for fuck's sake.

Who invented these tiny hooks that don't hook?!

"Freya? Are you in there?" Ruby's voice comes through the letterbox.

"Yes! Coming!" I shout back, shaking my arms out before getting ready to try again. "I'm just having trouble with the back of my dress!"

"Let me in, then I can help you."

"No, I need to do it!"

"Why?"

"Because! I have to work out how to do it on my own!"

"What are you talking about?"

"I don't have Matthew to help me with it anymore!"

"Yeah, but you have me!"

"You can't just come over any time I need my dress done up!"

"Why the hell not?"

"Because! That's ridiculous! You're busy!"

"Very rarely."

"I hate these hooks!"

"Oh man, not those little silver hooks that you have to try to attach through the little silver holes?"

"The exact ones!"

"You can't do those on your own. No one can!"

"I have to!"

"No, you don't! Now, please can you let me in?"

"What about the Uber?"

"It's fine, the driver's lovely. Him and Leo are having a nice chat, and he says he can wait."

"Have you just made that up?"

"*Let me in.*"

Giving up, I stomp down to the front door and open it. Ruby comes barging in and marches into the bedroom, as I spot Leo in the backseat of a car parked in front and give him an apologetic wave.

"Okay, turn around," Ruby instructs, as I trail into the bedroom behind her. She starts at the bottom hook. "They are very fiddly, these things."

"How am I going to get out of it at the end of the night?"

"I'll unhook it for you in the taxi on the way back." She finishes the top one at the neck. "Done. Now, what shoes are you going for and have you packed your clutch?"

This is a weird role reversal for us. Usually it's me giving Ruby instructions, while she flails about the place, leaving everything to the last minute. At university, I ended up keeping her purse in my bag because she always forgot it and there was nothing more annoying than when we'd finally get to the front of the club queue and she wouldn't have her ID. We had a bit of a running joke the past year about how different our weddings were going to be—mine, organized and coordinated down to the last minute; hers, a jumble of celebratory confusion. A few weeks after Leo proposed, I asked her whether she had any ideas for the big day.

"I know I definitely want food," she told me sincerely. "And also trumpets."

So, for Ruby to take over as the leader in our current scenario was mildly concerning. But I'm not going to argue when she's talking sense. I hurriedly select a pair of shoes and put them on while she takes my phone off charge and shoves it in the clutch lying on my unmade bed, along with my card wallet, before going into the bathroom and grabbing my lipstick and eyeliner.

"What are you doing?" I ask, putting on my earrings and watching her tear off some toilet paper, wrap it up, and slide that into my clutch, too.

"You should always have spare toilet paper in your clutch, Freya. You taught me that."

"Did I?"

"Yep. First year. I've never forgotten it."

"It is a good tip."

"You look amazing."

"So do you. I love your dress." I smile, admiring her red floral outfit and the way she's styled her hair, sweeping her black curls over one shoulder.

"Are you ready?"

I take a deep breath. "Yeah, I'm ready. I think."

"Remember, you have to be the last one standing."

She grins at me and ushers me out of the house. I lock up and slide into the backseat with Leo, while she takes the front, asking the driver if she can plug her phone in and have control over the music. As we make our way through London toward Stoke Newington, they fill me in on their news from the week and we discuss important wedding-related topics such as whether we'll be sitting at the same table and what option we chose for our main course back when we received the invitation. As we near the church, Ruby loosens her seat belt and swivels round to face us in the backseat.

"Right, Freya, how are you feeling?"

"Fine."

"Really?"

"Really."

I meant it, too. On the car journey, I'd had just one moment of feeling an immense wave of heartache when I looked out the window and wondered what Eva was doing right at that moment. Under an hour before her wedding, she'd be in her dress, surrounded by her bridesmaids, toasting a glass of champagne, posing for photographs, and no doubt experiencing an adrenaline-pumping concoction of nerves and excitement.

I smiled as I thought about her having those precious moments. And then I felt struck by a wave of intense loneliness. It was so complicated to feel so happy for someone at the same time as feeling so unbearably sad for myself.

But I can't go through these weddings resenting anyone for what they have, or feeling bereft about what I've lost.

I step out of the car determined to enjoy today. Leo offers me one arm and Ruby the other, and we join the trickle of well-dressed wedding guests ambling into the church. It's a really beautiful, small, old church that has stone floors and you know as soon as you see it that it's going to be freezing cold inside, even in the summer. I take an order of service from one of the ushers at the door and follow Ruby into a pew fairly near the back. Sliding in next to Leo, I spot Obi at the front of the church, nervously laughing with his best man. I catch his eye and he gives me a warm smile.

Obi was in our halls, too, so we were close throughout university and beyond, although he has drifted off the radar slightly in the last couple of years. I suppose that's natural as you get older and it's been trickier to meet up now that he's moved to North London, but every time I see him, I get that flurry of excitement that comes with hanging out with an old friend, when you both know each other so well. Obi is generous, kind, and laid-back and has a mischievous sense of humor. He's a secondary school teacher now and I bet the kids in his class love him.

He met Eva, a pediatric nurse, on a dating app—they have a lot in common, it's no wonder they matched. They're both extremely passionate about their jobs and very active outside of them. Obi plays a lot of football and Eva is on a local netball team. A couple of years ago, when I made the effort to trek to their end of London, I went with Obi to watch her play and I really saw another side to her. Eva seems like a gentle, quiet person, but as she plays center on a netball court she's extremely competitive, focused, and uncannily quick. She was zipping all over the place, I kept losing her. They're going to Canada for their honeymoon and plan to do "lots of hiking and water sports."

Not my idea of relaxing, but to each their own.

Some of Obi's extended family have flown in for the wedding and are sitting ahead of us, their colorful West African outfits striking and joyful. As the organ plays some background music while the guests chatter among themselves, I scan the pews. I don't know too many people, but then my eyes land on a whole row of those I vaguely recognize. I notice that they're glancing back toward me. I immediately feel my cheeks burning with embarrassment. I bet they've heard all about what happened.

"Are you okay?" Leo whispers, nudging my arm.

"Fine," I say, glancing back up at the row.

Some of them are whispering now. One turns slightly to look at me with a pitying expression. I look down at the floor, mortified by what they're saying and horrified to find my eyes welling up with the shame.

"I'll be back in a minute," I tell Leo, before standing up and quietly scurrying out.

No one is in the hallway bit of the church entrance, so I linger there for a moment, hoping that the ushers standing outside the doors won't turn round and notice me. There's a toilet to the right, but the wooden door has a laminated sign stuck to it saying OUT OF ORDER.

As I see some straggler guests approaching, I quickly duck into the loo, which is easier said than done thanks to the old, heavy wooden door. It doesn't matter if it's out of order, it's not like I need to use the facilities. I just need a moment of privacy to pull myself together.

The door creaks shut behind me, refusing to properly close. The lock is one of those old rusting metal latches, so it takes some force to get it done, but I get there eventually and heave a sigh of relief. There's no loo roll in there, so thanking Ruby for remembering my excellent piece of advice, I get a square of paper out of my clutch and dab at the corner of my eyes, careful to keep my makeup intact.

Come on, Freya.

What does it matter if people feel sorry for me because of

what happened? That makes them nice and compassionate human beings. I shouldn't be angry at them for that; I should appreciate their kindness. But I can also show them that it's unnecessary by having a fun time. Then, their pitiful looks will vanish.

Did you see Freya? they'll say. The one who got dumped in a broom cupboard the day before her wedding? Yeah, that's the one. She was partying all night! She looked fantastic! She was having the time of her life! Guess she's absolutely fine!

Ruby and Leo were right to give me this task. As absurd as it sounds, being the last one standing will go a long way to prove to myself, as much as anyone else, that I'm going to make it through this. I take a deep breath, feeling much better. I have given myself the pep talk I needed. Now, I just have to go out there and have a great day. I owe that to Obi and Eva.

I scrunch up the piece of tissue and pop it back in my clutch. I turn round to open the door.

The lock won't budge.

I try it again. It's really stiff. I tuck my clutch under my armpit and use both hands this time, rattling it as much as possible. But it is completely stuck.

Oh no.

I start to panic now as I keep attempting to yank it open. This is not good. This is *really* not good. I kick the door to see if that helps, but that doesn't seem to do anything. I use all my might to try lifting the lock again, and when it doesn't come free, I step back and stare at the door in utter dismay.

I've locked myself in a toilet. A really old church toilet. At a wedding.

This is *not* the cool, collected entrance back into society that I was hoping for.

"No, no, no, no," I mutter, desperately trying again and again until my hands hurt from all my useless attempts. "*Come on!*"

I quickly get my phone out of my clutch and start calling Ruby. She doesn't pick up. I try Leo. His goes straight to voicemail. I remember him telling us to put our phones on silent or turn them off as we went into the church. Argh! *Why did he have to be so sensible?!*

I call Ruby again, hoping that she might wonder where I am and check her phone in case I've locked myself in the old church toilet, but apparently my friends don't care about me at all. I send them some frantic messages and then get back to trying the lock.

I'm going to have to yell for help. Which I *really* don't want to do. But it's my only hope. I can't stay locked in the toilet for the whole service! And I don't want Obi to have seen me leave and not come back in!

"Help!" I squeak timidly, rapping on the door with my knuckles. "Ushers! Anyone hear me? Help!"

The organ music is loud, I can hear it muffled behind the door, so I'm going to have to raise my voice.

"Help!" I cry out, knocking harder on the door. "*I'm stuck in here! Help, please!*"

I check my phone, but there's still nothing. Why haven't Ruby and Leo come to check on me? Seriously, after I'm free from this toilet, we are having words.

"*Help! Someone please help me!*"

A shudder runs up my spine as I realize that the organ music has stopped abruptly. I press my ear to the door and hear some voices in the hallway. They sound excited.

Oh god. I think the bride has arrived. *The bride has arrived and I'm stuck in the loo.*

Maybe it's not her. Maybe it's some excited guests! Or the ushers! Either way, this is my chance to get someone's attention.

Promising myself that I will never, under any circumstances, use a church toilet *ever* again, I muster the courage to knock on the door of the loo and call out one more time.

"Help!" I say, knocking loudly. "Anyone out there? I'm stuck!"

Suddenly, a voice. "H-hello?"

"*Hi!* Oh my goodness, hi! I'm stuck in this loo! The lock won't budge."

"Someone is stuck in this loo!" the voice says in horror, clearly informing others in the hall with them of what's going on.

"But it's out of order!" another voice replies.

"Yes, the lock is broken!" the original voice replies.

Well, that would have been helpful information to know. *Maybe they should put that on the bloody sign next time.*

"Can you help me?" I ask timidly through the door, praying that the entire congregation can't hear me at this point. "What do I do?"

"Have you tried getting the lock unstuck?" the original voice asks.

Yes, of course I've tried to get it unstuck, you moron.

"I have tried, yes, thank you, but it won't budge," I say.

"Then, there's one thing for it. When this happened last time, we did manage to get them out, but that's why we put the sign up after, so it wouldn't happen again."

"Yeah, I wasn't actually peeing or anything," I explain through the door. "I just needed to . . . uh . . . get a tissue. So I didn't think the out-of-order sign mattered. I needed the cubicle but not the toilet if that makes sense."

Why am I telling them this? Why am I justifying my stupidity? It doesn't make the situation any less awkward! If anything, I'm making everyone out there *more* uncomfortable by yabbering away.

"Anyway," I say quickly, "if you could do whatever worked last time this happened to someone, that would be great."

"All right. Here, Gerald, you hold the Bible."

Gerald. Eva's dad. So it definitely is the bridal party. Excellent. And from the sounds of it, the person talking to me is the vicar. And just now I called the vicar a moron in my head! In a church!

That can't be good.

"Whoever is in there, please stand back," they caution in a commanding tone.

Stunned at this instruction, I shuffle back as far as possible, tucking myself into the corner next to the toilet. There's a moment of silence and I wonder what on earth is going on out there, and then there's a loud crash. I gasp as something slams hard against the wood, knocking the metal latch up by sheer brute force, and the door swings open, the vicar falling through with it.

He stumbles, regains his balance, and somehow avoids tumbling into the toilet.

I stare at him, openmouthed, astounded by his strength. He shimmies back out of the cubicle, holding the door for me, and runs a hand through his now-tousled hair.

"There you go," he says, gesturing for me to head out.

"Thank you!" I croak, looking at him in awe. "Are you okay? I'm so sorry!"

"I'm fine," he tells me kindly, rubbing his arm. "It will just be a little bruise. The ceremony is about to start, so if you could go on in and take your seat, we'll be with you in a jiffy."

I shuffle out of the cubicle to find Gerald, the bridesmaids, and Eva staring at me in bewilderment.

"Hi, sorry about that, you all look great," I whisper, plastering a smile on my face. "Eva, wow. So beautiful. Obi is a lucky lad. Anyway, I'll see you in there. Sorry again."

Any hopes for me to get to my seat pronto with no one noticing and without any further embarrassment are swiftly dashed. As I step through the set of doors onto the aisle, the wedding processional music strikes up and the entire congregation swivels round, expecting the bride. Instead, they see me, standing there like a deer caught in headlights.

So, what do I decide to do?

Give everyone an enthusiastic thumbs-up.

Yep. That's correct.

A thumbs-up.

And here I was thinking that the broom cupboard debacle would be my least favorite moment of the year. It just goes to show, things can always get worse.

CHAPTER TEN

The vicar broke down the door?" Leo stares at me in amazement. "That is very impressive."

We've taken ourselves off to a secluded corner of the reception, having just arrived here from the church. It's a very trendy place—an old warehouse turned wedding venue—with festoon lights hanging everywhere and long tables set up for the wedding breakfast lined with flowers arranged in various-size jam jars.

"I think it makes him sexy," Ruby says.

Leo balks at the suggestion. "What?"

"Come on! A vicar who throws himself against a door to rescue Freya? It's like a scene in an action movie."

"What action movies are you watching?" he asks, frowning at her.

"Face the facts, Leo," she sighs, "the vicar is now sexy in my head. That's just how it is."

"It was very embarrassing," I say, grimacing. "Are you sure no one in the church knew what was happening?"

"We could hear some strange sounds coming from the hall, but I never would have guessed it was you stuck in the toilet," Leo assures me. "Obviously, when you then came in and gave us a thumbs-up, I guessed that something had happened."

"The thumbs-up." I groan, horrified at the recollection. "Why?"

"You looked cool," Ruby insists, but her voice is just a little too high-pitched to be truthful. "And it's always fun to make an entrance."

"Not at someone else's wedding!" I hiss. "Eva must be fuming!"

"Nah, not a chance. If it happened at our wedding, I'd find it hilarious!"

"Yes, but you're my best friends! That's completely different. I need to apologize to her."

"You're overthinking this." Ruby gestures round the guests all mingling, chatting, and laughing. "No one else cares. They don't even know anything about the toilet incident."

"All I wanted was to get through this wedding with no fuss and my dignity intact. Instead, I've drawn more attention than ever."

"Nothing wrong with being center stage," Ruby opines, taking a sip of champagne. "Isn't that right, Leo?"

"Absolutely. Much better to stand out. What do you want, no one to notice you're here?"

"I would *love* that."

"Well, unlucky, because you're going to be the last one standing tonight," he says, flashing me an evil grin. His eyes drift over my shoulder as he spots someone. "Ah, here comes the happy couple."

I spin round nervously, expecting Obi and Eva to come thundering over, demanding why I ruined her entrance and almost caused their vicar to have a major injury, but they're all smiles as they envelop me in a huge hug.

"Thank you so much for coming!" Eva says in my ear, holding me tight.

"Congratulations, you two!" I enthuse, before pulling away to apologize. "I am so sorry for what happened at the church, I am completely mortified. You have every reason to—"

"Why are you apologizing?" Obi cackles, that infectious

laugh of his immediately putting me at ease. "Eva told me the story. I think it's brilliant. Who knew the vicar was such an action hero?"

"I know, right?" Ruby says, delighted at his choice of words.

"There was something quite sexy about it," Eva admits, causing Ruby to shoot a disgruntled Leo a very smug smile.

I nudge Obi. "So, how does it feel to be a married man?"

"Fantastic." He beams, showing me his left hand. "Although wearing a ring feels weird."

"You'll get used to it," I assure him.

Will I ever get used to not wearing one?

As Eva falls into conversation with Ruby and Leo, Obi wraps an arm around my shoulders and gives me a comforting squeeze. Maybe my expression betrays my thoughts.

"How are you?" he asks quietly. "You doing okay?"

"I'm great, thanks!"

"I'm so sorry about . . . what happened."

I force a smile, keen to move off the subject. "Thanks, Obi. Hey, this venue is cool and edgy. I'm guessing that it's down to Eva and not you?"

"Hey!" He chuckles. "What are you trying to say, huh? That I'm not trendy?"

"Well, judging by the fact that we went to see *High School Musical 3* in the cinema together . . ."

"You said you'd never speak of that," he says in a hushed voice, before breaking into a wide smile and laughing. "Ah, fine, the setting is all Eva, but wait until we get to the food bit of the day. That was all me. Nigerian cuisine will blow your mind, trust me. Oh, and I've also sat you next to a certain someone." He waggles his eyebrows at me.

"What does that mean?" I ask nervously.

"Oh, you know, it's a single guy; he's suave, charming, handsome . . ."

My jaw drops and I'm about to protest, but Eva sidles up to him and links her fingers through his, offering me an apologetic smile.

"Sorry, Obi, the photographer is calling us. So nice to chat to you three, see you in a bit!"

With a cheeky wink at me, he heads off with his wife and leaves me in a state of panic. Ruby asks me why I look so worried.

"Because Obi just insinuated that he's set me up!"

"What do you mean? With a person?" Leo asks.

"No, Leo, with one of the jam jars." I roll my eyes. "Yes, with a person!"

"Wait, what did he say?" Ruby probes, glancing around the room as though she might be able to spot who's single just from looking at them.

"He said that I'm sitting next to someone single, charming, and handsome!"

"He sounds perfect!"

"Ruby! I'm not ready for that!"

"Not ready for what?" She tilts her head at me. "To sit next to someone you don't know? You do understand that you're in control of what you decide to do, right? All this means is that you're at a table with a single guy. That doesn't mean you *have* to get with him. Just enjoy the company of a handsome stranger."

I take a deep breath. "You're right. That was an overreaction."

"You've got this."

"Right. Exactly. I've got this," I repeat, not feeling like I've got this at all.

When the time comes to sit down, I check the table plan and breathe a sigh of relief that Ruby and Leo are at least nearby, and make my way down the length of the table to find my spot. There's that awkward moment where you find your seat at a wedding, but no one's really sitting down yet, so you hover next to your chair, pretending you're just happily hanging out there, until someone else makes the first move to sit. I busy myself admiring the beautifully decorated place cards.

"Eva did those by hand, you know," a voice above me says. "Nice to meet you, Freya, I'm Obi's uncle, Chido."

"Nice to meet you," I say, as he takes his seat.

I can see from the place cards that Eva's friend Holly is sitting on my other side, so I'm going to go ahead and guess this was who Obi was referring to earlier. I must thank him later. Ruby and I share a bemused look. Chido is, at a guess, in his sixties, and certainly charming, handsome, and suave, but I think it's safe to say neither of us is looking for a setup. We exchange some small talk about how I know the bride and groom, then sit back for the speeches before the sharing plates of food are laid out in front of us. Chido makes sure to sort my plate before tending to his.

"What was Obi like as a student, then?" he asks, filling up my water glass.

"The life and soul of the party," I reveal, prompting Chido to chuckle, nodding in agreement. "He has a talent for making any situation seem fun."

A random memory suddenly flits across my brain. Matthew and I had invited Obi, Leo, and Ruby for dinner a few years ago, and it turned into one of those unexpectedly brilliant nights. We'd eaten and were playing Jenga, Ruby, Matthew, and me up on the sofa, Obi and Leo sitting on the floor round the game.

Before everyone arrived, I'd done a quick sweep of the flat we were in at the time, but really more of a tidy than a proper clean, because we'd got home from work knowing the guests wouldn't be far behind. I'd found my can of dry shampoo sitting on top of the coffee table along with a load of other crap and I'd just shoved it on the shelf underneath, out of sight.

"What's this?" Obi said, having taken his Jenga turn. He reached for the can under the coffee table and inspected it. "Dry shampoo. How can you have dry shampoo?"

"It's for when you can't be bothered to wash your hair," I informed him.

"It washes it without water?"

"It's sort of like talcum powder for your hair," Ruby explained. "It makes it less greasy."

Obi looked impressed and then pulled off the cap, before aiming the nozzle at his head and spraying it all over. We burst out laughing as a thin layer of white powder covered his hair.

"You're not supposed to hold it so close, and you have to rub it in!" I said, giggling uncontrollably along with Ruby. "You look like an old man!"

"Oh yeah?"

Obi jumped to his feet and came at us with the can, spraying it at my head and Ruby's while we tried to shield ourselves with our arms, laughing and spluttering. After his dry-shampoo attack, Ruby and I looked at each other and burst into hysterics, both now with white-gray locks. Obi cackled victoriously.

"I have to get me some of this," he declared, shaking the can again, looking for his next victim.

Matthew reached over and ruffled my hair. "Well, I've just had a flash-forward into my future. Even at ninety-five years old, you're a looker."

I'd laughed and squeezed his arm in response. It was a throw-away moment; I had forgotten it until now. But even then, we knew that we'd be together forever. He knew then.

"Freya?"

Chido's voice snaps me from my daze and I turn to smile politely at him.

"Sorry, I was in my own world! What did you ask? Sorry!"

"I asked a boring question about where you live," he says, brushing it away with his hand.

"That's not boring," I assure him. "I'm in South London."

"Do you live with family?"

"No, on my own."

"You have a partner?"

I hesitate. "I did. Things are a bit . . . unsure at the moment."

"Ah, I'm sorry."

"That's okay. What about you?"

"Widow." He gestures to the wedding ring on his left hand. "Five years now."

"I'm so sorry," I say, my heart sinking.

"You would have liked her." He chuckles, offering me more stewed beef, which I decline, having eaten my weight in rice. "She was very witty and quick. I'm not sure what she saw in me, but I'll be forever grateful that I was the one lucky enough to marry her."

I smile. "You must miss her, especially on days like this."

"Of course." He shrugs sadly, before a smile creeps across his lips. "But then, weddings are a celebration of the start of something, and I love that, don't you? It's so exciting."

I nod, swallowing the lump in my throat.

He watches me carefully. "This partner that you mention things are unsure with—are they here today?"

"No," I confirm. Normally, I would never talk about something like this with a stranger, but Chido's vulnerability makes me want to be honest in return. "We were meant to get married two months ago but he panicked and we broke up. I'm just not sure we're over forever. Well. I guess what I mean is, I'm sort of hopeful we're not."

"I see."

"I probably sound like an idiot."

"Not at all. The heart wants what it wants."

"If only it wanted something that wanted it back," I say, attempting to sound light-hearted, but failing miserably.

"You know, it will get better," Chido says simply. "It doesn't feel like it. But, with time, it will. One day, you'll be somewhere, could be anywhere, and suddenly it will hit you. You won't be expecting it. It will come out of nowhere." He claps his hands. "Bam."

"What? What will hit me?"

"The realization that you really are okay."

I look up to see him smiling warmly and hopefully at me.

"It will happen," he continues. "You may not believe it, but it will. It always does."

"My friends have set me a task for this evening," I inform him. "To keep me distracted. I have to be the last one on the dance floor."

He throws his head back, laughing in delight. "That's wonderful. I hope you intend to complete said task?"

"I'm not one to shy away from a challenge, Chido."

"I didn't think you were."

"But I'm not exactly a dancer."

"That so?"

"You any good?"

"Oh, terrible."

"That's great news." I smile at him. "You can join me then."

⁂

I step out of the taxi, holding the front of my dress up, the back completely undone.

"Thanks, Ruby," I say, slightly slurring, holding the door open and peering in at the backseat. "Without you, I could have been stuck in this dress forever."

"Without me, you never would have got into it in the first place," she points out, leaning across the seat to look up at me.

"That's true."

"Before you go, Freya, can I just say something," Leo begins, winding down his window at the front.

"Here we go." Ruby sniggers. "He's going to make an emotional statement."

"No, I'm not! I wanted to say I'm proud of you, Freya."

Ruby groans. "Told you!"

"You did it. You completed the task. That's all I wanted to say."

"Thanks, Leo." I smile at him through the window. "You're the best."

"You're the best."

"Thanks for looking after me today, you two. Now get home safe," I conclude, giving Ruby a wave and then shutting the car door.

The Uber driver, who has been very patient with my lengthy goodbye, pulls away, and Leo's voice echoes down my road as he calls out good night. I get my keys out of the clutch, unlock the door, and stumble inside, grateful to pull off my heels, slip off the dress, and get ready for bed.

I wipe off my makeup and brush my teeth, thinking about what a great time I had. Tonight, I had to dance like no one was watching. I had to force myself not to care about what anyone was thinking. Was it as liberating as all those inspirational quotes say?

No. It was not. It was horrible and I hated putting myself out there.

But now that it's over, it really feels like an achievement. And there was a moment when I almost forgot how embarrassed I felt, when one of Ruby's song requests came on—the almighty "5,6,7,8" by Steps: a song with formulaic dance moves that I happen to know, thanks to the necessity of doing it at school discos along with everyone else when it first came out. I could see Chido clapping as I swayed my hips to the "boot scootin' baby" line, moving into the "rodeo Romeo" side steps.

When the DJ wrapped things up, I was on the dance floor and remained there until everyone else had moved off to prepare sparklers for Obi and Eva's exit. I lifted my hands in the air and took a flourishing bow, as Ruby and Leo applauded my success, and then we hurried to join the crowd outside to wave goodbye to the bride and groom.

As I snuggle under the duvet, I smile into my pillow thinking about dancing to Steps with Ruby and Leo bopping around me, whooping and cheering, while a giddy Obi and Eva attempted to copy my routine, laughing their heads off.

The last thing I think on before falling into a deep sleep is how I felt at that moment, laughing and being silly with good friends. Matthew wasn't there, but it didn't matter.

My heart felt full.

CHAPTER ELEVEN

I've done something stupid.

This is so typical. There I was a few weeks ago, having a lovely time at Obi's wedding, thinking I was moving on, that I was doing really well, that I was set to embody this amazing gutsy woman that Uncle Chido thought I could be, and next thing I know, I'm calling Matthew's mum several times and, when she doesn't pick up, leaving her whiny voicemails.

Yes. I *know*. His mum. What was I thinking?

I blame Mary Berry. Last night, I was sitting on the sofa all cozy in my slanket—a blanket with sleeves; Matthew got me it as a joke one Christmas, but who's laughing now?—and I thought I'd watch some old episodes of *The Great British Bake Off*, because it's comforting and the cheerful world it portrays is one I'd very much like to be a part of. The competitors were baking away and there was Mary Berry, being supportive, encouraging, and lovely.

It made me think of Gail. She loved Mary Berry. She had all her cookbooks. We sometimes watched *Bake Off* together when Matthew and I visited. We'd spout our opinions about the various creations and cheer on our favorites. It was really quite adorable.

Now, I have to watch it on my own. And that's all Matthew's fault. First I felt sad about this, and then I felt angry. Because why do I have to lose Gail? Why do we have to never speak again? Why can't we be buddies? Surely, she wants to. Gail *loves* me.

Maybe she loves me a little less after seeing me karate-kick her son in the balls, but she has to admit that he deserved it. What if she's been really missing me all this time and feels horribly sad about everything that happened? What if she wants to check in on me, but feels she can't because of Matthew? What if she's been waiting for me to call her?

That's the line of thinking that made me do the stupid thing.

I didn't realize at the time that calling Matthew's mum was a stupid idea. I thought it was *brilliant*. It showed I really cared and I wasn't breaking any rules because I wasn't contacting him *and* it reminded him of my existence.

Genius.

Maybe she'd tell him I'd called and he would be really jealous, desperate to hear how I am, begin to wonder if he'd made a mistake and then come knocking on the door.

Last night, in my slanket, it all made perfect sense.

I called her and as it rang, I thought about how calm and collected I was going to sound. I would be like, "Oh hey, Gail, how are you? I was just sitting here watching *Bake Off* and it reminded me of you. I do hope you're well?" But I didn't get the chance to show her how cool and collected I was because it kept ringing and then went to voicemail.

I hung up and stared at my phone in betrayal. Why didn't she pick up? She might have been busy. *Or* she might have thought that I was calling her drunkenly, as people are known to do, but I wasn't (this time anyway). That made me think that it would probably be a good idea to call her again to explain that I wasn't drunk-calling her. So, I pressed her contact again and it started ringing.

When it rang out and went to voicemail again, I felt a little confused. The first time she missed the call is understandable, but the second? Unless, she really was busy. I put my phone down and got back to my television viewing.

Twenty torturous minutes later, she still had not called back. *No one* is busy for twenty minutes on a Thursday evening, right?

I picked up my phone determinedly and phoned her again. This time when she didn't answer, a thought struck me and chilled me to the bone. What if the reason she's not picking up is because she's meeting Matthew's new girlfriend? What if they're sitting round the table enjoying dinner and that's why she can't pick up the phone? What if they're watching *Bake Off* together? *How could she?!*

I almost started hyperventilating at this level of betrayal and I called her again to ask her how she could be so *fickle* and *shallow* and not even care *one jot* about me, even though I spent *years* picking out her birthday presents when Matthew couldn't be arsed.

When she didn't pick up that time, the anger subsided and the sadness set in. That's when I left the voicemail. It wasn't too long, *thank goodness*, but it was mortifyingly long enough. It went something along these lines:

"Oh hey, Gail, it's Freya. I was calling because I was watching old episodes of *Bake Off* and it made me feel so sad and now you won't pick up my calls and . . . oh god. Never mind. Sorry. Bye, Gail."

Then I realized what I'd done and had to call again to leave the following voicemail:

"Hi, Gail, it's me again, Freya. Please don't tell Matthew about this. Forget this happened, if that's okay. Thank you, Gail. I'm so sorry. Bye."

And then I buried my head under my slanket and remained like that wondering how I could be *so stupid* for a very long time until my phone vibrated with a message from her.

Hi Freya. I'm so sorry I missed your calls.

I was at the cinema watching a film about

a robotic hippo that gets out of control and
eats a lot of people. It wasn't a very good film.
I hope you're all right. Have a pleasant evening.
Gail

It's a miracle I even woke up this morning after reading a
message like that. I can't bear to tell Ruby and Leo about it yet.
I was already embarrassed enough about the whole episode, but
that message was the cherry on top. For starters, it's worrying
how much of it is dedicated to a film about a robotic hippo. And
she doesn't even *mention* the voicemails. But the "have a pleasant evening" is the clincher. So *formal*! So distant. Like a knife
twisted through the heart.

I slept badly last night because of the incident, writhing about
in the shame of Matthew hearing from his mum how pathetic I
am. In an ideal world, I'd stay in bed all weekend, hiding under
my duvet and pretending none of this happened, but unfortunately I can't do that because it's Isabelle and Ryan's wedding,
and I've taken today off work for the BBQ they're hosting before
the big day tomorrow.

I glumly pack my bag, trying to remember everything I'll
need for the next couple of days, and look up traffic to see how
long it's going to take to drive all the way to Devon. My phone
starts ringing and Isabelle's name flashes up on the screen. I
hurriedly answer, wondering if she needs me to pick something
up on my journey from London that the bridesmaids have forgotten.

I'm almost right. It's not something, but someone.

One of Ryan's friends, Jamie, who doesn't live too far and
is pretty much on my route, is supposed to be getting a train
to Exeter and then a taxi from there to the venue, but there's
been a problem on the line and the morning trains are canceled.
Isabelle was wondering if I could do them a *massive* favor and

give him a lift. I say yes, of course, because you do *not* say no
to a bride the day before her wedding (unless, of course, you're
Matthew and you're saying no to the wedding altogether), and
she thanks me profusely and tells me how excited she is for us
to arrive.

I don't mind giving this guy a lift and weddings do tend to
bring out the generosity of spirit, but I am slightly disappointed
that I'll have to be polite and sociable for a long car journey and
not have the chance to do what I was planning to do, which was
eat sweets and listen to uplifting podcasts about animals. Maybe
I can still do that. Jamie might also be into sweets and interesting
animal facts. We'll have to see.

Isabelle messages me his address and number, and I load the
car with my huge bag—I couldn't focus on what to bring because
of the Gail situation, so I ended up packing everything, which is
fine because I'm driving so there's no luggage limit. My phone
vibrates with another message, from the WhatsApp group I have
with Leo and Ruby.

Ruby

Have fun at Isabelle's wedding!

Don't forget your task for surviving this one

Get a guy's cuff links

Leo

And you can't tell him about the task

That would defeat the point

It has to be subtle

Shouldn't you both be working?

Ruby

I look forward to hearing about your attempt at

flirting

We'll need full details

Leo

We have full confidence in you

You can do this!

Go get 'em tiger!

Ruby

You're embarrassing yourself, Leo

I put my phone away, setting off toward Jamie's address. I was expecting him to be waiting outside, but there's no one here. I wait a few minutes, tapping on the wheel impatiently, and when no one appears, I get out and ring the doorbell. There's no answer. I double-check the address Isabelle gave me. This is definitely it. I ring the doorbell again, and when that's no use, I knock on the door.

"Oh god," I mutter under my breath to no one, "I'm going to have to call him."

Calling new people in these kinds of situations is so awkward, and when he doesn't pick up, I feel like the world is against me. First Gail, now this new person, Jamie. *Why* do people have phones if they're not going to answer them?

After calling through the mail slot and getting no answer, I reluctantly phone Isabelle, whom I really don't want to bother, but I'm not sure I have much choice. Traffic will be getting worse by the minute and I don't want to miss this lunch.

"I'm so sorry, Freya, that is so weird!" Isabelle says, when I explain what's happening. "Hang on, let me pass you on to Ryan. He knows Jamie better, so might know what's going on—" Her voice becomes a little distant as I assume she holds the phone away from her. "Ryan! *Ryan!* Come here! You need to talk to Freya. She's outside Jamie's house, but he's not there. Where is he? She's pressed the doorbell, he's not answering. You talked to him, right? Wait, what? Ryan!"

There's a weird scuffle and then Ryan's voice comes down the line. "Freya?"

"Hey, Ryan!" I say, trying to sound upbeat and excited rather than exasperated at the situation. "How are you feeling about your big day? Whoop whoop!"

I'm not really a "whoop whoop" person, so it sounds a bit sarcastic as I say it, but nothing I can do about that now.

"Very excited, it's going to be great," he tells me. "I'm sorry about Jamie, I haven't actually spoken to him this morning."

"He doesn't know I'm picking him up?"

"I know he was coming on the train, and when another guest let me know they were canceled this morning, I thought I'd message him and get Isabelle to contact you ASAP, so the crisis was averted."

"Very efficient of you."

"He hasn't replied yet, though. I was messaging him last night and he was out with his colleagues, so I think he probably had a big one knowing he had today off. If you keep ringing the doorbell, he should wake up."

"Uh—"

"Honestly, don't worry, he's just a heavy sleeper. Ring the doorbell a few more times, I'll give him a call, and if he doesn't appear, then we can say we tried! He'll have to come down on a train this evening if they're back up and running then, which fingers crossed they will be!"

"Okay. I'll do that. Thanks, Ryan."

"See you soon!"

We hang up and I sigh, shoving my phone in my pocket. This is ridiculous. He might not even be *awake* yet?! If that's true then he better get ready fast, because I do not want to hang around. I've already wasted time standing here on his doorstep. I ring the doorbell again. Part of me doesn't want him to answer, because then I have the excuse to get going.

But then I hear footsteps approaching the door. It swings open and I'm greeted by a man in his boxer shorts. I freeze, no idea what to say or where to look.

"Hi, sorry, I'm coming," he mumbles, squinting at me and pushing his scruffy hair back. "I'll be with you in a bit."

Then he just shuts the door again. Um. *Hello.* Where are his manners?! He didn't ask who I was or whether I'd like to come in and wait inside! He didn't even introduce himself! I remain on his doorstep with my hands on my hips, huffing to myself about what just happened, and then stomp back to the car.

I don't like this person.

And I can't believe he answered the door to a stranger in his boxers! That is very almost naked. I feel like I've violated his privacy or something, even though I had no choice in seeing him like that. We haven't even had a conversation, yet I've seen his nipples.

When he finally emerges from the house seventeen minutes later, his hair wet from the shower and a carryall slung over his shoulder, I decide not to judge him even though he slammed the door in my face, because it sounds like he is hungover and it's not really fair to judge a person in that state. After Obi's wedding, I didn't bother showering, spent all day in my dressing gown and Ugg boots watching TV, and ordered a large pizza for lunch and another pizza for dinner.

I like to think the delivery drivers didn't judge me that day, so I will extend the same courtesy to Jamie.

He opens the back door and shoves his bag in the seat, before coming to sit in the front. He makes himself comfortable by moving the seat back and then he turns to me.

"Hi, I'm Jamie."

"Nice to meet you. I'm Freya."

"Cool. Sorry you had to wait."

"That's all right."

"I had a few drinks last night. Hey, do you mind if I have a nap?"

I blink at him. "Sorry?"

"I would really like to sit back and sleep, but that's probably considered quite rude when I don't know you and you're driving me to Devon. So I thought it's probably better just to ask."

"Oh. Um. That's fine. Yeah, of course. Have a good nap."

"Thanks." He settles back against the headrest and closes his eyes. "I promise I'll be more human when I wake up and then you'll like me more."

Giving him a strange look, I turn the key in the ignition and set off. Within a couple of minutes, he's snoring. *Snoring.* I roll my eyes and put on a podcast about the secret life of lemurs, who, I come to learn, are fascinating little creatures.

I steal a couple of glances at Jamie, because I'm trying to work him out, but I don't want to take a good look at him as that seems creepy when he's sleeping. If he weren't so rude, I'd describe him as fairly attractive. He's tall with thick, dark, curly hair, bold eyebrows, and long, dark eyelashes. He is growing an unkempt beard, and as he shifts to face the window, I can just make out the top of a tattoo at the top of his back, most of it covered by the neckline of his T-shirt.

About an hour and a half in, I pull into a petrol station because I need to pee. Jamie has slept this entire time and wakes with a jolt as I park.

"Are we there?" he asks, rubbing his eyes.

"No, sorry. I just need to go to the toilet."

"Oh right. Cool. I'll get some food."

He climbs out and stretches, yawning loudly, and then plods into the petrol station. I follow him in and then, when I'm done, I wait by the car, watching him through the windows as he wanders about the aisles, looking confused. He eventually gets himself to the till and comes sauntering out with a plastic bag full of crisps.

"Did you only buy Quavers?" I ask him, when we're back on the road and I notice the contents of his shopping bag.

"Yep. Want some?"

"No, thanks. How many did you buy?"

"Five packs." He opens a bag and digs in. "Reckon that will sort me out. I also bought a Lucozade, so by the time we get to Devon, I'll be raring to go."

I smile politely, focusing on the road as he crunches loudly.

"I feel like a new man after that nap," he informs me. "I'm really sorry about that."

"Honestly, don't worry about it. We've all been there."

"Work nights out always get so unexpectedly big, you know? I only meant to join for a couple." He shakes his head and turns to look at me. "What do you do?"

"I work for Suttworth, the drinks company."

Usually, this information is met with impressed or, at the very least, nice reactions. Most people have heard of Suttworth and, if they haven't, then they know the drinks brands.

Jamie, however, is not impressed or nice. In fact, he is physically repulsed. He recoils in his seat, wrinkling his nose and looking at me up and down as though seeing me in a terrible new light.

"Suttworth?" he checks, disgusted.

"Yes, I'm a brand manager there," I say, a little unnerved by his reaction. "What's wrong?"

"You're the enemy."

"Excuse me?"

"I work for Dancing Bear."

"What? What's that?"

"Exactly." He shakes his head at me, as though I've disappointed him somehow. "It's a small independent brewery."

"Ah. So by the 'enemy,' you mean the big, bad corporation. Don't you think that's a bit of a stereotype?"

He snorts. "You can't argue that Suttworth is anything but a big, bad corporation, out to make as much money as possible with no real passion or love for its products."

"Hey!" I can't *believe* how rude and disrespectful this guy is! "I'll have you know that Suttworth is extremely passionate about its brands. In fact, if it weren't for us, a lot of small companies would have died out long ago."

"Yeah, because you take over the market and push them out. They have no choice but to let you buy them. Well, you're not getting your hands on Dancing Bear, that's for sure."

"I've never even heard of Dancing Bear!"

"That's because it's proper local stuff. We don't have global marketing campaigns or anything that threatens the quality of our product. You're a brand manager? So, you look after a few drinks brands I'm guessing."

"Yes."

"I bet you don't even like half of them."

"I love all my brands!" I lie, before glancing at him. He's raising his eyebrows at me, unconvinced. "Okay, *fine*, I don't love all of them, but not everyone has the same taste buds! And I love most of them. That's why I'm so good at selling them. I'm very passionate about what I do and, for your information, I'm very good at it."

"Maybe," he replies, "but I would safely bet anything on the fact that you don't know those drinks or the people behind them like myself and the team know Dancing Bear. We have true passion. Not passion we're paid to have."

I stare at him openmouthed. "You are such a snob!"

"I'm the snob?!" He raises his hands. "I'm not the one who works for the giant, posh, sleek company."

"Oh, let me guess, Dancing Bear is probably based in East London, and all your colleagues have scruffy beards like yours, wear checkered shirts and trainers to work, and listen to 'edgy' bands that are, in fact, terrible and that's why they're not popular." I take my eyes off the road to look at him smugly, pleased to see he's shifting in his seat as my words hit home. "You don't even know me and you've judged me straightaway and told me I'm not passionate about what I do. You and your team at Dancing Bear think you're unique and cool and trendy, when you're all the same: pretentious snobs, looking down your noses at everyone else."

"My beard is not scruffy," he mutters.

He looks out the window and I stare straight ahead, both of us remaining in angry silence for a good few minutes. This guy is a piece of work. Here I am doing him a massive favor and he spends the journey insulting me! I cannot believe Ryan is friends with him. You know, I always had a high opinion of Ryan, but it's hard not to judge him on the company he keeps.

"Fine," he says eventually, letting out a sigh. "I maybe shouldn't have jumped to conclusions straightaway. I don't know you, you're right. I'm sorry. That was rude."

I nod, but don't say anything. I'm not sure I'm ready to accept this apology and I'm going to stay up on my high horse a little longer. Clearly, I am a master at arguing my point.

"But I stand by the fact that by covering so many brands, it's unlikely you have the same passion that I do for Dancing Bear. And I'd also like to address the comment about 'edgy' bands. I can guarantee that my music taste is better than yours."

"You have no idea—"

"I have gathered some idea from the fact that on this car journey so far you have played a podcast about lemurs, followed by a playlist that included Take That and a song about swimming in the year 3000."

I narrow my eyes at him. "Don't even pretend you don't know who Busted are. And you were supposed to be asleep!"

"You are a true product of meaningless nineties mainstream, auto-tuned pop."

"*Ha!* Busted was in the noughties! So there."

He doesn't look impressed by this correction and I admit, it's not my best argument. But how dare he insult my cultural taste?! I am well aware that I'm not exactly a music maestro, but I also don't care. I have never met anyone so *smug* and *rude*.

We return to our silence and remain that way for the rest of the journey. I have to put on the radio just so there's something to listen to and purposefully turn it up loudly when a pop song comes on, just to make a point. He rolls his eyes and continues to stare out the window.

When we arrive at the country house hotel where we're staying for the wedding, and where the BBQ is being hosted, I get out of the car as soon as is humanly possible. As I lug my huge case out of the boot, he raises his eyebrows, but doesn't say anything. Oh, now he's judging how much stuff I've brought with me? What, I'm a bad person because I bring several outfit choices?

Who is this guy?!

"Thanks for the lift," he says, slinging his bag over his shoulder. "I'll pay you petrol money."

"No need," I snap, slamming the boot shut and locking the car. "Enjoy the wedding."

And with that, I turn on my heel and march into the hotel, determined to avoid him for the rest of the weekend and then, hopefully, for the rest of my life.

CHAPTER TWELVE

B ollocks."
    I step back from the seating chart in dismay. Niamh ex-
amines it next and turns to me, confused by my reaction.

"What's wrong? We're on the same table!"

"Yes, but so is that Jamie guy," I huff, leading her away so
the people hovering behind us can get a look at their fate. "The
one I had to give a lift to yesterday. The worst journey ever. He's
a nightmare!"

"He's actually really lovely. You must have got him on a bad
day."

I blink at her in disbelief. "You know him?"

"Yeah, he's good friends with Freddie. We met him through
Isabelle and Ryan, and now those boys hang out quite a lot." She
gives me a strange look. "I would have thought you two would
get on quite well."

I assure her we don't and then wander through the hotel ballroom to find our table, trying not to feel a little put out that "those
boys" didn't include Matthew as part of their crew. Oh well, I
suppose it doesn't matter now. And anyway, I'm pleased I haven't
had to spend any more time with this Jamie character than is
absolutely necessary.

At the BBQ yesterday, we purposefully didn't cross paths,
although I didn't really have many people to speak to—thanks
to the trains being canceled in the morning, the afternoon and

evening ones were delayed and overcrowded, so Niamh didn't make it until late. It was nice to catch up with some of the girls I'd met on the hen do, but I did feel a bit distracted by Jamie, who was right in the middle of things, apparently having a great time with Ryan and all his friends.

Whatever. I didn't even *want* to be at the hotel bar all night, which it looks like most of them were. I was very happy to sneak away to my room, have a bath, and then get to bed early before the big day today.

The wedding is elegant and stylish, just like Isabelle. Each table features a striking centerpiece of hydrangeas, roses, and greenery in tall, thin glass vases with tea lights dotted around the bottom. The earlier ceremony was outside, the bride and groom saying their vows on the terrace of the hotel prettily decorated with displays of white roses, matching the bouquets of Isabelle and her bridesmaids. We stayed there for the champagne reception before being ushered into the ballroom, complete with modern chandeliers hanging from the high ceilings and full-length windows that reveal beautiful views of the Devon countryside. I was very much looking forward to sitting down to eat, but now I've seen the seating chart, it seems distinctly less exciting.

Niamh and I get to our table, which is quite near the dance floor, and I seek out my place.

"Bollocks!" I mutter again on finding that Jamie is *right next to me* and Niamh is all the way on the other side.

"Ah." He comes up behind me and puts his bottled beer down at his place. "We meet again."

Without saying anything, I take my seat, hoping to chat to the person on my left side for the whole meal. Unfortunately, that person is one of Ryan's friends, who is really into Dungeons & Dragons and, after discovering that the person on their left is, too, pretty much turns their back to me for the time being.

"How is your meal?" Jamie asks, having also found himself with no one else to talk to.

"Great, thank you," I reply curtly, finishing my smoked salmon starter. "Yours?"

"Great."

We fall silent again. He takes a sip of his beer. I try to hold my tongue, but find myself unable to do so.

"Interesting drink choice," I blurt out smugly.

"Sorry?"

"Very mainstream." I nod to his bottle. "I think that's a Suttworth brand, isn't it?"

"Yes," he grumbles. "It is."

"I thought you were too good to drink something like that."

"Nothing I can do about what drink selection is served at a wedding."

"I'm sure you'll inform Isabelle and Ryan about their poor choice."

"Maybe they would have had more options if Suttworth didn't destroy the rest of the market with their low prices. That's not really an option for a small, independent company."

"You're against affordable drinks?"

He sighs, shaking his head. "Maybe we should change the topic. Clearly we disagree on this one and I'm not sure it's worth going on about."

"Fine by me. You were the one who attacked me yesterday."

"Yes, well I feel a bit bad about that actually."

I raise my eyebrows. "Really?"

"Yes. I blame it on the raging headache I was suffering under. I already apologized for that." He clears his throat and takes a deep breath, plastering on a smile. "So! Have you had a good day? Enjoying the wedding so far?"

"Yes, it's been really nice. They look very happy."

He glances over to Isabelle and Ryan, who are getting up from their table to go round and say hi to guests. "They do."

"The setting is stunning."

"It is. My cousin got married in Devon last year."

"Ah. How nice. Family weddings are fun."

"Yeah. My mum's Egyptian, so I don't get to see a lot of her side that often. A lot of the family flew over for it."

"Lovely."

I take a sip of my wine. He takes another sip of his beer. God. This is so painfully *stilted*. Isabelle rescues the situation by suddenly appearing between us.

"Hello!" She beams. "How are you guys? You like the food?"

"It's delicious!" I enthuse, as she gives me a kiss on the cheek. "You look so beautiful, Mrs. Warner! Your dress is stunning."

She's wearing a slinky, modern number with delicate spaghetti straps dotted with pearl beads, a dress which really shows off her gorgeous figure. Her nails are neon blue—her something blue, I take it—and she's wearing her hair loosely up with minimal makeup, looking fresh-faced and sophisticated.

She's already a little tipsy from the champagne, so I imagine some of the guests will be treated to some classic deep-and-meaningful Isabelle conversations this evening.

"Thanks so much, this is just the most amazing day," she declares, before turning to Jamie. "Isn't Freya the best? I thought I'd sit you two together because you have so much in common!"

"We do?" he mumbles, before repeating it in a more upbeat manner, having received a glare from me. "We do!"

"You're both in the drinks business, you have a similar sense of humor, you know, you're both quite sarcastic—" But before she can notice our confused expressions at that statement, she's distracted by someone waving at her from another table. "Got to go, I should say hi. Enjoy the day!"

"Thanks!" I say after her, before thanking the waiter as my starter plate is taken away.

"I didn't realize I was noticeably sarcastic," Jamie mutters.

"Neither did I. Still, I suppose there are worse things to be."

"True. I was once described as 'frivolous.' That was a bad one."

"Ouch. Who called you that?"

"An ex."

"Ah." I nod, before deciding I might as well be honest, since he was with me. "My ex called me 'pragmatic' and 'together.' And not in a good way."

"Whoa. Harsh."

"I'm not sure which is worse. That, or being brushed off as a product of nineties mainstream pop."

"Better than being labeled as a pretentious snob with a scruffy beard."

"I notice it's a little tidier today."

"Thought I'd make the effort for a formal event," he says, leaning back as our main course is placed in front of us. "What makes you so 'together,' then? The swish job at Suttworth?"

"I've no idea," I admit with a shrug.

"Isn't having your shit together a good thing? I thought that was what everyone is after in life," Jamie comments, digging into his food.

"Yeah, well, now my shit is very much not together, so he wins." I stab at a potato. "What makes you so 'frivolous'?"

"She said it after I made a joke about something she did."

"What did she do?"

He takes a swig of beer. "She cheated on me."

"Oh. Sorry. That's . . . horrible." I watch him curiously as he shrugs. "Why did you make a joke about it? Surely you were angry."

"Coping mechanism," he explains. "That's what my friend who's a therapist said, anyway. I told her to stop analyzing me, but it's very hard for therapists not to do that."

"I can imagine."

"Like a nervous tick for them."

"You made a joke about the cheating because you were trying to process it."

"So she says."

"I can understand that," I tell him, thinking back to the broom cupboard when I became oddly concerned about gathering the roaming peacocks after Matthew broke my heart and ruined my life. "Shock can make us behave in weird ways."

"I know someone who was so shocked when they were fired, they stole the vending machine from the office. They just unplugged it and walked right out of there with it. Completely out of character."

"What?" I stare at him. "That's ridiculous. You've made that up."

"It's true."

"You know this person?"

"A friend of a friend."

"How would they carry a vending machine out on their own?"

"They were really strong."

"No one is that strong."

"It was a mini one."

"Sure." I roll my eyes. "Though I actually do know someone who was so stunned when his boyfriend proposed that he punched him in the face."

"No way."

"I swear it. He was so shocked, he punched him right in the nose and then said yes."

"You're winding me up."

"I'm telling the truth!" I insist. "It's my brother's mate in New York. There's a photo of them at this rooftop bar, both crying with happiness, one with a bloody nose."

"Wait, the guy proposing still wanted to marry him, even though he'd been punched in the face?"

"Of course!"

"I'll believe you when I see this photo."

"No problem. I'll believe you when I see a picture of the vending machine in this person's house after they brought it home from work."

"They didn't get it home. They had to leave it in the lobby. Couldn't get it through the revolving office doors. They went down with it in the lift though."

I shake my head at him. "How would you get a vending machine in the lift on your own?"

"Easy. It's all to do with how you tilt it."

"You'd need a wheelie cart. No one's that strong."

Jamie looks thoughtful as he chews his mouthful. "I think I could lift a vending machine."

"What?" I snort. "No, you definitely couldn't."

"I lift a lot of barrels, you know. I'm not sure I've mentioned it, but I work in a small, independent brewery."

The corners of his lips twitch into a smile. I don't take the bait.

"A barrel is very different from a vending machine, which is a difficult shape and full of food and drinks and stuff," I point out.

"Yeah, and a barrel is full of heavy liquid."

"This is ridiculous, I refuse to argue with you any longer about whether or not you can lift a vending machine," I say, stubbornly. "How did we even get on to this?"

"People reacting strangely to shocking situations," he reminds me. He reaches over to grab a bottle from the middle of the table. "Top up?"

"Thank you," I say, sliding my glass across to him.

"Your brother lives in New York?"

"Yeah, he works in recruitment there."

"That's cool. Have you been to visit him?"

I nod. "Yes, and it's amazing. Have you ever been to America?"

"No, I'd like to go, though. They have some excellent craft breweries over there."

"And some excellent whiskeys."

He sniggers and then does a double take at my expression. "Oh, wait, you're serious?"

"Um, yes? You ever heard of bourbon? Do you live under one of your barrels?"

"I wasn't laughing about that," he tells me. "I was laughing at you being a whiskey fan."

"Oh my god, you are so patronizing!" I scowl at him. "What do you expect whiskey fans to look like? Old men smoking pipes and wearing trilby hats?"

He laughs at that, holding his hands up. "Sorry, sorry. I realize that came across as patronizing and I swear, I didn't mean to be. It's only because you work for Suttworth."

"You know, some of the best drinks experts in Britain work for Suttworth."

"Are you claiming to be one of them?"

"Of course not," I snap. "But you seem to have written Suttworth off as a company full of people who don't know what they're talking about. That's very frustrating. I reckon I'm better than you when it comes to whiskey knowledge and taste."

"Huge, bold claim," he says with a knowing smile. "But I like your confidence. Would you be willing to put your money where your mouth is?"

"You want to make a bet."

"They have a few whiskey choices behind the hotel bar here. We could do a blind tasting and see who wins."

I consider this proposition. I mean, he is so childish. Why do we need to make this a competition? He seems incapable of acting like an adult. However, at the same time, it is quite tempting, because I know I'll win.

An idea pops into my brain.

"If I win, you have to give me your cuff links," I propose.

He gives me a strange look. "Slightly disturbing request. You collect items from your victims?"

"Very funny. I just think it's a little less crass than money and still means I'm taking something from you."

"What do I get if I win?"

"An earned sense of satisfaction."

"Nice try." He leans back in his chair and thinks for a moment. "If I win, you have to come to the brewery, pay for a pint, and admit that Dancing Bear is much better than anything you have on your books."

"I won't be admitting any such thing. Where's the brewery?"

He hesitates, reluctant to answer.

"Is it by any chance in East London?" I ask innocently.

"Dalston," he grumbles.

I gleefully savor the moment of my judgment yesterday being snappy but ultimately correct. "Fine. You have yourself a deal."

As Ryan's best man taps the microphone and stands up, announcing that it is time for speeches, I hold out my hand to Jamie. He looks at it, smiles, and shakes it.

"You're wrong," I say confidently, tapping the side of the glass. "That's an Irish whiskey. At a guess, I'd say it was Tullamore Dew."

Jamie balks at the suggestion, crossing his arms. "That is another delicious scotch. I'm going to say Monkey Shoulder."

I raise my eyebrows.

"What's that face you're making?" he asks, laughing at my expression.

"It's an are-you-mad face. That is not Monkey Shoulder."

"I guess this is the deciding point then. So far we've both got one out of two; it's best of three."

He swivels on his stool to face the hotel barman, who has been thrilled to partake in our wager, pouring us three different whiskeys without showing the label of the bottles. We waited until after the first dance and then, on finding the wedding bar quite crowded, snuck away to the main hotel bar to play out our whiskey mission.

"Come on then, Neil, put us out of our misery."

With great dramatic effect, Neil pauses, letting the suspense build nicely, until he slides the bottle across the bar to us. It's Tullamore Dew.

"*Yes!*" I cry, cheering in victory.

"Noooooo!" Jamie buries his head in his hands. "How is that possible?"

"Thank you, Neil, those were some fine choices," I tell him, bowing my head in respect. "Jamie, I believe you owe me a pair of cuff links."

"Ugh." He undoes them from his sleeves and drops them into my outstretched palm. "Fine. Take them. Along with my pride."

"Aw, don't be so hard on yourself." I pop the cuff links safely into my clutch. "You got one out of three correct. Not bad for an amateur."

"You are going to be unbearable about this, aren't you?"

"If it was the other way round, would you be unbearable about this?"

"Yes," he admits gloomily.

"Then I think—"

I stop abruptly. I had just pulled my phone out from my

clutch as I put the cuff links in, and glanced at the screen. I have a message from Matthew.

Jamie glances down at the phone in my hands and frowns. "What's wrong?"

"N-nothing."

Just seeing his name on my screen. My ears are ringing, my heart thumping against my chest, my throat constricting, my stomach knotting. I feel sick, my mouth suddenly dry, and, at the same time, have an overwhelming and hopeless yearning to open this message and find him telling me he loves me.

Forgetting everything else, I open the message.

> Hi Freya. Mum told me you called her.
> I think it would be a good idea if you don't
> do that again, as it puts her in an uncomfortable
> position. Hope you're well.

"You okay?" Jamie asks, watching me. "You don't look so good."

"I . . . I . . . don't . . ."

I trail off, feeling as though I've been slapped round the face. How can he message me so coldly? This guy I've shared my life with all these years. The man I was going to marry. Now he concludes messages to me with "Hope you're well," the same language I use in work emails to strangers.

I remember once I was listening to a podcast in which a journalist was interviewed about the power of words. She spoke about how the careful structure of just one sentence can make all the difference and do remarkable things, like tip the scales of a crucial debate, uplift the spirit of a nation, and pierce the heart.

Hope you're well.

"Seriously, are you all right? You look as though you might be sick. You want me to get you some water?" Jamie asks, leaning forward in concern.

"S-sorry. I'm fine. Although water . . . yeah. Water would be good."

Waved over by Jamie, Neil gets me a glass of tap water, and I take several gulps.

Jamie watches, his forehead furrowed. "Better?"

"Yeah. Sorry." I place my phone on the bar, shell-shocked. "A message from . . . this guy."

"The one who had a problem with you having your shit together?"

I nod. "See how wrong he was about me?"

Jamie offers me a comforting smile. "I once got a call from my ex-girlfriend when I was in a kayak and I was trying so hard to get to the phone before it rang out that I capsized and ruined my phone anyway."

"Why were you in a kayak?" I ask, grateful for the distraction, forcing myself to be interested, even though Matthew's message reverberates in his voice around my head.

"I was trying out new things."

The band in the ballroom strikes up a well-known song and we can hear the wedding crowd go wild from here. I pick up my phone and put it in my clutch. I'll reply to him later.

"We should go back," I say, slipping off the barstool. "That was fun, though."

"Easy for you to say." He sighs as I lead the way out of the bar. "You won."

I force a smile, and when we get back to the ballroom, I find Niamh and Freddie still at our table, waving me over. I listen to conversations; I sit and watch everyone dancing; I enjoy a slice of wedding cake; I accept one of the espresso martinis Jamie carries over; and I hug Isabelle and Ryan goodbye, telling them I love them and to enjoy their honeymoon.

But a feeling of dread hangs over me all night, that message there on my phone, waiting to torture me over and over again.

Hope you're well.

CHAPTER THIRTEEN

I arrive at the meeting spot in King's Cross station ten minutes early.

There's no one else here yet, but I've already wasted as much time as possible wandering around M&S choosing tinned cocktails for the train. I thought that Niamh and Freddie or their best man and maid of honor might at least be here nice and early to greet their sten—stag and hen combined, of course—attendees, but it looks like none of them are that organized. We're going to Leeds for the weekend and our train leaves in forty minutes.

I linger next to Pret, scrolling through my phone so it looks like I'm busy, keeping the meeting point in my sight line in case someone else arrives. I go into WhatsApp and find Isabelle's name.

> Hope you're having an amazing honeymoon!
> Wish you were here this weekend

Isabelle
Freyaaaaaa!! MISS YOU!
Having a great time, although Ryan
got food poisoning last night. It was not sexy.
I'm telling you, he's lucky he put a ring on it
BEFORE I witnessed that scene yesterday.

> Oh no, is he ok?

Isabelle

He's fine now. Eating like a pig.

Omg wish I could be there this weekend!!

Please take SO MANY PHOTOS

And videos

Send them all to me please

I am there in spirit

Will do!

I glance up from my phone to see that someone has arrived at the meeting place. I wait a couple more minutes until others have joined them, and then when Niamh and Freddie approach to many cheers, I put my phone away, pick up my M&S bag of tinnies, and wheel my case behind me, strolling up to them breezily as though I've just arrived.

I'm offered a train ticket by the best man and then stand there like a lemon. The beginning bit of hen dos—and stags, I assume—is always a bit awkward when you don't know anyone else. I introduce myself to someone and we have a bit of pleasant small talk, but they then get distracted by one of their friends and I'm forgotten again. I know it will get better, but I really do wish Isabelle were here. At least on the train it won't be so obvious that I don't know anyone. Somehow standing here on the edge of the crowd feels worse.

"We have two tickets left," the best man announces, once it seems the group has assembled and it's time to get to the train. "Who are we missing?"

"Jamie is running late," someone calls out.

Jamie. Of course. I forgot that he was friends with Freddie and Niamh, but I didn't realize that they were close enough for him to be invited to the sten. I suppose it will be nice to know someone, even if it is him. We did sort of start getting on by the end of Isabelle's wedding. I didn't drive him back to London the following day, because one of his close friends had a space in his car and, according to Jamie, I was driving back "too early."

I set off at the time of checkout from the hotel, but whatever. Maybe he needed an excuse to get out of another few hours stuck in the car with me.

The return drive was very nice, mind you. I listened to my podcasts and Whitney Houston's greatest hits in peace.

Anyway, I'm not surprised he's late for the train. Having only just met him, I would safely assume he's late for everything. He seems so—

"Where's Matthew?"

I tense as the best man's question lingers in the air after he checks his list. My cheeks start burning with shame. I see the other hens and stags look to one another to see if anyone knows the answer. Freddie's eyes widen in horror and then he quickly clears his throat and says, "He's not coming anymore," with a wave of his hand, before encouraging everyone to move to the train.

I know Niamh is looking at me to check I'm okay, but I can't bear to meet her eyes, so I keep them firmly on the floor and follow the excitable group to the platform.

I'm fine.

Niamh and Freddie had, of course, invited Matthew to the sten, back when everyone assumed we'd be married by now. They must have forgotten to tell the best man to cross him off the list. Or maybe that's my job now?

I bought an unnecessarily large cookie in M&S that I was planning on nibbling later on in the journey if I got peckish, but I'll be needing that ASAP.

Our tickets take up a large section of the carriage, so the best man instructs us to pick any one of the many seats we've been allocated. I wait patiently as everyone sorts out their bags and gets themselves settled, and then quietly make my way to the back row of our cluster.

I chuckle as Freddie pops open a bottle of prosecco and pours some for Niamh into a plastic flute, spilling it everywhere and making her laugh. The maid of honor holds out two crowns for them both to wear, promising us all that the costumes will get a lot worse as the weekend continues. I hope the other passengers in this carriage don't mind sharing it with a rowdy bunch. I'm pleased to have two seats to myself and reach down into my shopping bag to find my cookie. Keeping my head down, I take a large bite.

Oh my god. So gooey. This cookie is officially everything to me.

A whistle is blown as the train prepares to leave and there's suddenly an eruption of cheers. I crane my neck over the seats to see that Jamie has arrived, jumping on the train just before the doors close. As the others pat him on the back in congratulations, he laughs, running a hand through his hair, looking frazzled.

After greeting his friends and giving Freddie and Niamh a hug, he starts strolling down the aisle looking for a seat as the train moves off. I sink into my seat, hoping he won't notice me or the empty seat beside me. There should be another spare one somewhere that would have been Matthew's, so he can have that one.

Look, it's not that I have anything against this guy. It's just that I was looking forward to being away from the crowd for the journey, hidden away here on my own with my cookie and the luxury of two seats to myself.

"Well, well, well," he says, stopping at my row.

I glance up, pretending I'd only just noticed he was here. "Oh, hi, Jamie."

"Hello, Freya." He grins, shoving his bag in the overhead

space above us, before slumping down next to me. "Looks like we're stuck on another journey together."

I grumpily shift toward the window as he knocks into my arm while digging into his own M&S bag to pull out a bottle of water and a can of craft beer. He really is something else.

"Why do you look irritated already?" he asks, unscrewing the lid of his water bottle and taking a few glugs.

"I'm surprised you found the time to do some shopping when you were running late."

"I wasn't running late."

"You literally just made the train by the skin of your teeth."

"Yeah, but I wasn't running late when I got to the shops. I was perfectly on time. It was the browsing that made me late. But, doesn't matter, because I made the train."

"I don't know how you're so calm."

"I wasn't a minute ago. I was running like a crazy person, shouting at people to get out of my way. I think I knocked over an old lady in my hurry to make it." His eyes drift to the lowered tray table in front of me. "That cookie is ginormous."

"I know."

"You have a sweet tooth?"

"A little bit."

"I'm more of a savory man myself. How long is this journey?"

"Just over two hours."

"Not too bad." He opens his can of beer. "And if we get delayed, then no one needs to worry about starving to death thanks to the giant cookie of yours. That would feed the five thousand."

I narrow my eyes at him. "There's nothing wrong with giant cookies."

"Never said there was." He takes a swig of his beer. "So, am I allowed to know the fate of my cuff links? You didn't use them in a potion to curse me, did you? Because I've had an extraordinarily bad week."

"Dancing Bear having trouble finding its rhythm?"

"Okay, that was a terrible joke so don't look so proud of yourself," he says with a sigh. "Work wasn't brilliant, but the week was shit because of my sister."

I can't hide my surprise. "Sister?"

"Yeah." He frowns at me. "Why do you look shocked?"

"I don't know. I thought you were an only child."

"Why would you assume that?"

"Not sure. Maybe it's because you seem so . . ." In lieu of an appropriate word, I do a strange little wave with my hand.

"What does that"—he echoes my action with his own hand—"mean?"

"You know."

"No?"

"Sort of . . . floozy."

"Floozy?!" He looks at me like I'm mad. "Floozy?"

"Yeah. In your own world."

He throws his head back and cackles. "That's not what 'floozy' means!"

"Floating through life."

"That's *not* what it means!"

"Really?"

"No, you dingbat!"

"Dingbat?!" I snort. "Who says 'dingbat'?"

"Who says '*floozy*'?! 'Floozy' is a word they use in, like, *Bugsy Malone*, to describe someone who sleeps around!"

"Oh. Well, it doesn't sound like that's what it means."

He shakes his head at me in disbelief. "That's not how language works. You should probably know what words mean before you use them. And for the record, I don't float through life. And I'm not an only child. I have a younger sister, Layla."

"What did she do that made your week so terrible?"

"It wasn't what she did. It's what I did." He takes a sip of beer.

"We had a fight and now she won't talk to me. And, on top of that, I dropped a barrel on my toe on Monday *and* I messed up some admin and had to start all over again. So, if you could cancel whatever curse you put on me that would be great."

"If I put a curse on you, it would be way more interesting than a barrel dropping on your foot and some boring accounts going wrong," I inform him. "I'd, like . . . send some locusts to attack you or something."

"Very original."

"You'd keep falling down wells."

"Okay, that one is actually original. I was being sarcastic before."

"I promise I didn't put a curse on you."

He lets out a long heavy sigh. "Guess this one is all on me, then. The last time I give my sister my opinion on anything, that's for sure."

"Ah."

"What? Why are you smiling like that?"

I shrug. "I know how it feels when you offer your opinion."

"Okay, the Suttworth thing is different," he says, shifting in his seat. "That was business. This was personal."

"Even worse."

"I know," he admits, grimacing. "You ever fight with your brother? The one in New York?"

"Yes, of course. Not so much anymore, but every now and then we'll have a scrap over something stupid."

"And how does he get you to talk to him again? Or vice versa?"

"It depends." I raise my eyebrows at him. "Did you say anything you need to apologize for?"

"A couple of things."

"Maybe start with that. Tell her you're sorry and why. It's a good icebreaker."

He rests his head back against the seat. "The classic apology, then."

"It's always a winner when you mean it." I pause, and then, because he looks a bit beaten, I reluctantly offer, "You want some cookie?"

"No, but thank you."

I shrug, reaching down into the M&S bag to pull out one of my drinks, placing it on my tray. He takes one look at it and snorts.

"What?" I ask defensively, opening the can.

"A pornstar martini. In a can."

"There you go again, all pretentious and judgy. I'm definitely on your sister's side for whatever it is you've fallen out over."

"Oh come on, you have to expect some backlash when you buy a canned cocktail," he argues, gesturing to my drink as I take a glug. "You could have at least gone for a good one like a classic gin and tonic."

"Classic? More like boring. Don't you ever want to mix things up and go for something interesting? You need to learn to live a little, Jamie."

"*Ha!* Says the woman who works for only the best-known brands and arrives early for everything."

"I like being organized and on time. It shows respect."

"I agree. I think it's impressive." He takes a sip of his drink. "But you telling me to 'live a little' seems mildly hypocritical, don't you think?"

"Oh, so you think because you have a tattoo and a beard, you're more exciting than me? Is that it?"

He frowns in confusion. "How do you know about my tattoo?"

"I saw it in the car," I explain, suddenly feeling embarrassed, as though I've invaded his privacy. "I didn't see much of it. Just the top bit."

"Hey, you two!" Niamh trills, appearing at our row and leaning on the seat in front of us. "Are you enjoying the journey?"

"Oh yes," Jamie answers, draining the last of his beer. I can't work out if he's being sarcastic or not on that one. "Are you having fun?"

"I'm already feeling tipsy," she admits, before gasping and giving me a sympathetic look. "Freya, I am so, so sorry about the whole Matthew thing at the station. Are you okay?"

As she says it, I realize that I had already forgotten about that awkward moment earlier. It's quite a nice realization, to be honest, although not so fun that it's come up again now.

"It was nothing!" I insist, plastering on a smile and holding up my pornstar martini. "Forget about it. I'm having a great time!"

"Phew!" She breathes a sigh of relief. "Freddie was meant to . . . well, anyway, I'm glad you're okay."

"Niamh! Come back here! We're playing a game!" the maid of honor yells down the aisle.

She winces at her name. "I hate these stupid games."

"All part of the fun," Jamie reminds her, before drinking some water.

She smiles at us and then makes her way back to her seat, wobbling and steadying herself as the train trundles on.

"Is Matthew your ex?" Jamie asks, as soon as she's gone.

"Yep."

"The one who said you were too 'together'? And sent you the message at the wedding that made you look like you'd seen a ghost?"

"The very one." I take two large gulps of my drink.

"Got it. I feel bad now about banging on about you being early for everything," he says cautiously, making a face. "Is that what he meant by you being too 'together'? You know, super organized or something?"

"Yeah, sort of. But I also think it was my lack of overt emotion, so I wouldn't worry."

He seems surprised. "Lack of emotion?"

I down the last of my can and get out another one. "When he compared us, he said that he was temperamental and emotional, and I clashed with that. I never really saw it that way. I might be more levelheaded, and more pragmatic about things, but I didn't feel that made us less compatible. I thought it was good that we balanced each other out. I don't know, maybe I was naïve."

I don't know why I'm giving this amount of detail to Jamie, someone I barely know. That pornstar martini has obviously gone straight to my head.

"He sounds like an idiot," he states.

I bristle at this description of Matthew from a stranger, even after everything. It's like a natural instinct in me to defend him.

"Why do you say that?" I ask grumpily.

"Because I barely know you and I can tell he's talking bollocks."

I stare at him, completely thrown. "But he's right, I'm not emotional. I'm sarcastic. Like Isabelle said at her wedding."

"You can't be both?"

"Of course you can, but I'm not."

"Okay, well I don't think it's fair to say you clash with someone temperamental and emotional," he argues. "I'm temperamental and emotional, and we don't clash."

I blink at him, surprised by this statement. "That's because . . . because we've barely spoken. And we did clash a lot at first. Wait . . . are you emotional and temperamental?"

"Yeah. That's why I have the tattoo. It's an eagle wearing a monocle."

"I'm sorry, what?"

He smiles apologetically.

"You have a tattoo of an eagle wearing a monocle?" I check.

"That's right. Remember the ex I mentioned? The one who cheated on me? We had a huge fight when we broke up and I marched straight to the tattoo parlor to get it just to piss her off."

"Why would a tattoo of an eagle wearing a monocle piss her off?"

"She hated tattoos and birds."

"Okay, but why the monocle?"

"I thought it made it more sophisticated. If you look at it, you can see what I mean." He turns to face away from me and reaches over to lower his T-shirt at the neckline to display the artwork in question.

I clasp a hand round my mouth. "Oh my god! It's ridiculous!"

"Kind of sophisticated, though, right?"

"Not at all."

"A little bit, though."

I can't stop laughing. "Okay. Maybe the monocle does make it a little bit sophisticated."

"Yeah, like you know that this eagle reads Shakespeare." Jamie turns back to face me, chuckling. "Worst thing is, she's never seen it."

"You're joking! After all this effort?!"

"I haven't seen her since we broke up." He shakes his head. "What an idiot. But honestly, I love it now. Life has a funny way of working out like that, I always find. Maybe that's because I'm a floozy."

I smile, looking down at my lap. "Floating through it all like a floozy. It makes sense."

"As I say, that Matthew guy didn't know what he was talking about. I'm temperamental, just like he claims to be, and here we are, getting on like a house on fire."

"I've known you for about two days in total and our relationship has already been rocky."

"On one of those days, I was too hungover to be a proper human," he points out.

"Okay, but in Matthew's defense, you haven't had to live with me for twelve years."

"You were together for twelve years?" His eyes widen. "Whoa. That's a hefty relationship."

"How long were you with your ex?" I ask curiously.

"Two years. That wasn't my longest relationship, though. I was with someone before her for three years. We're still friends, actually."

I nod and we fall into a natural silence. The train is hurtling through countryside now as we leave London behind, and I look out the window at the blur of fields and trees we pass. I can't imagine ever being "just friends" with Matthew, to be around him but not be with him. How would that even be possible? I can't get my brain around that idea at all.

An eruption of laughter from down the train prompts me to tear my eyes from the window and crane my neck over the seat in front to see what's going on. Freddie is standing in the aisle, telling an animated story and getting plenty of laughs from his captive audience. Niamh is sitting near him, burying her head in her hands as he relays an embarrassing anecdote about her to everyone. She reaches for his hand and squeezes it affectionately before he launches into the next part of the story.

Jamie nods toward Freddie. "Is this your only wedding this summer aside from Isabelle and Ryan's, then?"

"*Ha!*" I turn my attention back to my cookie, tearing a bit off. "No. I have five more this summer. Two down already."

He chuckles. "I have a fair few, too. I think three more."

I swallow my mouthful. "It's what happens when you're in your thirties. Hen dos, weddings, baby showers, housewarmings."

Jamie nods knowingly, reaching for a fresh can of beer. "Yep."

"Honestly, it's hard not to feel a bit lost when you're alone in the midst of all of it, with no idea where you're going, and everyone seeming to move on but you."

He pauses for a moment, and I feel my cheeks flush. I really said too much that time, didn't I? "You know what? I think everyone feels a bit lost. Even the people with high-flying jobs at giant drinks corporations, even those who seem like they have it—what's the word? Oh yeah—together."

"Guess you're right. I can attest to that."

"Muddling through is all we can do. And the best way, it's long been said, is to drink pornstar martinis from a can, go to Leeds for a weekend, and have a bloody good time."

"Those are wise words."

"I think it was Plato who said that."

"Surely Socrates."

"One of the two." He holds up his can. "Cheers."

"Cheers!" I happily knock my drink against his. "To muddling through."

Okay, so one of the articles I read about breakups said that making lists can help you to find the silver lining in a stressful and sad situation.

So, here goes nothing.

Things I would have done if
Matthew and I were still together:

* Got married
* Gone on an incredible honeymoon
* Returned happy and excited for our future

Things I have done because
Matthew and I aren't together:

* Kicked a guy in the balls
* Got into gardening and survived an attack by a killer worm
* Locked myself in a toilet and consequently been saved by an unexpectedly sexy vicar
* Spoken honestly about heartbreak to the charming Chido
* Broken out my old "5,6,7,8" Steps routine and victoriously became the last one standing at Obi's wedding, even though the Steps routine is very cringeworthy*
* Debated drink brands on a car journey with a rude, obnoxious stranger
* Beaten said stranger in a whiskey competition and won his cuff links
* Bravely attended a sten on my own, even though I only really know the bride, the groom, and the aforementioned rude, obnoxious stranger
* Drunkenly stole a traffic cone on a sten in Leeds after being egged on by the same stranger, who is now more of an acquaintance
* Returned said stolen traffic cone in the early hours of the morning after lying awake racked with guilt
* Told the new acquaintance that it was TOTALLY unacceptable behavior
* Secretly been proud that I had such guts I never knew of

*Everyone loves it, though, and if they say they don't, they're lying and probably work in an independent craft brewery in Dalston so have to pretend to be cool at all times. (Jamie has confirmed he loves the Steps routine.)

CHAPTER FOURTEEN

Ruby

Just booked a last minute bikini wax

I got mine yesterday

Hurt like a bitch

Haven't had it done since before the breakup

Ruby

I also haven't been for ages

Had a full on bush

I am SO ready for this holiday/wedding

Tomorrow, we'll be sitting by that pool in France in
our swimsuits, like hello boysssssss, yaaaas we
glamorous

Leo

Hello

Are you both aware that this is the group chat?

Ruby

Whoops

Soz Leo

Leo

I am also excited to sit by the pool tomorrow

And say hello boysssssss, yaaaas we glamorous

Ruby

Especially now you've had your eyebrows done

Leo

You said you weren't going to tell anyone about that

Ruby

Leo had his eyebrows done, Freya

His monobrow is no more

Super glamorous

Leo

I look very good, I have to say

Ruby

Own it, babe

Can't wait for that 6 a.m. glass of prosecco

in the airport tomorrow before our flight.

France, here we come!!

Cali and Dominic's wedding hotel is stunning. I can totally see how they fell head over heels in love with it when they came here to Aude on the hunt for a venue. It's very glamorous and grand, with this huge, amazing pool and stretching green lawns. The sun is shining, it's boiling hot, and that turquoise-blue water is calling us.

As soon as Leo, Ruby, and myself have checked in, we agree to meet by the pool immediately, rushing up to our rooms to get our swimsuits on. I love my room—there's something about hotel rooms, they're so much more exciting than normal bedrooms. Once I've managed to get the key card to work and get in there, I throw my bag on the bed and go straight to the window to check out the view. My room overlooks the pool, but I can also see the sea beyond. I take a deep, calming breath.

I have very mixed feelings about this weekend. I'm excited to be in this beautiful place with my best friends, and I can't wait to see Cali get married.

But Matthew is here.

It will be the first time we've seen each other since I kicked him in the balls. When I think about seeing him, I feel sick. I've played it out in my head so many times. I've imagined what he'll say, what I'll say, what I'll be wearing, how it will go. Ruby has told me that I have to pretend he's not there, that's the best way to enjoy myself, and I'm sure she's right. But how will I be able to do that?

I move away from the window and unzip my bag. Cali informed me that Matthew isn't flying in until later, so at least I have a day of relaxing without having to worry about him. I grab my towel, slide on my flip-flops, and prop a pair of sunglasses on my head. I won't think about the M-word.

"We saved you a spot!" Ruby calls out across the pool, as I come through the doors from the lobby and see her and Leo lounging on their towels already.

"This is glorious," I declare, plonking myself down on the sun lounger next to her and beginning the slog of applying sun cream.

"What do you think?" Ruby asks, gesturing to the wide-brimmed sun hat on her head. "Very Audrey Hepburn, right? I feel like a 1950s Hollywood actress who's just signed a major studio deal."

"It's amazing," I agree, noticing Leo's shorts that have turtles all over them. "Like your swimwear, Leo."

"Turtles are awesome," Leo comments without opening his eyes.

I finally finish applying my sun cream and then lie back on my towel, enjoying bathing in those warm rays. I close my eyes and exhale, feeling suddenly so relaxed. This is exactly what I needed.

"I've booked us a table for lunch, by the way, Freya," Leo says. "One of the tables outside. Dominic said the food here was really good, and the cocktails too."

"Perfect, thank you."

"Is it just me or is everyone who works here an Abercrombie model?" Ruby observes, making me laugh. "I'm being serious."

Leo clears his throat pointedly. "You know between that and the 'hello boys' comment in the WhatsApp group yesterday, I'm beginning to think you may have a wandering eye, Rubes."

"You have nothing to worry about, babe," she assures him. "And don't even pretend that you weren't drooling all over that hottie at reception earlier."

"I think you'll find she was the one flirting with me," he claims. "It's my irresistible charm. It reels them all in."

Ruby snorts. "Yes, she went weak at the knees when you asked her if there was an ironing board in the room. Sexy talk."

"I can make anything sexy."

"Go on then."

"Go on, what?"

"Say 'ironing board' in a sexy way," Ruby challenges.

"All right," Leo accepts. He pauses and then puts on a strange growl. "Ironing board."

Ruby and I both burst out laughing.

"That wasn't sexy!" Ruby declares.

"Freya, what do you think?" he asks.

"I reckon the receptionist was putty in your hands."

"Speaking of holiday flirtations," Ruby continues, "how are you feeling about your task this wedding?"

"Not very confident."

"Securing a good-night kiss."

"Yeah, I know I've said this several times since that night, but I'd like to remind you both that we were drunk when we created the Wedding Season list," I point out, opening my eyes and peering over at Ruby, who is sitting up and watching me smugly. "And I think I was a bit overzealous in my hopes of rehabilitation into the dating world by now. I'm not sure I'm ready to kiss anyone else."

"It doesn't have to mean anything. Just a peck. Why not?" Ruby suggests with a cheeky smile. "We're not in England anymore, Freya, we're in France. This is the country of romance and adventure!"

"And cheese and wine, which I'm more excited about, to be honest."

"Obviously the cheese and wine are the most important things, but you might as well throw in some romantic fun, too."

"I don't think I'm there." I let out a sigh. "Matthew is going to be here, too. I can't kiss anyone in front of him. It's not fair."

"Um. *What?*" Ruby gasps. "Leo, tell her how stupid that is."

"Freya," he says robotically, "that is stupid."

"You see? Even Leo thinks that's stupid!" Ruby exclaims, much to my amusement. "It is perfectly fair for you to enjoy yourself and not give two hoots about what Matthew thinks."

"Maybe, but it's not very me," I conclude.

Ruby sighs in disappointment. The three of us fall into comfortable silence and stay there until I feel a tap on my shoulder and find Ruby holding out one of her earphones. With a knowing smile, I stand up and push my lounger up against hers, then lie back down and take the earphone, pressing it into my right ear while she plugs the other one into her left.

"Do you remember when we used to do this at uni in the library?" she asks, scrolling through her phone for an acceptable playlist.

I grin. "We were supposed to be revising for our exams and you'd distract me by shoulder-bopping to R and B. Oh god, and when you went through that indie rocker phase."

"I loved that phase! I looked good in those checkered shirts and all that eyeliner." She hesitates, then adds quietly, "I'll admit the blunt block fringe was a mistake for my face shape."

I smile and shift to make myself comfortable on the lounger, closing my eyes, ready to doze in the sunshine. As I begin to drift off, perfectly content, a jarring memory flashes into my brain, despite my hopes to keep him at bay for today.

A couple of summers ago, Matthew and I were on holiday in Croatia. We were on the beach and I'd just been in the sea. I had come out of the water with a big smile on my face because it had been so fun and refreshing, and I made my way across the sand back to him, gearing up to tease him about not coming in. I'd tried waving to him from the sea and calling out to get his attention, but he'd been on his phone the whole time.

He didn't look up when I reached him, shaking my towel out from my beach bag and wrapping it round me.

"You should have come in! It was lovely."

"I got the job!" he replied excitedly, scrolling down his screen.

"What?"

"The promotion I applied for at work! I got it!"

I blinked at him. "Wait, what promotion?"

He looked up at me then, confused. "You know, Cate left and so I went for her role."

"I didn't know that Cate left. You never told me about this."

"Oh." He glanced back at his screen and shrugged. "I mean, it's not that big a deal, it's only an internal promotion. But still! We should go celebrate! Come on, grab your things. Senior Graphic Designer. Suits me, doesn't it?"

I felt completely thrown by this information. I brushed it off, pulling my dress on over my wet swimsuit and pretending like I didn't care that I was covered in salty seawater and my hair was straggled and dripping down my back, so we could go get a glass of bubbles straightaway to toast his success.

I smiled and congratulated him and loved that he was

suddenly in a much better mood than he had been that morning. He told me all about the promotion, filling in the details, and I nodded along, telling him how proud I was. I then pretended not to be humiliated when he video-called his mum and told her the good news, and it was obvious she'd known that he was applying for the promotion all along.

"Isn't this wonderful, Freya?" Gail said, delighted. "I told him he should go for that interview! And to think he was so nervous beforehand. Well done, Matthew!"

"Absolutely." I nodded with a fixed smile. "It's great. Really great."

The whole time, I wondered why he hadn't told me. When I brought it up the next day, he said he thought he had, but anyway, what did it matter now? He got the job!

Lying in the sunshine now, I remember it viscerally. The hurt, the embarrassment. I don't know whether he genuinely thought he had told me. With hindsight, it seems more likely that by then I had already begun to lose my position in his life as someone he wanted to share things with. If he'd forgotten to tell me something small, it wouldn't matter. That happens in relationships, it's usually not a red flag.

This was a big thing, though. Applying for a promotion and going through an interview process. How is it possible that he didn't mention anything on the day of the interview? He went into work, nervous and excited, without saying anything. And he returned home from work, relieved it was over, apprehensive for the news on how it went, without saying anything. I must have said something like "How was your day?" and he probably replied something along the lines of "Fine." How did he not think to tell me?

I was right there.

"If you could be the best in the world at any sport, what would it be?" Leo asks, drying himself with his towel and plonking back down on his lounger.

We had a lovely long lunch earlier, before returning to our places by the pool for a nice nap in the shade—watching Leo try to move the heavier-than-expected umbrella stand toward us without falling in the pool was utterly fascinating, but he got there eventually—and now we've emerged from a quick dip and are drying off in the late-afternoon sun.

"Good question." Ruby ponders for a moment. "Formula One, I think."

Leo is stunned by this response. "What? Why?"

"Because it's really cool," Ruby answers breezily. "I'd be really rich and get to drive really fast."

"It's also super dangerous."

"Yeah, but I'd be the best at it, so my chances of crashing would be slim. Why, what would yours be?"

"Golf."

"Golf?" Ruby wrinkles her nose. "If you could pick to be the best at *any* sport in the *whole* world, you'd choose golf? Honestly, Leo, I'm ashamed. I'm not sure we can get married anymore."

"It's the obvious choice," he argues, putting his sunglasses on and brushing his wet hair out of his eyes. "It's extremely difficult, so you'd be well respected. It's not dangerous, it's very calm, and there's no running necessary. Plus, the prizes are big money. Imagine, traveling all over the world on tours, strolling across those green lawns in the sunshine in the fresh air, playing excellent, satisfying shots. It's a classy sport."

"It's boring," Ruby says, aghast.

"It's not boring and if you bothered to watch it with me or try out some lessons, like I've urged you to, you would discover that. Although, I'm not sure you have the patience for such a precise sport," he grumbles. "Freya, what would you choose?"

"This is a very good question," I declare, lying back with my hands resting on my stomach.

"Yeah, I think it says a lot about a person," Ruby says, narrowing her eyes at Leo. "Golf?!"

"Tennis would be a good one, because winning Wimbledon looks like an epic moment in someone's life," I muse aloud, the others nodding in agreement. "A winter sport might also be quite fun, like ice skating, because it's very elegant and athletic."

"Ooh yes, and you get to wear *loads* of sequins," Ruby points out.

"I know," I say suddenly, clicking my fingers as an idea pops into my brain. "Fencing."

Ruby blinks at me. "What?"

"Fencing."

"Why on *earth* would you pick fencing?" she asks, bewildered. "Have you ever even done any fencing before?"

"No, but you get to use a sword."

Leo appreciates this sentiment. "I hadn't considered fencing. That's a very good point." His face lights up. "No pun intended!"

"Ha! Point! Good one!" I say brightly.

"Okay, did you two secretly have wine with lunch?" Ruby asks in disbelief. "You have the opportunity to be the best in the world at any sport and my boyfriend chooses golf and my best friend chooses fencing. What is *wrong* with both of you? Freya, nobody has heard of any fencing champions!"

"Well, that's not true, is it? There's bound to be diehard fans out there."

"You're not going to become rich through being the best in the world at fencing!"

"It's not all about money, Ruby," I say, enjoying how baffled she is at my choice. "And I wouldn't just be awesome at fencing in the Olympics and stuff, I could also be the stunt double for a

movie star in their sword-fighting scenes. I could do the chore-
ography for big action movies. Now, that is cool."

"That's really cool," Leo agrees. "And I could be the stunt
double for any movies that have golf scenes in them!"

"Yes, exactly." I nod.

"Ugh," Ruby groans, "I am surrounded by dweebs."

"You know, Ruby, we can't all live in the fast lane like yourself," Leo tells her. "I think you'll find that if you tried a golf
lesson, you'd be pleasantly—"

"Oh my god." Ruby gasps, looking out across the pool.

"Hear me out. Golf is—"

"No, not about that," she hisses, turning to look at me in
concern. "Matthew is here."

I jolt my head up so fast, I almost give myself whiplash. There
he is. He's wearing Wayfarers, and a light blue linen shirt with
navy shorts and flip-flops. He's grown his hair out and styled it so
it's smoothly swept back. He looks happy and relaxed, surveying
the pool and the restaurant terrace with what looks like great
satisfaction.

I quickly lie back down again, flattening myself against the
bed.

"What do I do?" I squeak in total panic.

"Stay calm," Leo instructs, looking mildly panicked himself.
"Everything is fine."

"Everything is *not fine*," I retort. "My hair is a bird's nest from
the swim! I'm all sweaty and covered in sun cream! I'm literally
a ball of slime! *I'm a slime ball!*"

"Okay, calm down," Ruby says under her breath. "You look
great and—"

"I need to get out of here! But if I stand up and walk round
the pool he'll either notice me or bump into me! I'm supposed to
look incredible when I see him for the first time! I'm supposed

to look sophisticated and sexy and easy! *This is not how it's supposed to go!*"

"We need to discuss you wanting to look 'easy,'" Ruby comments.

"Easygoing! You know what I meant! *Now is not the time for nitpicking, Ruby!*"

"Okay, maybe he won't see us," Leo reasons, keeping an eye on him. "Oh. Hang on."

"Has he seen us?" I ask, my voice strained.

"No, but he is coming this way."

"Oh my god."

"Why don't we—"

I don't wait to hear what Leo is about to suggest. I do the only thing I can do in that horrifying situation: I stealthily roll off the lounger and onto the ground.

"Freya? What exactly are you doing?" Ruby asks slowly.

Without replying, I then roll onto my front and push myself up onto all fours, hidden by my sun lounger, which is acting as a wall between me and the direction Matthew is coming from.

"Freya!" Ruby hisses, craning her neck to look at me. "You're not being shot at! You can't just crawl away!"

But at an impressive lightning speed, if I do say so myself, I scuttle toward a large potted palm tree. When I'm safely behind it, I kneel up to look through the leaves.

Matthew has *just* spotted Leo and Ruby, and is now wandering over to them with a nervous expression. I watch the scene unfold from behind the tree.

"Excuse me," a voice says behind me, making me yelp and *very almost* blowing my cover, but I check and am relieved to see that Matthew has not glanced this way.

I turn to the waiter who has disturbed me. "Yes?"

"Is everything . . . okay?" he asks.

I realize that I must look rather strange, crouching behind

this potted palm tree in my wet swimsuit, with no shoes on and very grubby knees thanks to all that crawling.

"Oh, yes, thank you," I whisper. "All fine."

He looks confused, but lowers his voice, too, in solidarity. "Are you sure?"

"Yes. I'm just . . . I'm getting some shade."

"I can move an umbrella for you if you need?" he offers quietly.

This person is annoyingly helpful. He's also, as an insignificant side note, very attractive. Tanned, dark, handsome, and the French accent is outrageously sexy. Leo should take note of the way this guy says "umbrella." Much better than that pathetic "ironing board" growl.

"No, I'm fine," I assure him in a hushed tone, desperate for him to go. I don't want Matthew to notice a waiter talking to someone hiding behind a tree.

"Would you like a drink?"

"No! Honestly!" I say in exasperation. "I'm fine!"

"Well, let me know if I can help." He turns to leave.

"Wait, wait!" I whisper, realizing that I'd be nuts to waste this opportunity and stopping him before he goes. "Do you do piña coladas?"

"Yes, of course."

"Large ones?"

"Yes."

"I'll have one of those, please."

"No problem. What is your room number?"

"One-twelve."

"Great." He hesitates. "Shall I bring it to behind this tree?"

"If I'm still here, then yes. Actually, make that three piña coladas. I should get a couple for my friends, too."

He nods and then tells me he'll be back soon. I'm actually surprised he didn't act more disturbed. Maybe he assumes crazy

English people hide behind potted trees, spying on people through the leaves while sipping piña coladas all the time.

I turn my attention back to Matthew. He's got his hands in his pockets now and he looks deeply uncomfortable. I wish I could hear what they're saying! While he's talking, he moves his left hand up to his ear and twiddles his earlobe. Is that a nervous gesture or is he talking about earlobes?! Is he talking about *my* earlobes?! I do have quite large earlobes! I've always thought so, but I've never said it to him. Is that part of the reason why he broke up with me?! *My freakishly large earlobes?!*

Matthew gives an awkward wave and then finally turns to leave, pretending to casually walk back into the hotel, although anyone can tell he's desperate to run away as fast as possible. When he's disappeared through the doors, I wait a minute or so just to be safe and then emerge from behind the tree and cautiously slink back to my lounger.

"What was that?" Ruby asks me as I slump back down next to her. "You looked like you were doing a bizarre army drill."

"Did he see me?"

Leo shakes his head. "No, you're safe. I think it was very clever thinking on your part."

"I think you're nuts," Ruby says, her lips twitching into a smile. "You all right?"

"What did he say? Did he talk about my weirdly thick earlobes? It's all right, you can be honest."

Ruby and Leo share a confused look before Leo clears his throat and answers, "No, Freya, your earlobes weren't mentioned."

"What were you talking about then?" I ask desperately.

"Well, I think it's safe to say he immediately withered under Ruby's evil glare," Leo explains, chuckling. "He just said hi and that it was nice to see us, but he wasn't met with such niceties from our side."

"I told him it would be best to avoid us if he knows what's

good for him," Ruby tells me defiantly. "At first, he chuckled like I might be joking, but I emphasized that I was not."

"I, on the other hand, tried to keep things civil, because I know that's what you want, Freya," Leo says, his eyebrows raised at Ruby. "I said that I hoped he enjoyed the weekend."

I nod, biting my lip. "Did he mention me at all?"

"He asked how you were," Leo says.

"We told him that you were doing great," Ruby says smugly.

"That was it? Nothing else was said?"

"That was pretty much it," Leo confirms, allowing me to breathe a sigh of relief. "He said he was heading out for dinner, so he'd see us tomorrow at the wedding."

"He won't come back out here then?"

Leo grins. "Highly unlikely after Ruby's comments."

"Thank god." I exhale and then turn to smile gratefully at them. "You two are the best."

"At least the first sighting is done with now. It wasn't too bad either," Leo comments happily. "It could have gone a lot worse."

"Yes, that's true," Ruby says dryly. "She could have dived into the plant pot."

"Three piña coladas," the waiter announces, appearing at my side holding a tray of delicious-looking cocktails, all with little colorful umbrellas in. "This looks much more comfortable than behind the tree."

I laugh nervously, as Ruby and Leo sit up in surprise. "Ha ha, yes, sorry about that."

"You ordered these from behind the tree?" Ruby asks, taking hers. "Impressive."

"Enjoy and let me know if you need anything else," the waiter says, flashing me a grin, before tucking the tray under his arm and walking off.

Ruby watches him go. "You see? Everyone here seems to be a model."

"You should hear him say the word 'umbrella.'"

"He did say to let him know if you needed anything else, Freya. You know what I think?" Ruby asks, smiling mischievously and taking a sip of her drink. "We might just have a suitable candidate for that good-night kiss."

CHAPTER FIFTEEN

The strange thing about being at an event with your ex is that you know where they are *at all times*.

When Matthew and I were together, I would go to a party with him and then we'd get chatting to people and naturally drift off in different directions, not needing to be stuck to the other's side like glue all night. I just left him to it and didn't really think about where he was until we needed to find each other at the end of the night to go home. But when we're not together as a couple, I know exactly where he's standing and who he's talking to at every minute of the bloody day. I'm so aware of his presence, even when I try not to be.

I'm not even facing him right now, but I know he's standing in a cluster of people a few meters away. I can see him in the corner of my eye and if I lean back ever so subtly, I can see him more clearly.

"What are you doing?" Ruby asks me, looking me up and down.

"What do you mean?"

"You're standing weirdly."

"No, I'm not."

"Yes, you are. Sort of leaning back and twisting sideways, like you're about to try a yoga pose," she insists.

"Don't be ridiculous."

"Are you trying to look sexy and flexible?"

"*What?* Why would I try to look sexy and flexible?"

"For the French waiter. He's here today, you know, helping to serve the drinks. Are you peacocking for him?" Ruby shares a grin with Simone, who arrived for the wedding on a late flight last night, completing our university group here to support Cali on her big day.

"No!" I roll my eyes, irritated at having to admit the truth. "I'm trying to keep an eye on Matthew."

"Oh, right." Ruby glances over to him with a repulsed expression. "Is he aware he's wearing the wrong shoes with that suit?"

"They're awful, aren't they? But other than that, he looks nice."

"He looks like a prick."

"Ruby's right," Simone says nodding. "He does."

"You would both say that no matter what he wore."

"No, we wouldn't. Anyone can tell he's wearing the wrong shoes, Freya. He doesn't have anyone to curb his disastrous flair for shit fashion anymore, that's the problem." Ruby sighs heavily, shaking her head at him. "Are you going to speak to him today?"

"I'm not sure I'll be able to avoid it."

The ceremony was lovely, outside in the sunshine on the lawn of the hotel, where Cali and Dominic said their vows under an archway of bright, colorful flowers. Cali looks stunning in an elegant strapless gown with a flowing chiffon skirt, perfect for the hot climate, and Dominic and his ushers are very smart in matching light beige blazers and navy trousers. We've just finished the wedding breakfast, which was absolutely delicious, and a jazz band is setting up, as all the guests mill about in anticipation of the cake cutting and the start of the evening festivities. It's such a beautiful, warm evening, and it makes for an excited, happy atmosphere.

Matthew and I never really considered a destination wedding because I'd always thought I wanted to have a traditional English countryside wedding at Dad's. But now that I'm here, and it's so magical and dazzling, such a spectacular escape from reality, I'm not so sure.

Not that I imagine I'll ever have to worry about a wedding again.

Which is weird to think about, actually. Will I ever get married? I wonder if I'll ever get to the stage where I can trust it will go ahead. If I ever even got engaged sometime far in the future, would I be terrified the whole time, wondering if it was real?

"You look stressed," Ruby observes. "Are you worried about talking to him?"

"I was actually thinking about whether I'd ever trust anyone ever again."

"Bloody hell." Simone wrinkles her nose. "Some nice, light thoughts for a wedding celebration, then."

"I'll likely become a cynical, bitter old bitch," I add.

"What do you mean 'become'?" Ruby raises her eyebrows. "You've already got the cynicism down. Whenever we watch a nice, happy, romantic movie, you go off on one as soon as it ends about how the couple won't stay together—"

"If it's set during their school years, then it's highly unlikely."

"—and don't think I didn't notice you mutter something snarky when we saw that couple kissing at the airport."

"I could literally see that the guy had a wandering eye. He's probably going to screw her over at some point."

"We didn't even speak to them."

"Yes, but I saw him checking out the flight attendants as they boarded the plane."

She smiles, amused. "Don't let Matthew warp your view of love."

"If I ever need proof that love prevails, I have you and Leo right here," I assure her, prompting Ruby to look down at her shoes bashfully. "Not to mention all the weddings this year. So don't worry. I'm not an old bitch quite yet, I just wanted to give you enough warning in case things start heading that way."

"In the hopes of never letting that happen," Simone says, jumping in, "I'd like to point out the hot French waiter is looking at you."

She nods in the direction of the bar. I glance over in what I hope is a subtle manner and spot him midway through opening a bottle of champagne. He catches my eye and smiles, before pulling out the cork in a swift and easy motion.

"Bloody hell," Ruby whispers, watching him, "I am unbelievably turned on."

"Ruby!"

"Sorry, but did you see the way he opened that bottle?" Simone gasps. "The way his arms actually flexed? I actually think I might need a glass of ice-cold water after that."

"After what?" Leo asks, returning from his trip to the loo. "Did the sexy French waiter say 'umbrella' again?"

"Who?" Ruby asks innocently.

"You're standing on the wrong side of the lawn, by the way," Leo continues. "On my way to the bathroom, I noticed they have trays of macarons on a table over there."

"*What?!*" Ruby's eyes widen to saucers. "You know my love of macarons and in France they're bound to blow my head off. Lead the way, Leo. As if I almost missed them!"

Leo laughs and instructs us to follow him as we weave our way through the guests. I'm bringing up the rear when I feel a hand on my arm and turn around to see Matthew. Leo, Simone, and Ruby don't notice, going full steam ahead toward the macarons. I'm on my own.

"Freya," he says in this breathy voice. "Hi."

"Hi," I manage to say. "How are you?"

"I'm good." He gestures to my dress. "You look nice."

I do, in fact, look quite nice. This is not an accident. In the knowledge of seeing Matthew today, I spent about five hours getting ready. I paid a small fortune for a blow-dry this morning with Ruby at the posh local hairdresser's that Cali recommended and spent ages getting my makeup just right, a look that I'd practiced at home with the guidance of some YouTubers, who seem to be about fifteen years old but really know their stuff. I ordered many, many dresses to try on for the occasion, took photos of my reflection in the mirror in each of them at different angles, and then studied those photos at my desk at work when Phil wasn't looking. I've gone with the open-back teal midi-dress with spaghetti straps, which is looking even better than when I first tried it on thanks to my savvy application of fake tan last night.

The best thing about my outfit, though, is the ring. I took Niamh's advice and decided to buy a ring to wear on my left hand. It's a big, statement green gemstone set in a gold band, sitting on my middle finger, that I found after scrolling through affordable-jewelry websites on my phone while watching reality TV. Whenever I catch a glimpse of my left hand now, I don't get a pang of sadness at what it's missing. I see my fabulous new piece of jewelry and feel all smug and kickass.

"Thank you," I say. "So do you."

Not your shoes, though. This is why you need me.

Why don't you need me?

"Thank you."

This is so painful. He's looking down at the ground now, not sure what to say.

"How have you been?" he asks finally.

"Great, thank you. Absolutely fine," I inform him, careful not to hammer home the point too much, but hopefully enough that he stops giving me those pitying looks. "How about you?"

"Yeah. I've been okay." He nods. "Look, about those phone calls to my mum—"

"They were a mistake," I interrupt, frowning at him, upset

that he'd bring this up. "I got your text, thanks, so there's really no need for you to talk about it."

"No, I wasn't going to . . . Sorry, I didn't mean to make you feel uncomfortable," he says hurriedly, blushing. "I was going to apologize for my text. I saw Ryan recently and he told me how it came across and I hadn't really thought . . . Anyway, the point is, I'm sorry if you read it in a cold way. I didn't mean it to be."

Huh. Interesting. This sounds like an apology, but at the same time, he's saying that I'm the one who read it in the wrong way, not that he wrote it in the wrong way. Was he always this blameless? Always this patronizing?

"No apology necessary, thanks," I say, bristling at his words. "I hope Gail can forgive me."

"Of course," he says, leaning forward slightly, and for a second I think he might be considering reaching out for my hand, because his sort of lingers in the air a bit and then drops down to his side. "Her and Dad send their love."

I nod, not saying anything. Their love? God, it's so hard being around him. I want out of this conversation. I am an overwhelming mixture of emotions. I want to run off and hide; I want to shout at him and throw stuff at him; but I also want to cry and hold him and beg him to love me again.

"I should go find the others." I smile politely up at him. "Nice to see you."

"Freya," he says, quickly, stopping me from escaping, "I also wanted to say . . . thank you."

I blink at him. "What?"

He exhales deeply, as though he's been holding his breath all this time. "I've been wanting to say it to you for ages, but it didn't seem fair. But seeing you here today and how . . . great you are. I just wanted to make sure you knew how grateful I was for the way you handled everything so well."

My brain feels stuck. "I'm sorry, I don't understand. Handled what?"

"The breakup! Me fucking up the wedding!" he explains, smiling as though I've said something funny. "I never expected you to go off the rails, because you're you, and I knew I could rely on you to be sensible about things, but still. And you kicking me wasn't very fun—" He chuckles at the memory. "—but even my parents agreed I deserved that one after what I'd put you through. Aside from that and the phone calls to my mum, you've really been amazing. So, I know it's maybe a strange thing to say, but . . . thank you."

I stare at him, my jaw on the floor. "You're thanking me for not going crazy at you when you broke up with me the day before our wedding."

Having been so confident, he suddenly looks unsure. Maybe it's my tone. He can sense that there's trouble brewing. And he is absolutely correct.

"Well . . . yeah. But not in a mean or disrespectful way," he says quickly, his eyebrows knitted together as he hopes that he's hit the right mark. "I'm trying to say that you've been really classy. It's a good thing."

"You could rely on me to be sensible about things." I watch him curiously as I repeat his earlier remark. "What did you mean by that?"

He shrugs, answering warily. "I meant . . . I meant what it sounds like. That you're a sensible, levelheaded person and you've taken everything in your stride. You're . . . a sturdy character."

"Sorry. I'm a *what*?"

"That sounds bad, but you know what I mean," he says, laughing nervously, while my deadpan expression doesn't flinch. "You're not one to lose your head, are you? You're collected and down-to-earth. I feel like you're upset by this, but it's a compliment, Freya. These are all good qualities."

"Really? Because the thing is, Matthew, these 'good qualities' sound a lot like all the reasons you broke up with me," I point out through gritted teeth, the rage boiling up inside of me. "I was so 'together,' remember? So 'pragmatic'? While you were away with the fairies, just an easygoing, laid-back kind of guy, who clashed with my sturdy, sensible ways."

"You know, when you say it like that it sounds bad. You're twisting it."

"It's nothing to do with the way I say it, Matthew."

"Freya, come on." He sighs as though this is all very tiresome. "I just wanted to give you a compliment, okay? I thought we were there, but clearly I was wrong."

Something snaps inside me. I can't pinpoint the exact thing that pushes me over the edge, but it's a mixture of his condescension, his scathing comments disguised as compliments, his manipulation of the conversation so that I appear to be the one overreacting, and those fucking stupid shoes.

"You know what, Matthew," I quietly seethe, being sure not to make a scene at a wedding, "you do not wear light blue shoes with a navy suit. You wear brown or black. And maybe some other colors that I can't think of right now. But you *never* wear light blue."

With that, I turn and march away from him across the grass to where Ruby, Simone, and Leo are waiting for me, all looking worried.

"What happened?" Ruby asks, her forehead creased in concern. "How long were you even chatting? We got to the macarons and realized you weren't with us! Then we weren't sure if you wanted us to come over and save you."

"Are you okay?" Leo asks.

"No," I hiss, leading them away from a cluster of guests chatting away nearby. "He said I was boring."

Simone gasps. "What? He said that?"

"In so many words. Oh my god, I feel like I might explode. I just . . ." I trail off, raking a hand through my blow-dried hair, probably ruining it for the night, but I don't care. "Is he still standing there or has he gone?"

"He's slunk away, don't worry," Simone assures me in a disgusted tone.

"What happened?" Leo asks, putting a comforting hand on my arm.

"He wanted to thank me."

"What for?"

"For being so sensible about the breakup. For not lashing out at him. For being so down-to-earth and boring," I explain, furiously.

"What the—" Ruby looks incredulous. "He thanked you? That's so weird."

"Weird and horrible!" I say, folding my arms across my body, suddenly feeling vulnerable. "It means he's happy with the way things are. No regrets. He wanted to thank me for making the right decision so easy for him. Ugh. I feel . . . I feel—" I sigh, shutting my eyes and wishing I could disappear. "—so small."

"He is such a dickhead," Simone says with so much feeling it makes me smile. "I hope you told him where he can stick his thank-you."

I wince at my parting shot. "Actually, I told him his shoes didn't go with his trousers."

They all burst into hysterics and their laughter is so infectious that I start giggling, too, even though I feel rubbish.

"I bet that cut him deep," Leo says, nodding. "He now has to feel stupid in those shoes for the rest of the day. Nicely played."

"I appreciate your support," I say, before throwing my head back. "How is this happening? Why did he do this to us? I want to feel happy again."

"You will," Simone says confidently. "And we're not going to let Matthew's horrible, stupid, gormless comments ruin Cali's wedding for you. You have to find the strength to forget about what he said tonight if only for her. She was so worried he would ruin her wedding."

I sniff. "You're right. Cali wouldn't deserve it if I fell apart."

"You know that phrase 'live like no one's watching'?" Ruby asks me.

"I think it's 'dance like no one's watching,'" Leo corrects, before receiving a sharp glare from his fiancée. He takes a sip of his drink.

"Whatever it is, change 'no one's' to 'Matthew's not,'" she instructs. "You have to enjoy this evening and act as though he's not here. Dance, live, whatever, have fun tonight like Matthew's not watching."

"That feels impossible," I admit, biting my lip.

"Freya." Ruby grabs hold of my shoulders. "It is imperative that you don't let him win."

"It's not really about winning," Leo mumbles, nudging her shoulder.

"Yes, I know, Leo, but for once, stop being so mature and wise," she huffs, turning her attention back to me. "If you sulk tonight, if you spend the wedding miserable, then he wins. But if you have a brilliant time, throwing caution to the wind and proving to yourself that you're worth so much more than how he makes you feel, who do you think wins then?"

"Um. Me?"

"Exactly!" she exclaims. "You are a winner! You are not . . . what did he say again? Sensible?"

"Collected. Down-to-earth. Sturdy. Not one to lose my head."

She closes her eyes in frustration at Matthew's words, before opening them and looking right at me, steadily and surely.

"Do you think you are those things?"

"Well, yeah. But he made them sound like flaws. And I'm not just those things."

"That's *right*." Her eyes light up and she jabs her finger at me, as though I've hit the nail on the head. "What else are you?"

"Uh . . . sarcastic, Isabelle said. Cynical, as we discussed earlier." I hesitate. "Wow. Why are you friends with me again?"

"Focus, Freya. You are kind. You are clever. You are silly."

"I can be surprisingly silly," I agree. "Like the other day when I was shimmying to music while I put out the washing."

"You're funny," Leo chips in. "Much funnier than Matthew. He doesn't really have a sense of humor. Some of his jokes were pretty crass. I hate crude humor."

I'm quite shocked at this revelation from Leo. But now that I think about it, I don't remember Matthew ever laughing much with my friends. Maybe that's why Freddie and Ryan never really included him in their crew.

"You're not a follower, you are a leader," Ruby continues, getting more and more riled up. "Would someone who 'doesn't lose their head' spend all night on the dance floor of a wedding and be the last one standing?"

"I don't think so."

"Would they steal a traffic cone on a night out in Leeds?" Simone asks pointedly.

"Definitely not. Although I do feel bad about that and I did put it back."

"Matthew is wrong about you," Simone declares firmly.

"Yes," I say, nodding, desperate for her to be right. "Yes, he is."

"Say it like you mean it!" Ruby demands.

"He's wrong about me!"

"Very good. Now, what are you going to do tonight?" Ruby asks.

"I am going to not be sturdy and down-to-earth," I say, clenching my fists. "I am going to lose my head!"

"And you're not doing it to prove anything to him," Ruby says firmly. "Who are you doing it for?"

"I'm doing it to prove it to myself," I reply, beaming at her.

"That's my girl." Ruby grins.

"Wow." Leo looks from her to me and back to her again. "I'm not sure how tonight is going to go, but I'm excited to find out."

"Me too, Leo," I say, feeling a fresh sense of determination as the horror of Matthew's conversation starts to lift. "Me too."

Okay, this is fun. The dance floor is fun. I like this song and I can sway along very happily here next to Ruby and Leo and Cali and . . .

Wait, what is Ruby doing? Oh *no*. She's creating a dance circle. Why does she love a dance circle? Aw, that's quite sweet. Dominic and Cali in the middle. Look how adorable they are!

Oh, nice, they're encouraging Ruby and Leo to swap in. Cali knows how much Ruby loves it there. Any minute now, she'll do her classic slut drop and . . . wait . . . there it is. The slut drop. Makes me laugh hysterically every time. Absolutely brilliant.

Why is she waving at me? Yes, you're very good at the slut drop, Ruby.

She's still waving at me.

Oh no.

No. No. No.

Being in the middle of a dance circle is actually quite fun.

But only for five seconds or so.

Interestingly, dancing back to the edge, doing a weird neck bop, feels more awkward.

Ah, there he is. I've been looking for him. Subtly, of course. But keeping an eye out.

"Excuse me!" I tap him on the shoulder.

The hot French waiter turns around and smiles at me. "Can I help you?"

"Please could we order some drinks? Or should I go to the bar?"

"I can get them for you. By the way, you were very good at dancing."

Oh *god*.

"Not really," I laugh nervously.

"You were. You looked great up there." He smiles at me.

Whoa. That is one hell of a smile.

"Are you a model?" I ask before I can stop myself.

Argh. That is *so embarrassing*. What am I thinking asking that question?! I sound like an absolute—

"Yes, I model swimwear." He grins, tilting his head at me. "What can I get you to drink?"

His name is Gabriel.

"Like an angel," I reply dreamily.

What is wrong with me?!

"Sorry?" he says, not hearing me over the music.

"Never mind."

Pull yourself together, Freya.

"This espresso martini is delicious," Leo tells Gabriel.

"It really is," Ruby agrees, smiling up at him in a daze. "You are very talented."

"I didn't make them." He laughs. "I just brought them over to you."

"No, she's right, don't be modest," I say, as Ruby and Simone nod along next to me. "You are very talented."

Not a good idea to take an espresso martini onto the dance floor. The shape of the glass isn't well suited for jumping around. Oh well.

Guess I'm rocking coffee stains the rest of the night.

See? I am so laid-back.

⌒⌒⌒

"I smell like coffee," I inform Gabriel after he delivers an order to another table.

"Sorry?"

What are you saying?!

Again?!

"Never mind."

⌒⌒⌒

"The pool looks so inviting!" Ruby says, carrying her heels in one hand. "The lights in that blue water."

"Look at the stars!" Leo cries out, pointing up. "They are so beautiful."

"So many of them!" Simone gasps, gazing upward. "Twinkling everywhere! You don't get this in London."

"No?" Gabriel looks up. "We get them every night here. Very romantic."

Ruby and I share a look. I try my best not to laugh at her wide-eyed expression. I glance at the pool. I know what Ruby means. It does look very inviting.

"We should go swimming under the stars."

They turn to stare at me.

"Huh?" Leo asks, putting his hands on his hips.

"Let's go swimming," I say confidently, bending down to take my shoes off.

"We're not in our swimming costumes," Ruby points out in confusion.

"Then we'll go in like this."

"In our dresses," Simone confirms.

"Why the bloody hell not?"

A wide grin spreads across Ruby's face. "Okay, then, wild child."

She flings her shoes to the side carelessly. One actually lands in the plant pot I hid behind yesterday, which feels like some kind of weird sign. Gabriel laughs and goes, "Okay." Leo shrugs, empties his pockets of his phone and hotel key card, and then sidles up to the edge of the pool in between Ruby and Simone, joining hands. I take Ruby's other hand. Gabriel takes my spare hand in his. He has very strong, warm hands.

"Ready?" Ruby asks, glancing down the line.

"Ready," we chorus.

"Three . . . two . . . one!"

We jump together.

⌒⌒⌒⌒⌒

Bloody hell. The white shirt has gone see-through. His *abs*.

Whatever swimwear he's selling, I'll buy it.

⌒⌒⌒⌒⌒

"You are a lot of fun, Freya," Gabriel says, after climbing out of the pool.

Ruby, Simone, and Leo are walking back into the hotel, giggling away.

"You think so?" I say.

"I think so."

I smile shyly, looking down at the ground. He comes closer and then as I lift my head to look up at him, he leans in to kiss me. In a sopping-wet white shirt, under a sky full of stars.

I appear to have stepped into a romance novel.

And it is *magnificent*.

CHAPTER SIXTEEN

Here's a question for you: How could a delayed flight home with a raging hangover and my ex-boyfriend on the same flight possibly get worse?

A call from my mother. That's how.

"Hello?" I answer, not bothering to check the caller ID because I can't muster the energy to open my eyes.

"Darling!"

"Oh god."

"Hello, sweetheart," she trills, delighted that I've picked up her call on the first go. "How are you? Are you abroad? I got the foreign dial tone beep!"

"Yes, I'm in France. I'm at the airport flying home. I'm actually at the gate and the flight is boarding so I'd better—"

"You sound very croaky! Do you have a sore throat?"

"No. I—"

"It's all that city pollution. It's not good for you, darling. I've always said that! I'll send you some hot drink recipes that will sort that throat out for you in no time, and no need to take any medication. Now, is fenugreek readily available to you?"

"Huh?"

"Fenugreek, it's a plant, darling. The seeds are just right for this sort of thing. Works wonders in tea form. Don't worry, I'll send all the ingredients over to you this week."

"The flight is boarding," I lie, holding my head in my hands as her voice vibrates through my poor little head, "so I should go."

"Of course, lovely to talk to you and we'll have a longer chat maybe when you're home. I wanted to discuss . . . well, I wanted to come see you! Do a little trip and spend some time with you. I thought that might be a nice idea."

"Right. Okay. I'll think about it."

"Wonderful," she says, with such sincerity that I instantly feel bad for being so distant with her. I have to remind myself that she didn't want much to do with me until recently. "Talk soon then, darling, safe flight! Bye now!"

I hang up and chuck my phone back into my bag. Ruby and Leo are next to me, Leo with his head resting on Ruby's shoulder, snoring gently, as she rests her head on top of his.

I take the opportunity to glance over at Matthew. He's sitting a few rows away from us, reading a book. Anxiety seeps through me as I watch him turn the page. There's no chance he saw me kissing Gabriel by the pool last night. He'd left the wedding a while before and he looked pretty unsteady on his feet when he went, helped by one of Dominic's friends. But I still feel guilty. Like I've done something wrong; like I've cheated. I know that's stupid. We're both single now. I can do what I want.

But it's strange, all the same.

The hangover is making the fear and guilt much worse. I keep telling myself this. When I woke up this morning to my alarm, I plodded into the bathroom to find my makeup all over my face. I was actually startled when I saw my reflection. I looked like a mess. I hadn't cleaned my face the night before and the stint in the swimming pool had caused my eyeliner and mascara to run all down my cheeks. *How* did Gabriel want to kiss *this*? I wondered, frantically scrubbing at my face.

Leo and I managed to get down to the hotel restaurant in time to eat some breakfast, which I think has helped, unlike

Ruby, who decided to get the extra sleep. Simone also opted for a lie-in, especially as she's getting a later flight. But Cali and Dominic were there this morning at breakfast, so it was nice to see them both before they headed off on their honeymoon.

"You were in great form last night," Cali whispered in my ear as I hugged her goodbye. "I haven't seen you so happy in a long time."

I'm not sure if she meant since the breakup or before, but I was much too hungover to analyze it. Leo and I went back to our separate rooms to get ready for the airport transfer—and to wake up Ruby—and we survived check-in, only to get here and find Matthew waiting for the same flight. Typical. I felt a *hundred* times more sick at that discovery.

When we're seated on the plane, I actually whisper, "Thank you," when it turns out that Matthew is right at the back and we're at the front. It is not surprising, when I think about it. I always select seats when booking flights, while he is happy to leave it to random allocation.

Maybe that's what he means about me being a sturdy character and him being laid-back. I'm predictable and he prefers to take chances.

Whatever.

"You're so tense," Ruby groans, whacking me on the arm as she tries to get her head comfortable on my shoulder. "What's wrong?"

"Matthew is on this flight."

"So?"

"So, that makes me tense."

She yawns loudly, nuzzling into my arm. "Just think about Gabriel in the see-through shirt. The abs of a sculpted god. That should help you relax."

"My eyes are closed, but I can still hear you," Leo grumbles from the window seat.

The flight is thankfully smooth and quick, and by the time I get home, I'm desperate to just crawl under my duvet and stay there forever, emerging only to get my takeaway dinner when it arrives, and returning straight to bed after I've consumed my weight in noodles.

The next morning, I wake up and not only is the hangover gone, but the guilt and fear are too. I turn off my alarm, glug down some water, and gradually sit up, gearing myself up to swing my legs out of my nice cozy bed, so I can start getting ready for work.

As I go to push the duvet off, I notice the ring on my left hand. I forgot to take it off last night. I smile at it. Gabriel didn't think I was boring. He thought I was fun.

I think so, too.

"Dad," I begin, looking out curiously across the lawn at the mound of soil next to a large hole in the ground with a spade lying nearby, "why are you digging up the garden?"

He comes to sit next to me on his garden furniture in the sunshine with two mugs of tea.

"I'm building a pond," he explains proudly. "It's my new project. Got a lad down the road helping me out with it. I want it to be a heavenly retreat for frogs, newts, insects, and other wildlife. Hoping for some dragonflies and damselflies. Will get some good plants for it, too. Can't think why I haven't built one before, to be honest, Freya. It will be nice to have some company when I sit out here."

"Are you talking about the frogs and newts?"

"That's right." He smiles into his mug, taking a sip of tea. "They've much better conversation than most people I know."

"You are, of course, referring to Adrian."

"Hey!" my brother says, eyeballing me through the screen of

my phone. "I have excellent chat. Much better than yours, Freya. Tell us that story about ripping the sleeve of your dressing gown on the door handle again? That one had me gripped."

"All right, children," Dad says in amusement as I stick my tongue out at Adrian. "That's enough."

"I think a pond will look really nice there," I muse, turning the camera round so that Adrian can get a view of the garden. "Water is very calming."

"I agree," Adrian says. "It sounds like a fun project, Dad. Although careful of your back with all that digging."

"I'm not that old, thank you," he replies haughtily. "Young spring chicken, me."

"Maybe when it's done, you can show it off to a new lady friend," Adrian suggests with a mischievous grin. "You can't keep something so magnificent, like a pond you've built, all to yourself. A good opportunity to get out there and date someone else who's interested in newts."

"Very funny," Dad says, rolling his eyes.

"I wasn't joking!"

"He's got a point, Dad," I say, propping the phone up on the table in the middle of us, so that I don't have to hold it all the time. "Have you thought about trying some dates?"

"What is this, an intervention?" He shakes his head. "I'm too old for all that nonsense."

"You just said you were a young spring chicken," Adrian points out. "If you're not too old to dig a bloody pond in your garden, then you're not too old to date."

"No one is too old to date," I add, Adrian nodding along as he bites into some toast, washing it down with his morning coffee. "Why don't we get you set up on some dating sites?"

"Thank you, but no," Dad says firmly. "I've told you before, I'm not interested. I'm too set in my ways. I don't need anyone coming in and shaking things up."

Adrian and I share a knowing look. Dad uses excuses like these all the time. Truth is, we think he's too scared to get back out there and be vulnerable with someone again. I don't want to push him into something he doesn't want to do, but it would be nice for him to have some company.

Aside from the newts.

"Speaking of someone coming in and shaking things up, I have a new love interest," Adrian announces. "We've been on three dates and so far I haven't managed to fuck it up. I hope you're both suitably impressed."

"That is exciting!" I say, leaning in toward the phone. "Who's the lucky guy?"

"His name is Nolan and he's New York born and bred. Very good-looking, very smart, highly successful."

"He sounds perfect," Dad comments, raising his eyebrows. "What's he doing dating you?"

"*Ha!* Good one, Dad," I say, nodding approvingly as he chuckles at his own joke.

"I'll have you know that in New York, I'm considered charming and witty," Adrian replies with a smile. "It's my English accent. It fools them all."

"How did you meet him?" I ask. "He sounds like a catch."

"Through a friend; he's her colleague. We're going to a baseball game today. He hasn't seen my competitive nature yet, so it will be a good test to see if he really likes me. I hope I don't put him off."

"It sounds like you're very excited about this one," Dad says warmly. "When do we get to meet him?"

"Dad! This is our fourth date. We're a long way from meeting the parents."

"You can bring him home when my pond's ready," Dad suggests. "When you see him today, tell him he's very welcome."

"Yes, Dad, great idea," Adrian says sarcastically. "I'll ask him on the fourth time I've met him to fly home to *England* with me, meet my dad, my sister, and a bunch of newts. Very sexy chat." He shakes his head, laughing. "Freya, how was France?"

"It was lovely, thanks. Very sunny and the wedding was gorgeous, as expected."

"Dare I ask how it went with you-know-who there? Or are we avoiding that question?"

"Dad tactfully avoided it when I arrived home earlier," I inform him.

"I was waiting to see if you wanted to talk about it," Dad reveals, shifting in his seat. "I didn't want to ask outright in case you felt uncomfortable."

"You can always rely on me to get straight to the point," Adrian says through a mouthful of toast. "So? What happened? Did you kick him in the nuts, Round Two?"

"Nope, I decided to go the more civil route. We didn't talk much." I sigh heavily, not really wanting to go into details and relive the "thank you" moment yet again. "Aside from his presence, it was a really fun weekend."

Dad reaches over to give me an encouraging pat on the hand. "Can't have been easy."

"I can't believe he had the audacity to go to that wedding," Adrian comments. "You'd think he'd have the respect to keep his head down for the summer at least and leave you alone."

"It's not that simple." I shrug. "Just because we broke up, he can't miss his friends' weddings. As much as I wish that were the case, I'm not sure it's very fair in the big scheme of things."

"Have you, like, talked it all out yet?" Adrian asks, resting his chin on his hand as he leans into the camera. "Has he come over to chat or are you happy to never see him again?"

"Obviously I don't want to never see him again," I say, looking down at my hands. "He's said we need space and that's how it's been left."

"So, he hasn't given you any closure," Adrian concludes.

"No, not really." I groan. "It feels like I don't know him at all anymore. He seems so . . . fine. Would it kill him to have *some* kind of reaction to leaving me after all those years together?"

"Just because someone acts as though they're fine, it doesn't mean they are," Dad muses, looking out across the garden. "Trust me, he won't be unaffected."

"He still owes me for ruining the peacock hire," Adrian huffs.

"The weirdest wedding gift of all time," I comment.

Adrian grins. "Weirdest or best?"

"Weirdest," I confirm, rolling my eyes. "Honestly, Dad, where did Adrian come from?"

"Don't look at me. I think we can all agree that he gets his . . . well, let's call it creative side from his mother." Dad hesitates. "You two spoken to her recently?"

"She rang me when I was suffering the hangover from hell," I inform them. "You can imagine how much better she made me feel."

"Her voice is quite shrill," Adrian notes. "She told me once that she likes to talk to the birds that sing in their garden. I think she's gradually trying to match their tone."

"She mentioned that she's hoping to visit you in London, Freya," Dad says, watching me carefully. "I thought that would be a very nice idea. Especially with Rachel's wedding coming up. Might be nice to have a little get-together before then."

"I agree," Adrian opines. "You can give her some ground rules before the big day, like how it's inappropriate to get up on stage with the band and perform a spontaneous song to the new bride without their permission. I hear she did that at a wedding recently with Evan's mates; she sang a Mamas and the Papas classic, apparently. He thought she was spectacular, but I'd love to hear the bride and groom's side of the story."

"She did *not* do that, did she?" I groan, burying my face in my hands. "How did you even hear about that?"

"From her very lips," Adrian informs me. "She's been calling and I've been picking up."

"Hey, I picked up that day of the hangover," I tell him grouchily. "And it's only recently you've been bothering to speak to her, so hop down from that high horse. Easy for you to encourage me to meet up with her when you're safe across the sea."

"It might not be a bad idea, that's all," he says with a shrug. "Break the ice before the wedding, so it's not so awkward on the day."

"Mum doesn't do awkward. It's always as though nothing ever happened and everything is happy-go-lucky. She'll wear a gigantic hat and swan about the place, gushing about love and soul mates, and how wonderful everything is."

"I wasn't talking about her," Adrian corrects me. "I was thinking it might be a good idea so it's not so awkward for you. I want you to enjoy Rachel's wedding, not feel weird around Mum. If you've already done the first meet in a while, it will be easier for you to relax."

"What about you?"

"Doesn't matter about me," he says firmly. "I'm not the one who's been through a big upheaval recently. I just want to make sure you're okay."

I smile, feeling an overwhelming rush of love for my little brother. "Thanks, Adrian, but you don't need to worry. I'm fine. Anyway, I'm not sure when I'd find the time to see Mum. I have so many weddings and hen dos this summer."

"Who's next up?"

"Niamh and Freddie in Dublin. Should be fun."

"Will that Jamie guy be there?" Dad asks casually.

I turn to stare at him. "How do you even know who Jamie is?"

"You've mentioned him a couple of times, love."

"Have I?"

"When I phoned you after Niamh's hen do . . . or sten, whatever it was. I believe you said that this Jamie person encouraged you into criminal activity?"

"Whoa." Adrian's eyes widen in excitement. "What kind of criminal activity? How come you're telling Dad the juicy details and not me?"

"Okay, I don't remember mentioning any of this to you, Dad," I say, aghast. "I remember telling you about the traffic-cone theft—"

"You stole a traffic cone? That is lame," Adrian scoffs.

"Yes, you said that Jamie encouraged it, and when you said it, his name rang a bell because I remembered that you gave him a lift to Isabelle's wedding," Dad rattles off. "He's the one who works at Dancing Bear."

What? I am clearly going mad. I must have mentioned these things to Dad in passing, but he's managed to retain this level of detail?! He can't remember where he left his car keys every time he needs them, but *this* he recalls perfectly.

"Who is this Jamie?" Adrian demands to know.

"He's a nice fella, from what I can tell," Dad informs him, as I'm too bewildered by all this to speak. "Into his craft beer, has a beard, and he's single."

"*Dad!*"

He looks at me innocently. "What?"

"How do you know all this?! Have you been *stalking* him?"

"What are you talking about?" He frowns. "You told me all this."

"No, I didn't!"

"Yes, you did." He chuckles, before turning to face the phone screen. "She doesn't even realize she's talking about him."

"A classic sign of subconscious desire," Adrian declares.

"*Oh my god!*" I cry in horror. "I do not have subconscious desire for Jamie! And can you not say stuff like that in front of Dad!"

"What, stuff like you desire a bearded man?"

"*Shut up, Adrian.*"

"You told Dad he was single . . ."

"As a passing comment! It wasn't a significant detail!"

"Sounds significant to me."

"Okay, enough about this!" I dramatically instruct, my cheeks burning with embarrassment as Dad laughs with great amusement. "Time to move on!"

"I couldn't have put it better myself. It is time to move on," Adrian grins, holding up his mug of coffee as though to cheers. "And this Jamie chap seems like the perfect way to do so."

I've discovered that when you suddenly find yourself single after living with someone for so long, what the other person contributed to the upkeep of the house becomes glaringly obvious.

For example, I've always been better at sorting bills because I like to pay and file them right away, while Matthew is the sort of person who tends to leave boring but important paperwork to "another time" (and a month later the bill is still sitting on the kitchen table, gathering dust). I'm also quite good at fixing things, like when the hot water is playing up, or the Wi-Fi isn't connecting.

Matthew was, of course, great in the kitchen and also quite handy at stuff that you don't consider very important until no one's doing it, like getting items down from high shelves without needing to balance dangerously on a wobbly chair, or hanging pictures straight.

But you know what? I'm now seeing all my disadvantages coming to light as a good thing, because it is an opportunity for me to improve on what I've always considered my weaknesses.

And the reason I am putting a positive spin on it is because of a certain *life-changing* incident that happened to me this week involving a bird.

Yes.

A bird.

So, thanks to this unforeseen but ultimately timely bird episode, I have now compiled a list of all the things I can improve on as a woman running my household single-handedly, and all the things that I'm already excelling in. See as follows:

What needs improvement:

* **Learning the days of the week for which bin collection**
  * This sort of thing is taken very seriously, and if I miss the recycling day again, I'm going to keep getting those disapproving looks from the nice drama students who live next door.

* **Mopping**
  * Okay, so who knew that mopping was such an essential chore?! I thought a quick hoover every now and then would do the job, but *no*. You *have* to do a good mop on those hard surfaces. It really makes all the difference.

* **Emptying the dishwasher in the morning**
  * I've realized that as much as it's a pain in the arse, if you empty the dishwasher first thing, then you can put things away in it throughout the day, rather than letting them pile up in the sink. This saves you from plodding into the kitchen just before bed and grimly remembering you need to unload and then reload all in one go. A tiny thing that really impacts the winding-down-before-bed routine.

* **Dusting**
  * What the fuck is wrong with me?! Why does my lifestyle produce so much *dust*?! I always used to take the piss out of Matthew going around with that little

duster, but my god, he was on to something. Humans are disgusting. Where does it all come from? *Where?*

* **Cooking**
  * Obviously. No need to expand on this one.
* **Remembering to close doors**
  * This is quite a niche one, but it turns out that I have a habit of leaving everything wide open. I must subconsciously barrel through doors and arrogantly expect them to shut themselves behind me, which leaves me open to burglaries and also, I've discovered, *birds* (see below).

What I'm excellent at:

* **Paying bills on time**
  * Easy. Get the bill. Pay it right away. No sweat.
* **Contesting bills if necessary**
  * These companies casually think they can raise monthly payments without good reason and assume I won't notice, do they? *Think again, utility world.* I have no issues ringing up and correcting them calmly but firmly until they lower those prices right back down again. I've got all the time in the world. (Although, not when *Love Island* is on. Then I need to be off the phone by 9:00 P.M.)
* **Electrical faults**
  * I have a knack for it. Maybe in another life I was a technician. Matthew was awful at this. He would stare for ages at the object and then whack it and hope for the best. It never worked.
* **Keeping the house neat and organized**
  * I put things back after I use them, unlike some people. Not naming names, but Matthew was terrible at this

very simple task. You take a folded blanket from the arm of the sofa, you refold it and pop it back there when you get up. You don't leave it strewn across the seat with the TV controller and Doritos lurking somewhere inside the folds.

* **Gardening**
  * Not to blow my own trumpet, but I'm smashing it.
* **Bathroom cleaning**
  * I really do not want to generalize or stereotype, but I am yet to meet a man capable of doing this properly and thoroughly. Very, very happy to be proved wrong. Please. Let me one day be proved wrong.
* **Assembling IKEA furniture**
  * It's like a puzzle to be solved and I love it, which was useful because Matthew was much too impatient and hated stuff like that. Sometimes when I'm doing DIY, I pretend to be Nicolas Cage in a British-inspired *National Treasure* spin-off and I have to assemble this excellent shelving unit to retrieve a clue to the location of the stolen Magna Carta. I know it sounds odd, but it really does make it so much more fun when you're examining each different screw and you've got an epic suspenseful theme tune playing in your head.

And finally, the capability I never would have known I'd had if Matthew and I were still together, because I would have forced him to deal with it:

* **Getting a bird out of the house**

It happened on a pleasant, tranquil Thursday evening. It was still light outside. A warm day. I'd gone out to the garden to check on my budding plant pals but when I came back inside, I must have left the back door wide open. I got some chocolate from the fridge and then I went to slob on the sofa and begin the process of going through the whole of Netflix to end up choosing something I've already seen a hundred times. I was very happily clicking my way through all the options when suddenly I heard what sounded like flapping wings.

Strange, I thought. Then carried on with the clicking.

It was at that moment that *an abnormally large London pigeon* flew into the lounge to join me for some television viewing. It swooped in and landed on the floor. I blinked at it. It tilted its head at me.

I admit, I may have overreacted at first.

I screamed my head off, jumped to my feet, leaped up on the sofa, and slammed myself against the wall as though the pigeon had cornered me with a rifle. My screaming, in turn, must have scared the pigeon, who then began to fly around the room in a panic, trying to escape this shrieking banshee, but finding no route of escape.

"*Oh my god!*" I yelped, sliding along the wall toward the door, as it knocked into the window and then landed on the sill. "*Please don't poo in here!*"

This was a silly request. Of course the pigeon couldn't understand what I was saying. It didn't speak English. And, also, it was a pigeon.

Still, as I've said before, shock makes you react in bizarre, surprising ways. Once I'd safely exited the living room, I stood in the hall slowing my breathing and collecting myself. I realized that I was going to have to deal with this unwanted visitor. No one else was going to do it.

"You've got this," I told myself, because, quite frankly, I didn't have a choice.

I marched into the kitchen and grabbed a tea towel. I marched back to the hall and opened the front door. Then I cautiously returned to the lounge. The pigeon was a bit more chilled now that I'd left it to its own devices. It was strolling around the floor, not really going anywhere or doing anything, just being a pigeon.

I snuck around until I was behind it and then I started waving the tea towel at it and going, *"Shoo! Shoo, pigeon! Shoo!"*

It jumped away from me and flew about a bit, often in the wrong direction, until *victory*, it managed to fly out into the hall, where it landed next to my running shoes.

Just where I wanted it to be.

I moved toward it again, covering the route to the kitchen, waving the tea towel at it and ushering it toward the front door.

"Shoo! Out you go! Shoo!" I repeated haughtily, like a house-keeper in *Downton Abbey*.

After a few irritated hops away from me, it finally got the message and flew outside into the warm evening air.

"Yes!" I cried, pelting after it and slamming the door shut.

I quickly ran to the other side of the flat and closed the door to the garden. I then put my hands on my hips and, with a great beaming smile on my face, felt an overwhelming sense of achievement. In the future, if any bird swoops into my home, I know that I've got it covered. Before now, I didn't know that I had that capability in the bag.

I was right, I thought, putting the tea towel back on its hook before returning happily to the sofa. I've got this.

CHAPTER SEVENTEEN

The Swill Awards celebrate the best wine, beers, and spirits of the year, and it's a pretty big deal for the drinks trade. It's usually held at a fancy hotel in London—this year, the Dorchester—and it's always a fun night out with the team and their partners, if they bring them along, plus a great opportunity to meet existing and potentially new clients.

This time last year, I was on my way to the awards and in a terrible mood. Matthew and I had had a big fight the night before and we hadn't spoken all day, both of us too stubborn to apologize. The argument kicked off when I was getting a black evening dress out of the wardrobe in preparation to bring it with me the next day to work so I could change into it before the awards, when Matthew arrived home from watching football at Akin's.

He was lying on the bed, his legs outstretched and crossed, his shoes still on, one hand holding his phone, and the other behind his head on the pillow. He had quite long hair at that stage, long enough that it fell into his eyes if he didn't push it back. He was growing it out and it didn't suit him as well as it did short. He also had the start of what he hoped might become a beard, but it grew too patchy, so didn't last long. I quite liked the beard, but was overruled.

"I like that dress," he commented.

"Good." I smiled, looking for the shoes I needed to wear with it. "What are you planning on wearing?"

"To what?" he asked, scrolling through his phone.

I found my classic black court heels and put them in my bag. "To the awards."

"I'm not going."

I stopped on my way across the room to get my jewelry. "What do you mean you're not going?"

He finally looked up from his phone. "I've got work drinks tomorrow."

"But this has been in the calendar for ages."

"In your calendar," he emphasized, frowning.

"In our shared calendar," I said firmly, getting it up on my phone to check. "I put it in a couple of months ago. Surely you saw it."

"Yeah, but I thought it was just you going."

"What?" Putting a hand on my hip, I smiled nervously as I wasn't quite sure yet if he was being serious. "You come with me to these awards every year."

"You didn't tell me I had to come."

"I assumed you knew," I said, my smile starting to fade. "Are you really not coming?"

"I've said I'm going to these work drinks and I can't back out now, especially as I missed the last ones because I had that family meal with Mum. If I drop out of these and say I have to go to my partner's work drinks instead, they'll think I'm using any excuse to get out of them."

"Swills isn't a 'work drinks' night," I pointed out, getting annoyed now. "It's a really important night to me, you know it is."

"Yes," he said slowly, also growing irritated, "but this year you didn't say I had to be there, so I made other plans. Sorry, Freya, but you can't just put stuff in the calendar for both of us and expect me to be there."

"We go every year together, I didn't think I had to specify that I wanted you to come!"

"That doesn't mean you can control the calendar without even talking to me about things and assume I'm okay with it! How would you feel if I put something in the calendar without mentioning it to you and then expected you to do it anyway?"

I hesitated, because obviously I would *hate* it if he did that.

"This is different!" I argued, even though I knew exactly what that sounded like. "It's an annual thing that you know all about. Why didn't you say something when you saw it in the calendar and decided you didn't want to go?"

"That's not my responsibility!"

"How is that not your responsibility, Matthew?"

"It's your responsibility to tell me I have to come to your work event," he said with a huff, sitting up on the bed, leaning back against the headboard. "I wouldn't put my work drinks in the shared calendar and expect you to come."

"You never put anything in the calendar! And honestly, I thought you'd want to come. It's a big night for me."

"Freya," he said with a long, drawn-out sigh, "you're always preoccupied with colleagues and clients at these dinners. Does it even matter that I'm not going? Why are we arguing about this?"

"Because there's a space for you at our table. Because it's embarrassing for me to tell my boss you're not coming at this late notice. And because I want you there!"

"I think it's really unfair that you're guilting me about this," he grumbled.

"I'm not guilting you about anything, I'm just frustrated you didn't tell me you weren't coming."

"Oh my god, I'm not getting into this, it's so stupid!" he snapped, swinging his legs off the bed and standing up. "You didn't talk to me about this, and now you're acting as though it's my fault I can't read your mind!"

He stormed out of the room, leaving me to stomp around as I got ready for bed. By the time he came in, I was in bed with my back turned to him and he turned off the light without saying good night. I remember making him his coffee as usual in the morning, but we were distant, both of us still seething.

I knew he had a point. I suppose it was unfair of me to expect him to come simply because I'd put it in the calendar. But I didn't tell him that until I got home after the awards, a little tipsy and elated from one of my team's whiskey brands winning "best new relaunch" with its refreshed packaging design.

This year, I'm in a much better mood as the taxi draws up to the hotel, because I haven't had to argue with anyone over phone calendars, which is a relief. I'm wearing a black cocktail dress with orange block-heel shoes with ribbons that tie in bows around the ankles and a matching orange clutch. I'm going for a professional-with-a-splash-of-color vibe.

Like everyone else on my team, I got ready in the toilets at work, so I didn't have the time or space to go too exciting with my makeup, settling on a bit of mascara, topping up my bronzer and lipstick.

My boss Phil hands both myself and his wife a glass of champagne as we enter the ballroom where the awards are held with the team and all take a moment to scan the sea of faces as guests mingle before the ceremony begins. Phil catches me craning my neck to look over the crowd.

"Are you looking for someone?"

"No, no one in particular," I say hurriedly.

This is a lie. It hasn't escaped my notice that Dancing Bear is nominated in the IPA category and I did wonder if Jamie might be here. It's not that I specifically want him to be here. It simply crossed my mind that he might be.

I go say hi to some of our clients and then, a few minutes before the ceremony begins, sneak away to find the toilets. I always feel guilty if I have to get up from the table and creep out during someone's acceptance speech.

I'm on my way back from the bathroom when I see Jamie. He's standing in the hall leading to the ballroom, where guests are mingling around some food stalls set up with different brands offering tasters and brochures. He's in midconversation when I catch his eye and do a small wave. A knowing smile spreads across his face and he excuses himself to come over. He's wearing a smart navy suit and when he leans in to give me a kiss on the cheek, I get a wave of his cologne. It smells good.

"You're here on time," I observe, clearing my throat and trying to not let his cologne go to my head. "Impressive."

"Is that all it takes to impress you? Good to know." He grins, his eyes drifting down to my shoes and back up again. "You look very nice."

"Likewise. You put on a tie and everything."

He reaches up and tugs at the knot as though I've just reminded him to be uncomfortable in it. "Well, when you know the likes of Suttworth employees are going to be at an event, you have to make an effort. How was the hangover after the sten?"

"Raging. Yours?"

"Terrible. A fun weekend, though."

"It was." I notice the hotel staff beginning to usher those out in the hall into the ballroom. "Looks like it's about to start. We should go to our seats."

He points at the stall next to us. "Before we do, have you tried this olive oil? These stalls are going to pack up once the ceremony begins, so you need to experience this now before it's too late."

I glance over at the slim, dark bottles of olive oil lined up on the table behind small taster pots and plates of sliced sourdough bread. The woman standing behind the stall straightens and smiles as she notices our attention.

"You have to try this," Jamie insists, leading me over. "This is the best olive oil I've ever tasted."

"Wow. That is a very bold claim, but I know you wouldn't say it lightly."

"Nicola, tell my friend here about this olive oil," he prompts, as she beams at him and holds out the plate of bread for me.

"Of course! This is produced in Tuscany and is made from a blend of olive varieties, but primarily Moraiolo and Frantoio. It's delicate, buttery, with a hint of pepper. Make sure you smell the oil first, that's important to the taste, same as if you were tasting wine."

"It's a family-run business, isn't that right?" Jamie adds, nodding to her.

"Yes, and it has been for generations," she confirms. "We're all very passionate about this oil, we use it at every meal. If everyone in the world consumed as much olive oil as my family, we'd be very rich." She grins satisfactorily as Jamie and I chuckle. "The farm where this is made is near San Gimignano."

"I bet it's beautiful," I say wistfully.

"I'm biased, but it's not bad. You get some good sunsets. I'm actually getting married there next year," she adds bashfully.

"Really? Congratulations!"

"Are you serving olive oil instead of wine at the wedding?" Jamie quips, looking pleased at himself for such a joke. It's quite cute.

"No need to choose, because we actually produce wine, too," she informs him.

"Wine and olive oil," I sigh, "what more could you want?"

"Bread," Jamie answers, before nodding toward the slice in my hand. "It's time to taste. I'm excited to hear your opinion."

I tear off a piece from my slice and hand Jamie the remaining bit, which he takes gratefully. I pick up the small paper cup and give it a sniff, as instructed, before dunking my bread in and letting it drip into the taster pot, careful not to get any on my dress. Jamie does the same.

"Cheers!" he says.

"Cheers!" I reply, before taking a bite. I chew and then turn to Jamie, speaking through my mouthful. "Oh my god."

"I know!" he replies wide-eyed, also still chewing.

"This is . . . incredible!"

"I know!"

Nicola laughs as I dip my remaining bread into my taster pot again, going for another bite. It really is the most delicious olive oil, so much flavor, smooth and buttery. The taste makes me think of Italy. I can see the family farm bathed in a warm, golden hue from a stunning sunset, long wooden tables set up for a wedding, the bride looking effortlessly chic and whimsical in a simple, floaty dress with flowers in her hair, the groom in a light suit, laughing with their family and friends, drinking crisp white wine, with a band playing in the background. I can picture it perfectly.

"I see the olive oil has put you in a daze," Jamie laughs, snapping me out of my vision. "That good, right?"

"It really is. Thank you, Nicola, and congratulations on the wedding," I say, gratefully taking the napkin she's offered. My cheeks flush as I feel strangely embarrassed about how one bite of good olive oil could cause me to lose myself in a romantic fantasy of a place I've never been.

The ceremony is about to start, so we thank Nicola again and make our way down the hall.

"Thank you for introducing that oil into my life," I say to Jamie, using my fingers to check I don't have any crumbs round my mouth.

"You're welcome. Good luck in your categories this evening."

I raise my eyebrows at him. "You're wishing Suttworth good luck?"

"I'm wishing good luck to those drink brands and the passionate, brilliant people behind them," he corrects, the corners of his lips twitching into a smile. "And, I suppose, although I'm not wishing good luck to Suttworth, I will wish it for you."

"I feel honored. Good luck to Dancing Bear, too. If you win anything, Suttworth might consider buying you."

He gives me a look. "That's not funny."

"Have a good night, Jamie." I smile, before heading over toward my table, leaving him to make his way to the other side of the room to his.

It ends up being a really fun event, and not just because one of our new brands won bottle design, but because it's nice to hang out with colleagues outside of the office in a relaxed atmosphere, where you can chat about things other than work. I was disappointed for Jamie that Dancing Bear didn't win the IPA category, but the fact that it was nominated is brilliant publicity for an independent and maybe he was secretly pleased after my parting comment. I didn't have the chance to ask him, because I left as soon as the ceremony finished, not wanting to stay on for drinks with a long day of meetings tomorrow. I tried looking for him to say goodbye, but either he was lost in the crowd somewhere or had already left himself.

I do owe him a thank-you, though, because the next day I'm sitting at my desk, looking over my notes of campaign ideas for Bodacious Gin, a British brand on my books that needs a fresh new angle, when I'm suddenly hit with a wave of inspiration. I quickly jot down some ideas.

During an informal brainstorm meeting with the team later that day, Bodacious Gin comes up and various ideas are discussed for the campaign, along with audience trends to help us focus our marketing. Finally, I speak up.

"At the awards last night, I tried this olive oil at one of the food stalls, and I spoke to the woman whose family produced it. She was telling me about the farm where it's made, and how the land has been in her family for generations. Then when I tasted the olive oil, I could really imagine it. It made the experience so much better."

"Olive oil, when it's done right, is sensational," Phil comments.

I blink at him, surprised at such sincerity from someone who has the same ham sandwich for lunch every day.

"Right. Exactly," I continue. "But I think that in the past, the advertising around Bodacious has solely concentrated on its taste. For the new campaign, we should consider telling its story, too. I think it's important to focus on the passionate, brilliant people behind the drink."

"That's interesting," Phil says thoughtfully, as everyone round the table nods.

"You see, Bodacious is family-run in Shropshire. But you'd never know it from their online presence. Bodacious social media has plenty of beautiful shots of the bottle next to a delicious-looking glass of gin and tonic, but there's nothing that makes the brand more human, nothing personal about it. The 'About' page on their website has a brief history of the company but no memorable details. They describe how they distill from British wheat and they infuse botanicals, which is important, but there's no mention of those at the helm, the passionate people who are actually doing the distilling and infusing. Personally, I want to know more about them and I think other people would, too. There's a sense of connection to a product, isn't there, when you know the hard work and passion that's gone into it, especially when it's homegrown. You end up remembering not just the great taste, but the great story, too—that sort of thing might bring about a fresh way of looking at Bodacious."

I finally pause, catching my breath, and look around the room expectantly. Everyone is staring at me, but they're still nodding, and Phil smiles encouragingly.

"Good thinking, Freya. Let's try that route and see how we go. I'll leave it in your hands?"

"Leave it in my hands," I reply confidently, excited for this project.

Like I said, I owe Jamie a thank-you.

CHAPTER EIGHTEEN

I've learned something new about Leo," Ruby announces, after we've finished ordering our food and handed the waiter our menus. "It's really weird and off-putting."

I look over at Leo accusingly. "Have you been cutting your nails in the shower again?"

"*Ew!*" Ruby stares at him, horrified. "You did that?"

"Years ago and it was only a couple of times until I happened to mention it to Freya and she told me I was never allowed to speak of it again," he explains, holding up his hands. "I promise I haven't done it since university. Not that I think it's that gross. The clippings go down the drain, so what's the—"

"It's absolutely disgusting," Ruby remarks, wrinkling her nose as she cuts him off. "I also don't want to know what you two were talking about so that that kind of personal information just came up in conversation. Anyway, this was *not* about that."

I sit back happily, sipping some iced tea through a straw, as we enjoy dinner on the South Bank. I'm biased, but there's something about London in the summer. It's such a good atmosphere, everyone is out and about, enjoying the sunshine. Maybe it's because such amazing weather is a bit of a rarity here that when it does strike, spirits are more easily lifted and everything seems that little bit brighter and better.

"So, what's this weird, off-putting thing?" I ask, intrigued.

Ruby adjusts her sunglasses. "Until now, Leo believed there was only one type of quiche."

"What do you mean?"

"I mean, he"—she jabs her finger in Leo's direction—"thought that there was quiche Lorraine . . . and that was it."

"I'm sorry. I'm lost." I hesitate, looking to Leo for clarification. "You thought quiche only came as quiche Lorraine?"

"That's correct. Who knew there were so many kinds? We had a mushroom and spinach one the other day. I thought it only came with bacon in it. That's how this all came up."

"What? How is this possible? How did you not know a quiche could have different ingredients?"

"I had the exact same questions, Freya," Ruby says, shaking her head at Leo in disappointment. "All these years, he's lived his life under the impression that quiche Lorraine was the only quiche in existence."

"This whole thing has blown my mind," Leo admits. "Talk about a roller-coaster week."

"Bloody hell." Ruby winces. "When did we get so old and boring that Leo's ignorance on quiche is the excitement of our week? We need other things to talk about."

"I think Freya will be providing gossip soon enough," Leo declares, grinning at me. "The next Wedding Season task is just around the corner."

"Oh yeah!" Ruby squeals, her expression brightening as she leans back to allow the waiter to place the sharing starters in the middle of the table. "Freya, are you ready to get naked?"

The waiter looks startled. "Uh . . . is there anything else I can get for you?" he squeaks.

"Nothing, thank you, this looks great," Ruby assures him, before he wanders off with a strange glance back at our table.

I blush furiously. "Thanks for that."

"He's probably thinking about you naked now."

"*Ruby!*"

"I'm joking," she laughs, breaking apart her chopsticks. "Sort of. Anyway, are you ready to strip down to your birthday suit and run around the hotel?"

"No, I am not ready to do that. I can't believe you got me to agree to this stupid task."

"Don't blame us," Leo says. "Blame the Spice Girls."

"Do I really have to do this?"

"You signed a contract, Freya," Ruby says in a serious, professional tone.

"I didn't sign anything."

"You committed verbally and you're sitting in front of the two witnesses," she tells me. "Think about how good you'll feel after. You were the one saying that you hated the implication that you're sensible and . . . what was the expression you really didn't like?"

I chew on my gyoza in dismay. "Sturdy. A sturdy character."

"Right." She shrugs. "No one who runs down a hotel corridor naked could be considered a sturdy character."

I sigh heavily, reaching for my drink. As much as I don't want to do this frankly *absurd* task, Ruby does have a point. It would help me prove to myself that I'm not the boring loser that Matthew made me feel like at Cali's wedding.

Not that I felt like a loser when I was kissing Gabriel, that's for sure. Which, when I think about it, was because of the Wedding Season survival guide. Maybe these tasks are helping.

"I suppose I signed a verbal contract," I say, giving in.

"Good lass." Ruby beams at Leo triumphantly. "I can't wait to hear about this one. You are going to feel so free afterward. I love being naked. Speaking of naked, how are you feeling about Gabriel?"

"What do you mean?"

"Was it weird kissing someone else? Getting back out there? All that sort of stuff," she explains with a shrug.

I take a moment to think about her questions. "I actually don't feel that weird about it. I guess it was strange kissing someone who wasn't Matthew and I did feel a bit guilty about it the next morning, even though I knew I shouldn't. But I definitely don't regret it. It was a bit of fun."

I don't admit the odd thing that happened to me the other day. I was in the shower and I suddenly had an overwhelming panic about Matthew dating someone else. It hit me out of nowhere. I've been putting so much energy into focusing on myself and taking some time, but a thought flitted through my mind of Matthew being on a date with another woman and I immediately started crying.

I've wondered if it was a delayed reaction to the Gabriel kiss. Whether me being with someone else made the possibility of Matthew being with someone else all too real.

The good news is it didn't make me want to die. The first few weeks after the breakup, the idea of Matthew meeting another woman made me feel crazy—a destructive mix of rage, betrayal, hurt, and disbelief would overwhelm me and I would sob at the thought. This time, I cried silently in the shower and let myself feel distraught for a bit, before washing my face, turning off the water, stepping out, drying myself, and getting on with my day.

That's progress right there.

Ruby puts her chopsticks down. "How do you feel about . . . dates?"

"I don't know. Kissing waiters at weddings is one thing, but dating is an entirely different ball game." I laugh, shaking my head. "Now I know how Dad feels when Adrian and I interrogate him about dating. It's very sweaty work being in the hot seat."

"Just something to start getting your head round, that's all," she says.

"Let's stick to me surviving the Wedding Season first."

"Exactly," Leo agrees, picking up his drink. "Who knows? Maybe once you're through this summer, you'll be ready to get back out there and into the dating game."

The conversation moves on, but the dating chat lingers in my brain all evening until I'm at home in bed, trying to read but finding it impossible to concentrate. Dating. Dating. It seems alien to me. The whole idea of it. I feel terrified at the thought.

I couldn't go on a date with someone who wasn't Matthew. What if he realizes he made a mistake and wants to get back together? If I was dating someone else, he might think he'd blown it for good, and not bother to tell me he'd had a change of heart! So, it makes sense to stay single just in case. Until I'm absolutely certain we're over.

Then again, he broke up with me the day before our wedding. He doesn't love me anymore. Shouldn't I want it to be over now, too? After all the terrible things he said?

Why am I holding on?

I have to find a way to stop holding on.

Complicated feelings for Matthew aside, I wouldn't even know how to go about dating. There I was telling Dad to get back out there, as though it were no big deal. What was I thinking? It's *terrifying*.

I pick up my phone and call Ruby.

"Miss us already?" she says as she picks up.

"I don't know how to date."

"What?"

"You know what you were saying earlier about me dating?"

"Yeah?"

"If I did feel ready, I wouldn't even know where to begin. What would I do? How do you date?"

"Hang on, let me put you on speaker," she says, then after a pause, "Okay, Leo's here, too. It's Freya, Leo."

"Hey, Freya," he calls out.

"I don't know how to date," I repeat.

"Everyone knows how to date," Leo says, seemingly unsurprised by my question. "You go meet someone, chat about stuff, that's it."

"You've made it sound very simple." I sigh. "It's a lot more than that. First you actually have to meet a person you even want to get to know further. Then you have to work out if there's a connection, if there's any frisson between you. All that riding on a drink or two at a pub? That's a lot of pressure."

"Exciting pressure, though," Ruby says enthusiastically.

"I'm not sure I'm capable of any frisson with anyone but Matthew," I admit, closing my eyes and resting my head back against my pillow.

"The word 'frisson' is quite weird when you think about it," Leo says helpfully.

"Look how far you've come!" Ruby insists. "A few weeks after the breakup, you told me that you'd never even watch a love story again. Now, look at you! Kissing hot French men by the pool like you're the star of your very own rom-com!"

"I don't feel like the star of my very own rom-com."

"The point is," she continues, "I bet you never thought you'd be ready to feel up some random guy's stone-hard abs and pinch-perfect bum in France, but here we are."

"I want to know if those descriptions were Freya's or yours," Leo mutters in the background. "I don't remember her ever saying that bum was pinch-perfect."

"Maybe you're right." I bite my lip. "I just can't imagine dating anyone else. Establishing that kind of intimacy? It seems impossible. How can I ever trust anyone again?"

"You'll learn," Ruby assures me. "And with the right person, you'll want to."

"I don't know," I croak, before admitting something I've been thinking, but haven't wanted to say out loud, because it makes

the fear even more real. "I'm scared I'll never really believe anyone if they say they love me."

He's late.

There we all are, boarded on the plane, ready to set off, and
guess who is the last person to come barreling down the aisle?
Jamie. Of course.

Everyone stares at him. This is why I'm early for flights. How
is he not shuddering under the gaze of every single person on
this plane? He casually makes his way down the middle, his bag
slung round his shoulder. He spots me and smiles, saying "Hey,"
as he passes before taking a seat a couple of rows behind. I glance
back as he puts his bag up into the overhead locker before plonking himself down in his aisle seat.

I face front, putting my headphones on, ready for takeoff.
I'm not surprised we're on the same flight to Dublin. A lot of the
wedding party are on this plane. I saw them greeting each other
at the gate and overheard them mention Niamh and Freddie. I
considered introducing myself, but then thought if I did that,
I might have to make small talk with them on the flight, and
actually I'd rather sit back, relax, and—

"Excuse me."

Someone taps my shoulder after we've taken off and the seat
belt sign has turned off. I look up to see a stranger towering
over me. I remove my headphones, panicking about whether I
should recognize them or if I've done something wrong without
realizing.

"Yes?"

"I'm sitting next to your friend back there, and he thought
you might want to sit together," she tells me with a warm smile.
"I would actually prefer the aisle seat, so it doesn't bother me at
all to swap."

She nods down to Jamie and as I swivel in my seat to glare at him, he gives me a big wave and mouths, "Come on!"

I admit that Jamie is growing on me—and his insistence that I try that olive oil at the Swill Awards really helped get me out of a creative rut at work. But I also carefully selected and paid for this seat. Not to mention, I've got my stuff all settled here now, and my case is right above my head so it'll be easy to access when we land.

But I don't want to appear rude to this kind stranger who has gone to the hassle of giving up her seat for mine—or rude to Jamie, who has arranged with said stranger for us to sit together—so I unbuckle my seat belt, gather my things, and slide out of my row, thanking her.

"Well, hey there," Jamie says, greeting me as I slump down into the seat next to him. "How have you been? I couldn't find you after the Swill Awards."

"I had to leave after the ceremony, but was the rest of the night good?" I ask, clipping in my seat belt and stuffing my headphones in my bag between my feet.

"Yeah, it was. Although I was disappointed not to carry on our conversation. We had a lot to talk about and we didn't get the chance in that brief meeting before."

"You wanted to talk more about the olive oil?"

"Sure, but also we haven't gone over that night when we stole stuff. That makes us officially friends, you know."

"Would you keep your voice down?" I hiss, as the person in the window seat shifts uncomfortably while pretending to read a magazine. "We did not steal anything. We borrowed a traffic cone drunkenly and I returned it almost straightaway."

Looking amused at my reaction, Jamie lowers his tray in preparation as he sees the drinks and snacks cart making its way down the plane. He then tends to mine. "You also haven't told me what happened with Matthew at the wedding."

I gasp, staring at him. "How do you know I saw Matthew at a wedding?"

"You told me at the sten that you would see him soon at the wedding in France."

"I . . . I did?"

Why do I keep telling people things and then forgetting?! I have never been open about anything, but now apparently I'm a blathering idiot, telling Dad about Jamie, telling Jamie about Matthew . . .

This breakup has made me careless.

"You said how nervous you were about seeing him at the wedding coming up, and I was like all 'You've got this' and then you were like 'What if I'm not strong enough to handle it,' and I was like 'I can tell you are.' Don't you remember this conversation? It was so meaningful and candid," he chuckles.

"Uh-oh." I shake my head. "I must have been a lot drunker than you were."

"Don't worry, you didn't say anything weird. It was a nice conversation. A real step in our friendship," he teases. He beams up at the air steward offering drinks. "I will have a Coke with ice, please, and I think my friend here favors single malts or a pornstar martini in a can if you have those?"

"Very funny," I say, before turning to the very confused air steward. "I'll just have a Coke too, please."

"Two Cokes," Jamie confirms, getting his card out from his wallet and stopping me as I reach for my bag. "I'll get these."

When he puts his warm hand on my bare arm, I flinch, but not in a bad way. It's like a jolt of electricity runs right up my arm at his touch. I know that sounds so ridiculous, but that warm hand of his really made me shudder.

It's different from the drunken excitement I felt when Gabriel showed interest in me. More nerve-racking somehow.

Oh no. I can't fancy Jamie. It's too confusing.

Firstly, he knows people who know Matthew, which means Matthew might find out and then hate me.

Secondly, I won't allow myself to fancy someone with such horrendous timekeeping skills.

And thirdly, I don't remember much of our drunken conversations in Leeds, but I'm almost certain I recall him insulting Taylor Swift's lyrics.

That sort of thing just won't fly with me.

He doesn't notice my reaction and continues normally, paying the air steward as he sets our drinks down on the trays with those tiny, flimsy airplane napkins. I try to ignore the heat rising to my cheeks at his touch, cracking open the can of Coke and pouring it over the ice. I blame the Swill Awards. His exquisite taste in olive oil, and the fact that he took the time to actually learn more about the brand, has thrown my whole opinion of him.

"Cheers," he says enthusiastically, knocking his cup against mine. "To Niamh and Freddie and a fun weekend ahead."

"Cheers," I mumble, before taking a sip.

"So, are you going to tell me how it went seeing Matthew? You don't have to if you don't want to, although I will feel mildly disappointed having experienced all the buildup without any of the revelation."

I smile into my cup. "It was fine. Sort of. I think."

"Come on, I know there's more to it than that." He holds up his hands. "No judgment here. You're talking to the guy who fell out of the kayak, remember?"

I sigh, placing my cup down on the tray and shifting to face him. "He insinuated that I was boring and I told him his shoes were the wrong color."

As expected, Jamie laughs. "What a great put-down! Well done!"

"It's a terrible put-down! Pathetic."

"Nah, I like it." He nods, looking impressed. "Besides, you

would never say anything really nasty. Were you perfectly civil and well-behaved the whole night, or did anything else exciting happen?"

"Nothing worth telling," I say, thinking about Gabriel and blushing. "The shoes comment was the low point."

"I'm sure it was a lot more cutting than you think. But do you ever get in an argument, only to think of the *best* comeback about an hour later? By which point it would be petty to bring it all up again?"

"Yes! All the time! I think everyone gets that, though, don't they?"

"Yeah, I reckon. Still, some people are so quick on their feet. When I argue, my brain gets jumbled by the confrontation, and I say a load of nonsensical crap."

"Better than my reaction, which is to shut down and worry out loud about random things that don't even matter."

"All the same, well done for seeing him and getting through it." He smiles sincerely at me. "I know how scared you were about it."

"Thanks."

We fall into silence as I ponder the electric jolt of his hand on my arm. He's so easy to talk to. Maybe that's why I got the shudder? After a terrible first impression, we've connected, that's all. My cheeks start burning again at the thought of his warm hand. Why am I even thinking so much about it?! What is *wrong* with me?! Am I really so cold and isolated that someone touching my arm has reduced me to a shuddering mess?!

Jamie is not a good fit for me. This is perfectly obvious. I shouldn't even be *considering* him as . . . well, as anything. I mean, if Matthew and I were too different, then there is no way that I could be a match with someone who is late for almost everything and got a revenge tattoo of an eagle wearing a monocle. We are *opposites*.

Except, Isabelle did mention that she sat us next to each

other at her wedding because we had things in common? Obviously, there's the drinks side of things—we may work for different companies but we are in the same, rather specific industry.

And when we're casually chatting, we do end up agreeing on quite a few things. He's fun to hang out with and there's no denying that he's hot in a rugged sort of way. He has gentle eyes and I really like the way he laughs. He throws his head back and wheezes slightly before letting loose and going full-on. It's very infectious.

Wait. What was the question?

Oh my god, I was meant to be focusing on how we would never work, not in a million years! Not getting sidetracked by his infectious laugh! I've lost my head.

Right, I have to say something. Something that isn't in any way sexy or leading or flirtatious. I have to forget about the jolt of electricity, because I am *not* ready for anything along those lines.

"My friend thought there was only one kind of quiche," I blurt out in a blind panic.

Jamie looks thrown. "Sorry?"

Oh, bollocks. What have I done? It is a decidedly unsexy topic, so that's something. I'm going to have to go with it now.

"My friend, Leo . . . it turns out he thought that quiche only came as quiche Lorraine. Weird, right?" I laugh nervously.

He raises his eyebrows in interest. "I can see how that would happen. Why don't the other kinds have strange names, too? Why is it even called quiche Lorraine?"

"I'm not sure. But it's a good point. Maybe I was too hard on him."

"If it makes your friend Leo feel any better, up until embarrassingly recently, I didn't realize that halibut was a fish," he admits.

"What?"

"I thought that it was a vegetable."

"Sorry?" I say, baffled.

"I thought it was a vegetable. The word 'halibut' sounds like a vegetable."

"No, it doesn't. It sounds like a delicious fish."

"You think that because you know it's a fish. But if you just heard the word, you'd be like, 'Oh, that must be some kind of potato.' The day I found out it was actually a fish, it threw me off completely. I couldn't concentrate on anything else."

"But when you'd ordered halibut in a restaurant in the past, didn't you realize then?"

"Ah, but here's the thing, I would never order halibut," he explains, "because I thought it was a potato and I didn't want a main of potato. I wanted a more exciting main, like fish. I would see it on a menu and wonder who was ordering a main of potato that often came with a side of potato."

"Wow." I nod slowly, letting it sink in. "That's bad."

"Don't be too judgmental. Let's not forget the 'floozy' incident."

"That's not even my worst one, to be honest. I used to think that quince was a jelly flavor."

He looks thoughtful. "What does a quince look like? I'm picturing a fig."

"It's more like a pear. When I found out it was a fruit, I googled it and saw pictures. It's like a bright yellow pear."

"Look at that." He lifts his drink to his lips. "You learn a new thing every day."

"So they say."

He smiles, setting his cup down. "You ever been to Dublin before?"

"Not for a long time. I was really little, so I don't actually remember anything about it."

"You going to do some sightseeing?"

"That's the plan for today."

"On your own?"

228 ••• KATY BIRCHALL

"Guess so. Isabelle and Ryan didn't have enough holiday to take today off after their honeymoon, so they're flying tomorrow morning."

"Yeah, I spoke to Isabelle last week and she mentioned that. Want to do some sightseeing together? I was planning on having a wander round the city, too."

I hesitate. "Yeah. Okay. That would be nice."

"We can spend the day dazzling each other with interesting facts."

"Absolutely. You can share some more halibut-type revelations."

"No problem," he says, before breaking into a knowing smile. "And you can tell me about the French waiter in the pool."

What the—

How could he possibly know?

Hello Isabelle
Old friend
Old buddy, old pal

Isabelle
Uh oh
What have I done?

You know when I told you
about kissing that French
waiter at Cali's wedding?

Isabelle
Yes

Did you tell EVERYONE
about that little secret of
mine?

Or just your new BFF,
Jamie

Isabelle
Ah

I've spent an hour flying
over to Dublin with him

Isabelle
Right

It was very interesting

Isabelle
Yes

He thought halibut was a
type of potato

Isabelle
That's weird

AND HE ASKED ME
ABOUT THE FRENCH
WAITER IN THE POOL

Isabelle
In my defense, he asked about you
and it just slipped out!

THAT'S NOT A GOOD
DEFENSE

Isabelle
Don't you think it's interesting that he
asked me about you, though?

Don't try to distract me,
you wily fox
It is SO EMBARRASSING

He's been interrogating me
about the kiss!

Isabelle

I think he has a thing for you

ISABELLE

Isabelle

Not that it's surprising
You're a total babe

You're buttering me up
IT WON'T WORK

Isabelle

Are you going to hang out with him today?
You're both there for the day
You should go sight-seeing together

You are a crafty puppeteer
And a TRAITOR

Isabelle

Remember that time I helped you with
your French homework in Year 5?

What?!

Isabelle

You said, and I remember this clearly,
you said "I owe you, Isabelle"

I did not say that

Isabelle

You told me you'd always remember
We'll ask Niamh. She was there
She'll remember your exact words

You're making this up
We were NINE YEARS

OLD
Lies!

Isabelle

The point is, you owe me
So you can forgive me for
mentioning your sexy pool kiss
I thought it might spur Jamie on

Spur him on for WHAT?

Isabelle

To not let you slip through the net

STOP TALKING IN RIDDLES

Isabelle

Uh oh, got to go
The boss is looking over
Can't wait to see you tomorrow! Xxx

WAIT, COME BACK
Isabelle????
YOU'RE IN BIG TROUBLE

CHAPTER NINETEEN

We're staying in the same hotel.

It's hardly a crazy coincidence when Niamh and Freddie listed three recommended hotels for guests on the invitation, but still. There were *two* other hotels Jamie could have been booked into, but no, he's at this one with me.

Why is that a problem? one might ask.

It's a problem because at some point I have to run *naked* up and down the corridor and I can't risk *anyone* I know either seeing it or hearing about it. I'm going to have to pick my timing very carefully tonight.

This is such a stupid task. Maybe I won't do it. I just won't do it. Anyone would understand if I didn't complete it. I mean, it's only Leo and Ruby who would know, anyway. I will tell them it was wildly inappropriate in a busy hotel on a corridor of people who know Niamh and Freddie. I couldn't possibly complete the task without potentially traumatizing someone for life. And as much as these tasks are important to me, they're not worth that.

So, it's not like I'm giving up or anything.

It just wouldn't be the right thing to do.

"Are you all right?" Jamie asks, slinging his bag on the floor at his feet while we wait our turn to check in.

"Yes. Why?"

"You look stressed."

"I was thinking about something I have to do." I brush it off with a wave of my hand. "It's not important."

He nods and then gestures for me to go to the reception desk first as the person in front of us moves off. I soon discover with great relief that I'm on the fourth floor and he is on the first. We arrange to drop our bags and then meet down in the lobby in ten minutes.

When I get to my room, I put some deodorant on, because I always feel gross after being on an airplane, and then touch up my makeup and spritz on a little perfume. I also accessorize a bit nicer than on the plane, adding some earrings and selecting a pair of sunglasses. I'm bound to take photos of my tour around Dublin, so I want to look nice for those.

And I want to look nice for Jamie.

Ugh. Oh my god, *no.* Stop it.

Jamie is waiting for me in reception, and leaps up when he sees me.

"Right, how about we start with a stroll around Trinity College, because it's such a nice day, then on to the Guinness factory, which is meant to have a really nice view of the city," he suggests, before pausing and looking me up and down. "You smell nice."

"Don't look so surprised when you say that," I say, my face flaming with embarrassment. I hope he doesn't think I've put perfume on for his benefit.

I have a bit, though.

Stop it.

"I want to go to Dublin Castle," I inform him in a voice that I realize sounds a bit like a snippy teacher's.

My tone gives me a sudden flashback of Matthew and me at Covent Garden one weekend when we ended up having an argument, because he said I was being too stubborn. We had a list of things we needed to do before meeting some friends later that afternoon and I wanted to go into the shops around the square to tick things off, but Matthew wanted to sit on the steps and watch a juggling street performer.

"We have so much to do," I moaned, scrolling through my phone. "Come on, we don't have time for this."

"I hate it when you put on that voice," Matthew huffed.

"What voice?"

"The teacher voice. You do it when you're annoyed at me."

"I'm not annoyed at you," I said, getting really annoyed at him. "We can't afford to waste any more time, that's all."

"It's not wasting time, Freya. It's nice to enjoy the weekends." He shook his head and sighed, sticking his hands in his pockets. "Come on then. Let's go and do your list."

I remember feeling irritated by him for most of the afternoon, and then later feeling guilty, because he was right. Weekends are so precious; it was silly to waste them on tedious jobs. Life is short and all that, I said when I apologized.

I imagine it was behavior like that and days like those that helped him make his ultimate decision we weren't suited.

But thinking back on it now, the jobs on that list were necessary. They were buying things for our home; picking up gifts for our friends' birthdays; one of the tasks I remember that day was to buy an anniversary card for his parents. All those things are important to the life you lead. Life is short, that I was right about in my apology. But I'd also like to look back and know I put in the work to make others feel special. Sometimes, that means you need to put on a teacher's voice to get things done on a Saturday.

You know, I don't think either of us were wrong that day.

"I think the college is this way," Jamie announces, having led the way out of the hotel into the glorious sunshine, and now studying the map on his phone. He nods down the road. "Let me know if you're hungry and want to grab some food. I managed to grab some breakfast at the airport, but shout if you didn't."

"Is that why you were late getting on the flight?"

"I was waiting for you to mention that," he says, walking along beside me. "They didn't have to do a last call out for me, so I was perfectly on time."

"That's not how you measure if you're on time for a flight," I inform him haughtily. "If I ever heard my name announced through the airport for a last call, I would feel sick with panic."

"You get used to it."

"Let me just grab a coffee," I say, stopping at a bakery. "You want anything?"

"I would love one," he calls out after me. "Flat white, please."

I head into the shop and put in our order, while he waits outside, scrolling through his phone. I watch him through the window. Matthew says he's relaxed, but Jamie actually looks relaxed by appearance. Today he's wearing a faded T-shirt and fairly loose-fitting jeans with trainers. It's not exactly stylish, but it's not not stylish. I wouldn't say he was a fashion icon, but he definitely would know not to wear light blue shoes with a navy suit.

Not that I'm comparing Matthew with Jamie, because what would be the point in that?

(But completely hypothetically, if I were to compare, then: Jamie 1, Matthew 0.)

"Please can I guess your coffee order," he begs when I emerge from the shop. "Okay, I know you have a sweet tooth, so . . . mocha?"

"Nope," I inform him, handing him his cup.

"Damn. Cinnamon vanilla latte with chocolate sprinkled on top?"

"Not sure that's a thing."

"Definitely is at Christmas."

"I have a coconut latte," I tell him proudly. "You don't know me at all. I, on the other hand, would have guessed that you were a flat-white person."

"On what grounds?" he asks, as we walk on toward the college.

"Not sure." I examine him for a moment. "Your beard?"

He splutters, choking on his coffee, before turning to me in amusement. "You guessed I drank flat whites because I have a beard?"

"Yeah. All cool, bearded men drink flat whites."

He bursts out laughing. "That's a sweeping generalization if ever I heard one. Also, let's focus on your description of me as 'cool.' Is that a new observation or have you been sitting on that since we met?"

"It's new. I didn't think you were cool until you told me the halibut thing. Then I thought you were quite cool."

"I can't understand if you're being sarcastic, which I know you're good at." He stares at me. "The halibut story was a very uncool thing to tell."

I shrug. "I can't explain it, Jamie. The halibut thing made you cool."

"I think you're mixing it up with cute. You think I'm cute."

"What?" I recoil. "I do *not* think you're cute."

"The halibut story is the sort of cute, adorable story that makes people go, 'Aw, he's dorky,' and then they're hooked."

"Are you admitting that you told me the halibut story on purpose so I'd think you were cute, adorable, and dorky?"

"Are you admitting that you're hooked?"

I narrow my eyes at him. "Nice try."

He grins, taking a sip of his coffee. Trinity College is a spectacular campus, the kind that makes you stop in your tracks and wonder what it must be like to study here. We stroll around, admiring the buildings, and I use my phone to read out interesting facts about the history of the place.

"Would you like a photo underneath the chamomile?" Jamie offers, gesturing to the famous, magnificent bell tower.

"The *what*?"

"The . . . chamomile," he repeats, less confidently this time. "You just called it that when you read out that thing about students being superstitious of walking underneath it."

I burst out laughing. "The Campanile!"

"That's what I said."

"You said chamomile," I inform him through giggles. "Like the tea."

"No, I didn't. I said camperpile, or whatever it is that you said."

"Campanile!" I shriek, wiping a tear from my eye.

"Camperfile."

"Cam-pan-ile."

"Campanile."

"Bloody hell, you got there in the end," I wheeze, still chuckling.

"That is one tricky word." He laughs, watching me as I collect myself. "You want a photo under it or what?"

"Sure." I hand him my phone and stroll back a few paces. "I guess it would be nice to send one to my dad. How should I pose?"

"What do you mean?" he asks, getting the phone ready.

"Should I do like a happy pose or an excited pose? Should I fling my arms out or point upward at the bell tower?"

"What the . . . I don't know." He looks flabbergasted. "Just stand there."

"I can't just stand here. It will look stupid."

"No, it won't. It's a photo of you standing underneath the campertile . . . camperfile. Whatever it is," he grumbles, making me laugh again. "Are you ready?"

"Wait, I need to work out my pose."

"This is ridiculous."

"All right, I'll just stand here and you take the photo and you'll see how stupid it looks."

"Fine," he agrees. "Ready? And . . ." He presses the button and then shades the screen with his hand to examine the snap. "Oh, wait. Yeah, you're right. That does look stupid. Why is that?"

"See?"

"Your arms are hanging there by your sides, all tense and straight. You look very awkward."

"Yes, thank you, it was to prove a point. You don't need to analyze it any further. I'll change my pose, let's take it again."

"Wait, give me a minute." He's using two fingers on the screen now.

"Are you zooming in?" I ask, putting my hands on my hips.

"Yeah. I want to find out why you look so weird in a simple standing position."

"Jamie! Can you take the picture so we can move on with our lives?"

"You were the one fussing about the poses, Freya. If you're only concerned about getting the picture of the bell tower, then it's already done," he says, before lifting the phone up again and pointing the camera in my direction. "I'm intrigued to see what pose you're going to pull for this."

"I'll do a selection."

I start by pointing up at the bell tower with an excited expression, as though I've just stumbled upon this amazing landmark. He smiles at that one. Then I throw my hands above my head as though I've just finished a performance and I'm giddy taking the curtain call. Then I move into the one-hand-on-the-hip look, with a smoldering expression.

I decide that's enough with the awful posing and start laughing, sauntering back over to him. "You get enough shots, Tarantino?"

He makes a face. "You know Tarantino is a film director, right? Not a photographer."

"Oh, yeah," I say, craning to look at my phone over his shoulder. "Who do I mean?"

Jamie looks pensive for a moment and then clicks his fingers. "Testino."

"That's the one! Well done." I smile up at him. "Okay, so, did you get enough shots, Testino?"

"You look very glamorous in all of them," he tells me, passing my phone over. "But I think my photography skills help to capture your emotion."

I scroll through the pictures. Some of them are really quite funny and I should probably be more embarrassed at how goofy I look in front of Jamie, but if I'm honest, it felt good to just be silly. There's one at the end that he's taken, though, when I had finished my poses. I'm smiling naturally and looking down at the ground, tucking my hair behind my ear.

"That's a good one," he declares, and I can't help but nod in agreement. "That's the one you need to put up."

"Put up where?"

"On Instagram or whatever. Unless you don't use social media?" He seems surprised.

"I do have an Instagram account, but I haven't posted on it since before the wedding," I say before I can stop myself.

My words linger in the air and I find myself feeling uncomfortable, having not spoken to Jamie about any of that before. He doesn't look confused, though. He doesn't look awkward, either.

"Yours and Matthew's?" he asks quietly.

"I'm guessing the others mentioned it."

"Yeah, they did. I'm really sorry that happened."

I shrug, looking back down at the picture. "I didn't realize you knew. Though I suppose everyone knows. It's the sort of thing that follows you round and sticks."

"Only in the same way a breakup does," Jamie says in this

gentle, comforting tone. "I know I can't speak from experience, but I imagine it feels like this open wound that people talk about, but over time, it fades."

"The wound? Or the gossiping?"

"Both, I reckon."

I nod slowly, letting his words sink in. "That was quite a good way of putting it."

"I write the copy for the Dancing Bear cans."

"An established writer, then."

"Oh, yes. You try describing the taste of a perfect craft beer in a few sentences."

"Hoppy and foamy. There. I've done it in three words."

He tries his best to suppress a smile. "I feel like we're having quite a nice moment, so I'm not going to ruin it by telling you how insulting that was, but I intend to bring it up later."

I laugh and then look back down at the photo. It is a good one of me, which is really quite rare. I've never felt especially photogenic. And I haven't thought about posting on social media in a while, because I wanted to hide away from the world, but I'm not sure I feel so hesitant anymore.

"I think I'd like to post this for my friends to see," I say out loud.

"Then I think you should," he replies.

He waits patiently while I log into my Instagram account, which takes me a couple of tries because I can't remember the password I use for it ("MattandFreya1," it turns out; I'll be changing that as soon as I get back to the hotel), and then I take a bit of time swiping through the filters.

"What do you think?" I ask, showing him it in black-and-white. "This one is quite classy and arty."

He wrinkles his nose. "No. I wouldn't bother with a filter."

"Of course, I bet you're really against filters," I say, smiling to myself as I carry on trying the different ones on the photo. "I wouldn't have thought you were a fan of social media."

"I have nothing against filters or people using social media," he says firmly. "I may not have it but we use it as an effective marketing tool at work. I just don't think that picture needs a filter."

"Because I'm so naturally beautiful?" I joke, swishing my hair dramatically behind my shoulder.

"But, of course!" He laughs. "I also like it with all its colors."

I look back down at the picture, going back to examine it in its original state. I see what he means. Maybe it doesn't need any tweaking.

"What should I caption it?" I ask.

He shakes his head. "No caption, in my opinion. It doesn't need one."

I take a deep breath and click on the post button. It loads before appearing up on my Instagram feed. "It's up."

"Yeah?"

"Here it is." I hold out my screen so he can take a look. "What do you think?"

"It's a knockout."

"As you can see, I took your advice and didn't put up a caption. I've let your photography do the talking."

"That," he says, standing so close next to me, I feel another jolt of electricity race down my spine, "and that beaming smile."

Niamh

OMG!!!

I LOVE YOUR PICTURE!!

Such a nice post, you look gorgeous!!

Are you having a lovely day??

Hey Niamh, you fabulous bride-to-be!

Are YOU having a lovely day more like?!

IT'S THE DAY BEFORE YOUR WEDDING

Are you excited?!

I can't WAIT! Dublin is the BEST!

The wedding is going to be perfect

Niamh

Aw I hope so!

I'm so happy you're here

You always make me feel calmer

You have a calm aura

Except when kicking people in the balls

I love how much you love that story

Niamh

I will forever regret not witnessing it

Until the day I die, Feathers

Until the day I die

Mum's having another meltdown, I'd better go

Thank you for everything, see you tomorrow!!

Xxxx

Can't wait to watch you get married

Xxx

Niamh

Oh, by the way, before I go . . .

Isabelle is flying out with Ryan tomorrow, right?

So, who took that picture of you?

CHAPTER TWENTY

As soon as we reach the bar at the top of the Guinness Store-house, which promises fantastic panoramic views across the city, it's clouded over and drizzling. The same thing happened when I finally made an effort to go to the London Shard. It was sunny in the morning and then as soon as I got to the top, it was raining and all I could see was murky mist. You don't get a free pint of Guinness at the top of the Shard, though, so this experience has won by a nose.

"I think I can see . . ." Jamie begins, squinting out at the view. He trails off.

"Yes?" I ask, trying to ignore the condensation creeping over the glass and focus on the sea of gray clouds beyond.

"Nope. Can't see a bloody thing." He takes a sip of his pint. "The Guinness is good, though."

We manage to get a couple of seats by the window and settle in. A girl sitting behind Jamie uses her finger to draw a smiley face in the condensation.

"How are things with your sister?" I ask. "I remember you saying in Leeds that you'd had a fallout."

He puts his pint down. "Not good. Although I did what you recommended and apologized, so we're sort of talking now, but she's still furious at me. She told me not to bother apologizing if I didn't mean it."

"Did you mean it?"

"No."

"Then she's right. You can't waltz in with an insincere apology. That's just another opportunity for you to get talking and make your point again and she'll see right through it. What is it that you won't apologize for, if you don't mind me asking?"

"I told her that her boyfriend was . . . unsuitable."

"Ouch."

"And that things were moving way too fast and she was being an idiot and didn't know what she was doing."

"Wow." I nod, leaning back in my seat. "I see you've taken the role of overprotective brother rather seriously. I'm sure she loved being told what to do by someone who took revenge on his cheating ex-girlfriend by getting a tattoo on his back of an eagle wearing a monocle."

He laughs, rolling his eyes. "When you say it like that."

"Why is her boyfriend unsuitable in your opinion?"

"He's in his late thirties."

"So are you."

"Hey." He points a finger at me. "I'm early thirties. Thirty-three if you're interested."

"Not particularly. Why is it a problem that he's in his late thirties?"

"She's twenty-five."

"You don't like the age gap?"

He runs a hand through his hair. "It's not the ages so much that I care about, it's the stages of their lives. She's only just starting her life in the big city and he's ready to settle down and get serious. She's already moved in with him."

"How long have they been together?"

"Two years."

"What?" I look at him in surprise. "I thought you were going to say a couple of months or something! If they've been together two years, that's quite a while. It's not exactly a whirlwind romance."

"But that's the thing, they met when she was twenty-three."

"What are you worried about exactly?"

He sighs. "That she's wasting her twenties."

I had to stop and ponder that one for a moment. After a brutal end to the relationship that had taken over a decade of my life, I had had similar considerations. Matthew wasted my twenties, I thought on several occasions, wailing into my pillow. All those people I didn't meet, all those decisions I didn't make, all those paths I never took, because of him and my commitment to our relationship. What a waste.

"Do you think years you spend loving someone are wasted, even when it doesn't work out?" I ask, not sure of the answer myself.

"How do you mean?"

"I don't know. I see why you'd be concerned for your sister but if she's genuinely happy, and he truly cares for her . . ." I shrug, looking out at the clouds. "That's what we're aiming for every day, isn't it? Happiness. The people in our lives to be loved properly. For her right now, that's him. So, I'm not sure that could be considered a waste of time. It would be a bigger waste to give up on it in case it goes wrong."

Jamie watches me carefully. "Now who's the writer?"

"We all have our moments." I smile at him. "Look, the way I see it is you have to work out if being right is worth risking your relationship with your sister. Personally, I don't think it is. Is this guy horrible to her? Does he treat her badly?"

He shakes his head. "No. He's a good guy."

"Then, she's safe and happy. If it all goes well, then marvelous. If it all falls apart, you're there for her. Either way, stop being a dick about it and apologize for calling her an idiot and not knowing what she's doing when you work for a company with a logo of a brown bear holding maracas."

He pauses, letting out a heavy sigh. "I guess I may have been a bit too harsh to Layla. I'll talk to her and apologize. Properly this time. My parents will be happy about that."

"They don't like it when you two argue?"

"They hate it. We don't argue often though. I think because we're not close in age."

"Did you say your mum was Egyptian?"

"That's right."

"Does she speak to you in Arabic?"

"No. She only speaks it when she's on the phone to family still in Egypt. Although, saying that, she does sometimes mutter in Arabic under her breath when something has pissed her off. Usually some kind of technology issue, like if the Wi-Fi goes wrong."

"My dad is useless with stuff like Wi-Fi."

"I think all parents are."

"Are your parents in London, too?"

"They live in Oxford with their dogs," he says, chuckling. "They have four rescues, the loves of their life. Mum just bought the oldest one a chaise longue."

"Wow. That's dedication."

"Your parents have pets?"

"If you count newts as pets, then yes. My dad is building a pond and it's become his new obsession."

"That's cool. I think I'd like a pond. Is he going to get koi carp?"

"No, newts and frogs are his main focus I think. How come you don't know what a halibut is but you know about koi carp?"

"You remember me mentioning my therapist mate?"

"I do. The one who can't stop analyzing you."

"Yeah, and you should hear what she has to say about how

I handle things with my sister." He rolls his eyes. "Anyway, her parents keep koi at their home and they are awesome. Have you seen how big they get?"

"Oh my god, yes! They are huge! Maybe I should persuade Dad to get some koi."

"They're a lot of work apparently. Expensive to keep and you have to get the water right. You have to be careful of herons, too."

"Maybe I'll tell him to stick to the newts."

"I do like newts," he informs me. "It makes me think about that bit in *Matilda* by Roald Dahl where that girl puts the newt in Miss Trunchbull's water. I found that hilarious."

"You still do apparently," I comment as he chuckles away at the thought. "I remember that scene. It's why to this day I don't like keeping water glasses by the bed."

"You're scared of newts creeping in in the night?"

"Spiders really. Imagine, you reach for your water in the dark, you take some gulps and unbeknown to you, a big old spider is in there."

"That makes me feel sorry for the spider. I like spiders."

"I respect spiders, but I don't like them."

He nods. "I can understand that. Like, you respect what they're about, but you'd rather not have one in your water glass."

"Exactly. Are you the kind of person that can pick up a spider with your bare hands to take it out of the house?"

"Yes, I am. How could you tell?" He narrows his eyes at me. "You can't say it's because of the beard. You've already used that for your stereotyping."

"I think because you seem quite levelheaded. I can see you being calm and no-nonsense with spiders."

"Why, do you run away into another room, screaming?"

"No, but I have to take them out using a jar or a glass and a piece of paper," I admit. "Although recently I had a significant episode with a pigeon and I managed to get it out of the house myself with no fuss. Quite proud of that."

"Nicely done. I can imagine that was quite stressful. London pigeons are very stubborn."

"It took some persuading but eventually it got the message."

He chuckles. "Does your dad live alone, then?"

"Yeah, just him and his pond." I take a sip of Guinness, careful to wipe my lip in case there's any foam left behind. "My brother and I would like him to get back out there and start dating, but I don't think it will ever happen."

"Too set in his ways."

"Those were his exact words."

Jamie laughs, impressed with himself. "Your dad and I are on the same wavelength. What about your mum?"

I hesitate. "She lives in the Lake District with her partner, Evan."

"I take it from your sour expression that you're not the best of friends."

"You could tell that from my expression?"

"Yeah, you looked irritated."

"And there I was thinking I was hard to read," I say, surprised. "Mum and I aren't close. We haven't been for a long time. She wasn't very interested in my life once she left my dad. Or even before she left, to be honest."

"What sort of terms are you on now?"

"Bad ones." I look out the window, frowning. "She's trying to make amends, though."

"You're not happy about that?"

"I don't know. My dad really wants us to have a relationship. I think my brother is starting to build one with her, too, which makes me anxious."

"Worried that she'll hurt him?"

"That, and worried about being left behind." I tear my eyes

away from the window and pick up my pint again. "I don't want everyone else to be all happy families again, while I'm still too angry to play."

"Maybe you need a bit more time to trust her again. That's not a bad thing."

"Yeah, maybe. She's been making quite a bit of effort since the wedding was called off. But it's hard to welcome her back with open arms when she didn't give a hoot about making an effort when I got my A-level results or my first job, or even when I got engaged. Those were important life moments, too. She didn't care about missing them."

"She might have a different side to the story," Jamie reasons. "She was too scared or other things were going on. I'm not making excuses for her, but I can see why she'd want to be there for you when you've been through a big heartbreak."

I nod, though I'm not convinced. "Are you close with your parents? Or do they prefer the dogs to you?"

"The dogs are definitely top billing, but we're close," he says, breaking into a wide smile. "We're quite different, but that doesn't seem to matter."

"Different, how? They have good music taste?"

He laughs. "They're big on Classic FM, so yes. Although apparently the dogs prefer Radio Four."

"How predictable."

"I guess my sister and I are a lot more open than my parents. They're gentle, quiet countryside types. They're thinking about getting some ducks."

"Sounds idyllic. I'm picturing them pottering around a garden, listening to classical music, chatting to friendly, gossipy neighbors."

"Sounds like you're imagining a scene from that murder-mystery series. What's the one set in that little village and everyone gets murdered by pitchforks."

I sit up straight. "*Midsomer Murders!*"

"That's the one!" He exclaims, looking thrilled. "Inspector Barnaby."

"What a show. I always wondered why people lived in Midsomer, though."

"So many murders," he says, nodding.

"So many!"

"The price they'll pay for those picturesque cottages and the charming countryside lifestyle. I don't think I need to worry about my parents being attacked by people with pitchforks, though. They get on well with their neighbors, a notion baffling to us Londoners."

"Actually, I'm on good terms with my neighbors, so don't blame that on London. There's a couple of drama students who live next door to me, who always say hello when we see each other, and then above me is a very nice man called Tommy and his little boy, Jaxon."

"You even know their names. That is impressive. Have you moved since the breakup?"

"No. Matthew moved out. I didn't see the need to find somewhere new."

I glance out the window and notice the rain has passed and the sun is breaking through the clouds again. The view really is brilliant across the city. Jamie follows my lead and turns his attention to the window, too, the both of us staring out across Dublin.

"Are you, by any chance, hungry?" Jamie asks.

"Starving. Shall we grab some food?"

"Yes," he says, downing the last of his pint.

"Let me google a good place to go."

"Or we could just wander around and see what we fancy," he suggests, as I start typing into the search engine.

"But then we could be walking around for ages."

"Better than trawling through a list of restaurants for ages.

Come on, it's more fun this way," he claims, getting to his feet and flashing me a grin. "You never know where you're going to end up."

I don't know how, but it's nearing midnight and we're in a pub in a buzzing area called Temple Bar, listening to a live band, and my jaw aches from laughing.

That's not just Jamie's doing—although he has made me laugh a lot today—because we've joined some of the wedding party, whom we bumped into as we came in and who gave a big cheer when they saw Jamie.

Apparently, he's quite popular among this crowd, something that became clear on the sten in Leeds. I've done well to make friends with him, because, by association, I'm now being included in conversations and don't feel like an outsider anymore. The band in this bar is *brilliant*, playing "lively, foot-stomping classics" all night, as Jamie put it, which I obviously teased him about. It has been such a fun day and I've completely fallen in love with Dublin.

"Are you Niamh's school friend?" a guy called Harry yells over the music to me as Jamie passes me a drink.

"Yes!"

"I remember her saying she's got two of her best school friends coming!"

"Yes, me and Isabelle."

"Are you the one who's just got married?"

"No, that's Isabelle. I'm the one who got jilted at the altar."

He stares wide-eyed at me in panic.

"Well, technically, it wasn't the altar," I elaborate for no reason whatsoever. "It was the day before. He jilted me the day before the wedding. In a cupboard."

Harry's eyes are darting about as I speak, no idea how to react.

Jamie is standing next to me attempting to suppress a laugh. I lean in toward him.

"I probably shouldn't tell strangers about it, huh."

"Why do you say that?" Jamie asks innocently.

"I think I'm making him uncomfortable."

"Nah, you're not uncomfortable, are you, Harry?"

"Not at all!" Harry replies, comically tense and wide-eyed, backing away from me until he's safely engulfed into a conversation with another group of people.

"I scared away your friend," I tell Jamie apologetically. "I shouldn't talk about it; it freaks people out."

"I think it's good you talk about it," he says. "Probably helps you process it better."

"Are you repeating what your therapist friend tells you?"

"Yes."

"When I talk about it, it doesn't feel like I'm talking about it. Does that make sense?"

"No."

"It feels like I'm talking about something that happened to someone else. Then I have to remind myself, 'Oh my god, that happened to me!'"

"Okay, I think that did actually make sense," he says thoughtfully. "I think what you're saying is, when you're talking about it, it's like having an out-of-body experience."

"Yes! It's surreal. Anyway, sorry for scaring away Harry." I take a sip through my straw before looking up at Jamie quizzically. "Do you think I'll always be that person?"

"The person who scares people away?"

"The person who got dumped the day before her wedding."

"No, Freya, you won't always be that person. You're not even that person now!" he says, looking exasperated. "You're . . . Freya!"

"Very helpful."

He laughs. "What I mean is, what happened doesn't define you. It's not who you are."

"Yeah?" I nod, letting his words sink in. "That was actually quite helpful. Thank you."

"Doesn't matter how the world sees you, anyway." He puts down his drink and then rests his hands on my shoulders. I inhale sharply as I'm forced to look up into his intense, dark eyes. "All that matters, Freya, is how you see you."

I can't stop thinking about that moment.

All that matters, Freya, is how you see you.

I'm lying in bed and I can't sleep, because I keep thinking about the way he was looking at me. With those eyes, he *pierced my bloody soul.*

I would love to claim that line as mine, but I'm pretty sure I've stolen it from a magnet on Cali's fridge. She loves an inspirational quote.

Whatever that line is from, it is ringing true for me right now. My soul has been pierced.

Do I want it to be pierced, though? That's the question.

I'm so confused.

Googled the quote because I can't sleep and it turns out it's from a Jane Austen book. A man called Captain Wentworth is writing a letter to Anne—not sure who she is, but someone important— and he says, "You pierce my soul. I am half agony, half hope," in the hopes of winning her back, which is very romantic.

I once got a drunk text from Matthew that read, "me like boobs."

So, guess Anne and I both know how it feels to be wooed with words.

One thing led to another and I just caught myself typing "what does Jane Austen recommend you do if someone pierces your soul" into Google search.

I think it's time to go to sleep.

CHAPTER TWENTY-ONE

I 've decided that if things drastically change for me and I somehow find a way of loving again, then I will fall in love with and
marry an Irish gentleman. My reasons for this are twofold. One:
the accent. And two: the wedding.

Irish weddings are *so fun*. I haven't stopped smiling since
the festivities started earlier this afternoon. The wedding is in
this grand Dublin hotel called the Shelbourne. Ever since she
booked it on her parents' recommendation, Niamh has joked
that it's much too posh for the likes of her and Freddie, but, of
course, it's absolutely perfect. She and Freddie have looked deliriously happy and at ease all day, and everyone is so friendly. And
despite the impressive surroundings, the general atmosphere is
relaxed and happy, and there's no sense of stiffness or formality.
As soon as the music started, the guests were all up on their feet,
no faltering or stage fright at the edge of the dance floor. The
best thing about it is that every Irish person here has made me
feel so welcome, like they are personally invested in me enjoying
myself.

"I need to reprogram my brain," I tell Jamie as we sit next to
each other at a table with our coffee, watching people gallivant
around the dance floor.

"Why in the world do you say that?" he asks, digging into his
slice of wedding cake.

We're at the stage of the evening where he's taken off his

jacket and tie, and has his first few buttons undone and his sleeves rolled up. I appreciate this look on him. It's very smart.

He's very sexy.

"I'm too cynical and standoffish," I explain.

"That's all part of your charm."

"But everyone in Ireland is warm and kind."

"That's a bit like saying everyone with a beard drinks flat whites. Slight generalization, don't you think?"

"So far, I haven't been proven wrong on either of those points."

"You know what I think?" he says, gesturing to the cake with his fork. "Fruitcake is awesome. And you know I don't have a sweet tooth, but this is really good."

"Yeah?"

"Why do people choose all these outlandish flavors for their wedding cakes these days? Salted caramel, lemon drizzle, red velvet. I say bring back the traditional fruitcake. It's delicious."

"Okay, grandpa, thanks for your opinion." I pick up my dessert fork and try a bit of the slice in front of me. "Oh wow. That is actually really good. I didn't think I was a fan of fruitcake."

"You didn't get a bit with the icing. Get a bit with the icing."

"I don't want a bit with the icing."

"Why not?"

"I don't like marzipan and I can see a layer of it there."

"Oh that's another thing that I was confused about for years," he says, reaching over to my plate with his fork and stealing my icing. I slide my plate nearer to his to aid the transference. "Marzipan and mascarpone. Got those two mixed up the whole time."

"They do sound similar."

"Are you good at baking?" he asks, putting his fork down.

"Terrible. That's not me being modest. I'm genuinely shit at it. You?"

"Quite good actually. I like baking."

"Even though you're more of a savory man?"

"You can bake savory stuff," he informs me with a shrug. "But I like baking even if I'm not going to eat it myself."

"You see, that is weird to me. What's the point in going to all that effort if you can't eat it yourself?"

He raises his eyebrows at me. "Oh, I don't know, because it's nice to make things for other people to enjoy? Maybe your brain really does need to be reprogrammed."

I roll my eyes.

He nods toward Freddie twirling Niamh round the dance floor as the other guests, including Ryan and Isabelle, circle them, cheering. "Does all this bother you?"

"Dancing? Only if people click their fingers at the same time. I really hate that."

"Not dancing," he says, laughing. "I meant weddings. They've got to be hard to sit through."

I hesitate, but decide I want to answer truthfully. "At first, I was terrified. I wanted to be there for my friends' big days, but I also dreaded it, because I thought it would be a constant reminder of what had happened—or not happened—to me. But, even though I've had my moments, it hasn't been as bad as I thought. Weddings are such happy occasions. It's hard to be gloomy when everyone around you is so full of . . ."

I trail off.

"Love?" Jamie suggests.

"Right. Love." I watch Niamh wrap her arms around Freddie's neck and kiss him. "Plus, my friends have been amazing at making sure I didn't fall apart at all the weddings this summer."

"Oh yeah? They rallied, did they?"

"They did. They created a—"

I stop myself. This is what's so annoying about Jamie. When I think about our conversations, I'm amazed at how much I've spilled about my life. I barely know him, I literally met him just a few weeks ago and already he's heard about my failed engagement, my disastrous relationship with my mother, and my dad's pond ambitions. I honestly had no idea until this summer that I was such a blabbermouth. Didn't Matthew break up with me because I was the opposite?

"Yes?" Jamie prompts, intrigued. "What did your friends create?"

"Nothing," I say, brushing off his question with a wave of my hand.

"No, come on." He grins, leaning closer toward me. "What were you about to say? I can tell it was something good. You have that twinkle in your eye."

"I do *not* have a twinkle in my eye."

"Yes, you do. Just like Father Christmas in that poem."

"What poem?"

"''Twas the Night Before Christmas.' There's a bit that goes 'his eyes, how they twinkled.' That's you right now, a cheeky, knowing twinkle. Spill your secret, Freya Scott."

"You have to promise not to laugh."

"Can't promise that."

"And you can't take the piss."

"Again, that will probably be an issue."

"Fine." I sigh. Here goes nothing. "They created a survival guide for the Wedding Season."

He blinks at me. "Explain."

"The Wedding Season. Everyone has one, right? Especially in your thirties."

"That bit I did understand."

"So, my best friends, Ruby and Leo, thought it might be a good idea if they set out a task list. For every wedding I attended, there would be a challenge to complete. That way, instead of thinking of Matthew at each event, I'd be focused on the challenge. It's kind of like a survival guide."

"Okay." He nods thoughtfully, crossing his arms. "I like it. What sort of challenges were on the table?"

"You'll be relieved to hear that one of them was to retrieve someone's cuff links without telling them why."

He brightens. "That does make me feel better! I was genuinely concerned about why you were so keen to win them. Hey, I feel like a celebrity! I was one of your tasks!"

"No, your cuff links were. But I'm glad you feel honored."

"This is fun," he claims, beaming at me. "I like your friends' style. Okay, tell me more."

"I had to be the last one standing at another wedding. That was hard because I'm sure by now you've witnessed, and no doubt laughed at, my dancing prowess."

"I notice you're a fan of the laughing trick."

I frown at him. "What's the laughing trick?"

"It's what you do on the dance floor. You laugh at everyone else, putting the attention on them."

"I do not laugh at people dancing! That's mean!"

"You're not laughing in a mean way," he explains breezily. "You're laughing in a 'Good move!' way. You sort of sway around, laughing and pointing at your pals as they fling themselves around. You're the one fueling their outlandish moves, which gets you out of having to be outlandish yourself."

I want to argue, but now that I think about it . . . he may be right.

"You know you do it, don't you?" he says, watching me with interest. "You've realized now that I'm right. This is going to really throw you."

"It will not throw me."

"It will when you next get up to dance," he predicts. "Anyway, keep going with these tasks. Any others?"

"Securing a good-night kiss."

He sits up straight. "I'm listening."

"I already completed that one. The French waiter, remember?"

"Ah yes, very nice. Hang on. We're at a wedding right now."

"Very observant of you."

"So, what's your challenge for tonight?"

"I'm not telling you that," I say, shifting in my seat. "It's against the rules."

"Oh, come on, maybe I can help."

"Trust me. This one I have to do all on my own," I say firmly, still considering how to back out without Leo and Ruby getting cross at me or thinking I'm a chicken.

"Fine. I look forward to hearing about it though. So, has it worked?"

"Has what worked?"

"The Wedding Season survival guide."

"Yeah, actually. I've dreaded a lot of the tasks, but then I think that was the point."

"If the tasks were easy, they wouldn't have been very distracting."

"Exactly."

We go back to sipping our coffee and watching the antics playing out on the dance floor. I realize that now would be a rather good time to complete my task. All the guests are here at the wedding, so I wouldn't need to worry too much about bumping into someone who recognized me at the hotel. In fact, it would be better to get it out of the way now, rather than wait up, trying to make sure everyone from the wedding has gone to bed.

"I'm going to sneak off," I tell Jamie, seeing Niamh being lifted up onto one of the usher's shoulders. "I won't disturb the bride and groom. If you join them on the dance floor, tell Ryan and Isabelle I'll see them back home."

"Wait, you're leaving?" Jamie looks shocked as I pick up my clutch from under the table. "You can't go now!"

"Why not? It's not long until guests have to leave anyway and I have an early flight tomorrow."

"You're not on the three P.M.?"

"I have to leave the hotel at seven A.M.," I say, wincing. "I don't know why I booked such a stupid flight all those months ago. It's been a fun weekend, thanks so much for the tour yesterday."

"Okay, well how are you getting back?" he asks, standing as I do, which is weirdly well-mannered and old-school of him. "Shall I come with you? I should come with you."

"Don't be stupid, you have loads of pals here and I've been hogging you. I'll get a taxi from outside or an Uber easily. Enjoy the rest of the night," I insist.

He looks a bit bewildered at my sudden exit as we lean toward each other to give a polite parting kiss on the cheek. I notice that he lingers slightly, or am I making it up? I think I'm making it up.

He smells so good.

"Night, Jamie."

"Night, Freya."

I pull away, smile up at him, and slip off out of the wedding. There are taxis lined up outside in anticipation, so it takes no time at all to get back to the hotel. I kick off my shoes and stand in the middle of my room with my hands on my hips.

Am I really going to do this?

No. This is ridiculous. I'm not going to run naked down a hotel corridor. That would be completely *absurd*.

Would it?

I quickly open the door and stick my head out, looking up and down the corridor. It's dead. Completely quiet and empty. Late enough for the early birds to be in bed; early enough for the night owls to still be out. I also check for security cameras. None in the corridor that I can see.

I pull my head back in, shut the door, and lean against it. If I tell Leo and Ruby I didn't do it and make an excuse, they'll be disappointed. More importantly, I think I might be disappointed, which shows how brainwashed I am by my stupid friends. I hate the idea of losing this challenge, especially when I've smashed all the others.

I don't know what's wrong with me. I can't believe I'm even considering this. I think it's because every time I even think about it I get this insane rush of adrenaline that genuinely makes me shiver.

It reminds me of laser tag, which Matthew once persuaded me to try. It wasn't something I'd considered doing before, I'd never been dying to try a game of shooting at someone with lasers while running around an indoor maze, but it was a few years ago when Matthew would organize these fun days out for us and I couldn't really say no. When I was handed my laser gun and the teams were organized, I remember thinking that Matthew was off his rocker to have thought I might want to spend a precious Saturday doing this, but when it started, I had such a good time.

I got really into it. I was running around, ducking, hiding, pretending I was in a real-life deathly-laser-gun-fight scenario. I started yelling orders at my team members, who were genuine strangers and I'm sure probably didn't appreciate me acting as some kind of self-appointed general, but I didn't care. I got a major adrenaline rush.

A few months before the wedding, Matthew and I walked past the Laser Quest where we'd done that day out years previously and I brightened, pointed at it, and went, "Remember that day? It was so fun! We should do that again!"

"Maybe," he replied, barely glancing at it. "It would be more fun in a group, though."

"Yeah," I agreed. "It would."

That way, I could shout orders at my loving friends, rather than strangers. We could go for drinks after and it would be a great day out with everyone. I didn't take what he said personally. I didn't interpret it as he would rather be in a group than alone with me. That he couldn't picture just us two having fun.

Now I wonder if he was giving little hints like that the whole time that we both missed.

I take a deep breath, cross my arms over my body, grip the sides of my dress, pull it up over my head, and drop it into a crumpled heap on the floor. With dramatic flair, I then remove my underwear, kicking it to the side.

Right. I am officially naked. This is no big deal.

I pick up my phone and *very carefully* take a selfie of just my shoulders, neck, and face (I do not want to scar Leo for life), sticking my tongue out at the camera, and send the picture to the group.

> **Time for the task!**
> **Wish me luck!**

I put my phone down. I'm going to do this. I'm going to run naked down this hotel corridor just like a Spice Girl. Oh my goodness, I have even more respect for those women now that I know they used to do this on tour.

No, I can't do this. *Am I actually going to do this?!* I shake my hands out at my sides, like athletes do before an Olympic race, because I'm sure we have a similar amount of nerves.

I creak open the door and stick my head out. There's no one there and—

Oh my god I almost forgot the key card.

Can you imagine? *Can you imagine?!* Wow. That could have been really bad. I actually would have died right there if I had locked myself out of my hotel room naked. I grab the key card and clutch it in my tingling fingers as though my life depends on it.

Here we go again. Opening the door, I look up and down the corridor again, and then once more for good measure. I listen for any sounds. There's no ping of the elevator; only silence from all the rooms down the way.

This is it. This is my moment. My moment to shine. I'm going to go for it.

I'm going to bloody go for it.

With a little squeak of excitement mixed with nerves, I creep through the door and then dash down the corridor as fast as I can, giggling my head off. Oh my goodness. *This is hilarious!* I can't stop giggling, like I'm a bonkers teenager playing a stupid prank or acting out an outrageous dare with a group of friends, when in real life I'm *on my own* running naked around a hotel! What am I doing?!

I feel so freeeeee!

I reach the end of the corridor, turn on my heel, and leg it back to my room.

I'm almost at my door when I hear a sound that turns my blood to ice.

"Freya?"

I yelp, looking over my shoulder to find Jamie standing in the door leading from the stairwell, his mouth wide open in shock.

"Oh my god," I cry in horror. "No, no, no, no!"

I slam into my door and desperately try to get the key card working, shaking the door handle at the same time, but *of course*, the light flashes red.

"What the—" he begins.

The light is green! I fly through the door, slam it shut behind me, and bury my face in my hands, shaking my head and desperately wishing to erase that moment. I feel like I'm on fire, my cheeks are so hot, and I run into the bathroom, ripping the dressing gown off from the hook and wrapping it round me immediately.

To no surprise, there is a knock on the door a few moments later.

"Freya?" he says, rapping his knuckles against the door again when I don't answer. "Hey, are you okay? Can I come in?"

"No!" I shout back, dying with embarrassment. "*Go away!*"

"Oh. Is someone in there with you? Sorry, none of my business. I'll go."

"No, *there is no one in here with me!*"

"Why are you so cross?"

"I'm not cross! *Go away!*"

He chuckles. "Come on, let me in. There's no need to be—"

"*Stop laughing at me!*"

"I'm not, I swear!"

"I can hear you!"

"I'm laughing at the shock of the situation! I wasn't expecting to . . . uh . . . see that."

"Oh, so me naked is funny?"

"No! No, you naked is . . . uh . . . Look, please can I come in? I feel like an idiot standing out here talking to a door."

He's not going to go away until he gets an explanation. It's also probably a good idea for me to give him one. I don't particularly want him thinking that I run about naked for my own amusement. With a heavy sigh, preparing myself for a *lot* of mockery and keeping my dressing gown wrapped around as tight as possible, I reluctantly open the door.

He comes in, walking past me to the middle of the room and turning round with a quizzical expression.

"Hello," he begins.

"What are you doing here? You were meant to be at the wedding!"

"Why are you running up and down the hotel corridor naked?" he asks, intrigued. "I'm not against it, but I'm just interested to—"

"It was one of the tasks, okay?" I explain grumpily. "The survival guide I told you about earlier."

"Oh right." He nods, shoving his hands in his pockets.

"Clearly, it's gone *very* wrong and I will be killing my friends as soon as I land on British soil."

"I don't think it's gone wrong at all. You did it, didn't you?"

I sigh, closing my eyes in despair. "Yes. But no one was supposed to see."

He holds up his hands, his lips twitching into a smile. "I promise I won't tell. If it helps, I didn't see everything, I just saw—"

"*Please don't detail to me what you saw.* Oh bloody hell, this is so embarrassing," I mumble, running a hand through my hair. "Please can we just pretend that didn't happen? You need to erase it from your brain."

"Okay. I'll erase it from my brain." He hesitates. "If you want me to?"

"*Yes*, I want you to!" I say, aghast that he'd even check. "Why wouldn't I want you to? You've just witnessed me running about with no clothes on!"

"And you think that's a bad thing?"

I frown in confusion. "Is that . . . is that a trick question?"

He stares at me. I stare back at him. Hang on. What's happening here? Is he . . . is he saying it's a good thing he saw me running around with no clothes on? Is that what's happening? And now that I think about it, how has it come about that he's seen me at all?

"Your room is on the first floor," I say out loud as my brain becomes muddled. "Why were you even up here?"

His turn to look bashful. His eyes drop to the floor guiltily.

"I was coming to see you," he admits eventually. "In case . . ." He trails off.

Oh my god. What do I do? *What do I do?* I feel like my throat has got really tight and I need to swallow, but my throat is so constricted that if I swallow it will be so obvious. I do it anyway and I can hear the audible gulp. I've given away that I'm nervous. I am nervous. I'm really nervous. And I'm scared. In a good way.

I like him.

Wait. I need to clarify what's going on. Technically, he hasn't explained exactly why he was coming to see me. He could have been coming to see me to ask if I had a spare shower cap he could borrow. It could be completely innocent.

I open my mouth to ask him what exactly he means, but I don't get the chance to. Because he's walking toward me with purpose and I can see exactly what purpose that is. I think the audible nervous gulp, as unsexy as it was, may have given away my position. He's so close now, right there in front of me, and as I tilt my head up to meet his eyes, he lifts his hand to the side of my head, while keeping the other hand in his pocket.

Yes. That's right. *That's how sexy and casual he is.*

Good lord, who knew? Who knew a casual hand in the pocket could be so *exciting*?!

I close my eyes and he kisses me, and it's quite soft and gentle at first, then it gets more urgent and his pocket-hand is suddenly round my waist and on the small of my back, pulling me closer to him.

My phone rings. It's on the table under the mirror, where I'd left it after messaging Ruby and Leo. I can hear it vibrating, but obviously ignore it because *hello* this kiss is outrageous and it's likely Ruby and/or Leo calling to ask how the naked run went.

If only they knew. I cannot *wait* to tell them.

I'm somehow up against the door now and he's kissing my neck and I can't believe this is happening, and I feel completely caught up in this incredible, passionate moment with Jamie, who I thought was so irritating and rude at first, but now he may just be the hottest guy on the planet, and I don't care if this is reckless or outrageous, I'm loving every second because it's nice to feel wanted and it's even nicer to feel wanted by Jamie, whom I want, too.

My phone rings again. I ignore it again.

I'm suddenly very much aware that I'm entirely naked under my dressing gown. He hasn't tried anything yet, but what if he does?! What do I do? I'm not sure I can handle being naked in one fell swoop. It's usually a gradual thing, with clothes being removed one at a time, so it's not so sudden, but I don't have that option.

Who cares?

There goes my phone another time. I don't ignore it this time and neither does Jamie, because three phone calls one after the other at this time of night isn't normal.

"Do you need to check that?" he asks huskily in my ear, and I know he wants me to say no, but we both know the answer is yes, otherwise we wouldn't have stopped.

I smile and release myself from his arms, walking over to check my screen in the hope that it's Ruby and there are accompanying silly messages, so I don't need to panic about it being anything genuinely serious. I look at the missed calls.

Matthew.

I inhale sharply, the shock making me numb. The phone rings out as I'm staring at it.

"Who is it?" Jamie asks. "Everything okay?"

It starts ringing for the fourth time: Matthew.

"Sorry, I . . . I should probably get this. Something might be wrong," I say to Jamie, before turning to face away from him and picking up. "Hello?"

"Freya," he says, and the sound of his voice makes me feel dizzy. "I need to talk to you."

"This isn't a good time, Matthew," I tell him, trying to be firm, but closing my eyes because it's exciting and painful at the same time to have him call me. "Is everything all right?"

"I miss you."

He's drunk. I can always tell when he's drunk, even if it's not obvious. The slight tilt in his voice. I know him.

"You're drunk," I say, my heart aching. "You can't—"

"No, I know. I know I shouldn't be doing this. But I do miss you. Okay? I just . . . I had to tell you. I saw your picture on Instagram and it made me smile, because there you are. It made me miss you."

Stop it.

"Matthew, please—"

"I think we should meet up. We need to talk. We haven't talked. But it's been enough time now, hasn't it? We'll talk it all through."

Please can he stop.

"Okay," I say, my mouth dry, "but you need to go, because you're drunk and you—"

"Stop saying that! I mean what I say. I'll message you tomorrow and you'll see."

What about Jamie?

"Fine. That's fine, you can message tomorrow. I have to go."

"I don't want you to forget about me, you know? That's what's made me so confused. I thought we'd made the right decision, even though it was so hard. Then I see you and the idea of not being in your life—"

Make it stop.

"Matthew, I'm going to go. Don't call again tonight."

I rip the phone away from my ear and press the red button. My brain is a mess and I suddenly feel like I might cry, but I'm also proud of myself. Because somehow I shut it down when I wanted so badly to hear what he had to say. But I have to hear it sober and not when I've got someone else in my room.

Jamie.

"I'm so sorry J—" I begin, spinning round, but there's no one there.

He's gone.

Hi Matthew, hope you had a good weekend and the hangover isn't too bad! I haven't heard from you, you said you'd message to work out a time when we can meet? Maybe an evening this week?
X

Hey, just tried calling again to try to schedule in this chat. As you said when you called, it would be good to see each other and talk everything through
X

CHAPTER TWENTY-TWO

I feel mortified.

How did I think it was in any way appropriate to pick up a phone call from my ex-fiancé while I was with another guy?! That must have made Jamie feel terrible. I wanted so badly to track him down and explain it to him, but I realized that I didn't understand what had happened myself, so what would I say?! Besides, the moment was over. I'd completely ruined it.

You know what the most annoying thing is? I hadn't even been thinking about Matthew. I wasn't thinking about the breakup or my sorry little story. I was having fun. I was happy.

And then Matthew swoops in with his drunken phone call and what happens?!

Just like that, I turn into a mess.

"You're not a mess," Ruby asserts, handing me a mug of hot chocolate with marshmallows on the top, as I curl up on her sofa, feeling very sorry for myself. "It's not your fault."

"It's completely my fault," I tell her. "I didn't have to pick up. I shouldn't have answered that phone. I didn't need to listen to a word Matthew had to say."

"He called you four times," Leo says, looking at me sympathetically. "I think anyone would have done the same. You'd be too curious not to answer."

"I feel so embarrassed, and Jamie must think I'm such a loser!"

Ruby can't help but smile. "Freya, he won't think you're a loser."

"Yes, he will. He'll think that I can't resist my ex-boyfriend even when I'm literally in the arms of another guy. Ugh." I slap my forehead with my hand. "I hate myself."

"Stop it," Ruby says sternly. "Leo's right. You were in an impossible situation. It's a complete headfuck. Anybody would understand you picking up when he was calling you so many times. Jamie would understand."

I wince. "He did say that."

"Who?" Leo asks.

"Jamie."

Ruby's eyes widen. "You spoke to him after?"

"Just over WhatsApp. I didn't know his room number so I couldn't go around shouting his name. I also didn't think he'd want to speak to me, so I sent him a message. Ryan gave me his number the first time I met him."

"What did you say?" Ruby asks, as I chew on a marshmallow.

"I apologized. I didn't give a long explanation. I just said I was really sorry about what happened."

"And?"

"And he replied saying, 'It's okay. I understand.'"

"That's it?" She looks confused. "You didn't have any other conversation?"

"Nope."

"Seriously? Nothing? After that steamy kiss?"

"That steamy kiss was ruined by me and my stupidity," I remind her, taking a sip of hot chocolate in the hope it will make me feel better, but all it does is burn my tongue. "What could either of us say? We probably both feel as embarrassed as each other."

"Do you want to speak to Jamie?" she asks curiously.

"Yes. No. I don't know." I scrunch up my face like a toddler. "I feel so confused. I really like him, you know? We click. It's weird, it's like we've known each other for a while and I feel happy in his company, just at ease and relaxed. But I can't think about that right now. I'm a mess. My head is all over the place. It's too much."

"What about Matthew?" Leo says, his eyebrows knitted together in concentration.

Ruby wrinkles her nose. "What about him?"

"It seems like a big deal, him calling," he tells her pointedly, before turning back to me. "What happened after the phone call?"

"Well, this is what makes everything so much worse," I say, grimacing at the thought of having to say this out loud. "Nothing."

Leo and Ruby share a questioning glance.

"Nothing happened after the phone call," I explain quietly. "I haven't heard from him. No calls, no messages, nothing."

Ruby gasps. "You're joking?"

"No, I'm not. So, you can imagine how much of an idiot I feel. All of that for nothing. He put my head into a spin and vanished again."

"Hang on," Leo says, holding up his hands before Ruby has the opportunity to explode into a tirade about Matthew, "have you reached out to him at all?"

"Yes, of course. I barely slept, I was all over the place after what he said. I messaged, called. Nothing." I sigh, leaning my head back against the cushion and closing my eyes.

Leo looks pained on my behalf. "Why wouldn't he at least message to apologize? He must have known how it would upset you."

"He's a coward," Ruby states simply.

"You know," I begin, clasping my warm mug in my hands as though it's a precious relic, "if I'm being crazily honest,

I loved getting that phone call. I did, I loved it. Even if it ruined my night. It made me feel so good that he was thinking of me enough to call me. It gave me some of my power back. The hardest thing about this breakup has been Matthew acting like a total stranger. I haven't been allowed to see him; the only messages I've received have been cold and impersonal. Sometimes, I've felt genuinely insane, like I was in that relationship for twelve years on my own. Or as though I'd somehow forced him to propose without my knowledge; that I'd fooled him as well as myself into thinking we had a future. And with one drunken phone call, I felt validated. He made me feel important to him again. It was an amazing feeling." I take a deep breath. "God, I am *such* an idiot."

Leo and Ruby listen patiently, their expressions full of sadness and concern.

"I'm back at the beginning again," I add glumly.

"No, you're not," Ruby insists, reaching over to rest her hand on my knee. "You know how I know that?"

"How?"

"The Freya who was engaged to marry Matthew would *never* have run down a hotel corridor stark bollock naked."

I give her a weak smile. "That's a fair point."

"What Matthew has done is pure selfishness," she says, suddenly serious again. "He's seen you moving on and he's panicked. Which is unfair, because it's not like . . ."

She trails off and glances at Leo. Something about her eyes, which are mildly panicked, makes me realize that she's not telling me something. Leo doesn't give anything away in his expression, but he shifts under her gaze.

"What's going on?" I frown at them. "What are you not saying?"

She looks nervously to Leo again and then down at her hands. "We were going to tell you, Freya, because we didn't want you finding out any other way, but then when you told us he called you . . ."

"Tell me what?" A croak in my voice betrays my panic, as I hurriedly sit up and face whatever's coming.

"We bumped into Akin," Leo reveals gently. "You obviously know he lives around here."

"All too well. What did he say?" I ask hurriedly, begging them to end this suspense.

"He told us . . . he mentioned that Matthew has been on a few dates," Ruby says so softly, it's almost a whisper. "He went out with some friends recently and brought along one of these dates and they put up some photos with her, too. Akin was worried that you'd see it on one of their Instagram pages and get upset, that's why he told us. He didn't know who you still followed out of the group and . . . I actually think he was trying to do the right thing by telling us." She pauses, watching me carefully. "I'm so sorry, Freya."

I can't really speak. I think if I open my mouth, a sob might come out, and I don't want that.

"Are you okay?"

I'm not okay. But I nod slowly and clench my jaw stubbornly as my mind races. I knew this would happen. We're both single now, and Matthew was going to start dating other people eventually. It was always going to happen.

Still. Even when you expect it. Even when it makes sense. It's heartbreaking.

Without saying anything, Leo stands and comes to sit on the other side of me and the two of them form a human cocoon around me. I don't know how long I sit there in silence, but it's a long time, because my hot chocolate goes cold and a thin layer of cold marshmallow goo forms on the top of it. Ruby holds my hand. Leo leans his head against mine. Neither of them say anything, because they both know me well enough to know I don't want them to. And even though I feel utterly broken, I also feel safe in this little human sandwich they've formed on their sofa.

The brutality of a breakup is hard.

Feeling replaced is worse.

"Darling!"

Oh god, here we go. The moment has arrived. I turn round to see Mum standing in front of me wearing an elaborate purple hat with a giant bow on it. Adrian tenses next to me and I can sense poor Dad literally steeling himself by puffing out his chest.

"Hi, Mum," I say in a strained tone, going along with her air-kiss-type greeting.

"You look so beautiful! So glowing! So sparkling!" she exclaims, a hand to her chest as she takes me in. Her eyes drift across to Adrian and she tilts her head and sticks out her bottom lip. "My baby! So grown-up! Adrian!"

Adrian is then subjected to the same greeting, but manages to look a lot more at ease with it than I do, giving her a warm smile.

"Hey, Mum. Wow, great hat."

"Oh thank you, darling, you know me!"

"I do," he says with a fake laugh.

We'd just had a conversation about how it was important to be nice to Mum because it was Rachel and Carley's big day and we didn't want any tension at such a happy occasion. Despite Adrian's advice, I hadn't made the effort to meet up with Mum before today, but I've promised him and Dad that I'll be on good behavior for Rachel's sake.

The wedding is on the grounds of a beautiful old house in Norwich, with a sailcloth marquee up on the lawn for the reception following the ceremony, which will take place in the Orangery. Rachel is our only cousin, the daughter of my dad's sister, Aunty

Em. We knew Mum would be invited even though it's Dad's side of the family—Mum is Rachel's godmother and Aunty Em really does love her, despite everything. Aunty Em even phoned Dad to discuss inviting her, a kind gesture he felt unnecessary.

Adrian and I have always got on well with Rachel and spent childhood holidays building dens with her or creating silly plays to perform to our parents. As we grew up, we saw her less, as she moved to Norwich to work for a house-renovation company there, but we've kept in touch, often checking in on each other, and she's been really supportive this summer, sending me messages and offering to come visit to make sure I've been doing okay.

We met Carley two years ago at Christmas, when she and Rachel were in London for a couple of days. The relationship was still new, but I knew Carley was The One—mostly because Rachel told me so when Carley nipped to the loo. Rachel wears her heart on her sleeve but it was obvious that the adoration was mutual.

As Mum turns her attention to Dad, Evan steps forward, having been lurking behind her nervously, and gives us an awkward wave.

"Hello," he says with a fixed smile. "Nice to see you both."

"Hi, Evan," Adrian says cheerily, offering a handshake. "How are you?"

We've never warmed to Evan. In our minds, he's the bad guy, who lured Mum away from Dad and destroyed our family. I was horrible to him when it all first happened, and I look back on some of the things I said with a touch of regret, because, affair aside, Evan does seem like quite a nice guy. He's kind, outgoing, and with a streak of quirkiness that matches Mum. Today, for example, he's wearing a mustard-yellow checkered suit with a matching bow tie. I'm surprised Mum let him wear something that clashes with her hat, but I suppose she's all about the free spirit, so telling someone how to dress wouldn't really be her vibe.

I can see that Evan is nervous around me, and part of me quite likes that, if I'm honest, because it gives me a sense of power over him. Then I remember how in Ireland, I banged on to Jamie about admiring those who exuded kindness. He may have been a target for a lot of my anger, but Evan really isn't the person I should be mad at.

After Adrian has performed his jolly greeting, he gives me a pointed look. I clear my throat.

"Evan," I say, plastering on a smile and stepping forward to give him a kiss on the cheek. "Great to see you."

He looks stunned and receives my olive branch overenthusiastically. In fact, he's so delighted, gushing about how wonderful I look and beaming at me so eagerly, that I wonder how much of a gremlin I must have been to him before if simply saying "Great to see you" has had such an effect.

I glance at Adrian, who mimes giving me a round of applause behind Evan's back. The three of us then smile at each other gormlessly, each pretending not to be listening to Mum and Dad's conversation, but of course we are. Still, it's all very cordial and pleasant, and it's not long before we are ushered into the Orangery to take our seats for the ceremony.

I find the service particularly moving, because all I can see when I look at Rachel is her as a little girl, mud on her hands and face, her red hair falling out of its neat plait by the end of our adventures. Now, here she is, a proper grown-up, in an elegant white jumpsuit and towering heels, saying her vows to someone, promising to love them forever, no matter what comes their way.

I look down at my hands folded neatly on my lap, finding it difficult to watch. I notice Mum watching me from across the aisle. Refusing to catch her eye, I remain facing forward and smile gracefully at the brides, even more determined to appear absolutely fine and unaffected.

"Lovely ceremony," Dad says afterward, as he, Adrian, and I clink our champagne glasses together and toast the happy couple. "Short, too, which I appreciate."

"Not sure you're supposed to say things like that out loud, Dad."

"No, I agree, it's all about keeping it short and sweet," Adrian pitches in. "Same can be said for speeches, so keep that in mind, Freya."

I scowl at him. *Damn it.* Why did I think it would be a good idea to tell him about the Wedding Season task for today?!

I'm dreading this stupid challenge of making a speech, even more than the naked hotel run. That was risky, but this is just downright mortifying. I even rang Ruby and Leo yesterday to double-check that I *had* to make a speech at this wedding.

"Of course not," Ruby said soothingly. "But you have to consider, would you be disappointed in yourself if you fail this task?"

She was playing me. I hated her for it, but I also had to respect her game.

"Are you making a speech today, Freya?" Dad asks, surprised.

"Don't say anything, it's meant to be off the cuff," Adrian tells him, tapping the side of his nose. "I think it's very sweet of you, sis. You've always been good at public speaking."

Dad makes a face. "Has she?"

"No, Dad, he was being sarcastic," I inform him, narrowing my eyes at my brother. "Permission to hit him over the head?"

"Permission not granted. Behave yourselves," Dad mutters. "Why are you making a speech, then?"

"Who's making a speech?" Mum asks brightly, appearing at Dad's side and almost taking him out with her hat as she turns her head to look accusingly at me and Adrian.

Ugh. Of all people, I do *not* need Mum's input on the topic. Evan comes sidling up next to her, carrying their glasses and handing her one.

"Freya is," Adrian says gleefully, nodding toward me. "You know she's always been good in front of a crowd."

"Is that right?" Mum looks confused. "I thought you hated that sort of thing. Remember when you, Rachel, and Adrian put on that play for us about King Arthur and the sword in the stone?"

"Oh yeah!" Adrian brightens at the memory. "I was Arthur, Rachel was Merlin, and Freya, remind us all of your role."

"I played the stone."

Adrian throws his head back and cackles loudly. Dad chuckles and even Evan feels that he can join in, sniggering behind his hand.

"That was because she refused to have a speaking role," Mum explains to Evan, patting my arm proudly. "The stone was a perfect fit for her and she happily sat there holding a big cardboard-cutout circle that she'd colored in gray pen to represent the stone in one hand and the sword in the other." She beams at me, adding fondly, "Even then, when she was so little, she knew exactly who she was, and she was not a performer. I've always admired that about you, Freya."

I'm taken aback by the sincerity of her tone. Mum is very good at saying what people want to hear, her flamboyant and excessive personality naturally lending itself to expertly crafted, exaggerated compliments, which is why she can easily be the life and soul of a party. But this remark was made quietly and earnestly, without flair or drama.

"Thanks, Mum," I reply uneasily, taking a sip of champagne.

Adrian looks stunned, too, and with a side glance to me, suddenly engages Evan and Dad in a conversation, turning his back on us slightly, so that we naturally form two new clusters. Mum and I stand awkwardly with one another, not sure who should speak first.

"You look really well, Freya," Mum says, breaking the ice.

"Thanks. You look nice, too."

"I'm just so sorry about what happened with the wedding." She gives an exasperated sigh. "It's awful and you've picked yourself up and carried on and . . . well, I feel terrible that you had to go through it. I'm sorry I wasn't there to look after you."

"That's kind of you, Mum, but I don't need looking after."

She snorts. "Don't I know that! Oh darling, you never did. You fell over in a playground once, and I ran to pick you up, but do you know what you did? You scrambled to your feet and with this determined little face, you clenched your fists and whispered 'Walk it off, Freya' to yourself."

"No way. Did I?"

"Yes!" She chuckles, smiling at the memory. "It was so sweet. You couldn't have been more than four years old. You must have heard your dad saying it to you or perhaps someone else using the phrase and you repeated it. We couldn't stop laughing." She hesitates and takes a sip of her drink, before continuing. "I think that sort of thing helped me excuse myself."

I stare at her. "What do you mean?"

She looks down at the ground guiltily. I've never seen her like this before, so vulnerable and apologetic with her body language. In fact, she's never spoken about memories of us as kids or even acknowledged that she simply left us. It's been all smiles and stories of her new life and how wonderful everything is.

"Look, I want to be a part of your life, Freya. I know I've made mistakes, but it would mean the world to me if we could find a way to spend time together. I miss you terribly and I've had time to reflect and . . . well, I wish I'd done things differently."

I don't know how to react. I clear my throat and take a sip of my drink.

"I'm not sure this is the time or place to talk about things, Mum."

"Well, I wanted to use this opportunity to ask you if we could find a time and place," she says gently. "There's a lot to say."

I don't say anything, but I give a vague nod. She brightens.

"Can I get anyone a top-up?" Dad asks, shuffling over to join us and pretending not to look overly concerned.

"You leave that with me," Mum insists, replacing her serious expression with a bright, breezy smile. "Champagne all round, eh? I'll be back pronto!"

She wanders off to get the attention of a waiter, and Dad turns to talk to me, while Evan continues to chat to Adrian about something he's deeply passionate about. From the snippets I over-hear, it sounds like he's filling him in on carrots, but that can't be right.

"Nice chat?" Dad asks, raising his eyebrows at me. "It didn't end in fisticuffs, I'm pleased to see."

"Fisticuffs? Showing your age there, old man." I nudge him affectionately. "It was fine. She wants to talk properly at some point."

"And?"

"And . . . I didn't tell her no."

A wide smile spreads across his face. "That's excellent news. You'll be pleased that you did."

"I'm not so sure about that." I sigh. "I don't know, it sounded like she really meant what she was saying, which is new to me."

"Oh, she means it. As you get older, you realize that when people don't mean it, they just won't bother. Too much effort," he informs me bluntly, before giving me a pointed look. "You also realize that people make mistakes and life doesn't always go to plan. I have no doubt that you and your brother can repair your relationship with your mum, and there will be happy times ahead. That's the trick to remember. Even when it doesn't feel like it, there will always be happy times ahead, so long as you surround yourself with people."

"The right people, you mean?"

He chuckles. "Not necessarily. The long and the short of it, Freya, is that people are what matter in life. They'll surprise you, amaze you, disappoint you. It's all part of the mess. And thank goodness! If we were able to plan everything, we'd never change; we'd never learn or grow. Take ponds, for example. It's the messy ones that are full of life."

I don't know when my dad got so profound. I always thought he sort of bumbled through life, but it turns out that underneath it all, he's bloody Yoda.

He catches me looking at him strangely.

"What?" he says defensively. "I thought you could use some wise words for your speech. Whatever you do, keep it under two minutes. I don't want you encouraging every Dick and Harry here to pick up the microphone and tell us their feelings, all right?"

That's more like it.

⌐——————⌐

"Hi everyone—"

Oh bloody hell.

"—my name is Freya, I'm Rachel's cousin—"

This is actually happening.

"—and I just wanted to say a few words."

I swear the number of guests has doubled since I took up the microphone.

Oh shit. I've just realized I've forgotten my notes.

They're in my clutch.

What have I done?!

"I promise I'll keep this short—"

Dad's nodding in agreement. Yes, thanks, Dad, I know.

Oh, and look, Adrian is filming with his phone, so we can watch this back whenever we want.

How wonderful.

"—I appreciate it's unusual for a cousin to make a speech, but I mentioned to Rachel and Carley that I had a few words to say, and they have graciously allowed me to do so."

I hate Ruby and Leo. Why am I friends with them?

"I'm not very good at this sort of thing, so bear with me."

What the fuck, how am I so sweaty everywhere, yet my mouth is so dry?

The moisture in my body appears to have become very imbalanced.

"I just wanted to say that . . . um . . ."

Mum is mouthing something at me. What's she saying? "Muck up"?

Why would she instruct me to *muck up*?! What is *wrong* with that woman?! And there I was thinking we were on better terms, well she better—

Oh. "Speak up." That's what she's mouthing. Speak up.

Okay, that's actually quite helpful.

"Sorry, let me hold this mic a bit closer. Can everyone hear me now? Okay, good. Sorry about that. Where was I?"

I'm going to ask Phil to send me on a public speaking course.

How have I got this far in my career with these *shite* skills?! I blame Phil, he should have pulled me up on this.

"Oh yes, I was right at the beginning. Ha ha. So yes, I wanted to say a few words about Rachel and Carley on their wedding day."

Deep breath, Freya. You can get through this. Even without your notes.

Just wing it.

"It has come to my attention this year that life is . . . uh . . . well, it's a big mess. But, so long as you have people around you who love you, you'll find that you're able to put one foot in front of the other just fine anyway, no matter where you're going or where you end up. Friends, family, partners in love, partners in crime—"

Satisfying chuckle from the audience here.

"—we help each other navigate the mess. We love each other, guide each other, don't give up on each other—"

Mum is smiling and dabbing at her eyes dramatically with a floral handkerchief.

Christ.

"—and we don't let each other give up on ourselves. What I'm trying to say is—"

I turn to my cousin and her new wife.

"—Rachel and Carley, we love you, we're happy for you, and we're also all here for you. You made your promises today, and now that's my promise to you. We are here for you on your journey together, whatever happens. So, I would like to raise a toast to putting one foot in front of the other." I raise my glass in the air. "To . . . feet!"

To feet. *To feet?!*

I just raised a glass . . . to feet?!

Well. That's it. I've officially lost my head. Case closed. The end.

Everyone, quite rightly, bursts out laughing. But by an extraordinary twist, they chorus "To feet!" in the most rousing toast of the night, and then the marquee erupts with applause and cheering. Rachel and Carley come rushing over and envelop me in a huge hug.

"That was so beautiful," Rachel sobs in my ear.

"I raised a toast to feet," I remind her.

"Yes, you did," she says, pulling away and cupping my face with her hands. "And it was perfect."

Things I miss about Matthew when I'm at a wedding:

* He is very good at talking to anyone, which is handy as I never had to worry about conversation with people we didn't know on our table as he'd chat away and put us all at ease.

* He really makes me laugh when he's dancing.

* If he noticed me really enjoying something on my plate, he'd give me his. For example, those delicious little sun-dried tomatoes that often come with a wedding char-cuterie starter. He always used to slide his onto my plate without even breaking conversation with the guest sitting on his other side. This is one of those small but affection-ate gestures in life that, when they're gone, you realize just how sweet they were.

Things I love about being by myself at a wedding:

* I can choose the wedding gift from the registry that I think is most appropriate for the couple without a partner remarking that it's "not very original" when they discover what I've selected (even though when they were asked for their opinion at the time of purchasing they didn't look up from their phone and said "Sure, yeah, get whatever you want, babe").

* I don't have to listen to someone whining about having to wear a tie on the way to the ceremony.

* I have the opportunity to sit next to people who can sing hymns in tune.

* I am able to chat to new people at my table without any-one talking over me or interrupting to tell the story be-cause they tell it funnier.

* I am focusing on my own dancing rather than anyone else's on the dance floor and, even though it's a slow pro-cess, I am gradually growing my confidence in this area.

* I no longer have to put up with ridiculous drunken arguments over nothing that ruin the night.

* The only person I have to worry about is myself.

That last one takes some getting used to and it can be daunting at first, but when you get there, it's like a weight you didn't even know you were carrying is suddenly lifted.

The more I think about it, the more I wonder if Matthew's idea of his self-declared "all over the place, temperamental" personality that didn't mesh well with my "togetherness" might just be translated as "lazy" and "often selfish." If you propose to someone and then spend the next year pondering "What if I could be happier? What if I've missed out?," while the person to whom you've proposed is putting all their spare time and effort into organizing the celebration of your marriage, who would be considered the more "emotional" of the couple?

He said he was in love. I was busy proving I was.

So, here's to only worrying about myself at a wedding. Here's to only worrying about what I want to do in my life, regardless of what he's doing in his. Here's to me putting one foot in front of the other.

Here's to feet.

CHAPTER TWENTY-THREE

I never thought I'd say this, but here goes: my boss inspired me. There's no denying that Phil is a nice guy, I just never thought he'd be the sort of person to influence me in any part of my life that wasn't a client meeting or whatever.

Here's how it happened.

Ruby recently reminded me that I had yet to invite an unexpected plus-one to Andy and Roshni's wedding, which is fast approaching. There was someone who instantly came to mind.

Jamie.

He'd never want to come. Asking him would have been a nice excuse to speak to him, though. But I wasn't going to humiliate myself even further by asking an impossible question, and forcing him to turn me down.

Still, I do wonder what he's up to.

During a work lunch break, I went through my contacts on my phone, hoping one would jump out at me, but other than Jamie, not one person would be appropriate. Not one. I started at the top again and then, when the second time through didn't prove helpful, I went onto dreaded Facebook to go through the hundreds of friends I apparently am connected with, the majority of whom I no longer even recognize.

I typed "who to invite to a wedding" into my work computer. Mortifyingly, the list of results that came up was all to do with guidance for a bride and groom agonizing over the guest list etiquette. I've already been there, done that.

I tried again: "Who should I invite as a plus-one to a wedding?"

A similar selection of results popped up. Third's time a charm, right? "I have a plus-one for a wedding. Who should I invite?"

Again, all these websites came up promising that they could help with how to address an invitation to a guest with a plus-one.

"For fuck's sake!" I hissed irritably.

Without thinking, I typed in, "I need someone to escort me to a wedding. Who shall I ask?"

I should have thought a bit more about my wording, but I was so caught up in how annoying the whole process was that I was genuinely shocked when a list of escort services was provided. I stared at my computer screen, my jaw hanging open.

There was a cough behind me.

I spun round to see Phil there with his eyebrows furrowed. He glanced at my screen.

Bollocks.

"Phil! Hi!"

I turned back to my computer and, fumbling for my mouse in such a rush that I knocked my hand against it, clicked something, and somehow caused the screen to *zoom in* on a search result titled, "Male and Female Escorts for Weddings."

"Oh god," I squeaked, closing the browser window and then looking up at him, my whole face on fire. "I can explain."

"Um," he began, looking more awkward and tense than ever, "I don't think—"

"I *swear* I was not just looking at escorts," I told him in a hushed tone, checking to make sure that most of my team were still, thankfully, out grabbing lunch. "I typed in something else and those results came up, but they were *not* what I was looking for. I especially would not be looking up those kinds of things on work time. Or any time, to be honest."

He held up his hands. "That's all right, Freya."

"I honestly—"

"I believe you." He looked pained. "I once searched how to clean a saxophone properly and I accidentally got one of the letters in that word wrong. You can imagine which one. It was . . . unpleasant."

I nodded slowly. "I bet."

"I came over to check you're feeling prepared about the meeting this afternoon," he said, acting completely normal and serious, as though we hadn't just had the weirdest conversation.

"Yes, thanks. I'm all good."

"Well, let me know if you need any help."

"I will." I hesitated. "Phil, I just want to reiterate that I really wasn't looking up escorts. I need to find a plus-one for Roshni's wedding next weekend—remember Roshni? And I'm just not sure who to take. I was looking for inspiration."

"Oh, well, that's nice news that Roshni is getting married. I didn't work with her for long, but she was a great member of the team." He raised his eyebrows. "Can you take a friend, or does it have to be a date?"

"Ah, well . . . uh . . . it's kind of a long story, but I have to take someone unexpected."

Why was I telling my boss this information?! He was *obviously* desperate to get out of this conversation! He was just being polite! He doesn't care about my life! He doesn't—

"Someone unexpected? Interesting," he said, stroking his chin and, much to my surprise, looking genuinely intrigued.

"It's a . . . uh . . . challenge sort of thing that my friends have set me." I laughed nervously. "It's stupid."

"I don't think that sounds stupid. Pushing yourself to meet new people and try new things is very important," he said matter-of-factly. "After all, it's thanks to giving the trapeze a go that I met my wife."

I blinked up at him. "Sorry?"

"I thought I'd try it out," he said with a shrug. "I've always been very into aerial acrobatics and things like that. Aerial yoga is fun, and a nice introduction into getting your feet off the ground. Anyway, all those years ago I'd spent too much time wallowing and moping around, pining after a girl I'd been seeing for just a few weeks who dumped me, and I thought I'd try something new and fun. My wife was one of the instructors."

I had no idea what to say to this. Phil is into aerial acrobatics?! *Phil*. He met his wife while honing his *trapeze* skills?

Good lord, nothing makes sense anymore.

I mean, this is the guy who always has a sandwich at his desk for lunch. Literally, I've never seen him go out and buy a different lunch, unless we go out for a meal with clients. Monday to Friday, he retrieves a homemade foil-wrapped sandwich from the fridge. He doesn't participate in any team-bonding activities; he's never shown any inclination toward having a passion for fitness; and, when pushed at the Christmas party, he admitted that one of the wildest moments of his childhood was when he styled his hair into a quiff.

That guy is a secret *seasoned acrobat*?!

"Have you tried speed dating?" he asked, as I simply stared at him openmouthed.

"Uh, no."

"Worth thinking about," he mused. "My brother tried it and didn't have any luck with the love side of things, but he did meet a magician that he's stayed close with."

What is happening?!

My brain couldn't handle this conversation. This was genuinely the most Phil and I had spoken about anything non-work-related ever.

"A magician," I repeated, still grappling with the trapeze stuff.

"Yes. She performed at my brother's birthday party a few years ago."

"Right. Wow. Any good?"

"The magician?"

"Yes."

"I have no idea. I actually wasn't there. I didn't get invited."

"To your brother's birthday party?"

He sighed heavily. "We're not . . . close."

"Oh. Sorry to hear that."

He shrugged. "It is what it is. The last time we spoke was at a wedding actually."

"Oh, really?"

"That's the thing about weddings, isn't it," he said thoughtfully. "They're little pockets of togetherness and happiness. My family seems to forget that we all don't like each other when we're at a wedding. Instead, we're perfectly civil and sometimes, even, forgiving. And trust me, that's not easy. My brother once tried to frame me for fraud. Denies it, of course, but we all know what he did."

I stared at him. "Wow."

"Anyway." He stood up straight, clearing his throat. "As I said, let me know if you need any help for the meeting this afternoon. And good luck with the plus-one dilemma."

"Thank you," I said in a daze, watching him walk away.

It took me a while to process our conversation. I stared at my computer screen wondering what the hell had just happened.

Aerial acrobatics. A dramatic family feud. Framed for *fraud*. Who would have thought it?

Later that day, I was sitting at home on my laptop, having a marvelous time buying colorful pens and glittery stickers for the hen-do book I was making Ruby—seriously, buying stationery is a lot of fun—when I found my thoughts drifting to something Phil had said about weddings in the midst of our bonkers conversation. He was right; they are a pocket of happiness. They remind you of what's important in life. What we're grateful for. They provide a perfect opportunity for forgiveness.

A plus-one idea suddenly popped into my head. A ridiculous and horrifying idea.

But it would certainly be unexpected.

"Darling!"

Mum approaches me in the hotel reception with her arms wide open. She's wearing the *loudest* orange and yellow dress I've ever seen, with eighties shoulder pads and a matching hat.

"Wow, Mum," I say, accepting her air kisses. "You look . . . bright."

"You are such a sweetheart, thank you." She gives me a twirl, her statement gold dangling earrings catching the light as they swing around and almost blind me. "My motto is, you can never be too much."

"Is it? How surprising."

"I am so happy to be your plus-one to this wedding," she informs me, reaching for my hand and giving it a squeeze. "Thank you, Freya, for thinking of me. What an honor!"

"Well, I thought it might be . . . uh . . ." I trail off.

"Oh, we are going to have the *best* time." She looks me up and down, her eyes welling up. "You are so tall! How did you ever get that tall?"

"Am I tall? I think I'm quite average, actually."

"Darling, when you see someone transform from the bairn you used to burp over your shoulder to the towering, confident goddess you see before you, then they seem tall to you no matter what their height!"

It was quite clearly a mistake to invite Mum as my plus-one.

Still, I'm trying my best to be proud of my decision to take the first step in building bridges. When I told Dad, he said he thought it was a brilliant idea, and Adrian was also quite enthusiastic. Ruby and Leo were definitely surprised, so they conceded that I'd smashed the challenge out of the park, but wanted to be sure I'd thought things through properly.

"You know, weddings are quite long," Leo said, giving me a pointed look.

"I'm aware of that, Leo."

"When you bring a plus-one, you have to look after them."

"I know."

"So, you can't just run away," he added, his eyebrows knitted together. "You have to talk to them and stuff."

"Not all night," I pointed out.

"Quite a lot of it, though."

"Yeah, well, maybe that will be a good thing for me and Mum. We'll be somewhere where we can't make a scene or lose our temper. We'll be forced to enjoy each other's company."

Of course, now that I'm here, I can see Leo's point. It's only been a couple of minutes and I'm already looking for exit routes. As long as she steers clear of poetry then maybe I'll make it through this wedding alive.

She suddenly reaches over, takes my hand in hers, and inhales deeply, closing her eyes.

"'Touch has a memory,'" she says, dreamily.

"Excuse me?"

"It's Keats."

Bloody hell.

Andy and Roshni are getting married at a castle looking over St. Ives Bay, and after suffering what feels like a much-too-long car journey from the hotel during which my mum filled me in on the St. Ives school of artists in the early twentieth century—

"What artist could not be inspired by this dramatic scenery, Freya? I have a mind to start painting myself just looking at these landscapes!"—we arrive at the venue as the sunshine breaks through the clouds. I know Roshni was concerned at how rainy it had been this week, so I smile for her as I climb out of the taxi.

"Aha!" Mum exclaims, inhaling deeply and closing her eyes in the sun. "I imagine someone thought to bury a sausage yesterday!"

"What?"

"It's a tradition, darling! To get rid of rain on your wedding day, you bury a raw sausage the night before."

"I've never heard of that."

"I've buried many sausages in my time," Mum announces loudly, just as she passes an elderly couple going into the venue, receiving appalled looks from both of them. "It works a treat."

"Mum, please keep your voice down when talking about burying sausages," I hiss, my cheeks flushing red.

"Not that rain is bad on a wedding day, of course," Mum continues happily, taking an order of service from one of the ushers before we find our seats for the ceremony. "In fact, it makes some of the most memorable pictures! Brides in wellies, holding umbrellas, smiling through the rain. Gorgeous, if you ask me."

"All right, thanks, Mum," I say in a hushed tone, gesturing for her to take a seat near the back.

"Isn't this decoration stunning?" She sighs dreamily, taking in the marigold flowers adorning the room. I give a sharp nod, hoping my lack of conversation will discourage hers.

"You worked with Roshni, is that correct?"

"A long time ago."

"But you remained friends! How lovely. It's so easy to lose contact with people, but you have to make an effort. It's always rewarded!"

I purse my lips. She doesn't notice.

"I'm so excited to be here," she rambles on, her eyes wide with excitement as they scan the other guests. "We'll have so much fun, Freya! I wonder what readings they've chosen."

She eagerly flicks through the order of service, while I take some deep breaths and try to remember what Dad had told me before the weekend. He'd wisely noted that Mum would probably be overwhelmed with both joy and nerves at receiving my invitation, so it was important for me to forgive her perhaps talking too much or being a little overenthusiastic about the day.

I'm surprised she showed up, to be honest. It's a long trip for her to St. Ives, and after the Peak District incident there's a part of me that always expects a no-show from my mother with an accompanying long-winded excuse. So, the fact that she's here at all is something.

When the ceremony begins and Roshni enters on the arm of her dad, I hear Mum inhale sharply and whisper, "Wow," under her breath. Roshni is wearing a stunning ivory *lehnga* detailed with rose-gold embroidery, and has intricate *mehndi* painted on her hands. Andy, in a navy-blue suit, looks like the breath has been knocked out of him at her entrance.

Theirs is a true love story with a meet-cute so ridiculously adorable, even us cynics have to acknowledge its charm. Roshni went to a secondhand bookshop in Brixton. She picked out a book called *The Eye of the World*, the first in the Wheel of Time fantasy series, by Robert Jordan. She was about to pay when she noticed the resident dog lounging on the sofa at the back of the shop. Naturally, she had to go pet him. After giving him a good fuss for a while, she straightened just as a young man appeared next to her, leaning down to give the dog a belly rub. She noticed the book in his hand. It was *The Fires of Heaven*, the fifth book in the Wheel of Time series. The man noticed her looking and then saw the book in her hand. His eyes lit up.

They got chatting about Robert Jordan and other fantasy writers they liked, decided to go for coffee to chat more about books, arranged to meet up for a date later that week, and that was that. They'd magically found the person they were going to spend the rest of their life with on a random Sunday afternoon in a poky bookshop in South London.

If ever there was an argument for fate, that meet-cute has got to be up there.

"Oh, look at them," Mum whispers in my ear, sniffing as Roshni makes her way up the aisle. "So happy. How lovely."

I smile in response, enjoying the harp music.

Mum clears her throat before saying quietly, "Of course, marriage doesn't necessarily mean happiness. I hope you know that, darling."

My mouth drops open, as I quickly make sure no one heard her over the procession music. "Mum!"

"I'm just saying," she whispers, raising her eyebrows at me.

The congregation is told to be seated and I give her a strange look as we do so. Who makes a comment like that as the bride walks up the aisle?! Thankfully, Mum manages to behave herself for the ceremony, and the only time she stands out is when her "aw" is louder than everyone else's when Roshni's cousin comes to the end of her reading—a passage from The Wheel of Time, of course.

Mum has a marvelous time joining the crowd to follow the *dholi*, an Indian drummer, leading everyone from the ceremony to the wedding breakfast. We're seated next to each other and we politely introduce ourselves to the guests on the other side of us, before she turns her attention back to me.

"It must be terribly hard on you to go to all these weddings after what happened, darling," she says, giving my arm a pat. "I want you to know that—"

"Mum, I really don't want to talk about it," I say sternly, baffled as to why she'd be bringing all this up, before promptly changing the conversation. "Doesn't this food look delicious?"

Luckily, the person on my right overhears and agrees that the food looks great. From that, I'm able to strike up a conversation with them, happy to ignore my mother for the time being until she stops being outrageous. Unfortunately, she catches me before the speeches without anyone to talk to and quickly jumps in.

"Darling," she says, leaning into me, "I want you to know, if you ever want to talk about Matthew, I will always be on hand to—"

"Mum! We are at a wedding!" I look at her as though she's lost her mind. "This is really not an appropriate time to talk about any of that."

"Why not? I think it's the perfect setting to reflect on one's own life and speak candidly about feelings, love, and . . . well . . . loss."

"Oh my god." I run a hand through my hair, trying not to lose it and plastering a smile on my face so that no one looks over and thinks we're having an argument. "Please just stop it, okay?"

She doesn't say anything more and the speeches start. I shake my head at her, furious that she's ruining what I'd hoped might be an opportunity for us to simply have a nice time together.

I should have known that we'd be unable to pretend that everything is just fine. I thought we could enjoy the wedding, have a bit of a laugh, and take that first step toward rebuilding a relationship. After today, we'd arrange a time for us to meet up, go for coffee or lunch, talk about some things. Little by little, we might develop a connection.

I should have known that she wouldn't see it that way. She wants to get straight into the drama; she's desperate for me to confide in her so that she can congratulate herself on being a good mother.

Well, that's not going to happen.

I can feel her eyes boring into me during the speeches and when they're over and dessert is served, I catch her out of the corner of my eye moving her food around her plate, distracted.

When the music starts up, she sits up excitedly, begging me to join her on the dance floor. I hastily refuse and, after looking at me all forlornly, she gives up on trying to persuade me and heads out there by herself. As I watch her shimmy up to a complete stranger, who holds out his hands cheerily and begins to twirl her around, Roshni suddenly appears next to me.

"Your mum is hilarious," she informs me after I've assured her the wedding is amazing. She nods toward Mum. "She's having a ball."

"She certainly likes being the center of attention," I say with a sigh. "Thanks so much for letting me bring a plus-one."

"Not at all, I think it's really nice you brought her," she tells me, pinching my fork and stealing a bite of my pudding. "I know you haven't seen eye to eye with her in the past, but it's great that you're patching things up." She puts my fork down as she catches someone's eye and quickly leans to whisper in my ear. "Bollocks. Got to go say hi to Mum's weird friend, I can't avoid her any longer. She always talks to me about boats. I know nothing about boats." She sighs. "The things we do for family, eh?"

"You're telling me," I mutter, watching Mum encouraging someone to take off his tie so they can use it for limbo.

A few songs later, Mum refuses to take no for an answer, and drags me over to dance with her. I roll my eyes and do a bit of swaying as she flings herself about wildly. I find myself admiring her a bit. You have to give it to her, she doesn't let anything stop her from having a great time and she clearly doesn't care who's watching.

When the time comes to wave off the bride and groom, I consider the evening a success. Mum and I made it through with just a few tiny blips. She didn't completely humiliate me and I didn't disappoint her with snarky but truthful comments about the past.

"Shall we go dance in the sea?" Mum suggests, taking off her shoes as we wait for our taxi outside the venue. "It's a short walk down to the beach, look!"

"It's time to go back to the hotel," I remind her, checking my phone. "We both have long drives home tomorrow."

"Oh Freya, live a little! Let go," she demands, marching toward the steps down to the beach.

"Mum!" I call out after her, glancing at all the other guests milling around waiting for their taxis. They're watching her with bemused expressions.

"Come on, Freya!" she cries, holding the rail and dancing down the steps, cheering and whooping as she goes. "The sand is calling out to our toes!"

For fuck's sake.

This is the sort of scenario that happens in romantic movies, except instead of a handsome man telling me to lose myself and beckoning me down for a spontaneous moonlit walk on the beach, it's my mother.

I have to follow her, because god knows what will happen if I don't, and I've lost sight of her now. Gritting my teeth, I tensely head over to the steps down to the beach and take off my shoes, my cheeks flushing with embarrassment in the knowledge that we're being watched by others. The steps are lit, but I need to use my phone's light to see the ground properly. When I hit the sand of the beach, I look up to see Mum with her feet in the water, hitching up her dress so that the waves swilling round her ankles don't splash her skirt.

"What are you doing, Mum?" I groan, folding my arms grumpily. "We have to go."

"Do you remember when we went to the beach in Newquay when you were little and you were scared of the jellyfish?"

"I'm not scared of jellyfish."

She chuckles. "Someone at school had told you some kind of silly horror story about them and you were asking us all sorts of questions. Was it true jellyfish could grow the size of sharks? Could their sting make you die? You were clearly terrified, so I said that you didn't have to go in the sea if you were scared of jellyfish. But you just looked up at me, shrugged, and went, 'I'm not scared.' You grabbed Adrian's little hand and the two of you pootled along into the sea. It was so sweet."

"As much as I love going down memory lane, we should—"

"But it's all right to be afraid sometimes, Freya," she says, turning to look at me.

"Afraid of what?"

"Everything." She shrugs. "The future. Change. Life. Jelly-fish."

I raise my eyes to the sky. "Right. Okay, thanks for the pep talk. Can we go back to the hotel now?"

"It just seems like you're holding your breath, waiting for him to come back and make everything okay."

It feels like a punch to my stomach. "Mum."

"It's true, isn't it? You're too frightened to start a new chapter without him, to step into the unknown."

"You don't know anything about me."

"I know that you won't admit when you're scared—"

"I'm not scared!"

"—and that you won't let anyone think you're anything but fine. But you need to face this head-on, let the emotions rage. You need to accept that you're walking a different path to the one you initially chose."

"Mum, stop."

"You have to let him go."

I throw my arms up in the air. "That's it. I'm not doing this. I'm going back."

"Freya," she calls as I turn on my heel, "you have to talk about how you're feeling!"

"Not with you!" I yell back over my shoulder.

"Why not?" she cries, having left the water and now following me across the sand. "Why won't you let yourself need someone?"

That's it. That's the stab. I stop and spin round to face her.

"I did need someone, Mum! I needed you when I was growing up! You weren't there, though, were you?"

Her eyes fall guiltily. "I admit that I should have made more of an effort to show up for things, and, of course, I've never forgiven myself for the time I missed picking you up from your school trip in the Peak District. You completely shut me out after that. If only I'd left on time, and there hadn't been that awful traffic—"

"That's the problem, right there," I seethe, pointing my finger at her, my voice cracking as the emotion threatens to bubble over. "It's not just the excuses, which are tiresome, Mum, really. And yeah, I did resent you for not showing up when you said you would, on multiple occasions. But it's so much more than that! Lots of mums are busy! There are times parents can't attend events! I knew that then and I know that now. But you can still be present for someone, even when you're not there physically. When you couldn't pick me up from the Peak District, you didn't call afterward to check on me, or even try to make amends. Not once. I wasn't a friend who you missed a coffee date with. I was a teenager, humiliated in front of her whole class because her mum stood her up. I could have forgiven you the lateness. But I couldn't forgive you for not worrying about how I might be feeling, for not caring whether I needed you."

"Freya," she whispers, looking distraught. "You were so closed off to me. You never seemed to want me around back then. I convinced myself of that."

"You're my *mum*! I needed you, whether it seemed that way or not, and it wasn't for you to decide that I didn't!"

Suddenly, I feel completely overwhelmed. I don't know if it's because it's been a long day, or a long week, or a long summer, but something finally snaps. I can't hold it back, as much as I try. I burst into uncontrollable, loud, heaving sobs, right there on the beach.

And, of all people, the person who wraps their arms around me and tells me it's going to be okay is the least expected of all.

My mum.

CHAPTER TWENTY-FOUR

The way I see it, life is full of chapters."

I groan into my knees, hugging them closer to me. "Mum, please no kooky analogies."

"Matthew has been there for several chapters of your book," she continues unfazed, completely ignoring me. "Now, he's written himself off the page. Which means you have some options. You can wait to see if he pops up later, letting the paragraphs waffle on with nothing much happening until he does. Or, you can embark into the next scene, ready to greet new characters that enter, experience a change of scenery."

I shake my head, listening to the calming sound of the waves. We're sitting at the bottom of the beach steps, our feet buried in the sand. I've stopped crying after what felt like forever, and gratefully took the tissues Mum handed me from her bag. I filled her in on everything. All the gory details of the breakup. I could have had a breakdown at any point this year in front of a number of much better suited people. Literally *anyone* would have been better.

Now I have to listen to my mum yabbering away about books and chapters.

"I'm not waiting around for Matthew, Mum," I say, but I'm not sure I'm convincing anyone, least of all myself. "I just haven't 'closed the chapter' or however you put it. We haven't talked it out yet."

She raises her eyebrows. "Do you want to talk it out?"

"Yes, and so does he. Or at least, he said he wanted to in that drunken phone call and then when I tried to arrange it, he never messaged me back. Maybe he's confused, too. Which is why we need to see each other. But when the time comes, I have no idea what he's going to say, and that's terrifying."

"Why aren't you asking yourself what you want to say? What do you want, Freya?"

"I honestly don't know. If he doesn't want to see me, then maybe he doesn't care. Maybe he never did. And that frightens me, because how is it possible that I've been with him all those years and was blind to it?" I sigh heavily. "I feel so lost."

"Matthew is acting cruelly, Freya. It's cruel what he's doing. It's selfish and unforgivable. You mustn't let him make you feel powerless."

"Well, he kind of stripped any power I had when he dumped me in a broom cupboard the day before our wedding."

"He didn't take anything from you that day. He gave you something."

I snort. "You're going to have to explain that one."

"He was giving you both a chance at true happiness."

"I was happy."

"Yes, but if he wasn't, then yours wouldn't have lasted long, darling. Matthew knew how much hurt and pain he'd cause you that day, someone who never did anything but love him, and he knew how much hurt he was causing himself. All the people he'd be letting down; the things people would say about him." She lets out a long sigh. "But he had to do it anyway, because it was the right thing to do. It could have been much worse if he hadn't."

I watch her closely. "You think I should be grateful to him?"

"I think, from what you've told me, he's forgotten himself this summer," she answers, peering out into the distance. "He's putting on a good show, but underneath he's just a frightened little boy, cowering from the consequences of his actions. If he can't face you, Freya, it's not because he doesn't care. It's because he's afraid."

"You really think so?"

"I know so. I know how it feels to be faced with the decision he had to make that day."

We fall into silence, looking out across the beach.

"I keep thinking about signs I missed," I admit eventually, biting my lip. "I analyze memories, wondering if I made it all up in my head that we were happy together."

She shakes her head. "You can't make that sort of thing up. I don't think that just because things didn't work out in the end, all of that time together was wrong somehow or unhappy or wasted. Things change sometimes, that's all."

I smile to myself. "It's funny. I told someone that recently. This guy I met, Jamie—"

"Yes, you've mentioned Jamie."

"Have I?"

She nods.

"Oh." I look back out at the sea in confusion. "Anyway, he was telling me about his sister and how he's worried that she's going to waste her twenties in a relationship that may not work out. It made me think about whether I'd wasted my twenties."

"Do you think you did?"

"I'm not sure. Matthew's thrown my life into chaos right at a time when everyone else around me seems to be finding their way and settling down. It seems so unfair. The idea of starting all over again. Maybe that's why . . ." I pause, feeling my eyes well with tears again. I swallow the lump in my throat. "Maybe that's why I'm still holding on to the hope that he'll come back and we can go back to the way things were."

"You can't ever go back," she tells me softly. "Even if you find a way to work things out together, it will be different. Not that that's a bad thing or a good thing. It just is what it is. Neither of you can change what's happened."

I sigh. "I honestly can't work out if I love or hate him."

"Probably a bit of both."

"I've had moments this summer where I've been genuinely happy. But then I always come back to Matthew somehow. I don't know what that means. It's like my brain won't let me move on. Or maybe it's telling me I'm not supposed to move on and I should hold out. I don't know."

"When someone's meant something to you, no matter how it ends, you can't simply erase them. They always leave something behind that becomes part of who you are."

"So, what do I do?"

She chuckles. "Oh, I have no idea. Nobody does. It's all very messy."

I hesitate. "Did you ever regret leaving Dad?"

She doesn't look shocked, but she takes her time in answering. "No, it was the right decision. But I regret how frightened I was of facing you and Adrian. I was so ashamed and I let that shame stop me from being decent. The truth is, I knew your father and I weren't quite right the day I married him. Don't get me wrong, I was so fond of him and I was pregnant with you, so I took the path that I was told was the sensible one at the time. But even though that's just what you did then, it wasn't the honest choice. And I knew that all along. Matthew was a coward for far too long, but if he had to face the truth, at least it was before the marriage. At least he didn't say those vows and break them, like I did."

I look down at the sand, burying my toes further into it.

"When Matthew called the wedding off, my heart"—she places a hand on her chest—"it ached for what you were going through. I knew you'd battle on, because I'd seen it before. I knew that you'd be relying on yourself to get through the breakup. And that's when I realized, more than ever, that I had failed you. Because the one person in life that you should have had at your side no matter what, the person you crumble in front of, it should have been me."

I let her words sink in, unsure how to answer them. She's right. It should have been her. After all these years, she's officially taken responsibility for her actions.

Maybe it hasn't been plain sailing for her, like I always assumed it was. Maybe she's been fighting demons, too, all along.

Maybe it's time to stop looking back.

"You're here now, Mum," I say gently, lifting my toes and letting the bulk of sand slip off them.

She sniffs, a tear falling down her cheek, and she reaches out to take my hand and squeeze it. "Thanks for letting me be."

The sound of the waves rolling in has been a soothing backdrop to this surprise heart-to-heart, but I suddenly wonder how much time has passed.

"We should go back to the hotel," I say.

"Hang on, you haven't put your feet in the water yet."

"So?"

"So, you should! You can't have a midnight walk on the beach without getting your feet wet. It's an unwritten rule!"

"Why? Then the sand will stick to my feet and it will be grainy when I put my shoes on."

She rolls her eyes. "Honestly, you are so like your father."

"Clever?"

"Sensible. No bad thing, of course, but that's why we need each other."

"You and me?"

"I mean, people who are opposites," she explains. "It would be a very boring world if we were all the same."

"Matthew used that as the reason for our breakup," I say,

getting to my feet. "We were too different, apparently. I was too 'together.' He was too 'emotional.'"

"Yes, well, I've done that plenty of times. Tried to explain away something that can't really be explained." She inhales deeply. "Are you ready to run into the sea?"

"I'm not running into the sea."

"Of course, you are, darling. I can tell that your toes are raring to go."

"My toes are happy where they are."

"It's very cold so prepare yourself."

"Mum," I groan as she grabs my hand, linking her fingers through hers. "Do I have to?"

"Yes, you do." She gives me a knowing smile. "I promise I'll protect you from any jellyfish."

"I'm not scared of jellyfish."

"Course not, darling." She clears her throat. "Ready?"

"No," I huff.

"*Let's go!*"

She darts forward, almost pulling my arm out of the socket as she runs down to the sea, and I have no choice but to reluctantly run with her, using my free hand to hold up my dress. She barely slows down as we reach the wet sand, running full pelt into the freezing cold water. I scream with the shock of my feet and legs hitting the icy water as Mum yelps alongside me.

"Isn't this refreshing, darling?!" she cries out next to me.

"No, this is horrible! I can't see if there's any jellyfish about!" I respond, shaking my hand free of hers and running out as quickly as possible to the safety of dry land, my calves now covered in goose bumps.

She comes running out after me, laughing her head off, and as the shock of the cold sea wears off, I start laughing, too. I realize then that I can't remember the last time Mum and I laughed together.

We still have a lot to process; there's so much to talk about and work through. But moving forward, I would like her to be a part of my life. So that's a good start.

Who would have thought that my broken heart would bring us back together?

CHAPTER TWENTY-FIVE

I t's like a scene from a movie.

Ruby, Cali, Simone, and I are having dinner in a restaurant in Soho, having decided to make the effort to come in to central London for once, something that we used to do all the time, but now is a rare occurrence.

"Everyone is dressed very trendily in here," Cali remarks, glancing around.

"Hello, that's because it's a trendy place," Ruby informs her proudly, having chosen the restaurant on Leo's recommendation. "You have to queue instead of booking a table, we're sitting on an uncomfortable bench, and they've served our wine in water glasses. Those are three signs right there that this place is all the rage."

"I want to eat everything on this menu," Simone says, glancing down the list. "I know already that I'm going to panic when they come to take my order."

"I would say we could order a few plates and share, but I know how you feel about that," I say, giving her a knowing smile.

"And don't you forget it," Simone replies. "If you split a meal with someone, you always have to hand it over, just when things are getting good. Like, I'm just getting into this burger and now I have to give you half and take half a fish or whatever. It doesn't make any sense."

"I tried to suggest that Dominic and I go for tapas the other day and he was having none of it," Cali tells us, rolling her eyes. "Apparently he never feels full after tapas, because lots of mini bites don't make up one big meal. I tried to inform him that that was ridiculous, but there was no arguing with him."

"Okay, strange question, but does it feel weird going back to work after the wedding and honeymoon?" Simone asks her curiously. "There's such a long buildup for this big day and then you have two weeks or whatever off from life and then—"

"It's shit," Cali confirms bluntly, making us laugh. "I don't know why we don't all live in Bali."

"It's a good question," I agree.

"Our surfing teacher was from London," she says with a sigh. "He'd had an epiphany one day on the tube."

"What kind of epiphany?" Simone asks, intrigued.

"He realized that he'd walked all the way to the station and got on the train without looking up from his phone. He hadn't noticed a thing around him. That's when it struck him that he was living in a haze. He quit his job and moved to Bali."

"Bloody hell." Ruby blinks at her. "Why haven't I had an epiphany? Why am I stuck in this city with a guy who, yesterday, got in a heated debate with me about jacket potatoes? I mean, our discussion lasted half an hour and I genuinely had to leave the room he was pissing me off so much."

Cali frowns. "What was the debate?"

"How the skin should be. Obviously crunchy. Leo—and I swear I feel repulsed at having to say this out loud—thinks it's better soft."

"What the fuck." Simone shakes her head solemnly. "You need to sort him out, Ruby."

"I know, I know."

The waiter appears at our table to take our orders and, after an entertainingly frantic and last-minute decision from Simone that involves her closing her eyes and just stabbing at something on the list, he takes our menus away.

"How's the gardening going, Freya?" Cali asks with a knowing smile.

"Great, actually. In fact, I went to B&Q the other day to get some plants to finish the little garden. I want to get it done before I move out."

Ruby looks stunned. "You're moving out?"

"Yep, I've spoken to the landlord and he's happy for me to give him two months' notice. He really loves what I've done to the outside space. He said I'd brought it to life! Anyway, I've booked viewings for some flats, so hopefully I'll find somewhere to buy."

"Hang on," Simone says, looking at me wide-eyed. "You're buying?"

"I always wanted to buy after the wedding, and it's been a few months since then, so I think it's about time, don't you?" I grin. "Obviously I didn't plan on buying on my own, but that's okay. It will have to be somewhere very small and probably a lot further out than where I am now, but I've got savings. I want my own little place."

"I think that's brilliant, Freya," Ruby says firmly. "About bloody time."

"This is great," Simone agrees, beaming at me. "New place, new start."

"It's a big step," Cali adds. "Just what you need."

"Truth is—and I don't mind admitting this to you three—I've been holding out hope for things to magically go back to the way they were," I tell them, although I'm certain they already knew this whole time. "But that won't happen, no matter what happens with Matthew. Which is why I finally sold my wedding dress."

Ruby's jaw drops. "You sold your wedding dress? When?"

"A few days ago. I put it up on a website and it went pretty quickly. It was at Dad's, so he took a few pictures of it for me—a process, by the way, which was long and taxing, but he got there eventually. Anyway, this lovely girl messaged me about it, went to try it on at Dad's and it fit her perfectly. I made quite a bit of my money back on it because it hadn't been worn."

"That's . . ." Cali searches for the word.

"Sad, but the right thing to do," I finish for her. "I felt a bit down, because I really did love that dress and it meant something to me. But this way, it gets to actually be worn by someone on their wedding day, and that does make me happy. Besides, I can't just stare at it on a hanger forever. It's a good thing it's gone to a deserving home."

"You're right," Ruby nods, smiling at me. "I'm proud of you."

"We all are," Cali adds.

"Thanks."

"So, let me get this straight," Simone begins, "you've sold your wedding dress and you're moving out of yours and Matthew's flat—"

"And I've booked myself on to some yoga classes," I add. "Time to give clearing my mind another shot. I think I'll be better at it this time round."

"Fucking hell." Simone exhales. "Is this all down to a chat with your mum? Because I could really do with getting my shit together and taking control of my life, so if she's got any free time . . ."

I laugh as our food arrives, leaning back and waiting until our plates have all been set down before continuing the conversation.

"Mum did say a few things that hit home, but it's all been a long time coming," I admit, admiring how good all the dishes look.

"Hang on, I've been meaning to ask you, did you ever meet up with Matthew after Dublin?" Cali asks, frowning.

I take a deep breath. "No, I didn't. He didn't reply to my messages or pick up my calls."

"Sorry." Simone puts down her fork angrily, having not even had the chance to try her beef yet. "Let me get this straight. He calls you several times when he knows you're in Dublin at a wedding, he tells you he misses you and wants to meet up to talk it through, and then . . . nothing?"

"Right." I nod, paying great attention to cutting up a tomato.

"I thought he promised to message you," Cali says, absolutely stunned.

"Yes, he did. But then, he also promised to marry me, so I have a feeling he might not be a man of his word."

"I'm sorry," Simone says again, more forcefully this time, her temper beginning to show itself. "He called you, after *everything* he's done, and then when you called back, he ignored you?"

I nod, chewing my mouthful. "I never should have picked up."

"He never should have called you!" Simone rages. "He never should have said those things! This is *outrageous*!"

"I know, right?" Ruby shakes her head.

"He shouldn't get away with this," Cali says firmly, her forehead furrowed.

"He won't. Not if I have anything to do with it," Simone seethes.

"Oh my god, *yes*, I love it when Simone's rage rears its head!" Ruby declares, a smile breaking across her face. "Remember when you laid into that guy for kissing someone else when he was meant to be seeing Cali?"

"Alfie!" Cali says, bursting into giggles. "I missed it because I was crying in the loo, but I remember the look on his face when I emerged and he was genuinely terrified."

"Yeah, well, I bet he thought twice before lying again," Simone huffs. "It's simple, if he wanted to kiss someone else, then he shouldn't have made things exclusive with Cali. Honestly, I have no time for cowards."

"Amen," Ruby mutters under her breath.

"Freya," Simone says, turning her attention back to me, "he never deserved you. Never in a million years."

"I just can't believe this is how he's acted," Cali comments, looking disappointed. "I'm so sorry, Freya."

"Don't be, I'm fine," I tell them with a wave of my hand. "I'm absolutely f—"

Matthew. He's there.

"What?" Simone asks, her eyebrows knitted together. "You look like you've seen a ghost."

"Oh, fuck it," Ruby whispers, having followed my eyeline. "Don't turn round, you two. Honestly, don't."

"Okay," Cali says slowly, putting down her glass. "Why? Who is it?"

"Matthew," I croak quietly, my whole body tensing as I watch him being shown to his table just a few tables from ours. "And he's with someone."

"Oh my god," Simone utters under her breath, her eyes narrowing. "A woman?"

Ruby nods slowly.

"What do I do?" I squeak, slinking down and ducking my head, trying to hide behind Ruby.

"Don't panic," Cali says calmly.

"Too late," I hiss, leaning back as Ruby leans back and then leaning forward again to mirror her. "Ruby, stay still! I'm using you as a fort."

"Got it," she says, freezing like a statue.

"Can I turn round now?" Simone asks desperately.

"Yes, but be subtle," Ruby tells her, jerking her head in the direction of Matthew's table.

Simone and Cali both casually look over their shoulder and then swiftly return their gaze to us, thankfully without him noticing.

"Just as I thought, he looks like a twat," Simone declares.

"He looks no different to when he and I were together," I say, glancing over again for confirmation.

"No, I'm with Simone on this one." Ruby takes a sip of her drink, staring over at him. "If I saw him for the first time now, I would think to myself: 'Twat.'"

"Is that the girl he's been dating, the one all over Instagram?" I ask, my voice wobbling slightly and betraying my feelings. "I never saw the pictures Akin was talking about. Ruby, did you see them? Cali, you might know through Dominic?"

"Uh . . . that's a different one," Ruby says carefully, her forehead creased in worry.

"Right." I swallow the lump in my throat as he throws his head back and laughs at something his companion says. "Wow. Was his laugh always that loud?"

"Ugh, he is such an attention-seeker," Simone claims, wrinkling her nose.

"I don't remember him ever laughing like that at my jokes," I say wistfully.

"Probably because he didn't get them because he's a twerp," Ruby points out.

"What do you want to do, Freya?" Cali asks. "Do you want to leave?"

"No. I was here first."

Simone nods. "That's right."

"But I'm also not that hungry anymore." I bury my face in my hands, before looking up and gesturing to their plates. "Please, keep eating, don't let it go cold because of this."

"We'll eat fast, in case you want to get out of here," Cali says, picking up her cutlery.

"Do not give yourselves indigestion because of Matthew," I say sternly. "He's already done enough."

"Please can we have a look at the wine menu?" we hear him

ask over the din of the restaurant. "Is it possible to taste the wines before choosing a bottle?"

"What a wanker," Simone says in absolute disgust. "Who does he think he is?"

"I wish I could throw my wine right in his face," Ruby snarls, watching him. "And say, 'There's your wine for you.'" She hesitates. "I feel that with more time I might be able to come up with a better line than that."

"Yes, I think so, too, but I love where your brain is going," Simone encourages.

"What if he looks over here? What if he sees me?" I ask in a panic. "I'm not wearing any perfume today! I forgot to put it on when I left the house!"

"He's not going to smell you from over there, Freya," Simone assures me. "Even though he may think he has a nose for wine."

Ruby smiles at Simone in approval. "Good one."

"You look stunning, Freya," Cali says brightly, bringing them back to the matter at hand. "Great outfit today and your makeup is perfect as always."

"Remember that time I bumped into my ex in that bird sanctuary?" Ruby recalls, her eyes widening. "And I'd just cried because of that owl presentation, so my makeup was all over the place?"

"Oh my god, yes!" Cali exclaims. "That owl story was really moving. I'm so glad her wing healed and they were able to reintroduce her to the woodland."

"Why were we in a bird sanctuary again?" Simone asks, frowning.

"We were in Suffolk for someone's birthday," I inform them, racking my memory. "It was a group of us from uni and we stayed in that cottage."

"That was it!" Ruby nods. "And he was there with his niece

and his parents, who lived in Suffolk. What are the bloody chances?"

"Didn't his niece pinch you?" Simone asks thoughtfully, as I reach for my wine.

"Yes," Ruby confirms. "She tried to pinch my vagina."

I burst out laughing and Cali spits her wine out everywhere, choking as it goes down the wrong way. Simone thumps her on the back.

"Why did she try to pinch your vagina?" Cali asks through splutters.

"She was very little and I think she was going through a pinching phase. It just so happened that her reach was toward my crotch area," Ruby explains matter-of-factly as the rest of us cackle with laughter. "The moral of the story is, don't wear mascara when visiting a bird sanctuary."

"Hi."

All of us snap our heads up at the sound of Matthew's voice. He's standing next to the table, his hands in his pockets, his eyebrows raised, like a teacher who's just caught a group of naughty students chatting during detention.

In that split second, Simone's expression has switched to rage, Ruby is glaring at him stony-faced, and Cali is looking at me in concern. My breath catches as I force myself to look him in the eye.

"Hi, Matthew," I manage to say.

"I thought I'd do the mature thing and come over," he informs us, glancing at Simone and Ruby nervously. "I saw you when I came in."

I nod, not sure what to say to that.

"Are you enjoying your meal?" he asks, attempting joviality.

"We were," Ruby says curtly.

He walked into that one.

"Okay. I see." He purses his lips. "I was just trying to be civil. Guess I'll leave you to it."

"Probably best, Matthew," Simone seethes.

"We'll pretend we don't know each other then," he says to me, holding up his hands. "Very mature. Have a good night."

He turns round and saunters back to his table, where his date is none the wiser, scrolling through her phone. The four of us remain silent for a while as we let what just happened sink in.

"Such an arsehole," Simone comments eventually. "Are you all right, Freya?"

"Yeah. Course," I say, my heart thudding against my chest. "But I think I'd like to not be here anymore."

"Absolutely, let's go," Cali says, catching the eye of a passing waiter and gesturing for the bill.

"I'm so sorry to ruin your night," I say quietly.

"You didn't ruin anything, we're finished anyway," Ruby assures me.

I can feel their eyes on me as our bill comes and Simone insists on paying for the whole thing quickly, saying we can just transfer her our shares later. We slide out from our benches and I silently follow them out of the restaurant, too mortified to risk looking over at Matthew, wondering if he's filling his date in on what just happened, painting me out to be the bitter, rude, obnoxious ex that just can't seem to move on. We step into the evening air and I take a deep breath in, the girls huddling round me.

"How dare he?" Ruby begins, shaking her head. "Honestly, I know you would hate me if I did this, Freya, but he really deserves to be taken down a peg or two."

"He thinks he's got the moral high ground?" Simone hisses furiously. "He was trying to be civil. You know what's civil? Apologizing for drunkenly phoning your ex over and over until they pick up."

"And what was that 'mature' comment, too?" Cali says. "Freya has handled this more maturely than anyone in the world. He's an idiot, he shouldn't have come over."

"The audacity," Ruby agrees.

"Let's get home," Cali says, rubbing my arm. "You ready to go, Freya?"

I don't know if it's because the surprise of the encounter is beginning to ebb away or because they're going over what he said again, but my shock is starting to change into something else.

Anger.

"Hang on," I say, my voice calm and steady. "Did he just imply that I'm the one pretending we don't know each other?"

Simone nods.

"He just referred to me, to the four of us, as 'very mature,' sarcastically," I say slowly.

"Yeah." Ruby looks at me curiously. "Are you okay, Freya? You look . . ."

"Enlightened," I finish for her, my eyes narrowing at the door of the restaurant.

Without saying anything else, I storm right back in there, pushing open the door and staring at him. He glances up and sees me.

"Do you need a table?" a waiter asks cheerily.

"No, thank you," I say, my eyes locked on Matthew. "This won't take long."

As I march over to his table, I hear the girls pile into the restaurant after me and then hurry to keep up, flanking me as I stop, ready for battle.

"Freya," Matthew begins nervously. "What are—"

"How dare you accuse me of acting as though I don't know you?" I say, my cheeks flushing hot with the rage I feel right now toward this man.

"Freya—"

"How dare you?" I repeat, louder now, noticing that other

tables around have stopped their conversations and are watching with interest. I don't care, though. I'm too angry to care. "I'm not sure if you remember, Matthew, but *you* broke up with me the *day* before our wedding. And then you told me not to contact you, because we needed time and space. Isn't that right?"

His eyes dart nervously around the restaurant as he grapples with everyone watching. His date looks horrified at my statement. He obviously hasn't got to the part about how we broke up, then.

"Then, *you* called *me* when I was having a lovely time in Dublin and you wouldn't stop calling until I picked up!" I remind him. "You told me that you missed me! That you wanted to talk things through! That you didn't like the idea of not being in *my* life!"

"F-Freya—"

"And *then* when I called and messaged you the next day to ask when we should schedule this chat you so desperately needed, *you never replied.*"

There's a satisfying gasp that ripples through the restaurant. Matthew is sweating, the beads forming on his forehead, his upper lip growing noticeably moist.

"You made me feel like a *fool!*"

I'm not sure why I'm speaking like I'm in a Shakespeare play, but I'm going with it.

"You acted like nothing had happened! Even though, *you* were the one who called *me!*" I cry, pointing my finger at him accusingly. "Now here I am, having a lovely meal in a lovely restaurant with my friends and you have the *audacity*—" Stealing your word, Ruby, thank you. "—to come sauntering over to our table while you're here on a date to tell me that I'm the immature one when I don't gush over you! That you are just trying to be *civil!*"

"Look," he squeaks, "I know—"

"No, Matthew. You don't know," I hiss at him. "You don't know anything."

I honestly am not sure what comes over me at this point. I've never been a dramatic person. As my mother kindly pointed out recently, I quite literally would rather be a stone than entertain the masses with my theatrics. But I don't feel like me right now. Like I explained to Jamie in the bar that time, moments like this are an out-of-body experience that I'll look back on and think, *Was that really me that happened to? Was it me who did that thing?*

I reach out and pick up his glass of wine.

"You wanted to taste the wine, didn't you?" I announce, the whole restaurant on tenterhooks. "Here you go. Have a taste."

And then I throw the wine right into his face.

Another, more enthusiastic wave of gasps this time, and I even hear someone right at the other side of the room go, "Yes, girl!"

Matthew looks completely shell-shocked, the red wine dripping down his face, all over his white shirt. Speechless and spluttering, he moves his fingers around the tabletop, feeling for his napkin to dab his eyes.

I'm about to turn around and leave, but Ruby steps forward to stand next to me and picks up the wineglass belonging to Matthew's date.

Uh-oh.

"Here's another taste!" she cries, and then pours that wine all over his head.

"What the—" he splutters, pushing his chair back.

Suddenly, Simone grabs a glass of white wine from their neighboring table.

"And another!"

With much greater flair than myself or Ruby, she throws the white wine at him.

Matthew scrambles to his feet and in doing so drops his napkin to the floor. He stands there dripping, his hair plastered across his forehead, his shirt stained pink, the droplets running down his jaw, his expression irate.

Cali steps forward. The restaurant-goers brace themselves excitedly. She swipes up the napkin laid out for Matthew's date.

"Here you go, Matthew," she says curtly, tossing it at him. "Clean yourself up."

That's our cue.

We all somehow know it, like a beautifully rehearsed girl-band stage exit. We each give him one last damning look up and down, and then the four of us turn around to leave the restaurant. Everyone watches us in silence, the waiters standing aside to let us pass without hindrance.

On our way out, I hear someone in the restaurant mutter in disbelief, "What just happened?"

It turns out that just as people can always surprise you, you can also completely unintentionally, and yet rather wonderfully, surprise yourself.

Hi Freya. I've been thinking about what you said last night. I think it would be a good idea if we meet up to talk. When would suit you?

CHAPTER TWENTY-SIX

I told Matthew to come to the flat.

It wasn't a rushed decision; I thought it out before I sent him the text. A public place didn't seem like a good idea for this kind of conversation.

I spent the morning cleaning and making sure everything was perfect. I had already picked my outfit, but that didn't stop me trying on some others just in case. It had to look as though I hadn't put much thought into it, but I also had to feel *very* confident in it, so it wasn't exactly an easy look to land on. It's a hot day, so I'm in a floaty summer dress and sandals, with gold hoop earrings.

The doorbell rings exactly five minutes after I asked him to be here.

Not bad.

"It's showtime," I whisper to my reflection in the mirror, because that's the sort of thing they do in films.

"Hi, Freya," he says nervously, when I open the door.

"Matthew," I reply, before standing aside to let him come into the flat.

Strong start, Freya. Civil, calm, controlled.

He walks into the sitting room, his hands in his pockets, his sunglasses resting on top of his head. He's wearing terrible denim shorts, for which I am utterly grateful. No matter what happens, at least I have that.

"It looks great in here," he remarks, scanning the room before his eyes land on one of my new B&Q purchases. "Cool houseplant."

"Thanks," I say casually, looking at it in admiration. "It's a peace lily. I needed something to fill that space. How is Percy, by the way?"

"Who?"

"Percy. The big Swiss cheese plant that used to be there. You took it when you moved out," I explain when he stares at me blankly.

"Oh right, yeah, the one with the funky leaves." He nods thoughtfully. "Yeah, Mum loves it."

Sorry.

What did he just say?! *Is this some kind of joke?!*

"Oh! You gave Percy to your mum," I comment, trying to keep control of my voice, but struggling to make it less squeaky. "How nice."

"You know how she loves plants."

"Mmm."

I clear my throat. This is not the time to explode. I mean, sure, some people might be very *hurt* and *insulted* by the news that the houseplant they gifted someone and took great care of when said houseplant lived under their roof was given away without a moment's thought. But this isn't the time to get worked up about a houseplant named Percy. I can't let this news throw me.

"Would you like a drink?" I ask, pushing aside my dismay.

"Maybe some water," he replies. "It's warm out there."

"Sure. Won't be a moment."

I leave him to go into the kitchen, taking long, deep breaths as I turn on the cold tap and let it run for a moment. My stomach is filled with butterflies. It's the strangest feeling, standing in our living room together, acting like strangers.

I return with a glass of water for him and one for me, setting them down on the coffee table before taking a seat on the sofa and gesturing for him to sit. He does so, reaching for his water and taking three large gulps, almost downing the whole thing. One of the things I always found irritating about him was how loudly he glugged drinks. It was one of those niggles you forgive your other half for, because you love them and these are the little things that make them who they are.

But that is bloody annoying.

"Feel better?" I ask as he puts the glass down.

"Yes, thank you," he says, before slumping back into the cushions and running a hand through his hair. He takes a deep breath and looks me straight in the eye, his voice softening. "How are you, Freya?"

"I'm okay," I respond confidently. "I really am. How are you?"

"Fine. A little nervous right now." He glances round him. "Feels strange sitting here."

"I can imagine."

He pauses. "That was a dramatic night in Soho, huh."

"It was."

"Can't say I didn't deserve it."

He looks at me and then lets out a sigh, shaking his head. "I'm so sorry, Freya. I'm sorry for a lot of things, but I want to apologize in particular for the way I acted in the restaurant. And for being there . . . with someone. It was a first date and we're not seeing each other again."

I nod slowly. "I appreciate the apology. I'm sorry for her that her date was ruined."

"It was for the best, I'm sure." He pauses, watching me with a pained expression. "I knew it would be difficult coming here, but shit. I feel so awkward."

"You don't need to feel awkward."

"I've been trying to work out what to say to you," he continues.

"How to get across . . . how to make sense of all of it. I do . . . I do miss you, Freya. Of course I miss you. You must hate me."

"I don't hate you. Well, I mean, I go through phases."

He gives a sad smile at that.

"I'm grateful to you for coming over today to talk," I add sincerely. "I needed to do this."

"It's so hard and confusing sitting here with you."

"I know, but we never sat down together and talked things out. You got to have your say when you called the wedding off. But there are things I need to say, too."

"It was too hard. You have no idea how difficult it is to face you after everything I've done. Everything I've put you through. And I know I've been shit with my phone and contacting you, but I was trying . . . I wanted to give us space."

"I can understand that. But there are better ways of doing it than simply ignoring me. It made me feel small. I didn't deserve that, Matthew."

"How could I face you after I'd canceled our wedding the day before? I'm the villain. Everyone was so mad at me. I thought I should just . . . leave it all behind for a bit. Sounds ridiculous, but it made sense in my head. I never wanted to hurt you, Freya, and one of the reasons I needed to stay away . . ." He trails off, looking up at me with wide, glistening eyes. "I do sometimes wonder if I made the right decision."

There it is. A knife to the heart.

"I know that's not fair," he continues hurriedly. "But please know, the reason I wasn't contacting you, the reason I had to be distant and cut you off, was partly because of self-preservation, Freya. And then I called you when you were in Dublin because I snapped and then I had to bring myself away again and I—"

"Matthew," I interrupt, because it's time to step in and take the reins. "You broke up with me after twelve years and then refused to talk to me about it. You'd given me a ring and made a promise. I wasn't sure if you were walking away from the wedding or from me, and whether you even knew the answer to that yourself. You cut me out to protect yourself, then expected me to act calmly and rationally. You expected me to simply accept your decision that affected both of our lives in such an extraordinary way without questioning it or needing anything more from you. I know I'm a 'sturdy' character and everything, but I'm also human."

"Yes, but as I just said, I was trying to do the right thing and—"

"I appreciate that. You break up with someone, you should give each other time and space. But you should also give an opportunity to talk. I had to push for today to happen. I had to go through the humiliation of unreturned calls and messages to get to this point, which you should have offered me when you broke your promise. You have every right to change and act on your feelings, but you don't have a right to minimize mine."

"Freya—"

"Like you, I've been trying to work out what to say to you today," I go on, ignoring him, desperate to get my piece across before I lose my confidence. "And that's actually a really big step, you know, because before I was flapping about, wondering what you were going to say to me. I didn't think about what I had to say. Mum reminded me of that."

He looks stunned. "Your mum? You've been talking to her?"

"It was like a switch in my brain. I realized this whole time, I've been holding on to something, because the idea of closing our chapter . . . it was almost unbearable. We've been through so much together. We know each other better than anyone else. The truth of it is, you're my best friend."

He swallows audibly.

"I mean, you were my best friend. And I was yours. I like to think that's why you waited until the last minute to call off the wedding. It was cowardly what you did. Truly cowardly."

He nods slowly. "I know. I've always said that, Freya, I'll never forgive—"

"But in the end, it was also the right thing to do."

As the words come out of my mouth, I feel the urge to cry. So, I let it happen. I don't try to stop the tears flowing. I let them spill over, falling down my perfectly made-up cheeks, probably leaving murky foundation lines as they go.

Matthew looks utterly thrown by this statement and, as I start to cry, his eyes well up.

"I wish it hadn't been the right thing to do," I continue with a defeated shrug, trying not to let my voice break. "I really wish it hadn't. I wish we'd got married and had a family and grown old together. That's what I wanted. I was in love with you. But you weren't in love with me, so that's that."

"Freya—"

"Please, Matthew, let me finish," I tell him firmly, refusing to relinquish control, despite how painful it is. "When you push aside all the mess of this breakup, forget all the wedding stuff, the only thing that really mattered to me was one question: Why didn't you love me anymore?"

He drops his eyes to the floor. I'm crying quite a lot now, so I reach for the tissues that I'd cleverly placed on the coffee table this morning. I dab my face and carefully wipe under my eyes, hoping that waterproof mascara is pulling through for me. From the lack of black smudges on the tissue, I can confirm that it is.

Thank you, Estée Lauder. Always got my back.

"I've been so preoccupied by what you told me in that broom cupboard; focusing on the reasons you gave as to why we didn't mesh well anymore. I think you've been trying to make sense of it, too. That's why you said I was 'together' and you weren't."

"I didn't articulate myself very well," he admits glumly. "And it was the same in France when I thanked you and when I think back on that, I feel like an idiot. The thing is, Freya, I just never felt needed by you. You had everything in hand. I felt like a spare part in your life. When we were together, I felt that I wasn't bringing anything to the table."

"It wasn't my responsibility to change that, Matthew. That's all on you."

"I know, I know. But that's the thing that I was getting confused about. It sort of dawned on me that maybe, I wasn't ready to bring anything to the table yet. I still feel like I have a lot of growing up to do and working out where I want to be . . . working out who I want to be. But you're already there, and for years, I just let you carry me along with you. You're . . . well, you're just so . . ."

"Together," I finish for him. And I say it proudly.

"Right." He shrugs. "Meanwhile, my head's all over the place. I've hurt you, I've hurt my friends, I've hurt everyone. And I still don't know whether this is right or whether I've been unbelievably stupid."

"Yeah, well, I've pondered those questions quite a bit and I understand now that if you really weren't sure you'd made the right decision, you'd be a mess. We'd be talking. We'd at least be messaging. You'd be back and forth. Your self-preservation, as cruel as it's been—and I mean that, Matthew, you've made a lot of cruel choices—comes from the right place. You know in your heart that you don't want to marry me; maybe you were avoiding me because you just don't want to face up to it and finally close the chapter on us either, because that means . . . that means losing each other. And we were happy a lot, too. That's what's so hard. But sometimes love just doesn't last."

I conclude there, because I need to blow my nose. It's not the most sophisticated way to end a very personal and emotional speech, but there you go.

Matthew exhales. "Wow. I . . . I wasn't expecting . . . I didn't . . ."

He searches for the words, but can't seem to find them, so we sit in silence for a bit, mulling over everything I've said.

"I'm sorry, Freya," he says quietly.

And that confirms it.

He could have argued against what I've said. He might have insisted he'd been in turmoil, that he thought he needed time and space, but now that he'd had it, now that he'd seen what else was out there, he knew he wanted to be with me; he'd been wrong and I was wrong now, he did still love me and he'd made a mistake, and despite all of this and everything that had happened, he wanted to fight for us.

He isn't saying that, though. And that's how I know.

It's over.

Finally.

"I'm so sorry," he repeats, a tear rolling down his cheek.

"I know."

"You didn't deserve this."

"It's not about what I deserve. It's just how you feel. You followed your heart and that's got to be the right thing to do." I give a small shrug. "That's what Disney movies always imply anyway."

He can't help but laugh. "That's true."

"I can't persuade you to love me again and I'm not sure I want you to. We're both different people now."

He brings his eyes up to meet mine. "I'm so sorry about ruining the wedding, Freya. I'm so ashamed."

"Yeah, well, that was particularly brutal. But I think it's best not to dwell on that. Time to look forward."

He reaches for the tissues. I slide them along to him.

"And, to be fair, I did get a bit of revenge with the whole wine-throwing thing," I add, making him laugh.

His face falls slightly. "Everyone hates me. I know that's my fault, but it's hard. Your friends. Dominic's pissed at me because of the situation I've put them in. Ruby and Leo . . . god, you should have seen their faces when I first saw them in France. I really let everyone down. I've been trying to ignore that feeling all summer, try to focus on new things, but it always comes creeping in."

This is the cue I need.

I've said what I needed to say. He's confirmed to me that we're over. He doesn't have anything more to add. I could ask him a load of questions, analyzing every aspect of our relationship, demanding to know what I could have done or said differently, but I don't want to. And I'm not going to sit here comforting him, either.

I stand up to signal he should go. He looks surprised.

"I'm meeting some friends," I lie, checking my phone. "I should get ready."

"Oh. Right. Sure."

He seems torn, as though he's considering protesting, but must think better of it. He pushes himself up off the sofa and we stand facing each other. I suddenly remember something. Something I'd tucked away on the shelf of the coffee table, ready to return. I bend down and pull out the engagement ring box.

"Here," I say, holding it out to him. "You should have this back."

He stares at it, crestfallen. "You . . . you should keep it."

"No, that's okay," I tell him firmly. "It doesn't belong to me anymore."

He reaches up slowly to take it, before sliding it into the pocket of his hideous denim shorts.

He waits a moment and then holds his arms out.

I step toward him and he wraps them around me. I close my eyes as I rest my head against his chest. I breathe in his smell. He kisses the top of my head. We stay like that for a few seconds too long. It's comfortable and safe and familiar, and we both know it's the last one.

"You're amazing, Freya," he says, his voice muffled in my hair.

I force myself to pull away, stepping back. His arms drop to his sides. He clears his throat.

"Thanks for having me over," he says. "And thanks for not kicking me in the balls."

"You're not out of the house yet. Still time."

Even though he knows I'm joking, a flash of panic crosses his face.

We wander out of the living room and linger awkwardly and silently in the hall, neither of us knowing quite how to wrap this up. We've already done the hug. I reach around him and open the door.

"Maybe I'll . . . see you around," he remarks.

I give him a small smile. "Goodbye, Matthew."

He nods slowly, before he steps out into the sunshine and walks away. As I shut the front door, I catch a glimpse of him looking back over his shoulder. The door closes and he's gone.

That's it.

I stand in the hall, leaning back against the wall. A sad end to our love story. Nothing anyone can do. No grand gestures, no words that can change the tide. It just didn't work out.

I'd better go water my peace lily.

CHAPTER TWENTY-SEVEN

The trapeze is not easy to master.

Look, I'm all for trying out new things and I appreciate the recommendation from Phil, but if I hate something straightaway, I'm not going to hang around. I lasted precisely eight minutes in the trapeze class, before I thought to myself *like hell I'm doing this* and pretended I needed the loo, walking out to go get a lovely chilled glass of rosé in a bar nearby in this glorious sunshine.

I give myself a little toast—"to trying new things"—and hold up my glass to no one, before taking a very satisfactory sip.

It's actually quite nice to have some time to myself.

Yes, I'm single and live alone, but things have been hectic recently. I never come to East London and this bar is the perfect place to people-watch on a sunny Thursday evening. I was annoyed at first when I realized how far it was to the trapeze class that Phil suggested, but I've discovered there's a direct train from Dalston to Forest Hill and it only takes half an hour. There are families out walking, groups of laughing mates headed for a night out, cyclists zipping down a path nearby, pissing everyone else off. This is London at its best and I'm going to take a moment to enjoy it.

It's been a few weeks since my official goodbye to Matthew and I've been sure to keep myself super busy. There's been a lot to do, what with work, flat searching, and organizing last-minute details for Ruby's hen do, which is this weekend. I haven't spoken to Matthew at all. I was surprised when he sent an unprompted text the day after we met up, emphasizing how sorry he was, that all he wanted was for me to get the happiness I deserve, and that he'd always love me.

I read it a few times and then I deleted it. Along with his number.

I can't get over how hard the trapeze is. I guess it doesn't look like a walk in the park, to be fair. You know from a glance that it's going to need balance, a good core, and a lot of upper-body strength, but *still*. I could barely get myself up on that thing, let alone twirl about with it. I'll just sit here, drinking my rosé, marveling at it instead.

My phone starts going and I grapple to get my headphones in as I answer a video call from Adrian, with Dad in on it as well.

"Where are you?" Dad immediately questions, peering at the screen.

"Who are you talking to, me or Adrian?"

"You, Freya," he clears up.

"I'm at a trapeze class."

"You look like you're at a bar."

"Well, now I am. But I was at a trapeze class."

"That's cool," Adrian declares, looking impressed. "How was it?"

"It turns out, I'm a natural."

Adrian raises his eyebrows. "You left the class early to go to the bar, didn't you?"

"The most important thing is that I tried the class," I say haughtily. "Where are you, Adrian? You look smart in your suit."

"I'm at work. Just on my lunch break. Looks like a nice sunny day in London."

"It's roasting."

"You need to wear a hat, Freya," Dad says, gesturing to the sun hat he's currently sporting.

"Thanks, Dad, but I think I'm all right in the evening sun," I chuckle.

"How are you, Adrian? All well?" Dad asks curiously.

"I'm good. The reason I'm calling you both is because I got my holiday approved for Christmas, so I can fly home!"

"*Yes!*" I cry, holding up my glass as I toast to the screen. "That's great news!"

"Excellent," Dad agrees, beaming at the phone. "I'm delighted."

"And . . . well . . ." Adrian sighs, before taking a deep breath. "I thought I'd ask Nolan if he wanted to join me for the trip. If that's okay with you."

"We would love to meet him," Dad says cheerily. "Tell him he must come!"

"I'm not going to force him, Dad." Adrian smiles, rolling his eyes. "But he mentioned the other day he's never been to England and would love to go, so I thought I'd take that as a hint. Things are going well with him, too. I really like him. He might think it's too early to fly all the way over to meet the family, and, of course, he might want to spend Christmas with his family but I thought—"

"Ask him," Dad interrupts. "If you don't ask, you won't know."

"Agreed," I say, grinning into the phone. "I'm so happy things are going well with him, Adrian. I can't wait to meet him! We'll make sure he feels right at home."

"Yes, he can admire my pond!" Dad exclaims. "It's coming along very nicely. Although I suppose it won't look so impressive in the winter. Will you take him to meet your mother, too?"

"I don't know. I think so." Adrian hesitates. "What do you think, Freya?"

"I think that's a good idea. Maybe . . . maybe we can spend

a few days with her over the Christmas break." They both look impressed and I roll my eyes. "Okay, don't make a big deal of this. We're taking things slow."

"Is Mum aware you're taking things slow?" Adrian asks, chuckling.

"Of course not. She's already phoned me three times this week just to 'check in.' And on one of those times, she insisted on reciting a poem about the unbroken bonds of family."

"Had she written it?"

"No."

"Thank God."

"I think it's lovely that she's making the effort," Dad interrupts, looking chuffed. "We're moving forward as a family and that's important."

"How are things going for you on the dating front, Freya?" Adrian asks boldly.

"They're not going," I inform them. "I don't think I'm ready."

"I don't think you'll know until you try," Adrian says with a shrug. "Maybe give it a go and if you realize it doesn't feel right, you're not ready. But I, for one, think you deserve some fun."

Dad nods, adjusting his sun hat. "You might meet someone very interesting, you never know."

"I guess. It's daunting, though."

"That's why I think you need to just get out there," Adrian insists. "If you keep putting it off, it will just get scarier."

"You may have a point there, Adrian," Dad says, shifting nervously. "It's not as scary as I thought."

"Hang on a second," I begin carefully. "Dad, are you implying that you're . . . dating?"

"Well, if you must know, I've been on a date this week."

"*What?*" I shriek, causing others in the bar to look over. "Why didn't you tell us?"

"Because I knew you'd make a big fuss," he says gruffly, adjusting his hat. "I didn't want any nonsense from you two shrouding my brain and making me nervous."

"Who is it? What's she like? Did it go well?" Adrian asks impatiently. "I can't believe you haven't said a word about this! It's great, Dad!"

"All right, don't go getting overexcited," he instructs, chuckling. "She's called Harriet and we met on the Life Evergreen forum."

"The what?"

"It's a website with tips and advice for gardening enthusiasts. One of my neighbors suggested I use it for help with the pond and so I started putting questions on the forum and these brilliant answers kept being posted by the same person: Harriet. She's extremely knowledgeable and we ended up chatting so much on this forum, we thought it worth seeing if a phone call might be better. Well, that went really well and before you know it, we'd chatted for over an hour! We discovered we didn't live too far and, inspired by Freya, I took the leap and invited her over to check out my pond and meet my newts."

"Wait." I hold up my hand to the screen. "What do you mean inspired by me?"

"I've long known that both of my children are much braver than me. Look at you, Adrian, moving to a brand-new city, working hard at your career, finding love. And Freya, we all know that you can handle almost everything—"

"Not jellyfish." Adrian smirks.

"Shut up, Adrian," I huff.

"When you told me about your conversation with Matthew," Dad continues, "I was reminded that it's not always easy to make the right decision for ourselves. It's downright terrifying. But I realized that I owed myself a chance, and so I worked up the courage and asked her if she wanted to see the pond in person. She came over a couple of days ago and it was a really nice evening.

We sat in the garden and she met Horatio Nelson and Francis Drake."

"You're talking about the newts, right?"

"No, Adrian, he's talking about the long-dead admirals."

"We're going on another date this weekend," Dad says, talking over us. "I'm taking her to the Crown. And before you say anything, Freya, I told her about the food there and she's now determined to work out if it really is microwave meals in disguise."

"She sounds great, Dad. I'm really happy for you," I say, beaming at him.

"Me too. Hey, maybe we can meet her at Christmas," Adrian suggests.

"Slow down!" Dad starts. "We've only been on one date. Don't want to scare her off too soon with talk of meeting the family."

"Yeah, Adrian," I say, shaking my head at him. "Be cool."

"And on that note, I have to go back to work," Adrian says, laughing. "Talk soon. Way to go with Harriet, Dad, and Freya, time to get back on that horse. You had a bad fall; the only way to get over it is to haul yourself back up. Otherwise the fear takes hold."

I raise my eyebrows. "I'll work on it."

We say our goodbyes, wave at the screen, and hang up. Swilling my chilled wine round the glass, I sit back, Adrian's advice whirring round my head.

It's not like I haven't thought about dating recently. Obviously, it's crossed my mind now that I'm officially single. I do spend a lot of time watching videos on YouTube of corgis shaking their fluffy butts to upbeat music. It's probably time to get out there and attempt scintillating conversation with other humans.

There's quite a few good-looking men at this bar, actually. East London is full of cool, trendily dressed guys, so maybe I should . . .

Wait a second. I think . . . I think Jamie might work somewhere around here. I mean, he has to, everyone else in this bar looks just like him! Well, sort of. They don't have his je ne sais quoi, but I would happily bet that some of these people work at independent breweries and consider my job supremely inferior even though I could kick their butts at a tasting any day of the week.

Jamie.

I get that weird tingling feeling again and suddenly feel nervous. I haven't even seen him yet, but just thinking about him makes my stomach knot. Every now and then I'll think of him and have this same reaction. I've thought about messaging him, but I always talk myself out of it. Would that be weird? Would he even want to see me?

I want to see him.

I smile as I think it. I want to see Jamie. And do you know what? It's so nice to feel excited about someone. About a guy. After feeling so confused and vulnerable for the last few months, it feels good to get butterflies.

We had a spark. And that doesn't happen often. At least, according to all the rom-coms I've been watching lately it doesn't. And if I've learned anything from Julia Roberts and Cameron Diaz these past few weeks, it's that you can't let this sort of thing slip through your fingers, even if you've been through a crazy summer of trying to get over your ex when you haven't really been trying at all.

I quickly get Maps up on my phone and google the Dancing Bear brewery. It's a five-minute walk from where I am *right this moment.* It's fate. I have to go see if he's there. There's a chance he might not be. He might have already gone home for the day. I shouldn't get excited. This could be a completely pointless exercise.

Or it might not be.

After finally catching the attention of the waiter, I pay for my glass of wine and scramble my stuff together, rushing out of the bar, my eyes glued to the map on my phone. I start thinking about what to do if I see him. Oh god, what *am* I going to say? I instinctively slow down, my feet dragging as my brain desperately attempts to come up with a plan, but it's too *scrambled* by the idea of potentially seeing Jamie again.

I wish I could call Ruby and ask for her opinion on whether I should be dropping in on him at work in the first place and, if it is a good idea, then what on earth I should be saying, but she's at a dinner with Leo's school friends this evening.

Bloody couples and their bloody couple dinners.

The Dancing Bear building looms into view. It looks just as I imagined it, down to the young hipsters sitting on the picnic benches dotted about wonkily in front of the brewery, drinking pints and stroking their beards while talking about Nietzsche.

(I made up the bit about Nietzsche. I have no idea what they're talking about.)

I wander in through the doors, stepping into a vast, cold warehouse-type room with high ceilings and metal barrels stacked around the edges. I'm about to approach one of the staff, when I suddenly realize a terrible, terrible thing.

I didn't think about what I look like.

Oh my god. What have I done? *What have I done?!*

I was in such a tizzy to see Jamie again that I've just strolled in here in my old, baggy gym T-shirt and leggings, with any makeup I had on for work today sweating off and my unwashed hair scraped back in a scruffy ponytail.

I need to get out of here immediately.

I turn on my heel and start walking at pace toward the exit when I hear what no one in this situation *ever* wants to hear.

My name.

"Freya?"

Grimacing, I turn very slowly to see Jamie strolling toward

me wearing a stunned expression. The good news is: he doesn't look horrified to see me. The bad news is: he's now seen me like this. He looks good in light blue–washed jeans and a colorful open shirt over a white T-shirt. His beard is more like stubble now and he's had a haircut.

"Hey," he says, a smile spreading across his face, which makes me feel at once comforted and terrified, "what are you doing here?"

"Jamie! Hi!" I begin, doing my best to seem startled at his appearance. This reaction, of course, makes no sense. We both know that I know he works here. "I was just passing and I thought . . . you know . . ."

I wave my hand about as though that gesture might perfectly explain what I mean. I don't even know what I mean, so I highly doubt Jamie does.

"Sure," he says, bemused. "Well, it's really good to see you. I'm glad you were just . . . passing."

He gives me a knowing smile. Oh, hang on. I see. Now he thinks I'm making this up and that I've come all the way to East London to bump into him and pretend I was in the area.

"I was trapezing."

He hesitates. "Sorry?"

"I really was just passing. I was doing a trapeze class nearby," I explain, making sure that he knows I haven't made the effort *just* to see him, and also that I only look like this after strenuous exercise (even if it was only five minutes of it).

"A trapeze class. Really?"

"Yes."

"Interesting. Any good at it?"

"Yeah, not bad actually. It's definitely not the easiest of hobbies. I mean, it requires a *lot* of strength and balance and dedication. And it's not easy to do it in front of other people watching. You know, because someone has to be there to make sure you don't fall off and break your neck."

He nods slowly as I speak. "It would be bad if that happened."

"It would be. Luckily, I'm all in one piece."

"That is lucky." He gives me a full-on grin as though he's been trying to hold it back. "Want to try some Dancing Bear beer?"

"Yes, I do."

"Come with me," he says, leading the way to the bar at the back of the room. "We have a few core beers—pale ale, lager, bitter—and then we have the small batches and the summer ones. There's a citrus one you might like. You want to taste a few, I'm guessing."

"I'm here for the full experience," I inform him.

"That's what I like to hear."

I pull myself up onto a stool at the bar as he slides behind it, dodging round the other staff who are busy pulling pints for the majority of customers sitting outside in the sunshine.

"Let's start with the flagship pale," Jamie states, reaching for a glass on the shelf under the bar.

"Sounds good. Thank you."

"So, how have you been?" he asks, preparing my first taster in a small glass and leaning out of the way as another staff member reaches round him for something. "Obviously you've been busy trapezing . . ."

"That takes up a lot of my time." I lean forward, resting my arms on the bar. "It's Ruby's hen do this weekend, so I've been organizing that. And work has been crazy. I've actually been working on this new advertising campaign for Bodacious, one of our gins. You may have heard of it?" Jamie nods. "It's distilled in Shropshire and they still follow this traditional recipe from the 1920s. Isn't that cool? They've had to move their production site a few times since it was first produced, of course, due to growth, but they've named each new headquarters 'Poppycock Lane' after the road their first distillery was on, so that they keep that sense of heritage. Anyway, we've been speaking to the family members who still work there, and we're going to do this whole campaign around its history and fantastic sense of humor, because obviously Poppycock Lane is a hilariously silly British road name and . . . and . . . oh my god, I'm so sorry. I'm rambling on and boring you."

"You're not!" Jamie assures me. "It all sounds really cool."

"Oh good. Well, I've been meaning to thank you, because you put the idea in my head at the Swill Awards."

He looks surprised. "I did?"

"You did. You took the time to get to know the family behind that to-die-for olive oil. And hearing you talk about what you're doing at Dancing Bear, the passion and knowledge of the people actually crafting the beer—that's what makes a product special. Anyway, all that gave me the idea."

He grins. "I had no clue my words carried such weight, but I'm pleased they've sparked something good."

"What about you? What have you been up to since I last saw you?"

"I haven't had any hen dos to busy myself with, but I've had a lot on with work too." He passes me my first glass. "Okay, here you go. It should be refreshing on the palate, citrus and peach notes. See what you think."

I thank him, and under his scrutinizing gaze I inspect the color and then take a drink. Taking my time before giving him a verdict, I wait a moment before having another sip, knitting my eyebrows together in what I hope is a pensive manner.

"Well?" he prompts.

"I like it," I tell him truthfully. "I like it a lot. I think I could drink that."

He smiles, his shoulders relaxing. "As good a compliment as I can get from you, I reckon."

"You know I'm not a beer drinker."

"I know," he says, getting my next taster prepared. "We'll move on to a lager next, I think."

"Sure."

"I hear you're moving?" He doesn't look at me, his eyes focused on his task. "Cali and Dominic mentioned something when I was out with them recently."

Maybe he's been asking about me.

"Yeah, that's right. I'm looking to buy my own place actually."

"Great."

"I've been to see quite a few flats, but haven't found somewhere yet."

"The right place will come up."

"I hope so."

"Here you go, our crisp and easy-drinking lager. See what you think."

I go through the tasting motions again, before concluding, "Delicious."

He raises his eyebrows. "Yeah?"

"Yes. I think I might prefer that to the pale ale."

"Noted."

"You look different," I observe, while he busies himself with the next taster. "You've trimmed back your beard."

He strokes his chin. "It wasn't my idea, but she was right in the end. I do think it looks better."

My insides churn and the heat rises to my face, causing my cheeks to feel as though they're on fire.

He has a girlfriend. Of course he does. People like Jamie don't just wait around. I'm *such* an idiot.

"Just goes to show," he continues, oblivious to the mental torture and humiliation I'm currently undergoing, "mums always know best."

Thank fuck.

"Oh right, it was your mum's idea. Yeah, I think it looks very smart."

"Smart?"

"You know. Nice."

"Thanks. Now, this next one is an IPA—the one nominated for the Swills, so brace yourself. It's probably going to be—"

"I ended things properly with Matthew," I blurt out.

His hand holding the glass is poised in midair. He blinks at me. One of his colleagues was standing just behind him as I spoke and, her eyes widening, she nonchalantly shuffles away from the bar to give us some privacy.

"Sorry," I say hurriedly, shaking my head, flushing once again. "I just . . . I thought you should . . . know."

"Oh." He puts the glass down. "I . . . uh . . . I'm sorry that you . . . I hope you're okay."

"Yes! It's a good thing," I say, flustered. "Technically we were over already, anyway, as you know. But we had a sort of . . . final talk, if you like. And it was my decision this time. As well as his. It was mutual. It's completely over. *Finito.* He's out of my life. See ya later, Matthew, you're gone! *Au revoir! Hola! Arrivederci!*"

"Actually, '*hola*' means 'hello.'"

"I realized that as soon as I said it."

There's an awkward pause.

I grimace. "Sorry, Jamie. I shouldn't have said anything."

"No! No, don't say sorry, it's fine," he says, looking a bit panicked. "It's good news. As in, I'm . . . you know . . . happy for you. If you're happy."

"Yeah. Yeah, it's good."

"Good."

We fall into silence. He stands awkwardly. I sit tensely. He slowly slides the glass across the bar to me. He clears his throat.

"So, here's the IPA. It's . . . hoppy."

"Right." I take a sip. "Yes. Nice and . . . hoppy."

Oh my god. This is more awkward than the time my ex-fiancé called when Jamie was in the middle of kissing me after I'd run about naked in front of him!

I've clearly made an error of judgment here. I've told him that I'm officially single and he's responded with a comment about the hoppiness of a beer. I made a stupid assumption about the stupid spark between us and now I've put us both in a really uncomfortable situation.

"I should be getting back home," I say firmly, tapping the side of the IPA glass. "That's really good. I'm officially impressed. You are very clever."

You are very clever?!

Sure, Freya, that's the sort of chat that will make him want to rip your clothes off.

Up your game, woman.

"Thanks so much for the tasting session," I continue, sliding off the barstool. "And it was nice seeing you again."

"Freya," he begins, frowning, "wait, you don't have to go. I—"

"No, no, I want to go! I mean, not that I want to go. I just have to go, because I have *so* much to do. Ruby's hen do, you know, there's a lot to organize. Food, games, penis hats—"

Why have you mentioned the penis hats?

"—you know how it is. Anyway, good luck with"—I gesture to the bar as I walk backward—"this stuff—"

"Freya . . ."

"Delicious stuff! It was delicious. Thank you. Okay, bye then."

I turn on my heel and get out of there as fast as I can before he can stop me, his stunned expression as I backed away from him burned into my brain for me to agonize over all the way home. What was I thinking? I shouldn't have brought up Matthew. Up until that moment, we were having a very nice time. For goodness' sake, Freya, he probably has a girlfriend! Or maybe he thinks we had our moment, I screwed it up, and life has moved on. I have a lot of baggage, too. And that kissing, we were in a different country and we'd had a lot to drink and we'd been at a wedding, so it was all romantic and . . .

He probably just wanted a one-night stand. And after ruining that, a few weeks later I've just marched into the place where he works, like I'm *genuinely* out of my mind, and told him things are over for real with my ex-fiancé, with no lead-up to that conversation whatsoever.

Clearly, I'm not ready to date anyone quite yet. I should continue spending my evenings focusing on myself and all the important things I've got going on right now, like watching corgi videos and ordering penis hats.

And I should absolutely forget about what just occurred.

Jamie who?

There. Sorted. No problem. I've completely forgotten about him already.

Things still to do for Ruby's hen do:
* Pack penis hats, photo book, paracetamol.
* Finish photo book. (Try not to accidentally somehow get glitter up my nose like last night. I sneezed so much on the way to the kitchen, I couldn't see where I was going and walked into the doorframe.)
* Confirm booking with stripper. (Do I need to provide the whipped cream and/or baby oil? Check this.)

I almost forgot to pack the inflatable male doll!

Bloody hell, that would have been *disastrous*.

I know this is going to sound weird, but I look surprisingly good in a penis hat.

I just opened the door for my takeaway and the pizza guy looked startled.

I forgot I was wearing the penis hat.

Sent Simone a selfie wearing the penis hat, saying, "Hope you're ready for Ruby's hen!"

To which she replied, "That reminds me of a wild night I once had in Amsterdam."

I'm going to take this hat off now.

CHAPTER TWENTY-EIGHT

I keep thinking about Jamie.

About exploring Dublin together, and how much we laughed and how the day flew by because we spent it together. Or the weekend in Leeds when he made me feel less alone and encouraged me to steal that traffic cone, like we were two silly teenagers acting out. I had a lot of fun with him. Thinking about him makes me feel excited and shuddery.

I was meant to wipe him from my mind and yet here I am on Ruby's hen do on a canal boat, surrounded by excitable women wearing penis hats and dancing around to Beyoncé, thinking about him *again*. Any time I consider dancing now, I know I'm going to do my laughing trick, something I wouldn't have been aware of were it not for Jamie.

"Freya has a crush," Ruby whispers in my ear as she slumps down next to me and giggles, her captain hat toppling from her head into her lap. "Whoops! Need that perched on the barnet, otherwise who will know who is running this ship, you know what I'm saying?"

"I do know what you're saying," I laugh, watching her shove it back on again. "Are you having fun?"

"The *best* time," she assures me, her eyes wide with sincerity.

Ruby had been very specific about the organizing of her hen do. She wanted it in London and I was repeatedly told that she didn't want any kind of strenuous activity. Relaxed with good food and drinks. That was my brief. The morning started with a bottomless brunch—is it even a hen do if a brunch isn't involved?—leading into a canal boat trip. After this we'll be heading off back to Cali's, where we'll be playing the classic hen do games and greeting a stripper dressed as a fireman, before a three-course meal in a private room of a nice restaurant and on to a VIP booth in a club where they put sparklers in the champagne bottles (a specific request from the bride).

"Why don't you just call him?" she says suddenly, bopping her shoulders to the music blaring out of the speakers of the canal.

"Who?"

"Jamie." She rolls her eyes. "You were thinking about him just now."

"No, I wasn't!"

"Yes, you were, you had that little smile on your face that you get when you have a secret crush." She wiggles her finger at me. "Everyone gets that smile when they have a crush and I saw it there on your face just now."

"I was actually enjoying your slut drops. It's admirable that you're still so good at them, even on a moving boat."

"I have abnormally strong legs," she assures me. "Well, even if you weren't thinking about Jamie, I think you should be. I like him."

"No boy chat on your hen do," I instruct, taking a swig of prosecco from my cup.

"Disagree, I want *all* the boy chat! Look, you can't blame yourself for what happened in Dublin. You weren't ready then for anyone, no matter how sexy they are with their beards and tattoos. Matthew was still looming."

"Yes, but he wasn't looming when I went to Dancing Bear, and I still managed to fuck things up. It's not meant to be."

"Do you believe in that sort of thing?" she says dreamily, slinking down on the bench a bit and resting her head on my shoulder.

"Yeah, I think so. What will be will be. I think it's a nice thing to believe in sometimes."

"Me too. We were always meant to be, weren't we?"

"Definitely."

"This is what I love about hen dos," she confesses. "All these women"—she jabs her finger in the direction of the girls dancing—"we've been through it all. Good times, bad times, relationships, heartbreaks, family shit. But here we are on a canal boat and I've never laughed harder. There's nothing like the friendship kind of love, is there?"

I shift to put my arm round her. "Ah, listen to you. So sweet and poetic."

"Fuck's sake. You won't tell anyone I just said that, will you?"

"It may come up."

"Can you not tell them I said 'the friendship kind of love'? That was the worst bit."

"That was the best bit."

"Don't tell Leo."

"He'll be the first to know."

"Freya!"

"What can I say, Rubes, life's a bitch."

"It really is." She sits up grinning. "Although now it doesn't seem too bad."

"No, now's all right."

"Want to shimmy along the canal boat to Lady Gaga?"

"Not really, but in the name of hen dos—" I stand up and hold out my hand to her. She takes it and I pull her up next to me. "—let's dance."

On the morning of Ruby's wedding, I find myself weirdly wanting to apologize to her for what happened at mine. Suddenly, I realize how hard it must have been for her when I sent her away with everyone else after Matthew broke up with me. Here I am in the position of best friend to the bride and I can see how much the day means to her just with one glance at her face.

I can see the worry and the stress as she checks everything is in place for the day, asking her mum a hundred questions as her hair is styled and makeup perfected; I can see the excitement and nerves as she looks at her reflection in the mirror. There's an overwhelming and unique sense of pride when your best friend gets married, because you know that they deserve every bit of the happiness that today brings; every hug and smile and moment of celebration that Ruby gets today, she has earned it by being this wonderful human being that honestly no one quite deserves, but if it has to be someone, it's Leo.

And that's why I suddenly feel horribly guilty that when that was all ripped from me, I sat in the broom cupboard alone, and Dad went round explaining what had happened and telling everyone to leave, including Ruby. She must have been dying inside for me. I know that because if anything happened to ruin today for her, I'd die inside for her. I'd want to protect her at all costs. I didn't allow her to do that for me. Not straightaway, anyway.

"Freya," she says suddenly, catching my eye in the mirror and jolting me from my recollections of those horrible days, "are you crying?"

"Absolutely not."

"Your eyes look teary."

"The eye makeup makes them glisten."

"Makeup isn't applied to your eyeballs, you doughnut."

I smile at her reflection. She smiles back.

"Can I get you anything?" I ask. "You want a drink? Or some food?"

"I'm fine, thanks. Actually, do you have any deodorant?"

"Yes, I do. Want me to get it for you?"

"Yes please. I can't believe I forgot to bring deodorant to my wedding."

"Of all the things you could have forgotten to bring, Rubes, deodorant is not a problem," I insist. "I'll be right back."

I leave her hotel room and amble down to mine, which is only a few doors down. Ruby and Leo are having a relaxed, intimate wedding in a marquee in a field in Herefordshire—they wanted a boho vibe, like a music festival only chicer and less muddy—and we're staying in a gorgeous boutique hotel fifteen minutes down the road. There are only ten rooms in the place and the beds are those four-poster ones that make you feel like you're royalty. When it rained last weekend, there was some panic because it's an outdoor ceremony in the field under a flower arch, but this week has been much better weatherwise. Today it's cloudy, due to get sunnier later in the afternoon. It will be perfect.

I get into my room and spot my deodorant on the dressing table next to my phone, which has just started buzzing loudly. I grab it and pick up.

"Hi, Mum."

"Darling! You sound sprightly today!"

"You got sprightly from two words?"

"Oh, I can sense moods from no words at all."

"Right." I roll my eyes. "How are you, all okay?"

"I wanted to check, do you eat chickpeas?"

"Yes, I do."

"Oh good! I'm making a casserole for you next weekend and it has chickpeas in it. I know they can divide people. It's the texture, you see. Quite powdery."

"Sounds delicious. Anyway, I'd better—"

"How is Ruby this morning? You can tell her that I buried a sausage last night in her honor!"

"Not the sausages thing again," I groan.

"Is it raining today on her wedding day? No. There you have it."

"Mum, you burying a sausage has no effect on the weather. It's science."

"It's faith, darling. Sometimes it's healthy to have some of that."

I lift my eyes to the ceiling. "If you say so."

"We are *so* excited to see you next weekend. We're going to prepare your room this week and we've worked out all the meals. Evan has booked one of our favorite pubs for the Saturday evening! Just you wait till you see the view!"

I soften at her enthusiasm. "Sounds really nice, Mum. I'm looking forward to it."

"I've asked Kian from the poetry club to bake one of his famous lemon and elderflower cakes for you. I don't know how he gets his sponge so moist."

I wince. "Okay, enough of the word 'moist.' That all sounds great, Mum, but I have to go."

"Yes, a big day ahead of you, and Ruby will need her right-hand woman! Before you go, though, I want to read something to you."

"Oh no, that's really not necess—"

"This is from *Anne of Avonlea* by Lucy Maud Montgomery," she announces, cutting me off and clearing her throat. "'Perhaps, after all, romance did not come into one's life with pomp and blare, like a gay knight riding down; perhaps it crept to one's side like an old friend through quiet ways; perhaps it revealed itself in seeming prose, until some sudden shaft of illumination flung

athwart its pages betrayed the rhythm and the music, perhaps . . .
perhaps . . . love unfolded naturally out of a beautiful friendship,
as a golden-hearted rose slipping from its green sheath.' There!
What do you think? I thought that was perfect to be spoken aloud
on Ruby and Leo's day."

"You know what, Mum? I was dubious at first, but I have to
agree with you. That is pretty perfect."

She sighs heavily. "Love can find us when we least expect it.
Keep that heart open, darling!"

"Mum, I really do have to go now."

"Have a wonderful time, I can't wait to hear all about it. Bye,
darling. Love you," she adds tentatively.

"Yeah, bye, Mum," I say, looking down at the ground. "You
too."

I know she's smiling into the phone as I hang up.

Armed with the deodorant, I make my way back to Ruby's
room. She raises her eyebrows at me in the mirror when her
mum opens the door to let me in.

"Where did you go?" she demands to know. "I've had to hold
my arms at a very awkward angle to get air to the pits."

"Honestly, Ruby," her mum mutters disapprovingly.

"Sorry, my mum called and I really don't know why, but I
picked up."

"Ah, how is she?" she asks, happily putting the deodorant on
and disturbing the hairstylist.

"She wants me to tell you that she buried a sausage in your
honor last night and that's why it's not raining today."

"What a hero."

"And then she read me a passage by someone I didn't know
about a knight and pomp and . . . uh . . . well the gist was that
you and Leo were pals first and then you realized you loved each
other. It was slightly more eloquent than that, though."

"No kidding."

"It was actually very meaningful."

"Oh, well, let's hope I hear it one day."

"How are you feeling?" I ask, sitting down on the bed.

"Sweaty."

"I just brought you antiperspirant."

"True. Now, a little less sweaty than before," she admits. "I hope the day goes to plan and everyone has a good time."

"They will."

"It's just, you know, a lot of my family have traveled all the way from Mauritius. They've made a *huge* effort to be here, so I really want them to have a good time and—"

"Ruby," I interrupt, "they're here to see you get married. That's all that matters. Everyone is going to have a wonderful day celebrating that. It's going to be brilliant."

She exhales as she gazes at her reflection, her hair almost finished. "This feels like a big moment."

"It is a big moment."

She bites her lip. "I'm nervous."

"That's normal. But everything is going to be amazing."

"Are you nervous? You should be."

"Walking up the aisle is a bit nerve-racking, but luckily everyone will be looking at you, so I reckon I'll be all right."

"I'm not talking about that," she tells me. "I'm talking about your task. The Wedding Season isn't over yet."

"Oh god, Rubes. How is it possible that you've been thinking about that when you've had so much on?" I sigh. "What are you going to ask me to do?"

"You'll see," she says haughtily. "Leo wants to be there when we tell you."

"Are you both mad?! Today is meant to be about you two!"

"Yes, and you are very much part of us. We've put a lot of

thought into this final task. You've been successful at all the others, but this one is a real game changer."

"You're not going to ask me to do anything crazy, are you?"

"Hmmm, well, what was it you said on my hen do? Ah yes, that was it," she says with a shrug. "Sorry, Freya, but sometimes . . . life's a bitch."

"Oh no," I whisper in defeat.

"I think we should open the bottle of champagne now, Mum, don't you? Time to celebrate," Ruby declares smugly, offering me a mischievous grin. "Not to mention, if Freya wants to survive the final day of the Wedding Season, I have a feeling she's going to need a little bit of Dutch courage."

CHAPTER TWENTY-NINE

S imone can barely speak she's laughing so hard.

"Do . . . you . . . have . . . any safety pins?" she manages to splutter through giggles and wheezes, putting her hands on my shoulders, her face creasing up with delight.

"Safety pins? No, although I think there may be some in the loos," I inform her. "Why would you need safety pins?"

"Dominic's ripped his trousers."

"What?"

"Right down the bum."

"*What?*"

"Look!"

She points to the other side of the marquee where Dominic is sitting on a chair, wide-eyed with panic, while Cali stands next to him, her face buried in her hands. Ruby and Leo are having a blast, twirling around the oakwood dance floor along the majority of guests as the band plays Arctic Monkeys.

The ceremony was brilliant. There was a brass band, so Ruby got the trumpets that she'd envisioned. Leo messed up his lines, breaking the ice early on and making everyone howl with laughter—"I, Ruby, take you, Leo . . . no wait! Other way round! I'm Leo!"—and then it showered during the photos, which turned out to produce some amazing shots of Leo and Ruby kissing and laughing in the rain, me holding an umbrella over Ruby in an attempt to protect her stunning bohemian lace gown.

The wedding cake, made by Leo's aunt, was produced to great fanfare and Ruby was horrified to see that it was bright red when she'd asked for a "rustic" look. Honestly, her *face*. She caught my eye and we got the giggles so badly, my eyes were watering.

"Do you like it?" Leo's aunt asked eagerly.

"Oh, yes. It's . . . uh . . . bright!" Leo said, shocked at the spectacle.

"A bright cake for bright, young things! And do you like the cake toppers?"

"Absolutely," he replied, peering at them. "Are they—?"

"Puffins!" she confirmed excitedly. "One is wearing a top hat and the other in the veil. Aren't they adorable? I saw them online and thought they were perfect for you two."

"Yes," Leo nodded robotically. "Perfect."

So far, neither Leo or Ruby has worked out why she'd see puffins and think of them, but to be fair, the cake is certainly unique, it tastes delicious, *and* no one will ever forget it. I actually feel quite boring that Matthew and I had gone for a traditional-looking cake with flowers on the top from our florist. Sure, it looked pretty, but if I ever have the choice again, I want my cake toppers to be something fun and ridiculous, like a puffin wearing a top hat.

The wedding breakfast food was delicious—Mauritian dishes served in sharing style—and Ruby gave a very moving speech, in which I got a mention as her "rock." A very fitting description for someone who once played the stone in the family's King Arthur production. They cut the eye-catching cake with beaming smiles and now here we all are, dancing away and ripping our trousers. Apparently.

"How did Dominic rip them?" I ask curiously as Simone collects herself.

"Didn't you see his flip?!"

"Dominic can flip?"

"No, he cannot," she says with a knowing smile. "But his attempt was spectacular and the rip down the back of the trousers, absolute perfection. Anyway, if there are any safety pins about, we can try to pin it so he doesn't have to sit down the rest of the night. Or at least hold them together long enough for him to get back to his hotel and get another pair of trousers on without flashing the whole guest list."

I agree that this seems like a good plan and head to the bathrooms to try to search for safety pins. As I thought, there is a pack in the basket next to the sink. I remember when I was helping Ruby with the task of preparing the toiletry baskets, I'd thought the safety pins were quite an odd addition to the deodorant, plasters, tampons, and paracetamol. I hereby stand corrected. I return to Cali and Simone holding them up triumphantly. While Dominic stands up embarrassed, the three of us crouch down to inspect how bad the rip is and work out the best way of temporarily fixing it with the tools we have to hand.

"What are you lot doing?"

Cali, Simone, and I look up from studying Dominic's arse to see the bride and groom looming over us with baffled expressions.

"I ripped my trousers doing a flip on the dance floor," Dominic cries out over the music.

"Attempting a flip," Cali corrects, rolling her eyes.

"We're trying to work out the best way of pinning his trousers back together," Simone explains. "At the moment his yellow boxers are on show for the whole world to see back here."

"Not the best day to wear the classic Tweety Pie underwear," Dominic declares. "By the way, great wedding. Such a blast."

"Well if that isn't a sign of a good party, I don't know what is," Leo laughs. "Hey, Freya, can we borrow you for a moment?"

"Sure," I say, straightening up, and follow them to another

table, where they pull out some chairs. "Do you need me to hand out cake?"

Ruby frowns, carefully arranging her dress as she sits down. "Why would we ask you to hand out cake?"

"Seems like a maid-of-honor thing to do. It really is delicious, too."

"Your duties are complete, Freya." Ruby smiles, reaching out and taking my hand. "We just want you to enjoy yourself now."

"Wait." I glance from her to Leo. "Is that my final Wedding Season task? To enjoy myself? I love it!"

"*Ha!*" Ruby narrows her eyes at me. "Nice try."

"Before the big reveal, I have something to say," I announce, clearing my throat. "This year hasn't been . . . my favorite. In fact, my life has felt like one big disaster. Everything I'd planned fell apart and I felt completely lost."

Ruby and Leo share a look.

"But," I continue, before they can jump in, "I can also say with complete and utter sincerity, that I wouldn't have made it through without you two and your stupid Wedding Season plan. I may have been heartbroken, but boy, did I laugh. It's reminded me to let go of my inhibitions every now and then. It's not so bad when I do. Something about this summer . . . the mix of having to cope with things myself, putting myself out there, renewing my relationship with my mum. It's given me this confidence I didn't know I had. I got with that hot French model! Me! I ran naked down a hotel corridor! Who does that?! Apparently, I do!" I pause as they laugh. "I guess what I'm trying to say is . . . thank you. For being there and for the Wedding Season. It's really meant a lot to me. And now here you are, married. Everything is as it should be. I couldn't be happier for my two best friends."

Leo's eyes well up. "Group hug?"

"I'm not sure that's necessary."

"*Group hug!*" Ruby wails, leaning forward to envelop me, with Leo following her lead but pouncing on me from the other side so I'm squished in the middle.

Closing my eyes for a second, I smile into Ruby's shoulder.

"All right," I say, patting them both on their arms. "Thanks."

"Wow," Ruby whispers into my ear. "Just wow." She pulls back to look at me, the corner of her lip twitching. "Thank you, Freya, for being so vulnerable. That was very emotional and touching. I feel touched. I feel moved."

I sigh heavily, muttering, "Okay. Here we go."

"It was just *so* beautiful," Leo joins in. "I feel like I've seen a whole new side to you."

"I wish I'd filmed that heartfelt speech," Ruby says wistfully. "I've never heard you so serious and in touch with your emotions."

"It's the perfect wedding gift," Leo points out, to which Ruby gasps and then nods along vigorously. "Thank you, Freya, for your words."

"I see, taking the piss, are we? Very classy."

"It was so meaningful and sincere," Ruby says, grabbing Leo's arm and squeezing it. "She really opened her heart."

"Proof that she has one," Leo remarks, prompting me to glare at him.

"We should remember what she said and get it printed on a tea towel," Ruby suggests.

"You're both evil," I tell them grumpily.

"Not that evil," Leo protests. "Your final Wedding Season task is actually quite a positive one, if you want my opinion. We could have been much nastier."

"It was really Leo's idea," Ruby says, giving him a dreamy look. "Truly inspired."

"It was a joint effort."

"Okay, okay," I jump in, rolling my eyes. "Time to put me out of my misery."

"You tell her," Leo says to Ruby.

"No, you tell her! It was your idea!" Ruby insists.

"*Someone* tell me, please." I fold my arms. "This is my grand finale. I'm waiting in great anticipation here."

"All right," Ruby says, grinning and taking charge. "The last task of the Wedding Season is this: ask him out on a date."

I blink at her. "Ask him out on a date? That's my task? That doesn't even make any sense."

"Makes perfect sense to me," Leo claims. "Does it make sense to you, Ruby?"

"Oh yes," she nods. "It very much makes sense to me."

"What are you talking about? Who is 'him'?"

Ruby nods to someone over my shoulder. Frowning in confusion, I swivel in my chair to look out across the guests on the dance floor. I have no idea who they're talking about. There are so many guys at this wedding, they're going to have to be a bit more specific. One of them dancing right there in front of me is Ruby's uncle, who has wrapped his tie round his head and is doing the chicken dance move with great aplomb. I bloody well hope they're not expecting me to ask him out on a date.

"I don't understand," I say, looking at Ruby and throwing my hands up in exasperation. "Who?"

"Him," Ruby insists, biting her lip and pointing behind me again.

I turn back around for another look, following the direction of her finger. This time, the crowd parts a little. And that's when I see him.

Jamie.

He's standing at the entrance of the marquee, looking a bit lost as though he's just arrived. Dressed in suit trousers and a white shirt with his sleeves rolled up, he's craning his neck as though looking for someone. He spots me. A smile creeps across his lips.

And suddenly it hits me. I'm ready for a new chapter.

I don't know what that chapter looks like or how it will pan out, but that's okay. Whether it turns into something, whether it's nothing at all, whether it's a little bit of something, whatever happens ahead. I'm ready to find out.

A conversation I had at Obi's wedding with his uncle, Chido, right at the beginning of the season, springs to mind.

"It will get better. It doesn't feel like it. But, with time, it will. One day, you'll be somewhere, could be anywhere, and suddenly it will hit you. You won't be expecting it. It will come out of nowhere. Bam."

"What? What will hit me?"

"The realization that you really are okay."

I turn back to Ruby and Leo with a big smile on my face.

"Thank you," I say, reaching for both their hands and giving them a squeeze.

Leo winks at me. "You go get him, tiger."

"Seriously, Leo," Ruby sighs, rolling her eyes. "Do you hear yourself sometimes?"

"Go enjoy your wedding," I instruct, getting to my feet and encouraging them to do the same. "I'll see you in a bit."

As the happy couple head back to the dance floor, where they are greeted with whoops and cheering, I take a deep breath and spin round to seek out Jamie. He's still standing where he was, this time much more at ease, leaning on one of the tent poles. He sees that I'm coming over and straightens to start walking to meet me in the middle, the two of us making our way through the crowd toward each other.

I feel unbelievably nervous, with all the signs of a gigantic crush. Heart thudding, butterflies fluttering, breath catching. I'm desperate to reach him, but also terrified of getting there.

As Ruby put it earlier, this feels like a big moment.

A memory flashes across my mind: my first date with Matthew. We'd swapped numbers at the audition and then had an awkward, small-talk, mildly flirtatious text exchange until he finally asked if I wanted to meet him for a drink. I remember Ruby being impressed that he'd suggested a nicer bar than the standard student ones we all congregated at. I remember Leo helping Ruby and me pick an outfit for me because we demanded a male opinion.

And I remember feeling just like this when I opened the door to the bar and saw him sitting on one of the stools. The nerves, the excitement, the anticipation of what might happen. It's such a wonderful, torturous feeling, isn't it? When you don't know what's ahead, but you're excited for it anyway. Matthew's face lit up when I walked in.

"I knew from the moment you walked in that bar," he told me a couple of years after our first date when we were lying on our sides, facing each other in bed and sharing his pillow, our noses almost touching.

"That we would end up in a relationship?"

"Yes." He grinned. "And I knew that I'd marry you someday."

In that moment, I felt so deliriously happy because I knew that, too.

But I'm glad we were both wrong. I may not always be this calm and accepting when I think back on Me-and-Matthew, but beyond the inevitable waves of anger and sadness, I will always be grateful we had a story together.

Jamie and I stop abruptly in front of each other.

"You're here," I begin stupidly, trying to control the excitement in my voice.

"I was just passing after a trapeze class."

"Right."

He smiles down at me. "It's nice to see you, Freya. You sort of ran away from me last time we met."

"I didn't run away."

"You ran away."

"I hurried off because I had something to get to."

"Was that something, by any chance, YouTubing videos of corgi butts?"

"I'm going to kill Ruby."

"It was actually Isabelle who mentioned that pastime of yours."

"I'm going to kill Isabelle."

"Why did you run away, Freya?"

I fold my arms across my chest, glancing around nervously to see we're being watched intently by Ruby, Leo, Cali, Simone, and Dominic. They quickly pretend they're not looking. (Dominic's trousers now look like they have been secured, which is quite the achievement.)

"I panicked," I admit with a shrug. "I told you Matthew was out of the picture and you didn't seem . . . I thought that maybe . . . you weren't interested and I'd made a fool of myself."

"You know, since then I've been in quite the spiral," he tells me.

"You have?"

"Oh yeah. You told me that you were single and my response was to give you an IPA and say, 'It's hoppy.'" He shuts his eyes in despair. "Those words have tortured me."

"'It's hoppy'?"

"It's hoppy. I felt like the biggest idiot on the planet."

"I felt like the biggest idiot on the planet!"

He hesitates, his lips twitching into a smile. "Two big idiots."

"Right. Although, I do want to reiterate that I was genuinely in that area of London for a trapeze class. I didn't come just to see you."

"Yes, I heard that the three minutes you spent at that class were breathtaking."

"I really am going to kill Isabelle."

"That one was Ruby."

"I'm going to kill them all."

He throws his head back and laughs.

I like him so much.

"Well, I have to admit that I wasn't just passing today," he says with a heavy sigh. "I came all the way here just for you."

I lift my eyes up to meet his. "Really?"

"Really. When I got the call from Leo and Ruby, I couldn't quite believe my luck. I was getting another shot. And this time, I'm going to say brilliant things that will dazzle you and not say things like 'It's hoppy.'"

"I'm a little disappointed. I think the hoppy comment is quite endearing."

"You do?" He raises his eyebrows. "In that case, let me tell you about many, many hoppy beers. There are lots of hoppy ones out there. They're all hoppy." He pauses. "For the record, I'm really sorry about my reaction when you told me about you and Matthew being completely over. I freaked out and fucked up."

I smile, shaking my head. "You have nothing to apologize for. If anyone does, it's me for the night in Dublin. I'm so sorry that I answered that call from Matthew. If I could go back to that night, I would do things differently."

He strokes his stubble thoughtfully. "It wasn't all bad. If tonight ends up in a similar fashion with you running around a hotel naked, I won't be complaining."

I grimace, lifting my hands to my face. "Argh. Bloody Wedding Season tasks."

His warm hands clasp round mine, lowering them so he can look right into my eyes.

"Those bloody Wedding Season tasks are why I'm here with you tonight, though," he says, and his voice has changed from teasing and jokey to serious and sexy. "For that, I am very grateful."

"Me too," I croak.

There was a time I was scared to like Jamie, but now I know that our differences—all those things I assumed would doom us from the start—none of that matters. Because if I've learned anything during the Wedding Season, it's that sometimes, love won't make sense. Sometimes it doesn't come all neatly wrapped up, all questions answered. And sometimes, even the relationships you thought you could count on change, maybe even fall apart. If you click with someone, you click with them. Sometimes you just have to go with it and hope for the best.

I swallow the lump in my throat. "Jamie?"

"Yes?"

"Do you want to go out on a date with me sometime?"

"Well—" He hesitates. "—it depends."

"On?"

He tries and fails to suppress a teasing smile. "Will we be going somewhere that serves pornstar martinis in a can?"

"I don't know, Jamie, maybe we'll go somewhere that serves halibut."

"That is one fancy potato."

"It will be a fancy date."

"Then, I'm all in."

"Good." I smile goofily up at him, unable to stop myself. "Me too."

"Well then."

He grins, his eyes sparkling at me. Without any hesitation, he moves forward. I lift my chin and we kiss, his hand on my waist, holding me tightly, the other tangled in my hair.

And then guess what happens?

Fireworks go off outside. I'm not even kidding. Fireworks.

Right at that moment. You can't make this up. There I was thinking that I'd had my rom-com movie moment under the stars in France, but that had absolutely *nothing* on this. I mean, really. Jamie and I start kissing and *fireworks* go off. *Literal* sparks flying through the air.

Turns out it wasn't purely down to our chemistry, but Ruby and Leo had organized a beautiful fireworks display for their guests. Everyone rushes out of the marquee to enjoy the magical, glittering colors lighting up the night sky.

Jamie and I miss the whole thing.

It really is quite the beginning.

Acknowledgments

I cannot believe how lucky I am to have Kim and Sarah, my absurdly talented UK and US editors, guiding me in my work. Thank you both for all your brilliant advice and for making me laugh my head off during the edits process with your hilarious comments throughout the manuscript. Let's get that Aude trip booked in soon, yes?

Huge thanks to Amy, Callie, Jenny, Rebecca, Mary, Marissa, Sallie, Kejana, and the teams at Hodder & Stoughton and St. Martin's Press for all your amazing work. I hope you're as proud as I am of this book. Thank you for making it look so good and getting it out into the world.

Without my fabulous agent Lauren, I'd likely spend the majority of my day panicking about life and getting nothing done, before watching back-to-back Netflix rom-coms starring Vanessa Hudgens. Thank you for your guidance, patience, and for always being there to say, "you've got this." Big thanks to the whole team at Bell Lomax Moreton.

To my family and friends, thank you for your endless encouragement and wonderful humor. I couldn't do any of this without you cheering me on.

In particular, I'd like to thank Laura and Rory for having me in stitches over the quiche saga; Nat, for your advice on Jamie's heritage; Lizzie and Jack for all your help brainstorming the Wedding Season tasks, and also, Lizzie, for your obsession with good olive oil; and Chloe for inspiring the pigeon scene after heroically chasing a crow out of your house.

Finally, thank you to my readers. I can't put into words how much your support means. I very much hope this book makes you laugh and cheers your day.

About the Author

Imogen Forte

Katy Birchall is the author of *The Wedding Season* and *The Secret Bridesmaid* as well as numerous books for young readers. A former editor for *Country Life* magazine, she studied English literature and linguistics at the University of Manchester, and currently lives in London.